Best Served Cold:

The Five Doors

By
Andrew Crossland

Published in the United Kingdom by:

off the ground publishing

Copyright © Andrew Crossland 2016

Artwork by Phillip Johnson

First printed in February 2016

eBook ISBN 978-0-9935374-1-7
Paperback ISBN 978-0-9935374-0-0

Chapter 1 – Seven Months Later

I placed my hands down upon the lectern in front of me. I spent a moment staring at my crisp black suit and plain green tie. I knew that I was distracting myself from what I was about to say, but I was glad; I enjoyed letting my mind wander onto pointless things. I thought about my clean-shaven face and my thinning black hair. I inwardly cursed my dad for passing these genes on to me. I wondered if *his* hair had been this way at the age of twenty two. I glanced upwards and saw the eyes of my audience burning into me. I knew that I could hesitate no longer. It was time to tell my story.

'Hello,' my voice echoed confidently through the large room. 'My name's Ian. I know that most of you know a version of this story now. You may have read it in the papers or seen it on the news, but now is your chance to hear it directly from me.'

I noticed a few members of the audience talking to each other; judging me, no doubt.

I remained confident as I spoke up, 'I'm sure you have all made up your minds about the subject already, but I assure you…this is a tragedy that befell *me!*'

There was no turning back now. It was time to give these hounds what they wanted. I decided to go full force with the story.

'My story takes place on the third floor in a block of flats that I owned; recently dubbed by the media as "The Bretton Flats". It was here that the love of my life came to an all too early end.'

Just speaking these words caused a tear to roll down my cheek. I had to remain confident. I decided to leave it to dry in the warm room

1

rather than show weakness by wiping it away. I had to tell this story *my* way. The media had warped and twisted it to an unrecognisable point. My love deserved better than that.

'She was killed by an evil person. A person who had far outstayed their welcome in this world. They're dead now. Dead by my hand. I was the one who removed that horrible creature from this world. Too late though. Too late to save the love of my life who was taken from me that fateful day seven months ago…'

Chapter 2 – The Blue Sock

I approached my building to the sound of the rain beating down on the plastic material of my dark green umbrella. I arrived at the front of my building and looked up. Light was pouring from some of the flats on the third floor. One of them was mine, which meant my wife must be home. All the other floors were in complete darkness. There were six floors so, including the ground floor entranceway, there were seven rows of windows. There are five flats on each floor, and with the stairwell window at either side, this meant that there were seven columns as well. Those lit up were 3B, 3C and 3D, the three in the exact centre of the building. I realised that I'd been staring up for far too long; my face was getting wetter and wetter until I could barely see. I moved my umbrella back into position to protect myself.

I stood still outside for a moment. I wasn't quite ready to go in yet. I was feeling happy and nervous at the same time. The tenant in 3D was new and I hadn't had a chance to really see how he was getting on. Kane his name was. He was a bit of a rough character. I didn't want him causing trouble, but I needed him there. The money was really helping too at this early stage. The flats were badly run down so I was using pretty much every penny I earned in this venture to renovate the building. It helped that my wife and I lived in the building too. That saved us a fair bit. I'd only managed to fill one other flat before Kane, so I was really happy about having another source of income. I looked down. I really was distracted. I hadn't noticed that I was standing ankle deep in a puddle and that the water had poured over the side of my shoe, drenching my sock. I wouldn't let even this annoyance throw me though. I'd finally got Kane living in the building and nothing was going to bring my spirits down now. Well, not unless he'd already caused some trouble in the short time he'd been here.

I looked around at the muddy grounds of the building. I thought of all the things I could do with this spare land should I find the time. No point fantasizing though; I must focus on the inside of the building if I am to continue what I'd started.

I looked further afield. The closest sign of civilisation, other than my building, was a main road about half a mile from here. Even at this late hour there were still plenty of cars to be seen. Bretton town was quite close. Close enough to walk to, but not close enough to cause a noise problem. A small smile grew on my face. This was the perfect location for me. It's not common for flats to be positioned all the way out here like this and the reason for that is they were not purpose built flats. Formerly it had been a hotel, and anyone who saw these grounds knew that it must have been a prestigious one. The Royal Rainford Hotel it was called. Some sort of incident had taken place years ago. I remember there being a fire up here; I was at the local university at the time and had seen it from my dorm room. After that, time took its toll and the place became very run down. It has been quite the challenge getting this place ready for my needs, but it has been a learning curve for me. It takes the kind of skill my dad would have most likely taught me, were he still alive, but hopefully it's something I can pass on to my children.

I took one last look towards the distant lights of the bustling town of Bretton and headed inside my building. I closed my umbrella and shook rain water from it outside before closing the door. I headed toward the mail boxes, one small box for each flat. Almost all of the thirty boxes were black, the way that I'd bought them. However I'd painted the ones for the flats that I was using in different vibrant colours which corresponded with the colour of the flat doors. The box for my flat, 3B, was green, my favourite colour. I opened it and reached inside to retrieve a handful of takeaway menus. One of the biggest downsides of living relatively close to town; menus! Every day! At least ten, and most were duplicates of ones I'd received only earlier that week. I placed the wad of menus in the bin that had been conveniently placed for just this purpose. I had plenty of the things in my flat already as my wife wasn't the best cook. Plenty of other things to love about her, though.

I made my way towards the stairs thinking about my past with her. When I first made my intentions clear to her, I never thought she would have gone for me. She was a whole ten years older than me, but I managed to woo her regardless. Age wasn't the only obstacle I had to overcome, either. She was absolutely stunning with a face that was far younger than her years. If I didn't know that she was thirty two, I wouldn't have believed her. She had gorgeous flowing dark hair that looked great whether it was tied up or hanging loose. She was really petite and slim with lovely shapely legs, probably from years of running. She took a keen interest in fitness, unlike me. Our lack of shared interests was another problem I had thought I would have to face if I was ever going to tie her down. But all these worries melted to nothing when I first got talking to her.

I got distracted again when I arrived at the first floor. I glanced down the corridor and saw the state that it was in. Musing that the residents might wonder why I had started renovating the third floor first instead of this one, I considered giving it a mild cosmetic makeover.

As I continued up the stairs, leaving the first floor behind, it didn't take long for my mind to wander to my wife again. We had met at a dinner party hosted by some mutual friends which I had only recently made. She was sitting opposite me at the other end of the large dining table, but I couldn't stop glancing at her. I didn't want her thinking I was creepy or anything, but she eventually noticed and, to my delight, smiled back. I'd bumped into her a few times after and we eventually got talking. Our shared friends faded into the background whenever I was with her. They all seemed, shamefully, irrelevant whenever I was talking to her. I would attend any event that they put on in the hopes that she would be there. It got to a point where I didn't even care about them; all that mattered was that I needed to convince this girl to go out with me. As our encounters increased she eventually agreed to go on a date with me. She'd hesitated over my age a few times, but I think she was more concerned what others would think of my youth. Anyway, I managed to convince her to forget all that and ironically, in the end, this was the thing she loved most about me, because no matter how beautiful I thought she was, she was always putting herself down. I couldn't believe it; this amazing woman would talk about shortcomings that she didn't even have. I wondered if she was just fishing for compliments but I didn't complain; it was these insecurities that led her to agree to marry me and in that, I'd achieved what I'd set out to do and I couldn't have been happier. Marriage at twenty two was something I never saw coming, though.

I headed up the stairs that led up to the second floor. This one particular stairway, and its mirrored counterpart at the other side of the building, was narrower than the others. I'd wondered why this was for a while before I figured it out; there is a little generator room on the first floor at one side, and a store cupboard at the other side. These extra little rooms on the first floor took the width from the stairwell leading up to the second floor, making it a lot narrower.

Arriving at the second floor I peered down the corridor, which was in an even worse state than the first. The damage here was severe. The fire that had happened here years ago had clearly originated on this floor; the whole area was heavily burned. One of the doors was hanging from its hinges. The fire hose box, of which there was one on each floor, had been ripped from the wall, and the hose itself strewn across the floor. This level definitely needed my urgent attention.

I continued up the stairs and arrived at the third floor. Recently improved and looking far better than any of the other floors, it was like something out of a children's book. Each of the doors was painted in a different, vibrant, colour. The numbers and lettering were all brand new and sat fastened perfectly in the centre of each door, their reflective gold surfaces clean enough to see your face in. Disappointment hit me as I looked up at some dirty polystyrene panels in the suspended ceiling. The majority of the panels were fine, but a few of them shared a rather large filthy stain. I'd been lazy in replacing these. My usual guy, Jim, who tended to all my D.I.Y. needs, didn't sell them and I hadn't looked elsewhere yet. I must make these my top priority, especially with the rest of the third floor looking so much better.

I stood in front of our flat, 3B, painted green of course, and reached for the handle. Before I had time to enter however, a suspicious-looking character entered the corridor from the opposite stairwell. He was young, probably of similar age to me or a little older, but other than that, nothing like me at all. He was wearing a black vest, showing off his fairly large arms, and some plain grey jogging bottoms. He had short blond hair atop his boyish round face. There was a very thuggish look about him which was emphasised by his many distasteful tattoos. His eyes, as he glanced in my direction, seemed particularly threatening. He proceeded to perform a coded knock on 3D, a brightly coloured yellow door, which was the home of my newest resident, Kane. Appearing at the door was Kane, a man in his early forties, with a shaven head, was also wearing grey jogging bottoms and the same red hooded top that I always see him in with the hood, as usual, up. He produced a bag of white powder which he promptly handed over to this unknown stranger. Clearly this young lad was a drug user and Kane; his dealer. His client in return handed over a wad of notes and promptly left the way he had come in. Looking shocked when he spotted me, Kane retreated back inside his flat and quickly shut the door.

I felt very uneasy as I headed inside my own flat. Kane could totally ruin things for me. If he's caught dealing drugs on my premises and the police start snooping around, everything could start to go wrong. Just as everything else is starting to go right! Everyone is always telling me how impressed they are with me. Running a property business is pretty impressive at any age, so when they see someone as young as I am doing it, people tend to be intrigued. I pondered the best course of action for Kane. I didn't want him to leave, obviously, but so far we'd only been taking rent from next door, 3C, so the money would be a tremendous help. My wife wasn't working at the moment, either, which didn't make things any easier. Anytime she got a job, she would get bored really easily and quit. She'd been a paramedic at one time and had loved the job. However one day she just quit and since then no job has satisfied her. She has never told me herself why she quit. It must have affected her badly so I don't like to bring it up.

I locked up and threw my keys onto a unit by the door. They slid across the wood making that sound that my wife hates so much. I saw her look over briefly from the living room sofa as I did this. But she soon returned her gaze to the television and the soaps that she watches every day. I felt a little disappointed at this; in happier times, her reaction would have been to give me a comic scowl at this to let me know that she disapproves, but that she isn't really serious. These days though, I don't even get that. A lot had changed between Layla and me in the eighteen months from when I met her to where we were now and I don't know why. Well, I do know, I think. I have been quite distant with her lately. I have been so preoccupied with other things that I've failed to give her much attention. We got married on our one year anniversary. Everyone told us it was too soon, but I had to make her mine. I didn't care what anyone else said, but it was shortly after we were married that we became like this. And as I started to get distant, so did she. It's not something I have the time to deal with whilst I'm doing all this with the flats, but maybe I should pay her more attention. For my own benefit if nothing else.

I sat down beside her on the sofa and she didn't acknowledge me.

'Alright?' I managed.

Layla gave me a grunt. I think this meant yes.

'Are you sure?' I repeated.

She duplicated her previous noise.

I pondered over what to say to further this fascinating conversation, but she beat me to it, 'You're home late. I wish you'd have told me, I could have been doing something else,' she said, reproachfully.

'Like what?' I asked.

'Anything!'

'Well you can do anything you want whether I'm here or not. I don't have to be out for you do something, you know.'

She went quiet at this for a moment. She seemed so aggressive suddenly. This was new behaviour from her. I knew that things hadn't been right for months now, but this was still out of character. She responded after a noticeable gap.

'Where have you been until now anyway?' You're never usually home so late.'

'I was meeting with a young couple. I'm hoping that they'll take one of the flats. They seemed really keen and they haven't even seen the flat yet so it's looking promising. They're coming to view the property in a few days.'

Layla returned to watching the television. I tried to keep the conversation going.

'We'll start to make decent money if we get those two here. You should have seen them. They were mad for each other. They've been together years and you'd think they'd only just met. If they move in I'll only have one empty flat left. Then I can use the rent money to make a start on the other floors giving us more room for even more tenants. Isn't that great?'

'Sounds good,' Layla responded, distantly.

'They're coming round the day after tomorrow to have a look at it. In the morning. And later that afternoon I'm off out to meet another potential tenant. It's gonna be a busy day. Good though.'

I left a pause to wait for a response and then decided to give up. I could see that she wasn't in the mood to try and talk to me so I got up to go to the bedroom, but as I stood up I saw that I'd been sitting on a sock. A blue sock. An unfamiliar blue sock.

I picked it up and decided to question its origins, 'What's this?'

'That's a sock darling. They keep your feet warm,' Layla replied, sarcastically.

'I know that. Why is it here?'

'Oh I'm sorry. Is the house not tidy enough for you when you come home?'

'Stop it, Layla! Why are you being like this?'

'Because I do everything around here and when one sock isn't put away you have to have a dig,'

'I'm sorry you do everything here, but you haven't got a job so…'

'So I should have to be the skivvy then?' Layla fired up.

'That's not what I mean. My money pays for everything so why shouldn't you do things to help around the house?'

'And what's wrong with the house? Do you see anything else out of place? No! Just one little sock and you have to comment.'

'It wasn't about the house, it's about the sock,' I replied, carefully. 'I don't recognise it.'

'What do you mean?' Layla replied, confused.

'Well it isn't mine.'

'Of course it is. Don't be silly,' she said, becoming a little flustered.

'Are you sure? I swear I don't even own a blue pair.'

'Ian, it's a sock. You grab a pair from the drawer and you stick them on. You probably don't know what any of your socks look like.'

'I suppose,' I said slowly.

I'd probably put too much thought into it, but suddenly, this small pointless sock had brought about a reaction I hadn't expected. Layla's attitude had changed abruptly.

'I'm sorry, Ian,' she said as she put her arms around me and gave me a hug.

'For what?' I replied.

'For being snappy. I just stay at home all day with nothing to do. I just want something interesting in my life.'

'Have you been looking for another job?'

'I have, but probably not as much as I should be.'

'Look, why don't we have an early night and just talk? Sort out whatever "this" is.'

'OK,' she agreed and gave me a loving peck.

#

I lay on the bed looking around at our nondescript bedroom. The mattress wasn't the best and I could feel every spring in my back. I'd buy a new one, but we don't exactly use it for I'd like to anymore. Next to our bed was my fairly large wooden desk where I did most of my work. It would be nice to have an office, but this suited my needs just fine. It even had a locked cupboard built-in where I could keep my private things. The bedroom wouldn't be so bad if I'd got round to carpeting it. I stared at the old floorboards that completely killed the room. Layla often nagged me to get a carpet down, but any spare money that I had, I would just spend on the flats…the ones with the *paying* tenants.

Layla lay beside me looking a lot better. I still thought that she looked really cute in her girly pyjamas. We lay on top of the duvet in silence for a moment whilst she wiped away a few tears. We had just grilled each other on the problems in our relationship, but I felt we'd taken a turn for the better now. She rolled over and cuddled up to me now that she'd composed herself.

'So how are you enjoying being the landlord of this big place?' she started.

'It's a challenge,' I said, thinking about my resident drug dealer.

'Is there anything I can do to help?'

'A bit of advice would be handy.'

'Advice about what?'

'I just realised that the new guy that's living in 3D is dealing drugs here.'

'*Just* realised? Come on Ian, you're more switched on than that.'

'You knew?'

'Of course I knew. Erica and I were talking about it this afternoon. We assumed that you knew. She isn't too happy that you've got him living next to her.'

'Do you talk to Erica a lot?'

'Not really. I think she's trying to befriend me, but I don't think she's my kind of person.'

'You should try with her. I think she's pretty funny.'

'I think I have more in common with her boyfriend actually.'

'Who, Lee? The man's a joke. You should see the way he is with their baby. He takes a backseat in that family. Do you know he used to be a policeman?'

'Yeah he has mentioned it. I wonder why he got fired.'

'Probably because he was shit at it!'

'Be nice, Ian. He could think that you're a shit landlord…you know…letting a drug dealer live here.'

'You're right,' I realised with a blank expression on my face. 'I suppose I should go round there and have a word with Kane.'

'Be careful Ian. You're only young. I think you're a bit naïve for his world.'

'I'll be fine,' I said getting up off the bed.

I threw on some clothes and headed out into the corridor. I knocked two doors up on 3D. Suddenly this yellow door didn't seem to suit Kane.

'Bit late, don't ya think?' he said in a gruff voice when he answered the door.

'Well, I knew you were awake,' I started confidently. 'You know I saw you dealing with that kid earlier.'

'What are you talking about? I wasn't dealing. He just owed me some money,' he responded, clearly getting defensive.

'Obviously I'm stupid,' I said, sarcastically. 'Look, I know what

11

you're up to here, and to be honest, I'm not overly bothered what you're doing as long as I'm getting rent. Just try and be a bit more discreet, OK? I don't want one of the neighbours complaining. It's hassle I don't need.'

'Alright, mate. That seems fair. But, whilst we're on the subject of complaints, that old man next door has his TV on really loud. It's every night. Come in and listen. He's watching it right now.'

I only had to step into 3D a short way before hearing exactly what he was talking about. Roger, who lives in 3C with Erica and Lee, was clearly watching a dirty film.

'You hear that?' Kane said, perturbed. 'That's every night I've lived here so far.'

'Yeah I hear it.'

'Who is he anyway?'

'He's Lee's dad.'

'They all live in there together?' Kane uttered in disbelief. 'Is there room for that couple with a baby and his dad?'

'They're a bit cramped, but they manage.'

'Well whatever, can you just sort it out for me please?' he said indicating the wall.

'I'll have a word tomorrow, OK?'

'Thank you,' Kane replied as he shut his door. I managed to glance inside his room before it was closed. It looked very dark and messy. I suppose that was to be expected though. I stood in the corridor and wondered momentarily about whether all this was worth it or not. It was only going to get harder as I filled the rest of the flats.

Chapter 3 – Dysfunctional

Erica stared at the mountain of ironing that she had to do. She set the ironing board up parallel to the television so that she could watch it at the same time. Not that there was much on it to interest her. Lee was watching some morning game show as usual. He doesn't seem interested in it himself, but he still sits there every morning. She looked over at him with a look of annoyance. She was the easy-going type who would rather do everything herself and hope that he would offer to help, but that wasn't going to happen. Lee was still in his pyjamas. He was a tall man. Tall to a point that Erica had to move her ironing board every time he shifted because he would block the television. He had thick curly blonde hair too, which didn't help. In his arms was their baby, Isaac. Erica was thankful that Lee was at least taking him off her hands for once. Isaac looked snug, fast asleep in his blue Babygro. He was what you would call a "good baby"; never any bother and rarely cried. This was just what Erica needed as she felt that looking after Lee was like caring for a small child. Isaac definitely looked more like Erica than Lee. He had her jet black hair and rosy cheeks. When he laughed, his eyes would almost disappear into those cheeks. Just like his mother's. It was part of their playful charm. Erica's hair was short and smart. No hair was awry. It framed her naturally pretty face. A face that required no make-up to look beautiful. In defiance of her surroundings, she always kept herself scrupulously clean.

'Are you going to look for a job in town today?' she directed at Lee.

'Maybe later in the week. I'm not really feeling it today,' Lee responded without taking his eyes off the television.

'They're looking for someone to work the night shift at our place. Want me to get you an application form? It would be good for us too as one of us would always be home to look after Isaac.'

'I'm not working in a supermarket,' Lee spat with a sneer.

'Oh I'm sorry, are you above that kind of work?' Erica replied sarcastically. 'It's alright for me though, I suppose.'

'You know I didn't mean it like that, Erica.'

'Well, that's what it sounded like.'

Erica continued to whittle down the pile of ironing as they both watched the boring program in silence. She ironed the last of her work shirts and made a start on pairing up all the socks. She got to the end and was left with one odd sock.

'That's strange,' she commented.

'What is?' said Lee, off-handedly.

'You're missing a sock. One of your blue ones.'

Lee turned at this, showing sudden interest, 'It's only a sock.'

'I know, but I never lose socks. I always make sure they're washed together.'

'Just throw it away, Erica.' Lee snapped.

'OK, no need to shout,' she responded as she discarded the lonely sock. 'Well that's the end of that then. Oh look. An hour of free time before I have to go to work! Oh, the joys of life!'

'It's not that bad, is it?'

'Not that bad!' Erica exclaimed. 'Look around you. We're all crammed into this poxy little flat. We're still living with your dad. We've got a baby that I hardly ever get to see. The house is always a mess because you never lift a finger,' Erica exhaled loudly.

'You're the one that picked this place, Erica.'

'Well I didn't have much choice on our current budget, did I?' she said as she calmed her breathing. 'OK, rant over, but I could do with a night off from it all.'

Seeing that she distressed, Lee headed over to Erica and put an arm around her, 'OK, how about tomorrow night you have a night to yourself. I'll take dad and Isaac out for the night and you can do whatever you want.'

14

'That would be brilliant, Lee. I might ask Layla if she wants to come round. We could have a girly night, watch a film and get drunk.'

'Layla? You talk to her a lot? I always got the impression that she wasn't too bothered about making friends.'

'She isn't…yet. But eventually I'll win her over with my charm. I know she likes her wine so hopefully that's enough to sway her.'

'Well good luck. I wouldn't have thought she was the kind of person you liked spending time with.'

'She isn't, but I'm not exactly spoilt for choice, am I? She's a bit boring, but who else am I going to make friends with around here?'

'My dad really likes your company.'

'It's not my *company* he likes.'

Lee's father, Roger, rolled himself into the room in his trusty wheelchair.

'Speak of the devil,' chuckled Erica.

'Morning, sweetheart,' yawned Roger.

'And that's my cue to leave,' Erica said as she kissed Lee on the cheek.

'You've got ten minutes yet, haven't you?' said Lee looking at his watch puzzled.

'I know, but I'm gonna stop by next door and ask Layla about tomorrow night. See ya!' Erica called as she left the flat with a smile.

'What's happening tomorrow?' questioned Roger.

'You, me and Isaac are going out tomorrow to give Erica a night off,' replied Lee.

'A night off from what?'

'I don't know. I think everything's just getting on top of her.'

'Oh right. Where are we going?'

'I don't know yet. I'll have to have a think.'

'Strip club?' Roger's face lit up at the thought.

'No dad. We can't take a baby to a strip club. Besides, Erica would kill me.'

'But it's not for you two. It's for me. I need some fun too, ya know.'

'Well, get yourself off then. I'm not stopping you.'

'I can't go on my own. Who'll push me?'

'Here's an idea; why don't you just walk?'

'Not doing that. It's bad enough that you've got me living on the third floor here. Getting up and down these stairs every day's a nightmare.'

'Yeah, I'm sure it's a real struggle sitting in your wheelchair whilst me and Erica carry you up.'

'Well, if I walked up those stairs every day I probably would end up needing a wheelchair for real.'

'What would be the difference? You never get out of the thing anyway.'

'Whatever. I'm getting some cereal.'

Roger wheeled towards the kitchen in his metallic blue chariot. His mostly bald head was kept warm by the horseshoe-shaped patch of grey hair that ran around the back of his cranium. He grabbed his silver bifocals from the kitchen unit where he'd left them the night before, then stood up with ease and reached high up for his favourite brand of cereal. He sat down again to pour them into a bowl.

'I'm sure Erica puts my cereal right at the top so that she can watch me struggle,' Roger called back into the living room.

'It's hardly a struggle though, is it, dad?' replied Lee.

'You'll be thankful I put myself in this wheelchair early before I needed it. This way I can still do a few things and don't completely rely on you,' he said as he grabbed the milk from the fridge.

'You're really considerate, dad.'

'I try,' said Roger virtuously as he poured the milk onto his cereal. 'OK Lee, it's ready.'

Roger wheeled himself into the living room. Lee stood up with a sigh and placed the still sleeping Isaac into a baby swing in the middle of the room. Lee sulkily headed into the kitchen to collect his father's breakfast. Roger stayed in the wheelchair which he'd now parked alongside the sofa. Lee grabbed a foldaway table from the kitchen, propped it up in front of his dad and placed the cereal on top of it before resuming his own seat back on the sofa.

'You forgot my spoon,' said Roger, genuinely amazed at the oversight.

Lee stood yet again and stormed into the kitchen, ripped open a drawer, removed a spoon and slammed it shut. When he returned he threw the spoon into the bowl causing a few splashes of milk to escape. Roger happily began to tuck into his beloved cereal. Lee began to flick through the channels of television showing little or no interest in everything he came across.

'What do you reckon to our new neighbour then?' said Roger through a mouthful of cereal and milk.

'Not spoke to him yet,' replied Lee with a shrug.

'Doesn't his kind of behaviour get your blood rushing again?'

'What do you mean? What behaviour?'

'I've seen him dealing drugs right out there in the corridor.'

'Really? Well it's not my problem anymore and it's certainly not yours, so stay out of his way.'

'Doesn't it make you miss it though? The police force?'

'No, dad. I'm fine as I am.'

'Twelve years though, Lee. Twelve years. And you threw it all away. And for what! Drugs? Maybe *that's* why our new friend doesn't bother you. Are you gonna start buying from him now, too?'

'I don't know how many times I have to tell you, dad. I have never taken drugs in my life.'

'Then why did they find some in your locker?'

'Look dad. If *you* don't believe me, how was I going to convince anyone else that they weren't mine? Someone must have put them there.'

'Oh give over. You've been watching too many movies. Who would want to do that?'

'I don't know. They'd been wanting to get rid of me for years.'

'Yes, and don't I know it! You don't know the things I had to do to keep you in that job. They'd have got rid of you two years before, if it wasn't for me,' Roger trailed off towards the end of his sentence, realising he had said something that he should have probably kept to himself.

'What do you mean?' piped up Lee.

'Well, it doesn't matter now. You threw it all away.'

'Whatever, dad. I shouldn't have to defend myself to you.'

'Well, you need to be on the lookout for a decent job. I don't want Isaac growing up and seeing his dad like this. We can't all live on Erica's wage forever.'

'I'll start looking again soon. I just want to enjoy my time off for a bit.'

'You mean you haven't started looking yet?' spewed Roger. 'Then where do you keep disappearing off to in the middle of the day?'

'You've noticed that?' said Lee anxiously.

'Of course I have. I had to make my own cuppa yesterday dinner time.'

'I knew you'd only leave your room for food or drink.'

'So where were you?'

'It's none of your business dad, and can you please not say anything about this to Erica.'

'Why not? Lee, what are you up to?'

'Nothing dad, just keep your mouth shut about it, OK.'

'Whatever,' said Roger as he dropped his spoon back into his now empty bowl. 'I'm off back to my bedroom to watch a film.'

'If you're going to be watching dirty films again, can you keep the volume down, please? We have a neighbour now, remember.'

'I was here first,' said Roger vigorously as he wheeled into his bedroom and slammed the door.

Lee relaxed back into his sofa for only a few moments before there was a knock at his front door. Puzzled at who this might be he sloped over to the front door and opened it. His heart sank as he saw Layla standing in his doorway. Normally this would garner a better reaction from him, but as he wasn't looking his best he felt embarrassed. He quickly ran his hand through his hair, which didn't help, and pulled his pyjama top out of the bottoms where it had somehow worked its way in. He felt his cheeks going red.

'What are you doing here? It's not like you to call unannounced,' Lee said, concernedly. 'What if Erica had been home?'

'Well, I knew she wouldn't be because she's just left mine. Did you know that she wants me to come round tomorrow night?' Layla said, clearly worried by this.

'Yeah, she did mention it before she left.'

'What am I going to do? I can't spend a full evening with her, but I couldn't think of an excuse fast enough.'

'So you agreed?'

'What choice did I have? I don't want her thinking I don't like her; she might get suspicious. Oh, and speaking of suspicions, I had a right job on explaining this.'

Layla thrust Lee's blue sock into his hand.

'Shit, sorry about that,' Lee chuckled. 'Erica noticed this was missing too.'

'What? We need to be careful. It's little things like this that will get us caught out.'

'I know, you're right. I shouldn't laugh.'

'Well, you don't take it that serious do you? It's alright for you. You're with a girlfriend that you aren't that bothered about. If Ian finds out, I could end up going through a messy divorce.'

'I *do* take it seriously. I have a baby to think about. Erica would probably stop me from seeing him.'

'Then maybe we shouldn't do it.'

'Yes we should,' Lee said desperately 'If I'm gonna get caught eventually then I want it to have been at least for something,'

'So what we've had so far is nothing then?'

'No, you know what I mean. It's been great kissing you and doing stuff, but I want you properly. All of you. I can't wait any longer.'

'I know. And we will. We just need to make sure we have enough time. I don't want to have to rush and ruin it. And I definitely don't want to get caught. I've only had your socks off so far and that nearly put an end to it. God knows what would happen if I got all your clothes off.'

'Magic! That's what,' Lee flirted. 'I promise I'll be the best you've ever had. In fact I could ask my dad to watch Isaac and I could come round and show you right now.'

'No, not today. I don't know what Ian's schedule is, so he could come back at anytime.'

'But I want you *so* bad!'

'I know, and I want you too. We'll have the chance soon, don't worry.'

'Soon when?' Lee responded giddily.

'Tomorrow afternoon,' Layla said with a grin.

'Tomorrow? Really? Just a minute; this seems too easy. I've waited for you all this time and now it's tomorrow?'

'Well Ian is meeting some potential tenants tomorrow. He should be out most of the afternoon. You need to wait until he's definitely gone though, because he'll be here most of the morning. He's showing a new couple one of the flats.'

'More people to hide from, then. Great! What are they like?'

'I don't know. He just said it's a young lad and lass.'

'Young lass eh?' said Lee jokingly.

'Hey! Aren't two women enough for you?' she said giving a teasing slap on the arm.

'I was kidding. With any luck Ian will cop off with the lass. It would be better if he found someone his own age.'

'Ha, I doubt it. He adores me. I don't know why. And anyway this young couple are supposedly mad for each other, so I doubt she will have a wandering eye.'

'That's a shame. Anyway, I can't wait for tomorrow.'

'Me too,' she said placing a caressing arm on his shoulder. She quickly drew it back as Roger burst into view.

'Who's at the door son?' Roger grunted in a perturbed way.

'It's just me, Mr Wilkinson,' said Layla sweetly.

'Oh, Layla. Hello gorgeous,' Roger replied with renewed excitement in his voice. 'Are you coming in for a coffee?'

'No, not today.'

'That's a shame. I know Isaac loves to see a different face around here. Especially such a pretty one.'

'Oh stop it dad,' Lee interrupted. 'Layla doesn't want you letching all over her.'

'Oh aye, and how do you know what she wants?' spat Roger scornfully. 'I was just paying the young lass a compliment.'

'No you weren't! You were being a pervert again.'

'Maybe she likes that sort of talk. I was just watching a film and it was about women who…'

'Dad! No one wants to know about your films.'

'I've got to go now anyway,' Layla interrupted awkwardly. 'Goodbye Mr Wilkinson, bye Lee.'

Layla's smouldering gaze lingered on Lee for far too long before she returned home to 3B.

'Now look what you've done. You've scared her off,' said Roger, annoyed.

'*I've* scared her off?' replied Lee, gobsmacked. 'You and your filth is what scared her off.'

Lee slammed his flat door, shutting them inside. He stormed over to the living room and back to his sofa.

Roger was hot on his tail with rapid strokes of his wheels, 'It was you! Talking back to me. You should respect your elders. Especially when I had company. She must have thought you very rude.'

'*You* had company?' Lee laughed. 'She wasn't here to see *you*.'

'Oh aye!' Roger commented with a raised eyebrow. 'Why was she here then?'

'She was just asking about bills and rent and stuff. Nothing for you to worry about.'

'I reckon she was just using that as an excuse to come round. She knows there's a sexy, virile, man living here and she's after a piece.'

'You can't say things like that, Dad. I already have Erica.'

'Not you, you imbecile. I was talking about me. I could see it in her eye. She wanted me.'

'Are you dreaming dad? She wouldn't go for you.'

'I'm the single one, not you. Why do you always get in my way?'

'Dad, you're a seventy nine year old cripple wannabe. She's far too young for you.'

'She's only in her early thirties. If anything that's bordering on too old for me.'

'If you say so, dad. Besides, even if she did, she has a husband,' Lee said scornfully.

'I see now. You're after a bit, aren't you?' Roger said with sudden realisation.

'No, dad!'

'Yes you are. Or maybe…you're already getting a bit.'

'Dad, stop it,' Lee said, panic sounding in his voice. 'If Erica hears you talking like that you'll upset her.'

'But I'm right, aren't I? I saw the way she looked at you when she left. And…' a moment of realisation appeared on his face, 'that's where you've been going all those times whilst Erica's been at work.'

'You're way off, dad,' Lee said, angrily as he stood and walked away.

'I don't think I am, son. And, as you've already said, you've got Erica. She's a good lass! And you've got a beautiful son. We've got it good here. She does a lot for us and I don't want *you* messing it up. You know if she found out she could take Isaac away from you. I love that little lad. I love that we all get to live together. Don't throw it away, Lee.'

'And what about what *I* want?' Lee said with sudden honesty.

'What do you mean?' Roger said, concerned.

'What if *I'm* not happy?'

'Sometimes, son, you have to put your own happiness aside for your children. Especially with Isaac so young. He needs his dad. You're just going to have to accept that your life revolves around him now. At least until he's a bit older.'

'I know. I know you're right, dad. And that's why I haven't left Erica before now.'

'Why haven't you ever spoken to me about this before?'

'Because I know how much you like Erica.'

'You can still talk to me about it though. So I was right about Layla then?'

'No, dad. I'm not having an affair,' Lee lied.

He thought about his dad's feelings for a while. Lee had never considered how his actions would affect *him* until now, but he was too excited for tomorrow to deal that at present. He couldn't wait for Layla any longer. He had to have her. All that was left was to think of a way to get Erica out of the flat.

Chapter 4 – A Storyteller's Woes

I looked around the room to attempt to gauge people's reactions. I know how my story ends. They know how my story ends. *But*, they don't know the full details of the journey along the way.

'I assure you it *is* all relevant,' I responded to a question which had been asked.

As sad as my story is, I hoped that no one was bored. Still, these people were here to listen to what I had to say. I have seen the whole thing distorted in newspapers and women's magazines. I need these people to hear my story for what it is and not how the world sees it. As I caught the eyes of a few members of my audience I could tell that they weren't losing interest yet, but could well be on the way. They looked attentive enough, but they were clearly waiting for me to get to the juicy bits.

I decided a few crumbs to keep them going was the answer, 'I suppose I'd better start telling you about Alex and Natalie.'

Chatter burst through the room at the mention of this. Alex Kendall. That's a name I'm not likely to ever forget.

'That's one of the main reasons that you're here right? To hear about *him*! The young man who caused me so much pain and anguish? Well, Alex joins my story very shortly, much to my pleasure…at the time. I had no idea what a nightmare having him there would be for me later on…'

Chapter 5 – Colour Crisis

I awoke to a loud knocking. Surely it was early still. Alex and Natalie wouldn't have arrived yet. I looked over at the clock. Seven a.m. They weren't due for another two hours. Maybe they were really keen to move in to the flat, which was an exciting thought. If I could convince those two to move in, I would have almost filled the floor. There was another loud knock at the door. Layla rolled over and poked me in the back as if to say "get the door, I don't want to move". I looked down at my pyjamas. It was either keep them waiting and get dressed or answer the door in my pyjamas. I chose the latter. I hopped out of the bed and ran to the front door. When I opened the door I was surprised to see a red-faced Kane standing there.

'Kane? What are you doing here? It's a bit early,' I said.

'Not for me it isn't,' he replied angrily. 'I've been up most of the night. I'd have come round earlier, but I knew you'd moan if I did.'

'Why, what's the matter?' I asked, concerned.

'Same as before. The pervy old man having his TV on really loud. It's last thing at night and first thing at morning. And a couple of times in between. I thought my choice of films were seedy, but the things I heard them saying last night *I'd* never even heard of.'

'I'll ask him if he'll mix up his film library from time to time.'

'It's not his choice of film I care about. I actually think it's quite funny that a man his age is still watching that stuff. What I don't find funny is being woken up two and three times a night by it. I've got a business to run and I need my sleep on a night.'

'I don't think you can class dealing drugs as a business.'

'It pays your rent.'

'Oh God!' I exclaimed, clutching my head. 'I'm going to prison aren't I?'

'Don't be daft, why would you?' Kane chuckled.

'Because you're dealing drugs on my property, and then using your drug money to pay the rent, and I know about it. I really wish I didn't.'

'Look,' Kane assured. 'I've been doing this a long time now. I'm not going to get caught. And besides, no one could prove that you knew about it.'

'I suppose,' I replied, easily convinced.

'All I need from you is to let me move to another flat. Now!'

'Can't we do it later? I have another couple coming to look at the flats in a couple of hours. I won't have the time.'

'You don't need the time. Just give me the key and I'll move all my stuff across myself.'

'I suppose.'

I thought about it for a moment and then headed back into my flat to grab another key.

'Here, you can move in next door to yourself, 3E,' I said, offering out the key.

'You're joking aren't you?' Kane laughed.

'What?' I said, puzzled.

'I'm not living in a flat with a pink door.'

'It's more of a salmon colour, I'd say.'

'It's pink,' he said, matter-of-factly. 'I'll just move into that one at the end,' he suggested, pointing at the flat next to mine. '3A…the nice red one.'

A smile spread across his face as he spoke.

'But that one's next to me,' I said worriedly.

'So?' he responded.

I thought for a moment and then gave in. I needed to keep him happy if I was going to keep him here. I let out a loud sigh, grabbed the key to 3A from my flat and shoved it into his hand.

'There you go,' I said, disappointed.

'Brilliant. I'll get moving my stuff now,' he said smugly.

'Do it quietly, though. Everyone else will still be asleep.'

'You'll barely hear me,' he said with a wide grin.

'Good. Make sure you post your old key when you're done. If I get a chance I'll come and help you in about half an hour once I've had my breakfast and got dressed.'

'No need,' he said, nodding towards his current lodgings. 'My mate will help me.'

I peered out of my doorway to see the drug user whom I'd seen previously, standing in front of Kane's, soon-to-be-abandoned, flat.

'He's early,' I said.

'He slept on my sofa. He couldn't sleep well, either,' Kane informed me.

'He stayed over? Excellent! Does he do that often?' I asked anxiously.

'Yeah he spends a lot of time here. Where he can get what he needs. I think it's like a second home to him. His parents aren't too accommodating of his habits.'

'Some parents are just cruel,' I replied sarcastically.

#

At ten minutes to nine, I looked at myself in the mirror. A professional looking man stood in the reflection. I felt confident about my upcoming meeting with Alex and Natalie. I thought about the loving relationship that the two of them had as I glanced over at Layla still in her pyjamas and in her usual spot in front of the television. That brief progress that we made the other day had cheered me up and I even got a loving kiss on the cheek from her when I went over to say goodbye. I saw my used cereal bowl on the kitchen unit. I was tempted to leave it for Layla to clean as I doubted she would be doing much else today, but decided against it. I washed the crockery, put it away and checked the time again. Five minutes to go. I was excited as well as a little nervous about having the two of them here. I decided that I'd better go and check if Kane had left his flat tidy for me. I headed out into to the corridor and braced myself as I placed my hand on the yellow door's handle. I entered 3D and my heart sank as I saw the state it was in. It was dark. It smelled. There was rubbish and used drug paraphernalia lying around on the sofa and carpet. I felt like an idiot. What did I think he was going to do? Move flats and have it spick and span within two hours? Alex and Natalie would be here any minute; I needed to do something fast. I sprinted out into the corridor, ran right to the end and banged on the red door that was 3A. Kane slumped through the door as he opened it.

'Ian!' he merrily slurred. 'Thanks for the new flat mate. It's loads better. Well actually. It's exactly the same, but this one has a red door. Look.'

He pointed and let his finger trail down the doorway and his eyes closed.

'What's the matter with you? You're not that tired are you?' I said.

'No, no, no. Well yes. I am actually. Now I can get rest finally.'

'Have you been drinking?'

'No, no, no. I just lit up to celebrate my new room. It's so much more peaceful. You're way better neighbours than that other family.'

'Kane!' I shouted at him. 'I needed you to leave your old room in a fit state. I have people coming to look at it any minute now.'

'What's wrong with it?' he asked, innocently.

'What's wrong with it? It's a right shit-hole in there. I need you to come and move all the drugs and rubbish out of there. Now! My appointment will be here any minute.'

'Urgh, fine.'

I dragged him as we ran towards the door, but I stopped us dead, halfway across the corridor. The sound of footsteps and laughter could be heard coming up the stairs. It was them.

'Quick, turn around!' I shouted.

'What. Why?' Kane asked, confused.

'Because I don't want potential tenants seeing you,' I said, ushering him back into his room.

'What's that supposed to mean?' he said stopping us in our tracks.

'It means I need to do everything I can to get them here and if they see you, it might put them off. Look. You've already screwed me out of showing them one of the flats. Now they only have one to choose from.'

I almost managed to get him back into his room when he decided to walk back himself.

'Fine, I'll stay out the way,' he said. 'But I'm not having you treat me like a third class citizen.'

I closed his door. This treatment of Kane was risky as I knew he could be very dangerous, but hopefully he was too tired to care at present.

Seconds later, Alex and Natalie came in to view. They were kissing whilst they were walking. I still found their passion for each other admirable. They soon stopped when Natalie looked up and saw me standing in the corridor.

Alex was an average sized young looking man. Even at the age of twenty five he could have passed for an eighteen-year-old. He had a bit of a stubble on his face which aged him somewhat. He was trim with some small evidence of being a gym-goer; not muscular, exactly, but a hint of something there. This look was reinforced by his skinny jeans. There was a bed hair look going on with his brown hair that I would normally assume was due to forgetting to do it, but it had been like that the last time I saw him too. He was dressed quite trendily in his branded t-shirt and bright green trainers. His t-shirt was a pale pink colour, which seemed like a good sign. My convincing them to live in the pink flat wouldn't be as difficult as I thought.

Natalie was the same height as Alex. Maybe a touch taller, but not really noticeable. What *was* noticeable was her perfectly straight fringe covering her forehead. The rest of her mousy brown hair was also perfectly straight and down past her shoulders. She was clearly protective of said hair as I saw Alex accidently touch it, whereupon she smacked his hand away. She was wearing a warm-looking purple jumper today, again reinforcing my confidence in being able to shift this flat, with the similar coloured door, onto them. If I couldn't, I would definitely need to rethink the paintwork of the doors.

'Alex, Natalie. Did you find it OK?' I called merrily, breathing a sigh of relief that I'd managed to stow Kane away just in time.

'Hi, Ian,' Alex called back. 'Yeah it wasn't too hard to find. Is my car OK out in the front? There's a sign saying I'll be clamped.'

'Yeah, don't worry about that,' I chuckled. 'I put that up to deter shoppers from parking here. Even though there's nothing else on the lane leading up here, people tend to park here and walk in to town to save on parking costs.'

'OK, thanks,' he said.

Natalie joined in 'I'm glad we're on this floor. The others look like they're in a right mess. I nearly got Alex to turn around halfway up the stairs.'

'Well, you'll be glad you didn't when you see inside the flat,' I said.

'Please tell me the green one is one of the empty ones. That's my favourite colour,' said Alex, lifting his foot to show me the colour of his shoes.

'Well, I have some bad news, actually,' I told them, warily. 'I only have *one* flat to show you now.'

'What!' Alex exclaimed. 'You've already filled the other one since we last saw you?'

I hesitated for a moment. I was about to tell them the truth, but then I thought that if I let them believe that this was the case, it would encourage them to reach a decision quicker.

'That's right!' I lied. 'They're not moving in for a while yet, but they've already secured the flat behind the yellow door. They're such good prices in today's market; people are crying out for flats like these.'

'OK, so which one's left?' said Alex, sounding worried.

'Just 3E I'm afraid...the pink one.'

'No,' Alex sighed.

'Yes!' Natalie said with a cheesy grin on her face.

'Of all the luck,' Alex sighed again. 'I can't live there. I'm sorry.'

'But, but look how cute it is, Alex,' Natalie begged. 'It's pink. I love it.'

'You would. You're a girl,' he said.

I attempted to save the situation, 'I could always paint the door another colour if you do decide to live here.'

Alex and Natalie gave opposing responses to my suggestion, and begun to have a comic argument over what action they should take.

'Why not just look inside first and see what you think?' I interrupted.

They agreed and all three of us went inside. As small as the space in these flats were, I'd prided myself on the décor of them. I thought this would be the only way to win these people over. I knew Alex and Natalie were on a low income, so as long as I made them an offer they couldn't refuse, they would be mine. Alex worked as an assistant mechanic and Natalie was a student, studying to become a doctor, so their current budget was quite limited, which, for me, was just what I needed to get them to rent a flat. The look on their faces told me that I had succeeded.

'I love it, Alex,' Natalie said to him. 'It's cosy, there's plenty of room for all our stuff and the fish will be really happy in that corner over there by the window. They'll be able to look out so they don't get bored.'

'Fish?' I said quizzically.

'Yeah, mate,' Alex said. 'They're like children to her. You should see her with them. She'd take them out for walks if she could.'

'Shut up, Alex,' Natalie said as she turned to me. 'They're exotic fish, Ian. They require more care and attention than your regular goldfish. They need to be treated right.'

'And they are!' Alex said sarcastically. 'My empty wallet every week is proof of that.'

'But they love you, Alex,' she said seriously.

'I don't think for one second those fish have any idea, so don't try and be cute with me,' he said.

'Of course they have, Alex. They know you're the provider. They really appreciate what you do for them. And so do I,' she said very lovingly.

I couldn't believe what I was hearing. This girl really did love her fish. I decided it was time to swoop in for the kill.

'So do you think there's something we could work out here?' I said sidling over to them.

'Yes definitely. We love it. As long as the price is right,' Alex said.

'And you keep the door pink,' Natalie requested.

We all had a little chuckle. I eventually discussed the price with them and they were understandably over the moon. This was a great step forward for me. My last challenge would be the hardest. Filling the remaining flat would be the most difficult. Especially now that I'd told Alex and Natalie that I already had tenants for it.

Chapter 6 – Intimacy, Intimidation and Intrepidity

Layla pulled the black bin bag of rubbish from its green metallic holster. It tore as it snagged on the pedal-lift lid. This annoyed her as she buys the more expensive, more durable sacks, but Ian had done the shopping most recently and bought these really thin cheap ones. She didn't want to make an issue over it, due to her not bringing a wage in at the moment, and he was clearly trying to save money. She fashioned a few makeshift knots in the sack to help retain its contents. The main bins were just outside the building. Ian had said that he intended to install a chute at some point, but for now she would have to walk all the way down.

As usual for her, it was midday and she was still in her pyjamas. She intended to make herself look presentable for when Lee came round shortly. But if she got changed before Ian left for the afternoon, he would ask questions. She threw her dressing gown on and stepped out of the front door.

'Still in your pyjamas?' said Erica, who was just passing.

'Yeah. Is that bad?' Layla replied.

'No, I suppose not. It'd be nice to sit around at home all day without a job or any dependants,' said Erica, giving a downwards glance to Isaac, who was strapped to her chest in his papoose baby carrier.

Layla gave an uncomfortable smile at this. She wondered if Erica was being sarcastic or genuine. It really was nice not having any responsibilities, but at the same time, she didn't like having to rely on Ian, especially with her recent dishonesty.

'Are you off to work?' Layla said, attempting to steer the conversation with a favourable note.

'No, I've got the day off,' Erica responded.

'Oh, are you off out, then?' Layla questioned, worried that her appointment with Lee would be cancelled.

'Yeah. Lee convinced me to take Isaac out for the afternoon. He says one of his friends is coming over, so I'll leave them to it. It's only fair I suppose, seeing as though he's giving us tonight.'

'Tonight?' Layla asked, puzzled.

'Yeah. You're coming over for a girly night, remember? Don't tell me you forgot!'

'No, no, of course not,' Layla lied. 'I'm looking forward to it,' she said skilfully lying again.

'OK. Brilliant. Just come over when you're ready. I'll see you later.'

'Will you throw this in the bin for me on your way out, please?' Layla said, holding out the bag of rubbish.

'Go on then, seeing as it's you,' said Erica, taking the sack from Layla. 'See you tonight.'

'Bye!' Layla forced.

As Erica left, Layla stood for a moment in the corridor, watching her. She thought about how she had got herself into this. If she was to continue this affair with Lee then she couldn't become too good a friend to Erica. That would make the situation ten times worse. Seeing her tonight, just the two of them, was bad enough. She stared into space for a long while, only to be interrupted.

'Alright love?'

A voice brought her out of her daze. In front of her, towering over, was Kane, looking very menacing. She'd already formed enough thoughts and judgements about him, but this was the first time she'd been face to face with him. She didn't know what to do, so ignored him; hopefully he would think she hadn't heard him. Kane did not take this well and raised his voice as he repeated his question. Layla managed a pathetic "hi" in response to this aggressive approach, but, like she always did, managed to avoid eye contact with him.

'Nice outfit,' Kane said, sleazily.

At a loss for what do, Layla ignored him yet again and headed back towards her flat. Kane marched over threateningly and placed his arm across her doorway, blocking her escape route.

'Where're you going? Don't you know it's rude to ignore someone when they're talking to you?' Kane said, suddenly seeming even more threatening.

'I'm sorry. I'm just tired,' she said, keeping her eyes focussed on the ground, trying to avoid his gaze.

'It's also rude not to look at someone whilst they're talking to you. But, I suppose I could let you off, seeing as though you make this corridor look so much better,' he said, creepily tracing his finger along the collar of her dressing gown and getting dangerously close to her cleavage.

He didn't push his luck. It was just enough to get Layla nervous, but not sufficient to cause her to act. She stood frozen, unsure what to do. She inwardly prayed for a miracle, which shortly came. The door to flat 3C opened and Lee entered the corridor pushing Roger. Kane responded to the presence of a third party by backing off towards the stairwell door.

He kept eye contact with her as backed away, 'Been nice seeing you.'

He pushed open the heavy fire door and left the corridor. Layla saw him turn and head up the stairs just as the door shut with a loud thud.

Lee brought Layla back to safety with a question, 'What was that about?'

'Just our resident perv,' she said with a moue of distaste.

'Oh dear, you're best off keeping your distance,' Lee said, trying to end the subject quickly.

'I don't like his sort,' interrupted Roger. 'Ogling young women for a cheap thrill. He should be ashamed of himself.'

Lee responded in disbelief to this hypocritical comment, 'You're one to talk. The other day you asked Erica if you could help her shower. You don't exactly treat women with respect, Dad.'

'Yeah, but I'm old. It's funny when I do it,' Roger chuckled.

'Anyway, I'll see you later, Layla. I've got to drop Dad off at the gym.'

'I didn't know you went to the gym,' said Layla, shocked.

'You know me, love,' Roger said confidently whilst loosening up his shoulders. 'I like to keep in shape.'

'No,' Lee interjected. 'What he actually does is sits in the Jacuzzi and stares at all the women.'

Roger gave his son a disgruntled look at what he clearly thought was an attempt to spoil his chances.

'Anyway,' Lee continued, 'the quicker I get rid of him, the quicker I'll be back.'

He gave Layla a wink and headed towards the stairwell exit. She allowed his hand to stroke her shoulder as he passed, once she was out of Roger's viewpoint. She quickly removed it, however, at the sound of a door opening and Lee followed suit by speeding towards the corridor exit with his dad. The noise was the sound of Ian exiting and locking 3E at the other end of the corridor. Layla breathed a sigh of relief when she had realised that he hadn't spotted her and her lover chatting.

Lee was long gone by the time he did notice her, 'Hi, darling,' he called, joyfully, as he came over to her. 'Alex and Natalie, that young couple I was telling you about, have decided to come live here.'

'That's brilliant, Ian. I'm really happy for you,' she said.

'You've just missed them actually. I was just putting a few finishing touches on the flat.'

'When are they moving in?'

'A week or so,' Ian responded, eyes sparkling with excitement. 'I'm going to have to dash though, love. I'm meeting those other hopefuls soon so I need to change my suit,' he said, indicating a few dusty marks on the one he was wearing.

Layla followed Ian inside their flat and watched as he changed suits. She thought about what she was about to do. She did love Ian, once upon a time, but things were too far gone for her now. She couldn't leave him, though. She had nowhere to go and she was too scared of breaking his heart. He clearly still loved her and did so much for her. She felt a tear escape as the feeling of guilt took over. But she had a much stronger feeling inside her. A feeling that vanished whenever she spent time with Lee. Claustrophobia!

#

With makeup done, nice clothes on, and Ian out of the house, Layla's heart raced when there was a knock at the door. Lee stood in front of her as she opened it. He didn't speak. A look between them assured him that he was free to enter. Enter, and do whatever he wanted.

He slowly moved towards her, shutting the front door behind him. She matched his speed as she retreated from him, staring deeply into his eyes, daring him to act on his impulses. He had been waiting for her for so long. She had been teasing him for weeks in the build-up to this moment, and now, he was about to have her.

She found herself backed against a wall. He ceased his advance, holding his positon just inches away from her, and stared into her eyes. She innocently looked back at him and bit her lip, seductively. That was all the invitation he needed and he locked his lips with hers; their tongues invading each other's mouths. Layla's heart dropped as excitement took over. She felt she was doing something, almost illegal.

A burning fire ignited inside Lee. He grabbed her behind and lifted her up as she wrapped her legs around his waist. He pinned her up against the wall with just enough force for her let out a slight gasp of mixed pain and pleasure. He could barely hold her steady against the wall as their vigorous movements couldn't be contained. He slid her across the wall and set her down on the windowsill.

She wrapped her arms around his neck and pulled him in into her. He passionately kissed her neck causing her head to drop back as moans escaped her open mouth. As he moved up and began to nibble her ear, his hand wandered down the front of her shoulder and curved onto her subtle breast. His hand lingered for a moment atop her clothing, however this was not enough for him. He slid his hand back up her chest before dipping it back down towards her breast, beneath her top this time. He could barely contain his excitement as he passed the lip of her bra and reached his desired destination. Her nipple. Hard. Erect. Perfect! His finger circled its circumference. Her light moans let him know that she particularly enjoyed this. He continued, revelling in her gratitude before grabbing her breast in full.

He pulled her off the windowsill; back on to her feet.

'Turn around,' Lee whispered in her ear.

She obliged, keeping her eyes on him as she did, and pushed her bottom against his growing bulge as she rotated.

'Look,' he indicated out of the window.

Far away, people were just visible walking by the main road. This safe thrill excited her. She watched, wondering if they could see them. The idea that they could turned her on even more.

The palm of his hand created a cold sensation on her belly as it moved slowly down. She held her breath in anticipation as his hand slid past the waist band of her thong. It felt like a lifetime waiting for his hand to reach between her legs, but when it did, she hunched over in pleasure. It was too much. She made a grab for his hand to stop him, but, using his free hand, he grabbed both her wrists in his palm and slammed them against the window. She was powerless to stop him as he expertly navigated around her, causing her moans to become more audible. She tried her best to keep her volume down, but this attempt was rendered inept when he plunged two fingers deep inside her. She screamed with pleasure as he explored her inner essence.

She let out a gasp as he retracted his fingers, but her pleasure doubled up when he ran his now lubricated fingers rapidly over her bud. She writhed and struggled against his powerful one handed hold against her. She couldn't contain herself. She climaxed, loudly, bucking her body against Lee's as she did. His fingers controlled their pace as she came down from her mind-blowing orgasm. He released her hands and her knees buckled, requiring him to support her with his now free arm.

Once she had found her balance he turned her around to face him and kissed her deeply again. After a brief moment he threw her on her back onto the sofa.

'You're amazing with your fingers,' she said.

'I'm even better with my tongue,' he said, pulling her jeans and underwear down and off her body to the floor.

'Enough foreplay,' she said, desperately, pulling his head back up to her level. 'I need you now!'

'I have to know what you taste like,' he said, hungrily.

She responded by running her own finger between her legs and seductively placing it in his mouth. His eyes closed as he tasted her.

He held the flavour in his mouth momentarily before agreeing with her. He needed her too.

He vigorously kissed her as she unbuttoned his jeans and pushed them down with her heels. She couldn't wait any longer. She was in a frenzy of lust. She felt an empty space inside her that he had to fill, immediately. She reached down and, not able to see, smiled with surprise as she grabbed his impressive manhood.

They continued to kiss as she manoeuvred his erection between her legs, wetting the tip so much that when it reached her hole, his downward force caused him to plunge fully inside her. She gasped at the sensation and wrapped her arms around his upper back, holding him close. She held him still, whilst she enjoyed the feeling of fullness. Her inner muscles squeezed tightly around his invading organ.

After a few moments, she released her hold on him. He lifted his head and looked into her eyes. Neither smiled, they just stared, lustfully at each other. Then Lee began thrusting, fast, catching her off guard. She couldn't keep her mouth closed as waves of pleasure overcame her.

Lee's long-awaited itch was being scratched. He overflowed with testosterone as he pierced her, filling her again and again, harder and harder. It was instinct. Animalistic. He could not slow down. He wanted to. He wanted to make this amazing feeling last longer, but he'd wanted her for too long. He couldn't hold back. He felt that amazing sensation travel up his shaft as he exploded inside her.

His rapid breathing began to steady as he finished. He gave her a worried look, scared that this short experience would disappoint.

'I'm sorry,' he apologised. 'I've just been waiting for this for so long.'

'It's fine,' she replied, happily. 'It was still amazing!'

'I can go again.'

'Really?' she said, excited at the thought that was, in fact, not over.

'Yeah. You turn me on so much.'

She could feel him still fully hard inside her. She hummed with delight.

'I can't believe we didn't use a condom,' Lee said.

'It's fine! I'm on the pill,' she dismissed.

Lee smiled and kissed her again.

'Let's go to the bedroom,' he said, lifting her up.

He carried her to the bed that slept her and her husband and closed the bedroom door, sealing their adulterous actions inside.

#

Layla woke. A brief moment to stretch before she realised where she was. In her marital bed with Lee still asleep besides her. She panicked and jolted her head around to her beside clock, almost decapitating herself. She breathed a sigh of relief as she saw it wasn't as late as she'd feared. They still had time, but she didn't want to push it. She needed to get all the bedding in the washing machine before Ian came home. She shook Lee to wake him up. He wearily rolled over and looked at her.

'Hi,' he said in a satisfied voice.

'Hi,' she replied, just as satisfied. 'I really panicked just now. I thought we'd slept longer than we had. That was stupid,' she said, relief still evident in her voice.

'Why, what time is it?'

'It's not that late yet, but I don't want to chance it. You should go!'

'In a minute,' he said, wrapping his arms around her and pulling her in for a cuddle. 'That was the best nap I've ever had.'

'It was really nice,' she said, removing his arms from around her waist. 'but you really need to go.'

'Fine!' he said climbing out of bed stark naked.

She grinned a little a she saw her newest toy swaying from side to side as he pulled his boxer shorts up. She watched as he got dressed and thought about her life and what she was doing with it. Here was someone who she had plenty of passion with, lots in common, and someone who she thought was worth risking all that she had. But then, on the other hand, she was married…to a much younger man. She wasn't sure if this was the problem or not, but she knew something wasn't right. Lee made her feel special physically, but Ian did so much for her. He treated her like a princess. Provided for her. Loved her. But it wasn't enough. That inexplicable feeling inside, the one that she had only ever felt with *one* man, wasn't there. It certainly wasn't there with Lee either, but Lee's feelings were less important in her situation. She felt she could have fun with Lee without worrying about hurting him. Neither him, nor her husband, could fill the hole in her heart that *he* had left. That's how she knew that neither men were truly right for her.

Dressed, Lee came back over to the bed and climbed on top of her still naked body and gave her another passionate kiss. She eventually fought her urges and pushed him off. After quickly throwing her clothes back on, she led him towards the front door. Peering out into the empty corridor she ushered him out. He gave her one last peck before disappearing back into his own flat.

She went back inside, quickly stripped the bed and stuffed the sheets into the washing machine. She glanced around the bedroom to look for any signs that would give her away. Just as she had satisfied herself that she was covered, a loud, unfriendly knock came at the door. She first suspected that Lee had forgotten something, but decided that his knock wouldn't be that aggressive. She opened the front door to a young man that she'd seen about the flats lately.

'Hello, darling! Do you know where Kane has gone?' he said, belligerently.

'Who?' she responded, still unsure who he was.

'Kane! He lives next door to you,' he said, pointing at the red door, the new home of the resident drug dealer. It was then that she realised that this young man was the friend who was his regular visitor.

'Oh, *him,*' she emphasised. 'I saw him leaving about an hour or so ago.'

'Well, he told me he'd be home all day,' he said, aggressively as though this was somehow her fault.

Deciding she'd entertained this stranger long enough, she attempted to end her involvement in his problem. 'I can't help you, sorry.'

She made a move to close her flat door, but the drug addict shoved his foot in the doorway, preventing it from closing.

Speaking more calmly now, as though this was an innocent action, he said, 'Well, do you know where he went?'

Layla was now shaking as she spoke, 'I already told you. I don't know. When I saw him leaving, he went up the stairs at the end of the corridor, but, like I said, that was about an hour ago.'

'Upstairs?' the addict questioned, puzzled.

Now that he'd mentioned it...that *was* strange. There was nothing else upstairs. Why hadn't she thought about that sooner? What was he doing up there? Well, no time to dwell on that now. She had this immediate threat to worry about.

'Just please leave me alone or I'm calling the police,' she said, timidly, whilst repeatedly attempting to close the door, only for it to bounce off his foot.

'There's no need to be like that. I was only asking a question,' he said.

'And I already told you. I don't know. Please just let me shut my door,' she said, breaking down now.

The drug addict just stood there and laughed at her. To make things worse, Kane joined them, quickly escalating the situation.

'What's going on?' he asked.

His friend turned his head to look at Kane, but kept his boot firmly in Layla's doorway.

'Where've you been?' he said.

'I just nipped to the shop for some fags,' Kane replied. 'What's going on?' he said, indicating his friend's foot.

'I was just asking this lass where you were, but she was being really rude,' the friend replied.

'Oh was she really?' said Kane now turning his gaze on her. 'Well then, love! That's twice today isn't it? You'll have to make this up to us somehow.'

He inched his way scarily close to her now. She felt very vulnerable as these two unsavoury characters invaded her personal space. Pointlessly, she attempted to talk her way out of the situation, hoping that Lee would eventually come from his room if he heard enough noise.

'I wasn't being rude. I just don't want your lifestyle knocking at my door.'

Saying this, Layla realised she'd been overly confident. Confidence which she did not have the courage to back up. She was hoping that it didn't sound as bad as it had in her head, but Kane's response confirmed that it, in fact, had.

'My lifestyle?' he shouted. 'You think you're better than me?'

She tried to backtrack, 'No, no. It's not that, it...'

'You know,' Kane interrupted, 'it's one thing to be funny with me, but if you start being funny with my client, then...well then you could cost me money. And if you cost me money, you'll have to reimburse me somehow.'

His final, sleazy remark made Layla more scared than ever, and it was this which triggered a distant memory of hers. A memory from when she'd been threatened by a man once before. Ten years ago. There was something about Kane which gave her an eerie echo of that man. She was getting desperate now and even more upset.

'Please, just leave me alone,' she managed.

'You know...' Kane continued harassing her, 'you've scrubbed up nicely since we last spoke.'

He was right, she panicked. Layla hadn't taken off her make-up since her time with Lee and if Kane noticed this, then so would her husband. Thinking she still had time to take care of this detail and make it look as though she hadn't done anything interesting all afternoon, she was shocked to see Ian turn up in the corridor. He stood in disbelief at the scene. Layla forgot about her appearance as relief set in. She now had someone to save her from this pair of villains. Even though Ian was young, he had a forcefulness about him that still made her feel safe.

'What's going on?' Ian asked, angrily.

'Ian!' Layla called over to him helplessly.

'Is everything OK?' he asked, walking over and squaring up to the drug addict.

'This man won't let me shut my door,' Layla informed him.

'Step back please, sir,' Ian asked, calmly at first. After no response he raised his voice to the drug user. 'Step back now,' he bellowed.

The drug addict begrudgingly walked away back towards Kane, allowing Ian to move between him and Layla, creating a protective barrier for his wife. Ian turned his gaze to Kane now. He knew he had to establish a strong position with Kane, or else he would walk all over him in the future. He needed him here, but he would have to take a risk. Call his bluff. Threaten to throw him out and hope that he needed this place too much to actually leave.

'Kane! If you enjoy living here, I suggest you change your attitude. I don't want you or your friend bothering my wife again. If you do, you're out!'

'Oh yeah!' the drug addict piped up. 'And who are you to threaten to kick him out?'

'I'm the landlord!' Ian replied, matter-of-factly. 'So if you don't want to cause problems for your friend then I suggest you heed my advice.'

Kane who had clearly fallen for the tactic, de-escalated the situation, 'Come on, mate,' he said to his friend. 'Let's get inside.'

Kane held his flat door open and waved his friend inside. They both returned to their narcotic lives behind the red door. Ian breathed a sigh of relief that his bluff hadn't backfired. Losing Kane would have been disastrous for him. His worries had clearly distracted him as when he stopped thinking about it he realised that Layla was clasped tightly around him. She was crying into his chest. He'd not seen her like this in a long time. Exhibiting vulnerability like this was something that she used to do very early in their relationship. It made Ian happy, which might seem a little sadistic since she was crying, but to him, it was a victory towards restoring her love for him.

'Ian!' she tearfully managed. 'I'm so glad you're here. That was awful.'

Layla suddenly pulled away from him as it dawned on her how close she had been to getting caught.

'How come you're back so early?' she questioned.

'That potential tenant cancelled, which is a shame, so I'm done for the day. Lucky they did really,' he added.

She gave an uneasy smile of agreement whilst her heart continued to race. And more so when Ian noticed what she feared he would.

'You look nice. Are you going somewhere?' he inquired.

'Oh…er…I was going to go in to town to look for a job,' she struggled.

'Well, just have a minute, you're still shaking,' Ian said, comfortingly as he pulled her in for another cuddle.

Layla lay with her head on Ian's chest, feeling terrible. Her young husband had been the saviour that she needed, but yet she'd still hoped Lee would have been the one to turn up. She felt guiltier than ever now. She could tell Ian loved her to bits, but she was so confused. His intrepid action had re-established the safe and secure feelings she had for him, but not blown away the doubts.

3C's blue door opened and Lee walked out into the corridor straight into Layla's eye line. They shared an uncomfortable glance where she could see that her loving embrace with her husband had upset him. He turned around and left the corridor via the fire door and went down the stairs. She sighed; just another layer of guilt to add to her mounting pile.

Chapter 7 – The Love of his Life

I tried to explain to my audience, 'I didn't know it at the time, but my wife's infidelity would cause major suspicion to be cast on me in the events to come. You should all know that I had no idea about her affair with Lee until after the event. I should have paid more attention to her. I shouldn't have let her fall into the arms of another man. It was my own fault. I accept that. I should have been there for her when she needed me. I should have paid more attention. Maybe then this wouldn't have happened.'

I started to think about something else as my audience chatted amongst themselves. I didn't want the memory of the love of my life to be tarnished by her affair and misdirection. She needs to be remembered as the most amazing person I'd ever met. I need to do her justice. I sat and thought about how to word this for some time. How to make them understand how great she was, regardless of what they would think if I told them the whole story. In the end, I decided against revealing anything about *that*. Let that remain our secret. Let them never know the real truth.

I realised that I'd been staring into space. I'd waffled again. I looked up at my information-hungry audience and decided to feed them.

'Later that day, in the evening, Erica and my wife had their "girly night" together. Understandably this was very uncomfortable for them both, but the love of my life was quite the actress. She managed to keep her cool throughout and feign a friendship. It was here that they began to learn a few home truths about each other…'

Chapter 8 – Truth & Wines

Roger pressed his ear up against the outside of his own blue wooden door.

Lee stood tall with Isaac strapped close to his chest. 'Dad!' he shouted to him from across the empty corridor. 'Come on, we're going to be late.'

Roger was trying to listen in to the flat that they had just left, 'I'm trying to hear what's going on in there,' he said with concentration on his face. 'Do you know the kind of things that happen at these girl's nights in?'

'Only in *your* films,' Lee laughed.

'Shh, I can hear something. I think they're comparing breasts.'

'Oh, whatever, dad.'

'I'm being serious. I can't believe it. My son's girlfriend and the neighbour that has the hots for me in some girl on girl action,' Roger said with growing excitement.

'Dad, come on, we're going to be late if you don't...'

Lee was cut short when he heard Erica loudly from behind the door, 'Come on, show me yours. I'll be showing you mine.'

Lee's attitude changed and he suddenly dashed over and pushed his ear to the door too. Roger and Lee scrambled for listening space. Roger shoved Lee out of the way a few times until they each found a comfortable spot and continued to listen.

'Come on. Are you ready now?' Erica shouted.

'But I feel silly,' Layla responded from what sounded like a room at the other end of the flat.

Lee and Roger gave each other a puzzled look, unsure as to what was going on.

'Remember, I'll be showing you mine,' said Erica, persuasively.

'I don't want to see yours,' Layla stated bluntly.

'Stop being so shy, everybody's got them.'

'But my husband is the only one that gets to see mine.'

'Don't be a wimp! Come on!'

'Urgh, fine!'

'We'll go together. On three. One. Two. Three!'

The girls were heard giggling. Roger and Lee looked at each other wide-eyed. Roger, unable to restrain himself, grabbed the handle and burst in through the door on foot, leaving his wheelchair behind. Layla and Erica, wearing ridiculous onesies, turned and stared at the gaping pair who stood frozen in the door way.

'What are you two doing?' Erica asked, angrily.

'Nothing we er…forgot…' Lee stammered.

'Did we miss the boobs?' Roger asked.

'Boobs?' asked Erica, puzzled.

'Yes!' Roger demanded. 'We heard you talking about showing each other.'

'We were talking about our onesies,' Erica chuckled.

'Onesies?' Roger enquired.

'Yes. These things that cover us from head to toe and leave everything to the imagination.'

'Oh,' said Roger disappointed. 'Come on, Lee, let's go. I told you we shouldn't have invaded their privacy.'

'What?' exclaimed Lee as Roger got back in his chair and wheeled down the corridor out of sight. 'I swear it was all him, he…well, I…we didn't…'

Lee continued to mumble until Erica cut him off, 'Lee! Go away.'

Lee obliged and fumbled his way out of the door.

'Sorry about that,' Erica said.

'You said you'd be the only one to see it. Now your boyfriend and his dad have seen me looking like this,' worried Layla.

'Oh come on, it's not that bad.'

Erica slouched on the sofa. Layla joined her, but couldn't relax. Erica admired Layla's predominantly green onesie. It had the Welsh flag in the centre.

'Have you visited Wales recently, or something?' Erica questioned.

'No, no. Ian bought me it as a gift. His obsession with green shows through everywhere. I doubt he even thought about the flag,' Layla laughed.

'Y Ddraig Goch,' Erica pronounced.

'What?'

'It means "The Red Dragon".'

'I didn't know you could speak Welsh.'

'I'm fluent in lots of languages.'

'That's quite interesting.'

'Not really. When I was growing up we were *made* to learn all sorts of different skills.'

'Really? Why?'

Erica became distant as she spoke, 'I was born into a *different* kind of life. It was drilled into us at a young age what was expected of us. What we had to learn, what we must achieve in life.'

'That sounds strict. Was it hard?'

'Sometimes, but…there was no falling behind. You had to keep up, had to learn everything, and fast, or else…'

'Or else what?' Layla quizzed after a long pause.

'You must understand that I grew up in a very different world to you. You did what you were told, or you were punished,' as she said this she lifted up the back of her shirt, revealing many scars and burn marks.

'Oh my god!' Layla said, sympathetically. 'But, you're adult now. Can't you report the people who did this to you?'

'It's funny isn't it,' Erica said, distantly again. 'Only when we are older do we see the benefit of our teachings. At the time I detested life, but now…I agree with everything that I was put through. It was required to make me the woman I am today. It made me stronger. And I see what they are trying to achieve.'

'You can't agree with that method of teaching, surely?'

'You wouldn't understand. It's all about the bigger picture. I see that now.'

'Where *did* you grow up?' Layla asked.

'I don't really want to talk about this anymore,' Erica said, diverting the conversation. 'Anyway forget all that. Let's crack the wine open and get a film on.'

Layla struggled with what she'd just heard. Erica had just divulged something so personal, but why? Was she perhaps expecting Layla to share something in return?

Layla decided to lighten the tone, 'I still can't believe I'm round here in a onesie.'

'This day and age it's not a proper girl's night in without a onesie,' Erica replied, clearly going along with this friendlier topic.

'I'll be fine once I start drinking,' Layla laughed, nervously.

'Can you handle your wine?' Said Erica, pouring them both a glass.

'Of course. I live off the stuff. You?'

Oh please. This stuff is like water to me.'

#

Halfway through the film and the majority of the wine, the girls were now getting merry. Layla had taken up a more comfortable position and Erica was sitting on the floor, using the sofa as a back-rest. More wine was poured as they watched the "chick-flick" they had chosen.

'Oh come on. Like you would ever do that!' Erica shouted at the television.

'Yeah, just dump him; you're way better than that!' Layla followed suit.

The film had reached a scene showing a woman taking back a man who'd been cheating on her.

'These films are so unrealistic. I don't know why so many girls cry at them,' Erica mocked.

'Me too,' agreed Layla. 'You wouldn't catch me sobbing over a soppy film.'

#

The film was at the end. The credits were rolling and both girls were now sobbing uncontrollably. They were both blubbering so much that they were barely audible to each other.

'She. Was. So. Strong,' said Layla, having to pause between each word through the tears.

48

'She. Deserved. So. Much. Better,' said Erica similarly.

'She. Was. A. True. Inspiration.'

They both continued to sob and wail until Erica finally composed herself. She crawled over to the television on her hands and knees and turned it off. Layla lifted the empty wine bottle upside down in a vain attempt to pour herself another glass.

'That's the last of the wine,' she said disappointedly.

'I'd have bought more bottles, but rent day is coming so I have to go steady.' Erica said, dismayed.

'Oh right, yeah,' Layla said, feeling a little guilty now 'You should have said and I would have paid. I forget that people have to pay rent.'

'Oh! Must be nice!' said Erica, sarcastically. 'One of the perks of being married to the landlord I suppose. What's that like?'

'It's OK,' Layla said, giving away more of her true feelings than she intended to.

'Ooooh, that doesn't sound good. Is everything alright with you two?'

'Well, things are a bit…'

Layla left a long pause as she thought about what she was saying. She didn't feel comfortable talking about her relationship with anyone, and here she is, spilling her guts to a woman she doesn't even like. Although that's probably just because of the affair she's having with her boyfriend. Would she dislike her as much if the circumstances were different? She decided to hold herself back rather than spill her most intimate feelings with this almost complete stranger.

'I shouldn't really be talking about this with you,' she added.

'Oh come on,' Erica insisted. 'That's the whole point of girly nights. If you can't talk about stuff like this, now, when can you?'

Layla thought about what she said. Even though she was in the wrong company, Erica's opinions could still help her.

'Go on. Things are a bit…what?' Erica pressured, impatiently.

'A bit…well…boring,' Layla conceded. 'It's like he's always got something else on his mind.'

'He probably has. Can't be easy running these flats, and trying to refurbish the rest of the building.'

'No, it's more than that. There must be more going on in his head than he lets me in on.'

'Why do you say that?'

'Oh I don't know. Like for example…he has this cupboard, in the desk in our bedroom that is always locked. If I'm honest, I'm not that bothered about what's in there…but that's the problem. I should be. I should want to know what he's hiding in there. I thought of asking him a few times, but I actually don't care.'

'Really? It would drive me crazy if there was a cupboard in our flat and I didn't know what was in it.'

'Exactly! I'm sure it's nothing. Probably just work stuff.'

'I wonder what's inside it.'

'If I ever find out, I'll let you know.'

'What kind of lock is it?'

'Why?'

'Well if it's just a lock on a desk cupboard then I'm sure you could get it open with a hairpin easy enough.'

'No. It's a padlock on a latch. One of those combination locks, so it's not like I could bang a hairpin into that either.'

'How many digits?'

'Four!'

'You should try important dates, stuff like that. I bet you could get in easily enough.'

'Like I said, I honestly don't care enough to try.'

'I think you're right, then. You probably *should* take a bigger interest in him,' Erica chuckled.

'I think we're both just into different things.'

'It's a bit late finding that out *after* you're married.'

'Yeah. Probably. I think it's our age gap. I'm starting to see the drawbacks of being married to a younger man. I sometimes forget he's only twenty two.'

'Oh yeah. That's easy to forget with all he's achieved. It's quite impressive for someone so young. So, are things between you really that bad at the minute?'

'No, not at all. He's really nice to me. He has no idea that I've been feeling like this.'

'It must be weighing on you a bit. Is that why you always look so tired?'

'No!' Layla said, slightly offended. 'Thanks for that, though,' she added sarcastically. 'No, recently I've been having these nightmares. I'm finding it hard to get to sleep.'

'Nightmares? About what?'

'About something that happened when I was younger. Back when I was a paramedic. I keep reliving something that happened. Something terrible.'

Layla sat for a moment as she thought about this inkling of truth escaping from her drunken lips. She must have zoned out Erica's next question as she had to ask it again.

'Come on, what did you do?' Erica asked, impatiently.

'Someone died and I lied about how it happened,' Layla responded, shocked at herself.

She worried at how easily she was talking about this. Erica was milking her dry of all her secrets. Layla decided to control herself and put a stop to it.

'Why would you lie?' Erica pushed again.

'I…I…' Layla hesitated. 'I'm not supposed to say.'

'What do you mean?' said Erica, becoming concerned and compassionate now. 'It's OK. You can tell me.'

'Please!' Layla began to panic. 'I shouldn't have said anything in the first place. Just forget it. Please!'

'OK, if it's really that bad,' said Erica, backing off from the subject.

Layla seized this victory and decided to pounce on the opening, forcing the conversation in a different direction, 'Anyway, what about you? How are you coping since Lee lost his job?'

As soon as she said this, she regretted it. She'd avoided the topic of Lee all evening. It was bad enough that she was here with his girlfriend, but to start talking about him was silly. Too late now, though. Her hasty question had backed her into another corner. A corner that was less dark and guilt-ridden than the one she had negotiated away from, but still, a corner she would prefer not to be in.

'Lost his job?' Erica laughed. 'You don't need to sugar-coat it, Layla. You mean "got fired"?'

'Well, yeah!' Layla awkwardly replied.

'I just wish he'd hurry up and find another job. I mean, no offence to Ian, but this place is just too small for us lot.'

Layla had the opportunity to move the conversation along again, but she suddenly had the urge to find out more about Lee. This was her chance to get some info that he wasn't likely to share with her himself anytime soon.

'How did he lose his job?' Layla asked, bravely. 'Well, don't let him know that I told you, but he was fired when they found drugs in his locker.'

'What!' said Layla, shocked. 'I'm guessing that didn't go down well, a police officer with drugs in his locker!'

'It didn't, obviously, but because he was already under investigation for negligence, they used this to finish him off.'

Layla was flabbergasted. She thought she knew Lee better than she obviously did. She would have never thought he'd be the type to indulge in drugs. She began to struggle with how she felt about this.

'I can't believe that Lee would ever take drugs,' Layla said, solemnly.

'He says they were planted,' Erica added.

'And what do you think?' said Layla, hopefully.

'I believe him. As for the neglect thing. That's probably true. I don't think that job was really for him. He was at it for over ten years and never really got the hang of it. He hates confrontation, so he used to just look the other way whenever he could for an easy life. But drugs? No way! Not Lee.'

'It's bad timing with you two just having a baby.'

'Isaac was bad timing anyway.'

'Why?'

'I'd only met Lee a couple of weeks before I got pregnant. He thinks that I trapped him.'

These words relieved some measure of the guilt that had been mounting inside of Layla throughout the evening. She had always thought they had a long history together. It was still bad enough that they had a kid, but now it felt more like they were together out of convenience. Maybe there wasn't any love there after all. If Layla did end up with Lee, perhaps there wouldn't be all that much heartache. She decided to dig a little deeper, selfishly, to alleviate even more guilt if she could.

'I always assumed you'd been together much longer,' Layla prompted.

'Nope!' said Erica, flatly. 'I doubt it will last. I think he's just sticking around for the baby. And besides, if anyone's been trapped, it's me.'

'What do you mean?'

Erica listed, 'He loses his job as a police officer, I have to live with his pervy old dad, *and* we all have to survive on my supermarket wage. How cunning I must have been to trap him,' she added, sarcastically.

'I didn't realise things were so bad,' Layla said, hiding a smile.

'I'm not overly bothered. It's all just extra bodies to help take care of Isaac. Once he's grown up, Lee can please himself.'

'That's a very relaxed way of looking at things. Good for you,' said Layla, sincerely.

'Well, I have to be relaxed, don't I? You see, the thing about Lee is…'

Erica was interrupted by the sound of keys in the front door.

'…never mind. Sounds as if they're back,' Erica said.

'…absolute nonsense!' said Roger, angrily as he was pushed through the front door by Lee. 'Where was all the smut and filth?'

'I hardly think a book called "The Secretary" was going to have raunchy content, dad,' said Lee, who was struggling to carry Isaac and a carrier bag at the same time.

'Well, I have a film with the same name and it's full of the stuff,' Roger added.

'I think that's a different kind of entertainment, dad.'

'So you three had fun then?' Erica shouted across to them.

'No!' said Roger, angrily. 'He took us to a book reading club. I hated it. People that read books are always posh, smarmy gits!'

'A book reading club?' said Erica, shocked. 'I bet Isaac was bored out of his mind.'

'No, he slept right through,' said Lee unaware that there was an issue.

'When I said take him out, I meant to do something fun, *for him,*' said Erica, slightly miffed and taking Isaac from Lee. 'Give him here. I'll put him in his cot.'

'You can tuck me in as well, whilst you're at it,' added Roger, cheekily.

'Tuck yourself in, you dirty old git,' said Erica as she marched out of the room towards the bedroom.

Roger followed Erica out of the room leaving Lee and Layla alone. Lee joined Layla on the sofa sitting uncomfortably close to her. It put her on edge knowing that Erica was just in the next room, but it didn't seem to faze Lee at all.

'So, how was your night?' he asked.

'It was OK,' she responded. 'I'm just feeling really guilty. Erica is so nice. It's so much worse now that I've spent some time with her.'

'I know and I'm sorry you've had to go through that.'

Lee looked around for any sign of someone else in the room and then leaned in for a kiss. Layla pushed him away.

'Not here!' she whispered, loudly.

'It's OK. She'll be a while yet,' said Lee as he leaned in for another attempt.

'I don't care!' said Layla, rejecting him again.

'When then?' sulked Lee.

Layla sat and thought about it. Although she knew it was wrong, sitting here with Lee excited her again. And after the other night, she wanted more. She felt it was getting riskier, but the greater the risk, the more she longed for him.

'I don't know when or how much time I will have away from Ian tomorrow,' Layla said, disappointed.

'But I *have* to see you again,' Lee pleaded.

'I know. I feel the same. What are we going to do?'

'Erica is working tomorrow and I can leave Isaac with my dad, so it just depends on where Ian will be.'

'I really don't know, so we can't use my flat. I wonder what the upper floors are like? Maybe there's somewhere up there we can go.'

'That's great, why didn't we think of that sooner? Erica will leave at about ten in the morning, so just come and get me when you've got rid of Ian.'

'OK, I'll try,' Layla grinned.

The pair sat and smirked at each other. Layla had a momentary feeling of disgust with herself at how easily she could abandon her morals. Only moments before, she was feeling guilty, but as soon as Lee had worked his charms, all that was forgotten. Her feelings on the subject were all over the place. Conscious again that Erica was only a room away, she moved a little further from Lee and tried to bring the topic to more neutral ground.

'What's in the bag?' she asked, pointing at the carrier that Lee had brought home.

'It's dad's birthday in a few weeks so I've bought him a mobile phone. I think it's time he had his own. I'm sick of him filling mine up with dodgy videos.'

'That'll be a nice surprise for him,' Layla laughed.

'He'll find it no before, no doubt. I was lucky enough to buy it just now without him seeing, but I'm sure he'll find it hidden in this small flat easy enough.'

'Then why don't I hide it for you? I'll keep it at mine and you can come and get it on his birthday.'

'That'd be great, but what if Ian sees it? Won't it look a bit odd?'

'I'll hide it in my underwear drawer, I can't see him going in there. And if he does, I'll just tell him the truth. Nothing suspicious about that. I'm just helping out a neighbour.'

'And you do help me out in quite a lot of ways,' Lee sniggered.

'I'll even wrap it up for you, I'm kind like that,' Layla said, cutely, moving her head close to his, dismissing her previous worries about his girlfriend's proximity.

'Too kind!' Lee said, moving in and finally getting his kiss.

Layla quickly put a stop to their throes of passion.

'OK, let's not push it,' Layla warned and stood up. 'I'm gonna get going. Say bye to Erica for me.'

'I'll see you out,' Lee said with a cheeky grin on his face.

Layla grabbed the present and they headed out into the corridor. There was no one else around so she gave Lee a passionate kiss goodbye. He simply smiled and returned to his flat. Layla walked back towards hers, but just stood in front of the door for a moment. She couldn't face going in just yet. She leant against the corridor wall and slid down it. She cuffed herself lightly on the head a few times with her palm. Her eyes were full of unshed tears as she sat there feeling sorry for herself. What was she going to do?

Chapter 9 – The Upper Floors

Layla awoke late the next morning. Ian wasn't beside her. She checked the time. It was well after ten. Erica would have gone to work by now. If Ian wasn't home she could meet Lee straight away. She leapt out of bed giddily and looked at herself in the mirror. A beautiful reflection stared back, but she could not accept it. She felt ugly. Perhaps it was due to her indiscretions, she thought. No. This was fixable. She really wanted to see Lee again this morning, after the teasing, fleeting moment they had shared when she had left his flat last night. Not knowing Ian's whereabouts was usually a risk she wouldn't take, but now that she'd had a taste of Lee, she felt the urge to take more chances.

With her make-up done, and dressed in the casual clothes that she felt accentuated her better features, she had one last look around the flat for any clue to where her husband might have gone. Nothing! She stepped out into the corridor and scouted for onlookers. No-one! She knocked on Lee's door. He answered so quickly that he must have been waiting.

'Finally,' he said, happily. 'I thought you weren't going to come.'

'I haven't long since woken up,' Layla grinned.

'Lazy! Anyway we're in luck. Dad is already watching Isaac. They're watching kids TV in his room. I bet his TV is thankful for the rest from bare flesh,' Lee chuckled.

'OK, come on then. Who knows how long we've got. We need to get off this floor before anyone sees us.'

They both headed to the closest stairwell and pushed open the heavy door.

'I wish he'd bought better fire doors,' Layla said. 'They're too heavy for little old me. I keep thinking I'm going to throw my back out every time I open one.'

They started up the stairs. As soon as they were in an area that they knew no-one would be, they began to kiss, passionately, all the while fumbling their way upward.

'How far up do you want to go?' Lee asked between locked lips.

'To the top,' said Layla, quickly, before continuing their frenzied activities.

When they arrived at the next floor, Lee stopped.

'What's the matter?' Layla asked.

'I just want to see what this floor is like?' Lee said.

'What? This is no time for that!'

'Come on, just a peek. I've never been up here.'

Lee pushed open a flimsy wooden door and stepped on to the fourth floor corridor.

'Well, these stairwell doors are much easier,' Lee laughed.

'Yeah, but I doubt they would keep a fire from getting through. Ian is quite thorough when it comes to health & safety. He'll probably replace these too when he starts renting out this floor.'

They both looked out onto the nondescript fourth floor. The fire hose box was still perfectly intact. Even the wallpaper was still in decent condition. The only odd thing was that there were cables and wires running out of 4B and into each of the other rooms.

'There you go, see. Boring! Can we get on with it now, please?' Layla asked, impatiently.

'You don't just want to stop here?' said Lee.

'Of course not,' Layla snapped. 'It looks like he could be doing some work on this floor. Look at all the wires. He could show up here at any time. Let's keep going.'

They returned to the stairwell and their tongue wars continued all the way up to the fifth floor, but they stopped suddenly when they heard movement down the corridor.

'What was that?' Lee asked, worried.

'It's probably Ian, quick, you go up to the next floor and I'll go and see if it's him,' Layla panicked.

Lee sped up the stairs two steps at a time, dragging himself up with the handrail. Once he was out of sight, Layla cautiously pushed open the battered stairwell door. This floor was in a much worse state than the one below. There wasn't even a door on 5A and 5B. The carpet was peeling and folded in multiple places and a large section was completely missing immediately outside 5D, along with some of the floorboards, leaving a sizeable gap. Furthermore, a couple of the windows in the corridor were smashed.

As she carefully proceeded along the corridor, she could hear loud banging and smashing coming from near the other end. It sounded like someone was searching for something.

She was about to call out Ian's name when suddenly, the door to 5E flew open. A bedside cabinet was tossed from the room, hitting the corridor wall, and smashing to pieces. Layla, very scared now, dropped back through the nearest door, which was 5C, and carefully shut herself in.

She could hear movement out in the corridor. It sounded like someone was now rummaging through the broken cabinet. An angry, disappointed grunt rang out. It sounded like a man having a tantrum, kicking things and shouting. Then, she heard him coming in her direction. She panicked and moved deeper into the flat, which mirrored her own, and dashed inside the bedroom.

It was quite dark in this room, likely due to the boarded-up window. The evidence that this had once been a hotel was very strong here. The bedside cabinet next to the bed, which looked identical to the one which had just met its end out in the corridor, had a Bible and a telephone on top. The phone had the usual hotel speed-dial numbers.

Still panicked, Layla lay flat on her stomach and inched her way under the bed. She'd positioned herself awkwardly facing the wall, so that her legs were pointing towards the entrance to the room, preventing her from seeing if the intruder entered. She was now too scared to move now, however. It was darker still under the bed. She heard faint movement and banging about off to her side. It sounded like the man was next door in 5D.

As she looked at the adjoining wall trying to listen, she noticed that the bedside cabinet was missing a small piece from its side. She could just about make out something white poking out of this small hole. She looked at the front of the cabinet and saw that the three drawers were higher up than the hole, which was in the backmost, bottom corner, meaning that this was a section of the cabinet which could not be accessed via the drawers. She reached in with a finger and thumb and pulled out a thick, glossy piece of white paper. There was writing on it. She drew her phone from her pocket and used its screen to illuminate it. "Me and the gang at The Royal Rainford Hotel" she read out, quietly. She flipped it over to see that it was a photo. Six men looked back at her. They were standing in front of the very building that she was in, except it was still a hotel in this picture. She recognised one of the men. It was her neighbour; the drug dealer, Kane. As she stared at him, she had the strange feeling that she had met him before he had moved into the flats. She couldn't quite put her finger on it.

She scanned the others in the photo. Her gaze settled on another man. She thought she recognised him from somewhere too. Maybe she was imagining it. What was strange, however, is that the other five men all looked to be in their thirties, but this one looked much younger. Late teens, early twenties, perhaps.

The light reflected something else inside this little hidey-hole. She poked her fingers through, but couldn't quite reach it. She needed to make the hole bigger. She grabbed the front of the cabinet and attempted to peel the veneer off. It was only held in place by some panel pins and the first few came away easily. Suddenly one part of the wood, held in by a nail, didn't tear away; instead, her pulling force caused the cabinet to topple over and crash onto the floor with a loud bang. The side panel had come loose now and she grabbed the thing inside. It was a piece of A5 lined paper with a message written on it:

"Kane. Don't worry man, I kept you out of it. We burned the couch, but something went wrong as you've no doubt heard. I wanted to tell you this in person, but they already suspect us of the fire. So that, coupled with our outstanding charges in America, could finish us. And you don't want to be associated with us. It could ruin your chances with your family. And that's the main reason I am writing to you. I happened across something very interesting. I wanted to leave it here

59

for you, but this room was taken when I came here again, so I've hidden it under the floorboards in the room I am currently staying in. Under one of the bed legs. It's room…"

Layla was suddenly dragged by her ankles from under the bed. She screamed, but was immediately silenced by a hand over her mouth. Her attacker flipped her over and straddled her, still gagging her with his hand. It was her neighbour, Kane. The man to whom the note was addressed. He raised a finger to his lips to indicate for her to be quiet. She nodded and he released her mouth.

'What are you doing here?' he ordered.

'Nothing, I was just exploring,' she lied. 'I've never been up here before so I thought I'd have a look. What are you doing up here?'

'Same,' he also lied. 'I was just looking around. I've never been up, either.'

'You're lying,' she blurted out, not thinking about the consequences. 'I saw you come up here the other day. What are you looking for?'

'I don't have to answer to you. What makes you think I'm looking for anything?'

'Why else would you be rummaging around and smashing things up?'

Kane went silent for a moment and then spotted the paper in her hand.

'What's that?' he said as he snatched the items from her.

He studied it and then looked at her.

'Did you read this?' Kane asked angrily. Layla kept silent. 'Did you read this?' he repeated at a yell.

'No,' she said, wearily.

She looked away, on the verge of tears.

'OK, here's what we're going to do. I was never here. Got it?' Kane barked.

It was in these words that Layla got the strange feeling of déjà-vu. She *did* recognise this man. It was driving her crazy now.

'Are you listening to me?' he barked. 'Look at me!' he shouted as he grabbed her by the chin and forced her to face him.

It was then, at this range, that she remembered. Her fear turned to dread as she felt the colour drain from her face. She wanted to get away from him, *now*. Suddenly the mystery of the photo and the piece of paper were irrelevant. She remembered where she had seen him before. The man who scared her only days ago, who had triggered the memory of the man who had scared her ten years ago, was, in fact, the *same* man. The man from the incident that she had been too scared to talk to Erica about on their drunken night in. She became more and more terrified and she needed to get away from him, fast!

'Oh my God, it's you. Get away from me!' she shouted.

She forced him off and ran to the bedroom door, but he got there before her and slammed it shut, trapping her in with him.

'What's me? What are you going on about?' he said, confused.

'I haven't told anyone! I swear,' Layla said, shakily.

'Told anyone what? Are you crazy or something?'

'You don't remember me,' she said, letting out a small breath of relief.

'No, not from before living here. I think I would…wait. I do remember.'

Layla's momentary peace of mind was replaced by overwhelming fear again.

'Ten years ago. At the cliff! You were the paramedic, weren't you?' Kane realised.

'Yes, that was me and I did what you asked, so please, don't hurt me!' Layla pleaded.

'That's good then. I appreciate that, love.'

'How can you be so calm? That day was horrible for me.'

'Well, it wasn't a walk in the park for me, either.'

'You got away with murder!' Layla shouted, surprisingly confidently.

'Keep your voice down, love!' Kane panicked as he looked around. 'Look. I'm sorry about what happened. I truly am. But I can't change the past. There's no point in ruining everyone's life over it.'

'No point in ruining your own life, you mean,' said Layla, bravely, in spite of herself.

'Listen!' said Kane, getting very angry now. 'I'm a changed man, but I can find my old self very quickly if I have to.'

As Kane got angrier, he relaxed his position. Layla used this chance to push him aside and run. She dashed straight out of the front door.

As she headed down the corridor towards the stairwell door, she looked back and saw Kane poke his head out of the doorway of flat 5C to shout to her, 'As long as you keep your mouth shut, we won't have a problem, you hear?'

Layla continued her escape and forced open the stairwell door. She was about to head home, but remembered that she had left Lee up on the next floor. She had to go and find him, but needed to calm herself. He couldn't see her like this, there would be too much explaining to do.

She stood halfway up the stairs between the fifth and sixth floor and allowed a small sob to escape her. She couldn't believe it; the man who had threatened her ten years ago, here, now, living next door to her! What were the odds? She'd lived in fear of him for so many years. True, he did seem somewhat different, but she was still terrified of him. Worst of all, she couldn't tell anyone about it. No one could know what she had done all those years ago. She would just have to grin and bear living next to that monster and hope she forgot about him. That seemed unlikely though. She was already having nightmares about the incident, so now that the man responsible was living next door to her, her dreams were likely to get a lot worse.

Layla collected herself and proceeded up the stairs to the sixth floor. This floor seemed perfectly intact, the way it must have been when it was a hotel. Nothing was out of place. Lee was loitering in the corridor looking a little on edge.

'What's wrong?' Layla asked.

'Aaaaah!' Lee jumped. 'You scared me. What was going on down there? I heard screaming.'

'Well, thanks for coming to my rescue!' she said, sarcastically.

'I just thought I'd better let you and him sort things out. It was Ian, wasn't it?'

Layla thought for a moment and decided it was best for Lee to believe that it was indeed Ian. It's not as if he was likely to ask him about it.

'Yes, we were just talking about stuff,' Layla lied.

'What kind of stuff?' Lee asked.

'I don't want to talk about it.'

She worked her head under Lee's arm and snuggled up to him.

'Is it safe to stay up here?' Lee worried.

'Err…yeah, he's gone out somewhere now,' Layla lied again.

'You look a bit upset.'

'I'm OK. It's just hard.'

Layla looked out of the window at the magnificent view. From the windows in the flats, you can see the town of Bretton, but from the corridor windows on the opposite side, there is just scenery. The gorgeous landscapes of Bretton and the tops of trees in the woods. Being this high up only added to its beauty. As she scanned across the horizon, far off in the distance, she could actually see Bretton cliff. The landmark which had caused her so much anguish for many years.

'It's really nice isn't it?' Lee said.

'I don't like it,' replied Layla, scornfully staring at the distant cliff. 'Let's go into one of the flats.'

Seductively, she led him by the hand into flat 6A. The flat inside was beautiful too, very dusty, but beautiful. They went into the bedroom. Lee pulled the dusty quilt from the bed and threw it onto the floor. The mattress sheet was perfectly clean, protected from the dust by the quilt. They lay on the bed, excitedly and began a repeat performance of yesterday's fun.

#

Layla woke soon after, shivering. Her nap must have been short due to the absence of the quilt. Lee didn't seem to be having any trouble, though. He was snoring away loudly. She poked him awake and grabbed all their clothes. She threw his to him and they got dressed.

'Come on. Let's go before our luck runs out,' she said.

They shared a final kiss, returned the flat to its original state, and headed out of the door. When they arrived back at the third floor, they said their goodbyes in the stairwell and Lee proceeded into the corridor first shortly afterwards, when she felt he'd had enough time to get home, Layla went through the heavy fire door and came face to face with her husband, who jumped when he saw her.

'Oh God, Ian. You scared me,' said Layla, clutching her chest.

'You scared me too,' he replied. 'I've been on edge for the last ten minutes.'

'Why?'

'Well, where've you been?' he asked.

'Just to town, window shopping.'

'Were you with Lee?'

'What?' Layla panicked.

'Well I just saw him and that's where he said he'd been.'

'Oh,' said Layla, relieved. 'No I didn't see him.'

'Well you can't have been that far behind him.'

'Why are you asking people where they were anyway?'

'Like I said, I've been on edge. I think someone has been watching me.'

'What? Why?'

'Just a feeling I had, but what really spooked me was, when I came home just now, I was sure I'd closed the door behind me. I threw my coat in the bedroom and when I came back out, I saw our front door ajar. Anyway, I didn't think much of it and just shut it again. But then, I went to the toilet and I could have sworn I heard the front door open and shut.'

'What?'

'Yeah. I thought maybe you had been home and I didn't spot you, daft as that sounds?'

'No, it wasn't me and now I'm really scared.'

'It was probably something else I heard. Like next door or something. I wouldn't worry about it.'

'Ian, if it's got *you* tense, then I'm petrified. Nothing gets to you.'

'I know. Like I said, I'm probably overreacting. Come on, let's get inside.'

Ian took her hand and walked her into the flat. Her emotions were in turmoil. How could she be doing this to him? He treated her so well, but she was just so much more excited when she was with Lee. He can never find out about them. If she does decide to leave him, he can't know that it's for Lee.

And all these dredged up memories of Kane and the incident at the cliff wasn't helping. And what else was he up to? What did the rest of that note say? And who were the others in that picture? *Was* someone spying on Ian? She suddenly realised that she had been oblivious to so many things. She'd been so caught up in her affair that she hadn't realised what else was going on in the building. But *had* she been missing something and only just realised, *or* had the doors of change only just opened?

Chapter 10 – The Young and the Old

The day that the young couple were to move in had arrived. To say I was excited would be an understatement. My excitement increased further when one of my contacts in the property business rang me to give me some good news about an old couple I'd had my eye on. I needed to handle their sale, personally, so I put the feelers out there. I agreed to let him have the sale of their house as long as I could handle their move into one of my properties. The couple agreed to see me this morning, which was ideal as I should have just enough time to see them before Alex and Natalie started to move in.

I threw my breakfast bowl into the sink and grabbed my coat. I felt a bit guilty about leaving my dirty dish for Layla again, but I was in hurry. She called over to me and I worried she would be having a go at me for it already.

'Just leave it, I'll clean it when I get back,' I called.

'No, it's not that, I'll wash that, I was just wondering where you were off to?' she asked.

'Another potential tenant meeting. They've been hard to snag, so I want to get out there and try and talk them round.

'How long do you think you'll be?'

'Only a couple of hours. I want to be back for when the new couple move in. Why?'

'Oh, no reason. I was just wondering.'

'OK. See you soon,' I said, placing an affectionate kiss on her cheek.

She's been asking me how long I'm going to be a lot lately. I wonder if she's starting to miss me more.

#

As I left the building I got the feeling that I was being watched again. I turned around and a figure on the third floor quickly disappeared from the stairwell window. Were they watching me, or just looking out of the window? I jumped into my green car and headed out. I couldn't quash my suspicions that someone had been watching me for the last couple of days. I thought of nothing else for the whole journey.

#

When I pulled up in front of their magnificent detached house, I felt extremely lucky. Their house was beautiful. Why they should want to move I had no idea. As I stepped out of the car, the elderly couple appeared in the doorway of their house. I knew their names were Seth and Ingrid, but this was the first time I had met them.

'You must be Ian,' Seth boomed across the driveway to me before I'd reached them. 'Seth Treant,' he added, extending his hand to me.

'Yes, pleasure to meet you, Mr. Treant,' I replied shaking his hand.

'Please, call me Seth,' he replied. 'And this is…'

'The lady of the house, Ingrid Treant,' Ingrid gushed.

I was immediately tickled by the unconscious humour of Ingrid's tone. When Seth introduced himself, he pronounced his surname "Trent", silent "a". But when Ingrid introduced *herself*, she was, Ingrid "Tray-ornt". I had an inner chuckle. I assumed that Seth's was the correct pronunciation as she would naturally have taken *his* name when they married.

'Lovely to meet you, madam,' I responded, taking my tone from Ingrid.

'Oh, a true gentleman! Maybe you could teach Seth a thing or two,' she said, happily.

Seth appeared to be in his late sixties. He was enormous in both directions, had a full head of short white hair and eyes that were almost slit like, but not menacing by any means. I noticed that he seemed only to be able to smile if his mouth was open. When it was closed, he just looked grumpy.

Ingrid was a mature woman in her early sixties and appeared to be very small. This may, in part, have been due to the fact that she was standing next to the towering Seth, but she was still tiny. She was well dressed with an abundance of classically styled brown hair.

'Would you like a drink, Ian?' asked Seth.

'If it's all right with you two, could we get straight off to the house? I hate to seem rude, but I have a new couple moving into some flats that I own soon, so I need to get back.'

'That's fine by me,' Ingrid chimed in. 'I want to see this new home of mine.'

'Calm down, Ingrid love. We haven't bought it yet,' said Seth.

'It looks absolutely wonderful from the photos. I just know I'm going to adore it,' she said.

'Then let's waste no more time. Let's get you down there. Would you like to follow me or do you want to travel in my car,' I asked.

'Oh we'll follow you in the Jag. Your car looks a tad uncomfortable for me and my back,' said Ingrid, disdainfully, peering over at my nondescript car.

'Ingrid!' Seth snapped. 'What my wife meant to say was, that we'll follow you so that you can get straight off when you're done. Seeing as you're in a hurry.'

'How very kind,' I replied with laugh.

#

I waited outside the large house that I was showing them whilst they spent some time exploring alone. When they'd finished, Ingrid came galloping out of the front door.

'We'll take it, we'll take it,' she called, merrily.

'As you can tell, it looks like we'll be taking it,' said Seth, who'd followed her outside.

'It's everything I'd dreamed it would be. It's so glamorous. Just what I need to spend the next few years.'

'The next few years?' Seth snapped. 'If I'm buying you this house, we're in it until we die.'

'Oh don't be such a commoner, Seth,' she laughed, sincerely.

'She's not for real,' Seth told me.

'How soon can we move in, Ian?'

'Right…well…' I said cautiously.

'Oh no!' Ingrid gave an anguished cry. 'I knew there would be some dire news. Go on, what is it?'

'No, no. Nothing dire. As you know…' I said, turning to Seth, 'it's best to get your current house sold as quickly as you can. That way, you're not out of pocket.'

'Yes, makes sense,' Seth agreed.

'Well, whilst you were looking around the house, my friend at the estate agents who are selling your house, rang me to tell me he had a buyer,' I continued.

'That's brilliant. I didn't think it would be so fast,' said Seth, with a smile.

'What's the "but"?' Ingrid asked.

'They want to move in, in two weeks. This is really important to them,' I said.

'Well that's fine isn't it, Seth, darling? We can be packed and ready to move by then!' Ingrid stated, confidently.

'Yes. Easily,' added Seth, just as confident.

'The problem is…' I said, nervously, '…is that the tenants of this house aren't due to leave for three weeks.'

'But the house doesn't look lived in,' Ingrid pointed out.

'Well, the owners haven't been spending much time there lately. That's why it's easy to show people around.'

'Well if they aren't that bothered, can't they just skedaddle sooner?'

'I'm afraid not. They're on holiday at the moment. They'll be moving as soon as they come home, but until then, this house is theirs.'

'So we'll be homeless for a week? I don't think so!' Ingrid spat.

'No, no. I wouldn't let that happen. The flats that I mentioned earlier; I have one going spare over there. You could stay there for a week, just until this house empties,' I suggested.

'A f-lat?' Ingrid gasped, nearly fainting at the thought. 'I'm not living in a flat!'

'It will all be free of course.'

'I don't give a monkey's if it *is* free. I wouldn't live in a flat if you paid me.'

'I don't know what else to suggest, I'm afraid. Do you have family you could stay with?'

'No. Not really. Not anyone I could impose upon at the drop of a hat. You will just have to tell the new buyers they can't move in yet.'

'I'm afraid that's not an option. They urgently need somewhere.'

'But it's only another week.'

'They were adamant. I'm afraid that they will have to go elsewhere if you aren't ready to sell.'

'Well tell them to do that, then! We shall sell to someone who is a little more patient.'

'Come now, Ingrid, dear,' Seth interjected. 'We can't be picky. Who knows when we'll get another buyer?'

'But Sethy-poos. You know I can't live like that,' Ingrid exclaimed.

'Shall I call my friend and cancel,' I asked, worriedly.

'No!' Seth panicked. 'You sort it all out, Ian. I'll deal with her.'

'I'd like to see you try. Nothing you do or say to me will get me to live in a flat,' Ingrid said, adamantly.

#

When I returned to home, I noticed a large white van parked outside alongside another car, neither of which I recognised. Alex and Natalie must have arrived already, I assumed.

I grabbed the usual junk mail from my post box and dropped it straight into the nearby bin, before ascending the stairs. I could hear banging coming from the third floor. It sounded as if they were making a good start on the move; Layla must have let them in. When I pushed open the heavy fire door onto the third floor I saw the hustle and bustle of activity. More action than this building has seen in a long time. Natalie stood out in the corridor playing on her phone as Alex walked past her carrying something heavy. He went straight into the flat.

'Keeping busy?' I shouted over to Natalie.

'Huh? Oh…' she chuckled. 'Yeah. I was helping, but the stuff's getting a bit too heavy now.'

'Hello?' said an unknown lady as she popped her head out of flat 3E. 'You must be Ian,' she said, extending her hand to me.

This lady, who I assumed must be Natalie's mother, based on her identical, perfectly straight, fringe, was very tall. She had smooth skin that looked like it required the help of little or no make-up. Her hair was bright blonde, unlike Natalie's brown hair, but they shared the same style. I realised I must have been staring when Natalie's voice brought me back to reality.

'I know she's beautiful, Ian, but take your eyes off my mother. My dad will be back soon and he won't like it if I tell him,' Natalie chuckled.

'What do you mean I…I mean hello Mrs…' I stammered.

'Goddard. But you can call me Brenda,' flirted Natalie's mother.

'And you stop it too, Mother. I've just met his wife. He's into the older woman,' said Natalie.

'Layla's not that old,' I protested.

'She looks a good eight or nine years older than you, Ian.'

'Ten, actually!' I admitted.

'Leave him alone, Natalie,' Brenda Goddard stepped in. 'He's obviously a man of taste,' she said, giving me a wink that made me a little uncomfortable.

I was saved when the corridor's fire door swung open and a very short man walked through. He was quite wide, looking almost as if the heavy fish tank that he was carrying had squashed and flattened him. He had short, cropped, black hair and a full moustache, which was almost curly at the ends. This could *not* be Natalie's dad. Her parents would be a real mismatched pair.

'Be careful with that, dad,' said Natalie, correcting my impression. 'And hurry up. I want my fish back in their home as soon as possible.'

'Maybe if you helped, sweetheart, things would go a little quicker,' said Natalie's dad. 'Hi, I'm Tim,' he said to me in passing as he disappeared inside the flat with the large tank.

'I can help if you need a hand?' I offered.

'That would be wonderful,' said Natalie's mum. 'What a gentleman! Tim's van is just outside. It should be unlocked. Just bring whatever.'

'Mum! You're making me cringe,' said Natalie, disgusted.

'I'll just go grab some stuff,' I said, escaping to the nearest stairwell door.

#

With flat 3E filled with the young couple's belongings, we all sat down to a cup of tea which Natalie's mum had made. Alex was still pottering about adjusting things, "trying to get it all right" he'd said. Natalie's mother was definitely making an extra effort with me; "Super Hunk" was printed on the mug she'd selected for me when making us all a drink of tea. Her husband seemed oblivious to her pointed flirting. Either that or he was used to it and just not bothered.

'I have to say, Ian,' started Natalie's dad. 'It's not a bad little place for the price, which, I must say, is very reasonable. Far below what the current market is at. It's not about to collapse or anything is it?'

'No,' I chuckled.

Natalie's dad laughed nervously before a more serious question. 'OK, so, seriously, what's wrong with it?'

'Nothing at all,' I said, getting a little miffed.

'There must be something for you to rent them out so cheaply.'

'It's not that. Alex and Natalie seem like good kids who aren't going to cause me any trouble. I'm only just starting out in the business so I'm not up for battling with the competition. I'd rather just offer really good prices so that I can get off the ground.'

'Fair enough,' he said, seeming satisfied.

'Enough business talk,' interjected Natalie's mother. 'Let's just enjoy the first cup of tea in our daughter's new flat.'

'Are your parents coming to visit soon, Alex?' I said.

'I doubt it,' he replied. 'I haven't even told my mum I'm moving.'

'Why not? Are you just gonna up and leave home?'

'Oh, I don't live with her. Natalie and I have been together for ages, as you know, and eventually, Brenda and Tim let me move in with them seen as though I was at their house all the time anyway and I've lived with them for the last few years. My mum was always at work so she didn't really miss me. It's not like we don't get on or anything, we're just not that close.'

'What about you dad? Are your parents not together?'

'No I never knew him,' said Alex, not fazed in his response that made the rest of us uncomfortable.

72

'Oh, I'm sorry. I didn't mean to...' I stammered, before being saved by him.

'No it's fine. You weren't to know, I don't really talk about him. What about *your* parents? I bet they're helping you out with this place. I mean, you're younger than me. You can't tell me that you own all this by yourself.'

'My mum died through illness when I was about four. And my dad died when I was bit older.'

'Oh God! Now *I'm* sorry! I'm a proper idiot assuming they would be helping you. Was your dad's death through illness too?'

I didn't feel comfortable sharing this in front of all these people, but I'd told them now, so I had to give them something. Plus, Alex had shared with me so I felt that I had to reciprocate.

'He was killed in a...in a bank robbery,' I said.

'Oh, that's awful,' piped up Natalie's mother. 'What is this world coming to?'

'Alex!' shouted Natalie, interrupting the depressive talk.

'What?' said Alex, who had been in the middle of moving the fish tank.

'Be careful with that. You shouldn't be moving it whilst my fish are still in it.'

'I'm not taking them all out again. I've only just got them back in.'

'*Why* are you moving it at all?'

'Well, I thought that if we put them over there,' he said pointing towards a darkened corner next to the television, 'then my cabinet could go here.'

'You can't do that; they won't be able to see out of the window.'

'They're fish! What do they need to see the view for?'

'So they don't get bored.'

'They'll forget they're bored seconds later. Oh look a road and some grass...' he said, mimicking fish, 'that's nice...oh look, a road and some grass, that's nice. Hey Barry, look at this road and grass, I've not seen that before.'

'Grow up, Alex. I hope the move wasn't too stressful for them,' she said, sincerely.

Alex put his palm to his face at this as Mr. and Mrs. Goddard and I laughed, heartily.

Chapter 11 – George

I strolled back to my flat, happy that Alex and Natalie were satisfied with their new home. Their parents had just left, so I took that as my cue to leave as well. I was sure they would want some alone time. My front door was unlocked so I looked around for Layla. She wasn't in the living room or kitchen so I headed for the bathroom, which, like in all the flats, was connected to the bedroom.

When I opened the door to my room, I was shocked to see a figure, in a bright orange hooded coat, crouching down in front of the locked cupboard in my desk, a crowbar in hand, attempting to prise it open.

'Hey!' I shouted, feebly.

The intruder spun around and dashed towards me. Head down, they barged past me, clubbing me, hard, on the side of my arm with the crowbar, knocking me to the ground. The uninvited guest then fled the flat.

I *knew* someone had been watching me. It wasn't just in my head. And now I know why. They wanted the contents of my locked cupboard. All those years of keeping *that* safe. But no one knew it was here. Were they just guessing? Only Layla knew about my locked cupboard, but even she didn't know what was inside. I have protected it for too long to let it slip away. It was dangerous. I could allow no-one to have it. I had been careless, keeping it locked inside such a flimsy cupboard. If I'd arrived home any later, they'd have got through that lock, no problem. It must have been someone who knew I had been in Alex and Natalie's flat. But then anyone watching me would have known that! As far as I'm aware, no-one knew what I was

74

keeping there, so why would someone be after it? Would Layla go this far just to find out what's inside? Perhaps this was just a petty crime. I would make sense that my locked cupboard is where I would keep any valuables.

I'd got careless; I'd assumed just locking my flat door was enough. *Had* I locked it, though? To be fair, I was a little trusting when it came to that. I often left it unlocked, but not when I had been out of the building itself. When I'd come home just now it was unlocked. So either Layla had been home and forgotten to lock it again when she left, or…someone who could pick locks had got in.

I decided I had to move it. My current efforts were not enough to protect it from anyone who really wanted it. I had to hide it. My eye fell on the floorboards in the bedroom. I was suddenly happy that I hadn't got around to carpeting this room yet. I grabbed a knife from the kitchen and studied my bedroom floor, speculating where best to create my new safe-place. I decided a floorboard under the bed leg would be best, so I shifted the bed and slipped the knife down the crack between two boards. I was about to apply pressure on the knife to lever it up, when the floorboard popped out easily. Strange? I mused. As I removed the floorboard and placed it to one side, I noticed something brown and furry. I jumped thinking it was a rat, but when I peered back in, I saw that it wasn't moving. That would be a great start to my business, rats, I thought, laughing to myself. I reached in and squeezed it up through the gap. It was an old, worn, teddy bear. There was a blank envelope tied around its neck with string. I tore it and pulled out some lined paper. It was written on in crayon in a child's handwriting. It simply said: "I luv you dady I mis you". I sat and wondered how long it had been there before pushing it back inside the envelope.

I pulled something else up from under the floorboards too. It was a photograph of a young woman passionately kissing an older man. She was very pretty with dark, curly red hair. Her face was heavily made-up, but she looked good for it. She appeared to be in her early twenties, whereas the man was in his fifties. He had a bald head and a grey beard. Definitely an unlikely pair to be kissing like that. I turned the photograph over. A note was written on the back in marker pen: "This should be all the evidence you need mate. Good luck! – Alan".

I contemplated discarding these items. They were no use to me; they'd most likely been here for many years. No one would be looking for them now. But my curiosity got the better of me and I decided to swap them with the objects that I had under lock and key. I crawled over to my locked cabinet, took the key from my wallet in my pocket, and unlocked it. The damage caused by my intruder was quite severe. A few more seconds and they would have been in. I took out a thin green folder, opened it and thumbed through the documents inside. It had been a while since I'd last looked at them, but I still didn't understand any of them. I closed the folder and grabbed a supermarket carrier bag which was on the bed. Layla must have left it there after she'd been to the shops earlier. I put the folder inside and wrapped it up, to protect it from the dirt and dust, and dropped it through the gap and under the floor. I took out a small black box, about the size of a light bulb carton, and placed that under the floor as well, before replacing the floorboard to conceal my new hidey-hole.

I returned the bed to its former position. Its new job as "floor guard" was the best thing I'd used it for in months, I begrudgingly mused, thinking about mine and Layla's waning sex-life. I grabbed the teddy, the letter, and the photo and put them into my cupboard and locked it.

#

The next two days passed without incident, but I'd been at home. Again, there were a few moments where I felt that I was being watched, but nothing happened. I was sure that this was due to my presence in the building, and that the perpetrator was just waiting for another opportunity.

Alex and Natalie had seemed to settle in OK. This being their first time living alone together, they didn't leave the flat much, understandably. Whenever I had knocked on their door it looked as though I'd disturbed them; they'd be barely dressed and very flustered. It must be nice to be seeing that much action, I thought, yet again, about Layla, who wasn't home.

Emotionally, things seemed better between the two of us, but she'd gone out for long runs these past couple of days which she hadn't done for a while. With me staying home these past two days, I thought she might have appreciated the time together.

There was a knock on my front door. I got up to answer it, but when I opened the door, there was no one there.

'Hello?' I called down the corridor.

There was no one visible, but the furthest stairwell door from me was just slowly closing. I dashed towards it and pushed it open. Alex was just about to head down the stairs, but he jumped in shock as I emerged. He was dressed in his burgundy mechanics overalls. On his way to work, no doubt, as this was the only time I ever saw him leave the flat.

'Jesus, Ian. You scared me,' he said with his hand on his heart.

'Sorry about that. Did you just knock on my door?' I asked.

'No.'

'Did you see anyone?'

'No. I've only just come out.'

'Someone has only just knocked.'

'I didn't see anyone, sorry. Anyway, I've got to go. She kept me in bed for ages, again. She's always making me late.'

'Must be nice,' I joked.

He laughed and hurried down the stairs. I returned to my flat and closed the door. I considered locking it, because, unusually for me, I was a bit scared, but I decided not to let the fear control me; it was the middle of the day and Layla would hopefully be back soon.

I walked towards the kitchen to make myself some food, but as I stood at the units, I felt a searing pain at the back of my head. Then, everything went black.

#

I felt cold. The quilt must have fallen off of me. I kept my eyes closed as I could feel the light was on. I threw my arms about, trying to feel for the quilt. I couldn't feel Layla next to me, either. How inconsiderate! She's got up already and left me in bed with the quilt off and the light on. Charming! Then, I suddenly realised that I wasn't laying on my spongy mattress, but a cold, hard, floor. I let my arms drop to the floor and my right arm stung. It felt like pressure on a bruise.

I forced my eyes open through the burning light. I looked at my arm, which was very red. I must have banged it. I looked around to see that I was on my kitchen floor. Now I remembered; someone hit me on the back of my head. I must have fallen on my arm when I went down. I touched the back of my head. It didn't feel wet, but it was horribly painful to the touch. As I brought my hand through my hair, I did feel some wetness on my forehead. I sat up and looked at my reflection in the oven door. There was a cut on my forehead which was bleeding, but it didn't look serious. I noticed some more blood on the kitchen unit. I must have banged my head on that too, after I was hit.

I got up and ran a piece of kitchen roll under the tap to clean the cut. Then, I suddenly panicked. I ran to the bedroom and saw my cupboard prised open. Someone had succeeded this time. Inside, the teddy and the other items that I'd stashed in there had clearly been disturbed, but obviously these weren't what the intruder had been looking for. I closed the cabinet door, which did still close properly, but I didn't bother trying to lock it. There was no point now. I picked up the broken latch. I rolled the combination lock to 1808, to open it, and removed it from the latch, which I discarded. Looking at the small padlock, I realised that I'd been very careless putting something so important behind something so feeble. It was lucky I'd just moved the items that my assailant was clearly searching for.

I didn't want Layla to see the cut or the damaged cupboard as I didn't want the questions. You couldn't really tell that the cupboard had been broken into, once I'd removed the latch. I checked around the flat for a plaster for my cut, but couldn't find one. It definitely needed one, maybe even stitches.

From my kitchen, I heard next door's front door slam shut. There was the distinct sound of Roger's wheelchair as well as the sound of a baby in the corridor. I heard Lee talking to his dad as they went further down. Great timing, I thought. Erica could get me patched up and she wouldn't say anything. And with those lot out of the house, so much the better for me.

I went round and knocked on 3C's blue door. Erica looked happy to see me when she answered the door. I don't think she's had many visitors for herself whilst she'd lived there.

78

I ended up staying over for a cuppa after she'd got me cleaned and patched up. We had a good catch-up on all the goings on in the flats. I told her about the break-in, but made out that I must have spooked my attacker and that just a bit of jewellery had been taken. I had a good time round at hers, but my mind was elsewhere. I couldn't shake the feeling that there was more going on in building than I was aware of.

#

I'd stayed at Erica's for far longer than I'd intended. Back at mine, I pushed open my front door, which, again, was unlocked. I really need to start locking it, but I hadn't meant to stay out this long. I was shattered. I thought being knocked out would have been as good as a sleep, but clearly not. I headed for my bedroom, intending to have a nap, but sheer horror filled me at what I saw; my bed had been moved and the floorboard was up, exposing my hiding place. I rushed over to the hole and slid onto my knees. I looked in…nothing there. "No" I silently screamed. But then…relief. A few yards from the hole…was my stuff. The folder, out of the bag now, the bag itself, and my box. What was going on here? If this isn't what the burglar was after, why *did* they break in?

It was no good. Either way, the items weren't safe here. I needed a better place to keep them, somewhere far away. I put the stuff into my briefcase, restored order to the room.

I grabbed my phone, thought for a moment and then touched "James" in the phone's contact list. After several seconds, I heard his voice.

'James!' I said down the phone. 'I need your help!'

James, my old friend from university. We'd studied business together, but he had become far more successful than me. He was running his own fancy restaurant in America. A long way to go for a favour, but he owed me one. A big one too, so I knew I could trust him with this. I told him as much as I needed to, mainly the fact that I had something that I wanted keeping safe, and after a long discussion I decided that the best thing I could do was deliver it him. I couldn't take the chance of posting it to him so I told him that I would fly out there.

When I ended the call, I went straight onto the internet on my phone to check for flights. This was urgent. I didn't feel comfortable leaving the flats with everything going on, but I needed to get it done before the old couple moved in. I found a flight for the day after tomorrow which returned five days later. No time to lose. I paid for it there and then. James had said on the phone that he knew a decent hotel nearby that we could stay in.

#

Layla came home soon after. She was very red and sweaty. It must have been a tough run. I always thought she looked really cute in her purple running gear. When I told her the news of our surprise "holiday" she didn't seem too enthusiastic. She managed to feign some excitement once she'd come around to the idea. I mean, I know I was just using it as a cover to get my stuff out of the country, but still, a holiday to America should be a thrill for anyone.

She asked about the cut on my head, but was easily diverted with a lie about me banging into a door.

Soon after, pleading tiredness, she went to bed, and I lay on the sofa. I felt my eyes closing. I was still shattered. With the trip to America, Seth and Ingrid due to move here in just over a week and everything else I have planned with these flats, the next couple of weeks are going to be busy. Then I remembered that flat 3D still needed cleaning after the state that Kane had left it in. I couldn't imagine what Ingrid's face would be like if she turned up and it looked like that. I would have to do that as soon as I returned from America, I didn't want to focus on anything else other than protecting my stuff before then. Depending on how the next few weeks played out, this might be my last bit of free time in a long time. I put my head back on the sofa arm and enjoyed the rest.

Chapter 12 – Motivations

Alex, dressed for work, walked into the corridor, dragging Natalie, who had wrapped her arms around his neck and was trailing her toes across the floor. She hung limply in her effort to slow him down.

'Please!' she begged.

'I have to,' he replied.

'Please!'

'I'd love to stay, but someone has to pay for this place.'

'Please.'

'Do you want to be back living with your parents?'

'No,' she sighed, sulkily.

'If it helps, you make it very hard to leave,' he said, turning to her and removing her arms from his neck.

'Anyway, you need to get studying. When you're a rich doctor, I won't need to go to work anymore. The life of a student can't be that bad. All these extra days at home you get. I'd love it.'

'It's just lonely without you.'

'I'm sorry. Anyway, I need to go.'

'Fine! At least I have my fish for company.'

Alex laughed and backed towards the stairwell door as they blew each other kisses at each other. Unfortunately, he misjudged his distance and banged the back of his head into the heavy stairwell fire door. Natalie laughed at him before returning to the flat.

She flopped on the sofa and lay there, letting a substantial amount of time pass as she played endless games on her phone. She looked over at the overflowing bin and had an inward tantrum over the fact

81

that she'd forgotten to ask Alex to empty it on his way out. She had no choice; it needed doing; some of the contents had already spilled onto the floor. She walked over to the kitchen area and scooped up the bag of rubbish, fastidiously returning the stray items to it, before heading out of the flat.

As she went down the corridor, she held the rubbish bag with both hands at arm's length, scared that the germs would leap out of the bag and infect her in some way. She got to the heavy fire door at the end of corridor and struggled to push it open with her back.

'Need a hand, sweetheart?' a creepy voice came from further down the corridor.

She saw a man in a wheelchair heading in her direction. He had a large, open packet of crisps on his lap and there were crumbs all over his chin and jumper. Natalie pushed with all her strength to get through the door before he got to her, but she failed.

'Let me get that for you, doll,' said Roger, slimily.

He parked his wheelchair and, to Natalie's surprise, stood and pushed open the door for her.

'There you go,' he said, blocking her path.

'Thanks, if I could just squeeze past you now, that would be great,' pleaded Natalie.

'Just have a minute. I haven't introduced myself yet. My name's Roger.'

'I'm Natalie, nice to meet you.'

'You must be the new bit of crumpet living in the pink flat.'

'I'm just Natalie,' she said as she tried to edge past.

'Well, you're no fun,' he said, letting go of the door and returning to his wheelchair. 'Let's change that, shall we?'

He proceeded to wheel into the back of her legs, causing her to fall on his lap.

'Weh-hey! Steady on love. We've only just met,' Roger chuckled.

Natalie jumped up and composed herself immediately, but felt violated. She started to move away from him, but he put his arm on her thigh as she passed.

'Where are you going, we were just getting to know each other better,' he grinned.

'I'd rather not, thanks. You're disgusting,' Natalie said, repulsed and smacking his hand away.

She walked off towards the other side of the corridor, deciding to take the stairs at the opposite side instead. As she walked past, Lee walked out of his flat, with Isaac strapped to his chest.

'What are you running off for, dad? You know you won't go down the stairs on your own,' he said.

'I was just getting better acquainted with this young lassie,' Roger replied.

'That's your dad?' Natalie asked Lee.

'Yes. And I'm Lee. Nice to meet you, neighbour.' Lee answered.

'You too,' she said. 'Your father is vile,' she added as she walked towards the other stairwell door.

She struggled again, but this time, with more determination, managed to get through. She heard Lee giving his dad a telling off before she disappeared out of earshot.

She carried the large black sack of rubbish down the stairs. This was the first time she'd had to do it since they'd lived here; up until now, it had been Alex's job. If only she had waited for him to finish work; she hated any sort of labour, especially if it was dirty. When she got to the staircase that led from the second floor to the first, she didn't notice that it was narrower than the rest, and the rubbish bag got wedged between the sides, jamming itself in the passage, causing her to walk into it. As the bag touched her, she gave a girly scream, and let go of it, spilling half the contents. "Oh no" she sighed to herself. She put the considerably lightened bag down carefully and had a moan to herself.

She headed back up the few steps that she'd descended and onto the second floor to look for a brush. There was no stairwell door to this floor; or so she thought. She eyed a flimsy looking wooden door on the floor not far from where it should have been. She was shocked at the state this floor was in. Black scorch marks and ash were everywhere. She couldn't believe that she only lived one storey above this. Even some of the ceiling looked burned. She hoped that the structural integrity of the building was sound.

She checked the rooms for any sort of dustpan and brush using the torch on her phone to illuminate her search. She opened door 2A and looked inside. Nothing! Then she checked 2B. Again, nothing! Flat 2C's door was hanging on by only a single hinge. She edged it open, but as soon as it was halfway there, it dropped off the frame with a bang and fell towards her. Natalie, cowered behind her arms and tumbled away from it into the room, dropping her phone as she did. She landed on a large pile of soot and ash. Clouds of filth flew upwards and into the room, before settling back down on her. She stood up and tried desperately to brush the dirt from her, by now, ruined pyjamas. Why was there just a random large pile of muck here? Then she noticed with dread that part of her phone was sticking out from under the fallen door. She prayed as she reached down and picked it up, waiting a few moments before daring to look at it, as though this would somehow reduce the likelihood of it being broken. It didn't. The screen was smashed and it wouldn't turn on.

'Great,' she said putting her head into her hands.

She felt the thick dirt on her face. She was filthy. All she wanted to do was get a shower. She looked around for anything to help her with the mess she'd left on the stairs. If there *was* something, she couldn't see it now that her light source had been destroyed. "Oh well" she thought. She was a mess now anyway. She may as well just go and pick all the rubbish up by hand.

She quickly returned to the site of her disaster and begun to place all the items back into the bag. She didn't want anyone to see her, so she hurried to the ground floor and placed it into one of the large bins down there.

She turned around and jumped when she saw Kane stood there, looking at her.

'Who are you? The cleaner?' he asked.

'No, I live here now. I'm Natalie, I live in 3E,' she replied.

'I'm Kane, 3A. Well, it's nice to have someone so young in here for a change. How old are you?' he said flirtatiously.

'Oh, not you too! Is there anyone decent living here?'

'What do you mean? I only asked a simple question.'

'I'm twenty-five, I'm studying at university to be a doctor, I keep exotic fish as pets and that's about it.'

'I don't need your life story.'

'Well, I thought it better to just get everything out of the way. And how old are you?'

'I'm thirty-nine. Just the right age for someone like you.'

'I don't think so, plus I have a boyfriend.'

'You're a feisty one, aren't you? I bet you're filthy.'

'I *am* filthy. I'm covered in muck and dirt and God knows what else, so if you don't mind, I need to go and shower.'

'Why don't I join you? We can shower in my flat, together. *I'll* get you cleaned up,' he said with a wink.

'Pig!'

She was about to storm off, when she gave a double-take. She had a sudden feeling that she had met him before.

'Do I know you from somewhere?' she asked.

'I doubt that, princess, but we could rectify that,' he replied.

'No, seriously. I'm sure I know you from somewhere.'

'Like where?' he asked, approaching her.

'I don't know, but it's going to bug me all day.'

Finding that Natalie didn't rise to his usual goading, he decided to leave, 'Whatever. See you soon, hopefully,' he said, before giving her a resounding smack on the bottom.

He exited the building, leaving her stood, gobsmacked, wondering about the kind of place she had moved herself into.

#

When Alex returned home, Natalie was waiting for him on the sofa with an angry look on her face.

'What's the matter, babe?' asked Alex, as he removed his work overalls, tossed them on the back of the sofa, and sat down beside her.

Natalie explained to him about her experience with their new neighbours, and about breaking her phone.

Alex stood, 'I'm gonna go round and see both of them.'

'No, don't bother, it's not worth the hassle,' Natalie responded.

'Defending your honour is not a hassle,' he said, doing a patriotic salute as a joke. 'Seriously though, I should go and see them. The earlier we nip this in the bud, the better. And I wouldn't worry about your phone. It's insured. We'll send it off later today for repairs.'

'Don't go round. The old guy is just a pervert, I wouldn't bother. But the other guy looks dangerous. Let's just see what happens.'

Alex sat and thought for a moment before replying with renewed vigour, 'No! I'm not having it,' he said, storming out of the flat.

'Alex!' Natalie protested, as he closed the door.

He made his way over to the blue door. It had been left slightly ajar. He'd noticed this a few times whenever Roger had left the flat. Probably because of his wheelchair he couldn't be bothered to turn around and shut it. But did this mean he wouldn't be home, he thought. Maybe he leaves it open when he returns too. Alex pushed open the door and was about to shout inside to get someone's attention, but he was stopped by an angry female voice.

He peered into the flat, but couldn't see anyone, which meant that she probably wasn't shouting at him. He stepped just inside, not wanting to intrude, but wanting to get someone's attention. Then he heard a few worrying words in her conversation, like "dead" and "murder". His curiosity got the better of him, so he sneaked into the room a little further. Across the living room was an open door to what he assumed was the bedroom. The flat was of almost identical layout to his, which the exception of an extra room, presumably another bedroom that slept Roger. Alex crept across the living room to the open door and peered in. He saw the woman who lived here, Erica, talking angrily into the phone and pacing up and down. He'd only met her briefly up to now.

'Jessica, listen! You need to stay focussed,' Erica said, angrily into the phone. 'I have a lot going on here at the moment. What I'm doing is very important. You need to take care of it yourself. I have given up too much for this to go south now...yes...Jessica...yes, I know...OK...stop getting upset. I know you have made sacrifices too. What happened to Nicola was terrible. But you need to stay strong...Jessica stop it now...no I'm not trying to manipulate you...I'm sorry I haven't contacted you since, but I knew you would get through it. I need to focus on what *I'm* doing...Forget about him! You didn't really love him did you, otherwise you wouldn't have done what you did so easily. You need to stay where you are and carry on. Sort it out. We're gonna need money when the time comes, so you just keep doing what you do best. I'll join you when I can...It should be soon...I'm still working on it. It's harder than I originally thought. You have no idea the elements that are at play here. So many things are coinciding with each other and I'm gonna end up caught in the middle of it if I'm not careful. Believe it or not, I'm actually at your old base of operations...The hotel. The one that had the fire. I need to get going anyway, just...'

Sensing that the phone call was coming to an end, Alex decided he'd better flee in case she left the room straight away.

When he got back to the corridor, he stood for a moment to process what he'd just heard. Something sinister was going on there. It gave him an uncomfortable feeling in his gut. Were he and Natalie safe here? He was sure he was just being paranoid, but, either way, this Erica woman was up to something very suspicious.

Alex decided to move onto Kane and confront Roger at a later time. He headed to the end of the corridor to the ominous red door. This was ajar also. Alex wondered if this was common practice here, or if this had just been coincidence. He pushed it all the way and saw a woman kneeling down on the floor in the living room. It was Layla, the landlord's wife. She turned and looked at him, shocked.

'Oh, Alex. You scared me.'

As he walked further into the room he noticed stuff all over the floor. Cupboard doors were open and the contents seemed to have been pulled out. Was Layla responsible for this, he wondered. She was holding a photograph in her hand.

'Layla, is it?' Alex asked.

'Yes, sorry we haven't met properly yet,' she said.

'What are you doing in here?'

Layla didn't respond. She looked like she was trying to formulate a lie, but she couldn't find the words. She suddenly burst into tears. Alex, unsure how to react, moved over and put his arm around her.

'What's wrong? Where's Kane?' he asked.

'He's not here,' she replied.

'Has he done something to you?'

'No...not recently, anyway.'

'What do you mean?'

'It doesn't matter. Look, just please don't tell anyone about this, OK?' Layla pleaded.

'I won't if you tell me what's going on.'

'It's nothing. The other day we had a bit of a run in, is all,' she dismissed.

'A bit of a run in?' inquired Alex.

'Yes, I really don't want to talk about it.'

'I can't promise not to say anything unless you tell me what's going on. I'm sure you're not, but for all I know, you could be robbing him.'

'Fine, just please don't say anything!' she reiterated.

'I promise,' he replied, sincerely.

'I'm not going into details, but a long time ago, he did something bad to me.'

'What was it?'

'I said I'm not going into details,' she reiterated. 'The point is, that I know he's bad, and the other day, when we had our run in, it was because I caught him sneaking around upstairs. He was looking for something, but I found it first.'

'What was it?' Alex asked, intrigued.

'It was this photo,' she said, giving it a wave in her hand, 'and a note. I didn't get to read the whole thing, that's why I came here, to look for it. I don't want to make the same mistake I did all those years ago.'

'What mistake?' Alex asked.

'Keeping quiet,' she said, absently. 'Whatever he's up to now, can't be good and if I don't do anything about it, then I'm just as bad as I was back then.'

'And you think that if you find that note, you'll find answers?'

'It's not just the note. You must understand that I'm not the sort to break in and risk my safety like this. To be honest, I'm petrified just being here, but I needed to see this photo again,' she said, handing it to Alex. 'Besides Kane, I recognised someone else, but I can't remember where from, or who he is. It's driving me mad, I *had* to see it again.'

'Well I can help you with one of the men,' said Alex as he stared intently at the photograph. 'This man here,' he pointed, indicating one of the other men in the photo.

It was not Kane, nor the other man that Layla had recognised.

'This man's name is Alan Kendall,' Alex stuttered.

'How do you know him?' asked Layla, puzzled.

'He's my father.'

Alex dropped the photo, confused at what he was seeing. He couldn't remember his dad. He only ever had some old photos of him.

'What's he doing in a photo here? With Kane?' Layla asked.

'I don't know, but it says a lot about the type of man he was. And why he abandoned me,' Alex said, troubled.

'I'm sorry.'

'Don't be. This is all just coincidence. I don't really care to know what he's up to.'

'I just wish I could remember where I know *him* from,' she said, pointing at the man in the photo that she recognised. 'Maybe if I find the note…'

She continued to search through everything she'd pulled out of the cupboards.

'I don't think this is a good idea,' Alex said. 'We need to get this place back to how it was, before Kane comes home.'

'It's a little bit late for that,' said Kane, stunning the other two.

'Kane!' Layla panicked.

Kane was standing over them with a menacing look on his face. Alex and Layla got to their feet.

'What the hell do you think you're doing?' he asked, angrily.

'I…I…I just needed to see this photo again,' Layla stammered.

'So you broke in?'

'No. I just borrowed my husband's master key.'

'There's a master key? Well it's good to know that we have our privacy,' Kane said, sarcastically. 'Why are you so interested in seeing that photo again?'

'I recognised one of the other men in this photo. Who is this?' she said, pointing at the man she felt she knew.

Kane looked at who she was pointing at, then looked up at her.

'Get out!' Kane said, angrily, snatching the photo from her hands.

'What's going on?' asked Alex.

'Something happened here,' said Layla, confidently. 'When this place was a hotel. He knows something,' she said, nodding at Kane.

'What was it? And this man here…' said Alex, pointing at his father in the photo. 'What's he doing here with you.'

'Why do you care?' Kane asked.

'He's my father,' he replied.

'Your father? Ha. Small world.'

'What happened here?' Layla asked.

'Believe me…you don't want to know,' said Kane, reminiscently.

'Was it really that bad?' Alex asked.

'Nothing I'm not used to. My life has been full of bad choices, as *she* already knows,' he said, nodding towards Layla.

'What?' said Alex, confused. 'What is going on between you two? What aren't you telling me?'

'It doesn't matter. Now I want both of you to get out of here and keep your mouths shut!' He focussed on Layla now. 'Don't mention my history with this place to your husband and I won't report you for breaking into my flat.'

Layla looked at him for a moment and then left. Alex and Kane stared at each other for a moment.

'Well?' Kane asked. 'What do you want?'

'I want to know what my dad is doing in this picture with you,' he replied.

'I think it's time you got lost. You don't want to push me.'

'You don't scare me. That's the real reason why I'm here. I want you to apologise to my girlfriend and never touch her again.'

'Your girlfriend?'

'Yes. You met her in the lobby. Sexually assaulted her.'

'Oh stop exaggerating. I gave her a friendly smack on the bottom.'

'Well, don't let it happen again.'

'You do not want to threaten me, young Kendall.'

'I already told you. You don't scare me,' Alex reiterated.

'Ha. Just like your dad. Just as cocky. We were good friends, you know. That's the only reason I'm going to let you off lightly. Now get out.'

'You'd better stay away from my girlfriend,' Alex said, firmly, before leaving the flat.

Kane stood for a moment and stared at the photo. He looked at his messy flat and began to tidy up. He reached into the cabinet that had recently been emptied. He felt around at the roof of the cupboard and pulled off a taped note. The one he had recovered the other day. He read it again:

"Kane. Don't worry man, I kept you out of it. We burned the couch, but something went wrong as you've no doubt heard. I wanted to tell you this in person, but they already suspect us of the fire. So that, coupled with our outstanding charges in America, could finish us. And you don't want to be associated with us. It could ruin your chances with your family. And that's the main reason I am writing to you. I happened across something very interesting. I wanted to leave it here for you, but this room was taken when I came here again, so I've hidden it under the floorboards in the room I am currently staying in. Under one of the bed legs. It's room 302. Sorry I couldn't leave it in our usual hiding place, but I'm taking a big enough risk just by coming here again so I'll leave this note with Jack and get him to hide it in the usual spot. Jack can't talk to you either so I'm hoping you come back looking for the stash you left here. Sorry to disappoint, but I told Jack he could take it as payment for risking coming back here again, but when you see what I've left you, you'll know that it's worth it. I hope it cheers you up. After this, I'm going to disappear for a while. Good luck, my friend."

Kane was struggling with the note. He wondered if he'd misunderstood something on it. The note said that Alan had found something for him. What was it? When he'd snuck in to next doors,' flat, where it was supposedly hidden, he'd found something that was definitely *not* for him. A folder full of documents that he didn't understand and a box containing some sort of electronic chip. Kane wasn't sure what these things were, but he *was* sure that they hadn't been left for him. Maybe whatever *had* been left for him was long gone. It had been three years after all. Who knows what had happened between then and now?

Kane screwed up the note and threw it into the corner. He sat down on his sofa in anger and started punching the sofa cushions. A few tears escaped as he began thinking about his daughter. He'd messed his life up so much. What did Lisa look like now? Would she remember him if he ever saw him again?

Chapter 13 – A Late Realisation

I continued my story, 'I found out later that the break-ins were done by two different people. One was by Kane. The other two must have been by someone else. I never found out who. It was just sheer coincidence that I had swapped the locations of the two treasures before their respective burglaries. Of course, at the time I had no idea, but Kane filled us in on his part in this on our final night at the flats.'

Looking around the room people were getting a little confused, so I tried to explain it a little simpler, 'Basically, as best I understand it, the first burglary attempt was committed by an unknown assailant who was trying to get to my belongings. I interrupted them and they fled, at which point I moved my stuff. The second attempt was by the same intruder. They were successful in accessing my cupboard this time, however I don't think a teddy bear is what they were after. The third break-in was done by Kane who was after said bear. Unfortunately he was also too late as I had now moved *his* prize.'

"What has all this got to do with the incident?" one person asked. "Nothing" I told them. Nothing at all really. But these parts of the story were as much for me as it was for them. I was trying to fill in the gaps myself. To understand what was going on beneath the surface of everything that *I* was doing. Our lives were intertwined so much more than I ever knew. Some would call it fate.

Someone else had asked what was in the documents and the box I'd kept hidden. I refused to tell them, of course. They were never found and never would be if I had anything to do with it…

Chapter 14 – Across the Pond

'Ian! Are you ready yet?' Layla said as she came into the room from the bathroom, putting in her last earring.

She looked amazing. It had been a long time since I'd seen her dressed up like this. I should have probably taken her on more dates, just to see her like this. She was wearing a long blue dress that showed off her perfect figure and exposed her gorgeous shoulders. It was sparsely covered with shiny specks that made her glow.

I was still lying naked in bed, but I knew it would only take me two minutes to get dressed. I needed a little down time. We had just made love, if you could call it that. It was so dull; her input was minimal. I could tell that she wished that she was elsewhere. I'd hoped being somewhere different would have excited her a bit more, but sex was definitely worse now than it had ever been. I didn't want her to leave me anytime soon. I needed to find out the problem and win her back.

'Come on, Ian. Get dressed!' Layla demanded, somewhat annoyed.

'I will in a bit. I just want to relax. We are on holiday,' I replied.

'Yes. We are on *holiday*. New York has so much to see and I don't want to stay cooped up in here.'

'But I thought we could just relax a little bit more.'

'Look. You sprung this holiday on me, without warning, so you're going to get into it.'

'I thought you'd be happy for the break.'

'Of course I am. I'm not going to be ungrateful when you take me to America on a whim, am I? But I want to see the sights. This restaurant you've booked for us sounds pretty posh too. I'm excited.

Now get dressed; I'm almost ready.'

Layla went back into the bathroom. I climbed out of bed and opened my suitcase. I peered into the bathroom; Layla was busy brushing her teeth so I removed my secret folder and box and slid them both under the bed. I grabbed the jeans that I'd thrown on the floor earlier and rummaged through the pockets to find my hotel room key card. I got dressed and put the card into my pocket. Then I joined Layla in the bathroom to groom.

'Have you got your room card?' I asked.

'Yeah, it's in my purse, why?' she replied.

'I can't find mine is all and I can't be bothered rooting round for it,' I lied.

'It's fine. We only need one.'

I finished brushing my teeth and looked at her. I hope this all goes OK. I didn't want the questions so I had to keep her in the dark.

#

'Your table, sir,' the waiter said, seating us at a private table in the corner. He took our drink order and left.

'This place is amazing, Ian. How can you afford to bring me to America and still have the money to splash out on fancy restaurants?' Layla asked.

'I can't put a price on our relationship, Layla,' I replied.

'What do you mean?' she asked, puzzled.

'I know things aren't going great between us at the moment. I just want to try and salvage something before things get worse.'

Layla looked down. I could tell she wasn't expecting me to be so direct.

'I didn't think that…that, well…that you thought there was anything wrong,' she managed.

'Of course I do. I know I've had a lot on my mind, but the last thing I want is to lose you,' I said. 'What's wrong? What can I do?'

'It's nothing that you've done. You've been brilliant. I just felt a bit distant from you. I don't know what's wrong with me.'

'I need your help. Tell me what's wrong, Layla. Let me fix this.'

'I don't even know myself.'

'Do you not know or do you not want to tell me?'

'A little of both, I suppose.'

'When did you start feeling like this?'

'I don't know,' she sighed.

'It's been a while now, hasn't it?'

'Yes. We got married so fast. We had so much fun at first. I know I probably rushed into it, because I thought I would never find anyone who would want to marry me. But that's the wrong reason.'

'We were still getting to know each other,' I agreed. 'I'm sorry it happened like this. It was just lust at first. I got caught up in a whirlwind of emotions and I thought that's what you wanted. We should have slowed things down.'

'I was the same. I didn't see a problem with it at the time. Being without a job hasn't helped. I've needed you. I don't know where I would have gone without you.'

'So you're just living with me out of convenience?'

'Not at first, but…I'm not going to lie. I might have left if I hadn't depended on you.'

'And that's what I want to avoid. Can we work it out?'

'Let's see how we get on this week.'

'And don't ever think that you wouldn't find someone who wouldn't want you. I think that you're one of the most beautiful women I've ever met.'

'That's because you're so young. You haven't met enough yet,' she joked with a hint of seriousness.

'Just take the compliment, would you. I would have booked for two week if I had the money.'

'Don't be daft. I'm lucky that you're even paying for me to come at all after how I've been with you.'

'If it helps, I have been really busy these last few months. I haven't been paying any attention to you,' I joked.

'You sod,' she said, giving me a playful slap. 'I am lucky, really. More than I realise. I mean, look at this place. It must cost a bomb to eat here.'

'To be honest. I'm getting a bit of a discount.'

'Really. Why?'

'I know one of the owners. In fact, here he is now.'

I pointed at a man that was approaching our table. Layla looked at him and her smile quickly disappeared.

'Ian!' the man called over. 'Good to see you, friend.'

'Good to see you too,' I said. 'I can see you're doing much better than I am. Layla, this is James. We studied business together at uni.'

James was only a little older than me; twenty three. He was a little taller than me, skinny and with a full head of short brown hair. His round spectacles made him look geekier than he actually was, and whenever he took them off, girls would tend to compliment him on how much better he looked.

'Great to meet you, Layla,' he said, extending his arm.

Layla didn't take his hand right away and just stared at him.

'Are you OK? Have I got something on my face?' he said.

'Sorry, no...no,' Layla stammered. 'Sorry, I just recognise you is all.'

'Really?' he replied, shocked.

'It's probably from an old uni photo of us that I have,' I solved.

'Yes!' Layla shouted, over excited. 'That's where I recognise you from.'

Both James and I were a little taken aback by her sudden outburst.

'Yes. That's what I just said, darling,' I reiterated.

'Yes. I know. Sorry. I was just trying to work it out. I saw you and I couldn't remember,' Layla said, unconvincingly.

I was really confused. Layla seemed to be acting a bit odd around James.

'So you both went to uni together then? In England?' asked Layla in a clear attempt to steer the conversation.

'Yeah,' said James. 'I moved here after uni to start my own business.'

'I think you'll find that you left *before* you'd finished,' I corrected.

'So, what are you doing with your degree, Ian?' he said, diverting the attention to me.

'I own a block of flats that I rent out. Nothing as glamorous as this restaurant, though.'

'We all have to start somewhere. This restaurant took some getting going.'

Layla was still looking at James in a strange way.

'I'm just going to the bathroom, if you'll excuse me,' Layla informed us as she stood.

'The ladies is just back there,' James said, pointing towards the toilets at the far corner of the restaurant.

When Layla was out of sight James quickly took her seat.

'OK, quick. We might not have long,' I said.

'OK what is it?' James asked?

'I don't have time to explain, but the contents are of grave importance. I can trust your discretion can't I?'

'Of course you can. I told you. Anything I can do to help, I'll do it.'

'I just need it keeping somewhere safe. Until it's OK for me to get it back. And I'd prefer if you didn't ask questions.'

'I understand completely. Keep it safe. That's all I need to know.'

'Thanks, James. I owe you.'

'You don't owe me. We're just even. So where is it?' he asked, looking around my vicinity.

'I couldn't bring it. I didn't want to have to explain to Layla. Here!' I said, producing my room card key. 'This is a card to the room at the hotel I'm staying at. It's the Griffiths Palace, room six seven four. It's all under the bed.'

'You want me to go and get it from your hotel?'

'Yes. Will that be a problem?'

'Well, I might struggle to get off tonight.'

'How long will you need?'

'I might be able to slip away for ten minutes in an hour, maybe.'

'OK. I can keep her busy until then.'

'Jesus, man. I hope whatever it is will be worth it. So, tell me about your flats, then.'

'It's just an old run down hotel. Not far from the uni, actually.'

'You don't mean The Royal Rainford Hotel do you?' asked James with sheer dread written all over his face.

'Yes, why?'

'I just…I have a bit of a history with that building.'

'Does this have something to do with the night of the fire?'

'I can't say. It's best you don't know.'

'You can't say that and not tell me,' I said, curiously.

'What's the thing I'm getting from your hotel room?' James asked, pointedly.

'Fair point. I won't ask,' I said, defeated.

#

We walked the city streets whilst our dinner was settling. We were heading back to the hotel. James would have had enough time by now. We'd stopped for all the novelties of New York. Best of all was the ice cream vendor. We were still both happily tucking in to our mint chocolate chip ice cream cones.

'Have I got any on my face?' she asked, closing her eyes and pulling her face taut.

'You've just got a little bit here,' I said and kissed it off the side of her lip.

She opened her eyes and briefly smiled. This was soon overwritten by a look of sadness.

'What's wrong?' I asked.

'Nothing. I…urgh…it's just what we were talking about at dinner. About us. Sometimes, like just now. I love it so much. And then other times, I don't know.'

'What is it that you want? Tell me and I'll try,' I said, just as my phone buzzed, alerting me to a text.

I checked it whilst Layla was trying to talk to me. It was from James. "Only just got away from restaurant. Stall longer". My heart sank. We weren't far away now. I zoned back into reality. I'd missed what Layla had been saying to me. I needed to stall her anyway.

'Sorry darling. Say again,' I requested.

'This is what I mean,' she stressed. 'It's like you've always got something else on your mind. Always.'

'I'm sorry. Please tell me what I can do.'

'I just think you're too young. It seems silly now, because of course I knew that when I married you, but…I don't know. At the time you seemed so mature, but I want you to be...I want…'

'I can be whatever you want. Just ask,' I pleaded.

'I just want a bit more excitement in my life.'

'But you don't exactly put the effort in yourself. Like in the hotel room, when we had sex, it was like I was on my own up there.'

'Because it's always the same,' she stressed again.

'So why didn't you say something?'

'I didn't know how. But now you know.'

'Now I know,' I said, dismayed. 'This whole thing is about sex.'

'I just can't see us getting back from this.'

'But I'm going to try. Starting right now,' I said, firmly.

'What do you mean?'

I grabbed her and dragged her down a nearby alley.

'Ian! What do you think you're doing?' she said.

'Making things exciting again!' I replied.

The alley was a dead end, but had a little lip we could just about hide behind, out of view of passers-by.

'This isn't what I meant,' she said, looking around at the filthy alley.

'I sense your body tells me differently,' I said as I slipped a swift hand under her long dress, causing it to ride up, and felt her moist knickers.

'Ian! What if someone…'

She trailed off in delight as I expertly manoeuvred my fingers around the outside of her knickers, hitting all the right spots. She started to moan and her feeble protests at the gritty nature of where we were, vanished. It wasn't about stalling her anymore. It was about showing her that I still knew what I was doing. This was exciting for me too. I've been so focussed on the flats that it was nice to let loose. Do something risqué, naughty, dangerous!

As she hungrily unzipped my jeans so that she could play too, I started to get a sense of what she really wanted. She wanted this daring, rough man that I was currently impersonating. I pushed her knickers aside and we began to have sex in the public alley. Looking at her face, seeing the pleasure in hers eyes as I thrust, told me one thing. I had been handling her all wrong. I had been too focussed on other things and wasn't being the vigorous lover that she wanted. I didn't have long to change her opinion. I could lose her too soon. The moment I felt that I had lost her was the moment I was able to turn things around, literally. I spun her around and continued in this new position. I wasn't making love to her anymore. This was simply rough sex and her body gave me all the responses I needed to tell me that this is what she wanted. I won't deny that I didn't love every second of it. It was a win-win situation, really. No love was lost, she was happy in the moment. And James had plenty of time to get my stuff.

Where would we go from here? I felt that she didn't love me anymore, but she clearly loved what has happening right now, but…is *this* the only thing that would keep our relationship together?

Chapter 15 – The Jailbreak Party

Erica stared worriedly at the hand written poster that had been shoved under her door. "Jailbreak Corridor Party – Please take part in a corridor party tomorrow – open your flat door and mingle. All invited. Bring as many friends as you can. Leave booze and snacks out in your flat and feel free to enter other flats and help yourself to their booze and snacks. Let's have a blast!" She clutched the poster tightly in her hand. Ian would be back in a few days and he'd asked her to keep an eye on things. He trusted her more than any of the other residents, so she didn't want to let him down.

This had to be Kane's handiwork, she thought. She left her flat, marched over to 3A and knocked politely on the red door. Kane's friend, the drug user who is usually there, answered.

'Is this Kane's doing?' Erica asked, holding up the tatty flyer.

'Well, it was my idea, but Kane is sorting it out, yeah,' he replied.

'Who are you anyway?'

'Tony. I'm here a lot.'

'I know that. I'd think you lived here.'

'Who is it?' said Kane, appearing at the door.

'You can't really be serious with this, can you?' Erica asked, thrusting the poster into his hand.

'Of course I am. Why not?'

'Because Ian will flip his nut if we wreck the place.'

'We're not going to wreck the place. Besides, it would be worth it. Corridor parties are the best.'

'Never heard of them.'

'You don't know what you're missing,' enthused Tony. 'They're the best kind of party.'

'So let me get this straight. You want us all to have our doors open for anyone to wander in and out?' Erica asked.

'Yes. It's about trust,' Kane said.

'Exactly. I haven't got any,' she replied. 'Especially not where you and your friend are concerned. And why's it called "Jailbreak Party", anyway?'

'Well, the main reason I'm having the party is because some of my friends have just recently got out of prison, so I thought I'd throw them a party to celebrate.'

'Oh yippety-doo-daa,' she said, sarcastically. 'Well, that's all right then. What were they in for?'

'Only robbery.'

'Only!'

'There's three of them. They all got sent down together and they've all just got out together. They stuck together through it all. I just thought I'd throw them a party; invite a few other friends, the neighbours, *their* friends. Plus, it's a great chance to meet new people. Look,' he said, trying to sway her, 'if I promise to clean the whole corridor *and* flat 3D afterwards, would you be on board?'

'What's flat 3D got to do with this? There's no one living there.'

'I know…but I still have the key. It'll make a great extra room.'

'I suppose anything I say won't stop you.'

'So you'll join in?'

'I'll *come*! Just to keep things under control, *but* you're not using my flat. I'll have to leave my partner in there with my baby so you'll only have the two flats.'

'Three, actually. The young couple have already been round to confirm their attendance.'

'Alex and Natalie are taking part?'

'Yeah. Said they can't wait.'

'Don't forget the old man too,' Tony reminded him.

'Old man? Oh no!' Erica sighed.

'Yeah. Your dad isn't he?' Kane asked.

'He is *not* my dad. He's my *boyfriend's* dad,' Erica corrected. 'I should have known he'd be up for it, the dirty old git!'

'He got really excited when we told him there'd be girls here,' Tony said.

'I've no doubt,' said Erica.

A look of worry spread across her face. Surely nothing good would come of this.

#

The next evening, noise was echoing through the flats.

'Maybe we should just join in,' Lee said, hopefully.

'I'm not letting a single one of those people in here,' said Erica, determinedly.

'Well, do you want to take Isaac then and I'll go and check on dad?'

'Nice try. If I let you go to that party, I won't see you for the rest of the night and I'll be lumbered with Isaac all night.'

'Lumbered? That's our son.'

'Oh, don't try and play that card.'

'So it's alright for you to party and have fun though?'

'I won't be partying. I'm going to be running round like a blue-arsed fly trying to make sure they don't turn this place into a shit-hole. I don't want Ian to have to come back to that.'

'What do you care? *Our* flat will be fine.'

'It's about having a little respect, Lee.'

'But it's not *your* responsibility.'

'That's not the point.'

A loud bang came at the door as though someone had been thrown at it.

'See what I mean?' Erica said, angrily. 'If the music doesn't wake Isaac, the banging about *will*. I need to get out there.'

Erica left Lee in the living room and opened her front door. Alex lay on his back, curled over, laughing hysterically.

'Shh,' said Natalie, appearing from further down the corridor. 'They have a baby in there.'

'Yes, we do,' shouted Erica, grabbing Natalie's attention. 'Nice to see that you're both getting into the full swing of the party.'

'We were...' struggled Alex, who was still in hysterics on the floor,

103

'we were just...just...'

Alex gave up and just carried on giggling.

'What's wrong with him?' Erica asked Natalie.

'He's not much of a drinker. A bit of a lightweight,' replied Natalie, also struggling to contain her laughter.

Erica gave up on the two of them. She stepped over Alex's wriggling body and marched over to 3A. The door was wide open, as expected. She edged her way through some men who were standing in the doorway. One of them slapped her behind. Erica spun around, grabbed his wrist and held it up with incredible strength, causing him to wince.

'Do that again, and I'll snap it off,' Erica said, forcefully.

Ignoring this threat, the man quickly brought his other hand around in an attempt to strike her. She blocked him, and swept his feet with her leg, knocking him easily to the floor. She held him in place on the ground as the onlookers laughed. They were playing to an audience of seven or eight other people.

'Ha-ha, Derek,' said one of the other men. 'How did *you* survive in prison?'

They all began to laugh. Erica was comforted by the lack of camaraderie; it meant that she was unlikely to be attacked by the others. This Derek, wearing a vest and some mucky jeans, looked like your stereotypical ex-con. Tattooed arms, shaved head, stone jaw. Average build, but nothing Erica couldn't handle.

'So you're one of the robbers then?' chuckled Erica. 'What did you rob, an old folks home?'

Everyone laughed again. Erica let him up and he loosened his shoulders.

'You don't know who you're messing with,' said Derek, gruffly in an American accent.

'Don't threaten me,' laughed Erica, 'unless you want embarrassing in front of your friends, again. Who are the other two you were put away with? I want to know who *not* to worry about,' she mocked.

'They're in the other room with Kane,' said Tony, appearing from the back of the crowd.

'3D?'

'Yeah!'

104

'Right, I'll go and see him. And can you turn the music down just a smidge please. I don't want my baby waking up.'

Erica left the group of men who were drinking heavily. She ignored Derek's scowling on her way out. 3D's door was closed. She pushed it open to see Kane and two other men; one was doing a line of drugs. They looked up as she entered.

'Great! So this spare room is the drug den, yes?' Erica asked, sarcastically.

'Hey Erica! This is Erica everyone,' said Kane, being over-friendly.

'Hi Erica,' said the other two men.

'This is Jack and Paul,' Kane said indicating them in turn.

Jack was a little weedy in the width department, but of average height. He looked much more run down than the others, possibly as a result of years of drug abuse. He was also heavily tattooed. He had short, thinning black hair.

Paul was stockier, but quite small in stature. He had short ginger hair and stubble. Unlike his friends, he had no tattoos that she could see. Both Jack and Paul spoke with American accents.

'Hello,' she replied, politely. 'Are all your friends American?' Erica asked Kane.

'Just these two. Oh, and Derek. I think he's over in my flat. You should go meet him. He's a sound guy,' said Kane.

'Yeah, he sounds peachy,' said Erica, sarcastically. 'Look, Kane, you're gonna have to try and keep it down. I wasn't expecting silence when you told me about this party, but we need to meet each other halfway.'

'OK, OK. I'll have a word with everyone.'

'Thank you. Nice to meet you both,' she said to Jack and Paul as she left.

'She's a bit of alright, isn't she!' said one of the Americans to Kane as she left.

Erica didn't look back, but just rolled her eyes as she returned to the corridor. Alex and Natalie were now nowhere to be seen. She wanted to make sure that they were keeping out of trouble, so she went to their flat, 3E. The door was wide open, presumably as they were taking part in the 'open-flat,' policy, but she *was* shocked by the scene before her. Roger was receiving a lap dance in his wheelchair from a topless woman. There were also two other women in skimpy underwear in the room being playful with each other. Alex and Natalie were sat on the sofa; Alex was in his element, watching the scene, and Natalie, looking grumpy.

'What's going on?' Erica asked.

'Kane said these women could use this room,' Natalie replied, scornfully.

'*Use* the room? Are you friends of Kane's?' Erica directed at the women, who didn't reply.

'I don't think they speak English and I don't think they're friends. I think they may be paid professionals.'

'Oh,' said Erica, uncomfortably. 'Shall I get Kane to move them?'

'You'll do no such thing,' said Roger, piping up.

'I thought I might find you here, you dirty perv!'

'Oh don't you start on me as well. I've already had an earful off him,' he said, pointing at Alex.

'Why, what's wrong?' Erica asked Alex.

'He was harassing my girlfriend the other day. He needs putting on a leash,' Alex responded.

'I said I was sorry. What more do you want?' Roger replied, tetchily, before turning his attention back to the women.

At this point, four of the men who had been in 3A came in loudly. They crowded around the women. Natalie buried her head in hands, clearly upset.

'Not what you were expecting?' Erica asked.

'Not at all,' Natalie replied. 'We just thought it was gonna be a party. We're in way over our heads.'

'We'll be OK, Natalie. It's not as bad as you're thinking,' Alex added.

'It is, Alex,' Natalie responded, clearly frustrated. 'All our stuff. It isn't safe here. I feel so dirty.'

'Here! Take this,' Erica said, pulling a key from her pocket. 'This is the key to 3B, Ian's flat. I can see that this isn't your scene. It's not mine either, but I've dealt with this kind of scum plenty of times before. I'll stay here and keep an eye on your stuff until they're gone. You two go and have some quiet time.'

'Really?' said Natalie, ecstatic. 'Thanks, Erica. Come on Alex.'

She grabbed him by the wrist and dragged him out of the flat, leaving Erica to guard their possessions.

Derek stood with his back to the wall between 3A and 3B. Natalie hadn't met this charming individual just yet so gave him an awkward smile as she let herself into 3B. They sat on the sofa together. This was the most exhausted she'd felt at any party.

'Have your eyes gone back in yet?' Natalie asked Alex.

'Don't be daft, babe. Those girls do nothing for me,' Alex responded.

'Oh, whatever. You couldn't take your eyes off them.'

'I could. I was just gobsmacked at what was happening.'

'I could see your excitement at what was happening,' she said, nodding at his trousers.

'That's only because I was sat next to you, babe.'

'Oh whatever.'

'You know, being here, in a different room, is kind of a turn on.'

'Really?'

'Oh yeah. I've always wanted to do it someone else's home. Just the thought's a thrill.'

'You've never told me that before.'

'Well, now I have, let's not waste this opportunity.'

Alex dragged Natalie to the bedroom and threw her onto the bed. Even after ten years he couldn't get enough of her; the only girl he had ever been with. She looked extremely sexy in the low-cut top and short skirt that she'd selected for the evening. The outfit that had drew so much attention from Kane's friends throughout the evening, but which had also excited Alex for the last few hours.

He wanted to make sure that she was fulfilled in every way possible. To her delight he motioned down between her legs, held her skirt up with one hand, pushed her knickers aside with the other, and began to give her the amazing oral sex that she had become used to. She was not so delighted when he was interrupted only seconds into his performance. She suddenly sat up as she heard the front door creak open.

'What was that?' she asked.

'What was what?' he replied, looking confused.

'I think I heard the front door,'

'You're just imagining it,' Alex said, returning to the task at hand.

However, the sound of men talking made Alex spring back up.

'You heard that, then?' Natalie whispered to him.

Alex grabbed Natalie's hand and dragged her into the bathroom. He carefully closed the door and they both pressed their ears against it.

'I told you it was unlocked,' said an American voice as it entered the newly vacated bedroom.

'But I tried earlier and it was locked,' came the sound of Kane's voice.

'What are they doing here?' Natalie whispered to Alex, who simply shrugged.

'I saw two young uns come in here. That's how I knew it was unlocked,' said the man's voice.

'Well, where are they?' replied Kane.

The sound of a third man's voice, also American, came, 'We've just checked the rest of the flat and there's no one here.'

'They're not under the bed are they?' came the sound of a fourth voice, again, American.

'No, I just checked. Try the bathroom,' ordered Kane.

Alex and Natalie looked at each other. Thinking fast, Natalie dragged Alex into the bathtub and they both stood behind the shower curtain. Paul entered the room. Luckily he only gave it a quick glance and shut the door, returning to the bedroom to join the others.

'No one there,' Paul told the others.

'Good!' Kane replied. 'I need your help finding what Alan left for me.'

'I thought you said you found the note I'd left you in our old hiding spot,' said Jack, confused.

'I did. And it said he left me something in room 302. That must be *this* flat, 3B.'

'What else did the note say?'

'It said he hid it under *that* floorboard,' Kane said, pointing at the location he had previously searched. 'But I checked and there was something else in there. The guy that lives here must be using it now.'

'I'm sorry, mate,' Jack said, dismayed.

'It's OK. It *has* been three years. I don't know what I was expecting. I was just hoping to find out more about Lisa and how she's doing. That bitch Laura ruined my life, just as I was getting it sorted too. It's probably for the best that I didn't find it. I never intended to come back here, but when I was offered the flat, I thought I'd be stupid to pass up the opportunity to get my stash. I couldn't even remember where our little hiding place was, so whenever I got the chance, I was checking all the spare rooms upstairs, looking for it. When I finally found it and saw the note that you'd left me, Jack, I became obsessed with finding whatever *Alan* had left for me.'

'I can't believe I'm back here,' said Derek, piping up.

'I know,' added Paul, 'but now that you've given up on the search for what Alan left you, you can move out, can't you? It's crazy for you to stay here. It's crazy for any of us being here. Returning to the scene of the crime like this. Us three have only just got out of prison; if the police find out what we did here, we'd be straight back in.'

'That was three years ago,' Derek interjected. 'No one is looking for who is responsible anymore.'

'Good for you then!' Paul sneered.

'What's that supposed to mean?' he replied, angrily.

'You know what it means. You legged it and left us to sort it all out. Makes you look guilty as sin.'

'It had nothing to do with me. I just wasn't sticking around to get the blame for it.'

'We're lucky Alan kept a cool head. We'd have been screwed if not for him,'

'Where is Alan anyway?' asked Derek, in friendly tone, hoping to divert the conversation. 'I thought he would have been here tonight.'

'He's gone into hiding,' Kane said. 'I haven't seen him since, but it's probably a good thing he *didn't* come.'

'Why?'

'You know that young lad, the one you said you saw come in here.'

'Yeah…'

'That's his son,' Kane revealed.

'What? That's crazy!' said Derek, shocked. 'Anyway, Alan's lucky. I hate being here again.'

'Come on, let's get back to the party. All this is depressing me.'

The four of them left the bedroom, heading for the front door of the flat.

'I still have nightmares about what we did to that girl,' said Jack as they reached the front door.

'Just try to forget about it,' Kane urged. 'We can't change what we did. I've done some pretty bad things in my life and the more of it that stays buried, the better. Enough of my past is already cropping up.'

'What do you mean?'

'You remember when I told you about that bloke who fell off the cliff, ages ago. Must be like ten years now.'

'Yeah!'

'The paramedic that I threatened to keep quiet is living here too. This is *her* flat, actually.'

'No!' Jack stressed. 'You need to get out of here, man. Your history with this place, and now her! It's just too risky.'

'But it suits me at the moment. I think I'm gonna stick it out,' Kane decided.

'Rather you than me.'

'Anyway, I'm going back to the party. You three stay out of trouble. We don't want a repeat of three years ago.'

Kane left the flat, leaving the other three in the doorway.

'I'm off back to Kane's flat,' Derek said. 'The rest of this place sucks!'

Derek strolled out, but Jack and Paul held back.

'Should we tell them?' Jack asked Paul.

'No way, man!' he replied. 'I don't even remember which floor we hid the body on.'

'I think it was this one.'

'Well the less they know the better. I don't want them getting curious. Who knows what state she's in now? It was a bad idea coming back here.'

The two of them left the flat as well.

Alex and Natalie were trying to process what they'd heard from the bathroom.

'I know you said you weren't bothered about knowing what your Dad was up to these days, but Kane appears know him quite well. You should think about asking him,' said Natalie, concerned.

'I have no interest in knowing my dad. What I am interested in, though, is what they were all saying when they left the bedroom. I couldn't hear them. Could you?' Alex asked.

'No, nothing once they'd left the bedroom.'

'I wonder what happened here three years ago. Something bad by the sound of it. We'd better stay on the right side of Kane.'

'I know I recognise him from somewhere,' Natalie said, thinking hard. 'Urgh! I can't think properly. This party's given me a right headache. See if there's any painkillers in the cabinet, we haven't got any in our flat.'

Alex opened the bathroom cabinet. There were no medicines in the cabinet, but a panel with many switches. Each row of switches was labelled with the flat numbers. At the end was a master switch.

'No medicine in here,' Alex told her. 'Just some sort of fuse box.'

Natalie looked in the cabinet and got an idea, 'We should flick the master switch off. That'd put an early end to the party.'

'Good idea,' said Alex who was long sick of the corridor guests.

He flicked the switch killing the power to the building. They both listened and grinned as they heard the moans of the partying crooks. The building still took a good half an hour to clear at which point they returned the power to the building.

When they finally set off back to their flat, they saw Kane, true to his promise to Erica, cleaning flat 3D.

Chapter 16 – The Last Door

My audience were looking increasingly interested, if somewhat confused.

'I didn't expect to enjoy my trip to America as much as I did. I thought it was going to be more business than pleasure,' I said with a reminiscent look on my face. 'Had I known about my wife's affair at the time, perhaps I would have treated her a little differently. I suspect that the extra effort that I'd put into our relationship abroad had delayed her leaving me, but my relaxation time was over. I had work to do. To my surprise, 3D had been cleaned whilst I was away. When I went to reclaim the key from Kane, he informed me that it was his doing. That took a load off my plate, because it wasn't long after I'd returned home that Seth and Ingrid moved in. Ingrid didn't half make me chuckle. I'm glad that she wasn't involved in the incident, because I'd really grown to like her over the few days I spent with her…'

Chapter 17 – An Inexhaustible Vocabulary

'It's just this yellow one here,' I said, coming to a halt in front of 3D with an eager Seth and an unhappy Ingrid. 'I know it's not much to look at, but I'm sure you'll feel right at home whilst you're waiting to move into your new house.'

'You expect us to live *here*?' came the shrill sound of Ingrid's voice. 'We're not peasants you know.'

'I'm sorry, I didn't realise it would be a problem,' I worried.

'It's just for a few days, Ingrid, love,' said Seth in his welcome, reasonable tone. 'We'll be out of here before you know it.'

'Oh Seth, I can't possibly live in such squalor!' said Ingrid, disgusted.

She had no shame at all. She wasn't bothered in the slightest that her words might offend me in some way.

'I'm sorry, Ingrid,' I started. 'You know how much of a nuisance vendor chains can be, I'm hurrying along the process to get you into your new house as soon as possible.'

Ingrid completely ignored me and turned back to Seth, 'Can't we just holiday in Peru until our new abode is ready?'

I inwardly laughed at her choice of words.

'Come now, dear,' said the ever reasoning Seth, as he peered inside the room. 'It doesn't look too bad. Not for free anyway.'

Ingrid didn't let up, 'Oh, but, darling, I could never live like this. Not after so many years of luxury. A woman, like myself, accustomed to the finer things in life requires only the most exquisite accommodation. You know how pernickety I am,' she said, before turning her inexhaustible vocabulary on me. 'I told him he'd struggle to get me into a flat, but he pestered and pestered. I agreed to come and look at it, but I can't see me living here. He's very wealthy, as you can no doubt imagine. Did I tell you he was once a successful inventor? Back in his glory days! He should put us up somewhere decent instead of being so tight-fisted.'

'Tight-fisted?' Seth boomed back at her. 'I've skint myself buying a new house because you wanted to move! I don't know what was wrong with our old house.'

'Now, Seth, it was time to move on to pastures new. I didn't realise that we'd be making a pit stop at pastures decrepit, first,' she said, giving the inside of the flat a look of disgust. She then turned her gaze on the mucky polystyrene ceiling panels which were unfortunately situated right outside her flat. 'Just look at the state of the roof! Oh I hope it doesn't smell!'

I felt it was time to step in and defend my beloved building, 'There are plus points to living here; everyone on this floor has the whole block of flats to themselves, there's no one living on the other floors. Also, this used to be a hotel so we have quite a lot of land around us. No busy roads nearby. It's only a short walk to town. And because there's nothing else up the lane leading here, we don't have drunk kids wandering over, causing trouble!'

'Well, I should hope not,' she said before turning her attention on Seth again. 'Oh, darling, we can do better than this, surely!' she pleaded.

'Not for free though, dear,' Seth reiterated.

'Well, what about your rainy day fund? I would certainly call this a rainy day wouldn't you?'

Seth looked stunned at this. He grabbed Ingrid and pulled her to one side in order to have a private word with her. Of course, with Seth's loud booming voice, I could hear everything.

'How many times have I told you, Ingrid? That money is not for us. There is only one person entitled to that money,' he said, firmly.

I felt awkward at being able to hear every word of this obviously private conversation, but with Ingrid now having been silenced by Seth, I seized the opportunity to go in for the kill.

'So, will you be staying in the flat?' I asked, hopefully.

Seth looked at Ingrid and raised his eyebrows, to which she let out a sigh, 'I suppose we can give it a whirl,' she reluctantly agreed.

'Excellent!' I exclaimed, happily. 'Here are your door keys,' I said, hastily thrusting a key at each of them. 'I'll let you get settled in and I'll pop round in the morning to see how you're getting on.'

'Not before ten thirty please!' Ingrid remarked. 'I like to be properly roused before I can entertain guests.'

Ingrid and Seth headed inside flat 3D leaving me standing in the corridor, smirking. No time to breathe a sigh of relief, I spun around to see the family from flat 3C heading down the corridor, chelping at each other.

'Come on boy,' Roger moaned at Lee who was pushing him. 'Get me inside. Sex in the City will have started already. Hopefully I've only missed the "city" part.'

'You should have just walked up the stairs yourself then, Dad,' Lee responded to this attack.

'I did, for that one bit.'

'Only because we had to fold the wheelchair in,' Erica said, joining in. 'Otherwise you'd happily sit there whilst we struggled.'

I let out a chuckle as I watched them in their comic life.

'Why does the corridor get narrower down there, Ian?' Erica asked, spotting me.

'The stairwell between the first and second floor?' I confirmed. 'There's a couple of small rooms on the first floor that eat into the width of the stairwell.'

'Well, that's daft,' piped up Roger again. 'You want to get that sorted out.'

'I'm sorry, I never expected to have to accommodate a man who gets around in a wheelchair, but is perfectly able to walk,' I responded, sarcastically.

'Come on,' he said to Lee, defeated. 'Get me inside before they get their clothes back on.'

Lee pushed Roger home into 3C. Erica, holding Isaac, gave me an apologetic smile on her way inside. I stood in the corridor, alone, as I thought about my achievement. I could finally relax. The hardest part was over. I had filled the third floor with tenants. I was happy.

115

#

Layla had carried two heavy bags of shopping up the stairs. She used the last of her energy to push open the stairwell door and get onto the third floor. She saw Kane who was standing right outside his room, smoking. He looked at her, which, in turn, made her study the ground, as usual as she walked past him.

'You look at me like I've got some kind of disease,' he said, menacingly stepping out in front of her.

'I'm sorry. I don't mean to…' she said, keeping her head down.

'I don't want your apologies,' he said, interrupting. 'I just want you to look at me like I'm a human being.'

Layla kept her head down, not wanting to respond.

'Look at me!' Kane shouted.

Again, Layla just winced and refused to meet his eye, still scared of this monster who had frightened her all those years ago. Kane grabbed her chin and forced it up so that her eyes met his. A tear slipped down her cheek.

'Now then,' Kane began, 'I think we should have a little chat about you breaking into my flat the other week. Don't worry, I didn't forget whilst you were on holiday.'

'I apologised for that,' she replied.

'I know. You just wanted to see that photograph again. What do you know about those people?' Kane asked, angrily.

'I saw one. James, his name is. He's…'

'How do you know James?' Kane snapped, and slammed his palm on the wall besides Layla's head, causing her to wince. 'What do you know about what happened here?'

Layla remained quiet. Terror silenced her. She'd finally seen the man in photograph; James. In America. An old friend of her husbands, that's where she recognised him from; In a picture from when they were at uni together, but should she tell Kane any of this.

'You'd better start talking,' he demanded. 'I don't need to remind you about ten years ago, do I? And what will happen if you don't do what I say?' he threatened, loudly and menacingly.

She stood in silence. He'd shown himself to be the same man he was ten years ago. It was the same threats all over again. She prayed for a chance to flee and it came; the door to 3D opened and Kane looked over. Layla used this opportunity to break away and flee back into her flat, shutting out the horrors of the corridor.

'What *is* all the commotion?' came Ingrid's shrill voice as she marched out of her flat. 'My sister Martha can probably hear you from Paris.'

She pronounced Paris, comically, in a French accent.

Kane replied nastily, 'Mind your own business you nosey bitch!'

He returned to his flat and slammed the door, leaving a shell-shocked Ingrid.

'Well, I never!' she said to herself.

Before she had the chance to collect herself, Roger came wheeling out of his flat into the corridor.

'Now then,' he started, rubbing his hands together. 'What have we got here?'

'Excuse me?' responded Ingrid, only just noticing him.

'Hello toots! My name's Roger!'

'My word! Should a man in your condition be living in a place like this? On the third floor no less.'

'Don't worry about me, sweetheart. I can be very active when I want to be,' he said, finishing with a cheeky wink.

'You don't look very mobile. How do you possibly clamber the stairs on a daily basis?'

'Climb aboard, I'll take you for a spin and show you.'

'Well, honestly!'

'Who are you talking to, Roger?' said Erica, joining the pair of them from her flat.

'There's a bit of totty roaming the corridor,' he replied.

Ingrid was gobsmacked, 'A bit of totty? I've never been so insulted in all my life.'

'Are. You. OK. Love? Are. You. Lost?' Erica said, loud and clear.

'I can hear perfectly well, thank you,' she said, angered by the assumption. 'And no, I'm not lost; I'm temporarily residing next door.

'Oh, bless you. If you ever need anything, dear, just pop round and ask.'

'Are you the hired help for this elderly gentleman?'

'The help…yes! Hired…no! I wish I got paid for the things I have to do for him!'

'Oh really. Like what, may I ask?'

'Like toilet duty.'

'What you on about?' Roger intervened at this attack on his character. 'I go regular at six, every morning.'

'I know,' said Erica, coolly. 'Trouble is…you don't get out of bed until seven. And that's not the worst of it…' she said, turning back to Ingrid now, 'I have to push him around everywhere, which would be OK, except that he's perfectly able-bodied. He's just lazy.'

'That's absurd!' responded Ingrid. 'Why don't you just stop pushing him and make him walk.'

'You've got more chance of pushing smoke up a cats arsehole with a knitting needle than you have of getting him to walk anywhere.'

'She does it because she's family,' said Roger with an affectionate leer.

'You mean to say that you both live here? Together?' Ingrid said, shocked.

'Unfortunately,' said a dismayed Erica.

'Don't you find it a little petite for the two of you?'

'Everyone ready to go?' said Lee, appearing from out of 3C with Isaac strapped to his chest and joining the growing crowd.

Ingrid looked disgusted, 'Good heavens, there's more of them. I'm surrounded by poverty everywhere I look.'

'This old mare's giving me the right hump!' said Roger, clearly getting a little miffed now.

'Mare? Old?' Ingrid screeched.

'You need cooling off doll. Hold on, I've got just the thing.'

Roger leapt from his wheelchair with very little effort. He marched over to the firebox and began to reel out the hose which he proceeded to point at Ingrid. She screamed in terror as Roger pulled the lever and blasted her with the hose, knocking her onto her bottom, to Erica's great amusement.

'Dad!' Lee shouted, before wrestling the hose from his father's hands and turning it off.

'I was just trying to teach the old bird some manners,' Roger said, defending himself.

'My clothes! My beautiful visage! Ruined!' sobbed Ingrid, motionless on the floor.

'Are you OK?' Lee asked, concerned.

'Just get away from me!' she snapped, still refusing to move and looking pathetic with water dripping from her.

'Come on, let's leave her to it,' said Erica, encouraging the others away.

They all left the corridor via the stairwell exit, leaving a drenched Ingrid behind. She struggled to her feet, holding her arms stiffly.

Ian emerged from his flat looking determined and completely missing the fact that she was wet through, 'Ah, Ingrid. My wife has just come inside in floods of tears, but she won't tell me what's wrong. Did you see anything?'

'I could just about break into floods of tears, myself,' she said, wearily. 'I've just met some of my charming neighbours.'

'Oh good! They're not bad, are they!' he replied, still oblivious.

'Not bad?' she shouted, regaining her strength. 'Look at me! They're horrendous.'

'What…what happened?' said Ian, finally noticing her sodden clothes.

'Like I said…my neighbours. Moments into meeting them, I was shouted at, sworn at, laughed at…and…and, I was dowsed in water by a very unhygienic man in a wheelchair. It was a tirade of abuse. And that was just from the neighbours in the flat at one side of me. I dread to think what lives in the one at the other side,' she said, indicating flat 3E.

'Oh, there's nothing to worry about there. That's where our young couple, Alex and Natalie, live. I assure you, they are model residents. Very quiet! I never hear them swearing and they are very hygienic.'

As if the universe saw a perfect moment to destroy Ian's credibility, Alex slid out of his flat, hair messy, naked, as far as they could see, with his duvet wrapped around his waist and trailing behind him on the floor. He reached down and very indiscreetly began scratching at his pelvic region. He was carrying two black bin bags full of rubbish as he ungracefully glided down the corridor. Ingrid looked on in horror. Before she had a chance to comment, Natalie poked her head out of the flat door, in a similar state, and held out some underpants in her hand.

'Alex!' she whispered, loudly. 'At least put some pants on when you leave the flat.'

'I'm only nipping to the bins,' he said, turning back to look at her briefly. 'I'll only be a minute.'

He continued down the corridor towards a petrified Ingrid and a smirking Ian.

'Hi, Alex,' said Ian, as he moved past the pair of them. 'Late night?'

'No night!' he said, giving Ingrid a nudge and a wink.

Alex disappeared through the stairwell door. Ian turned back to look at Ingrid who was staring at him, angrily. There was a moment between the pair of them as Ian struggled to contain his laughter.

'What?' he asked, almost letting a giggle escape.

She did not look impressed, 'You can wipe that effulgent smile off your face. What on earth was that thing?'

'Thing!' shouted Natalie from the other end of the corridor. 'That's my boyfriend you're talking about!'

'You two should take more pride in your appearance.'

'What are you trying to say?' responded Natalie, stepping into view.

Ingrid looked her up and down. She was filled with disgust. Natalie had dirty clothes draped over her body, two cereal boxes on her feet, which she could only assume were makeshift slippers, and she even saw some food in her hair.

'I rest my case,' she said to Ian, but with an arm indicating Natalie. 'How will I possibly see out the weekend like this?' she asked despairingly as she returned towards her own flat.

Natalie was dismayed when she saw Ingrid go into the flat next door to her.

'She lives next to us?' she asked Ian, disheartened.

'She's got a name!' Ingrid stated. 'I am Ingrid Treant. And I shall be adding a touch of class to this wretched hive we call a home.'

'I can see you becoming the best of friends,' he said, sarcastically answering Natalie's earlier question.

Alex returned from his trip to the bins, still looking tired and rough. He made his way back towards his flat, but as he passed Ingrid, he stepped on the quilt's trail and fell to ground, landing on his back and exposing himself.

Ingrid screeched in horror and hurried inside her flat.

'Lovely,' said Ian, who looked away after catching an eyeful.

Alex quickly grabbed the quilt and ran towards a giggling Natalie, before disappearing inside with her.

Ian just stood there and laughed. He knew it was going to be a difficult weekend with this cast of characters.

Chapter 18 – The Day It All Began

'I'm sorry if some of you feel that I have wasted your time thus far,' I said, looking at some of the confused faces in the audience. 'I wanted to build up to it. Make sure that you had all the facts, knew a little about everyone before…well…you know. But, here we are. D-day! The day everything went wrong for me. The day my life was turned upside down. The events that led to me standing up here in front of all of you, telling this tragedy. I hope that…I hope that at least some of you will see things as they are meant to be seen. Understand things as I did. And that some of you will see things as I came to realise…only *I* realised too late. Anyway. Here goes. That morning I headed over to Seth and Ingrid's flat, as promised, to see how their first night went…'

Chapter 19 – Decorum

'Now then, Ian, a few problems,' said Seth as he indicated an armchair in his flat for me to sit in.

'Straight to the point, I see,' I said.

I looked around at the generously furnished flat which had once been used as a site for Kane and his drug buddy. To say they thought they were only staying a few days, they had furnished the place extravagantly; hung portraits, fancy throws on the sofa, photos and ornaments over every surface. The thing that looked most out of place was the chair that Seth had sat himself down in. A very small, rickety looking wooden chair. The paint was chipped in several places and the joints looked like they were barely held together. I marvelled at its durability; holding this large man who was spilling over the sides was an incredible feat for such a miniscule chair. There was a full sofa he could have sat on, but he looked perfectly content, albeit a little uncomfortable, sitting in this small chair.

'Right,' he said, 'I want to get a few things sorted out quickly. Even though we'll only be here a short while I don't expect to be…'

Ingrid interrupted him from the kitchen, 'Tea, Ian?'

'Oooh, yes please!' I gratefully responded.

'It's an own brand I'm afraid. I left our Earl Grey back at the house.'

'I'm sure I'll survive,' I said, sarcastically.

'As I was saying,' Seth continued, 'at our age, my wife and I don't want…'

Ingrid interrupted him again, 'Would you like anything, Sethy-poos?'

'No thank you, dear,' he replied. 'Where was I?' he said, returning to our conversation. 'Ah yes…'

'Are you sure?' she said interrupting him for a third time. 'We have coffee, too.'

'No thank you, dear,' he said, getting a little frustrated, but still forcing politeness.

Seth left a pause before attempting to talk to me this time, holding his breath and keeping his gaze on her as she busied herself in the kitchen. There was a long pause with nothing from Ingrid, so he tried the conversation again.

He inhaled, 'So…'

'Are you sure, dear? It's Nescafé Gold Blend,' she shouted over with impeccable timing.

Seth was getting more frustrated now, but still managed to feign politeness through gritted teeth, 'I'm OK, thank you, dear, but our guest may have died of thirst by the time *his* drink arrives.' He turned to speak to me again, 'Right, onto business…'

'How about a slice of cake, then?' she attempted.

'Ingrid!' boomed Seth. 'I don't want a tea. I don't want a coffee. I don't want a piece of cake. I don't even want a hot chocolate with whipped cream, marshmallows, fudge, or any sprinkles. I just want to sit here and have a discussion. Do you think you could possibly stay in the kitchen for ten minutes whilst Ian and I have a chat?'

This outburst from Seth kept the three of us in silence for a few moments, before Ingrid finally broke it, 'Well, that's charming, that is,' she said, deeply hurt. 'I'll just have to eat this millionaires short-bread on my own.'

She didn't say anything again. Her actions in the kitchen however, were distinctly audible as she quickened her pace, letting us now that she was peeved. Seth took a few deep breaths to calm himself before trying to speak to me again.

'Right,' he said, finally 'I need to discuss the noise problem with you.'

'Noise problem?' I asked, confused.

'Yes! Surely you must have heard it. That strange old man from next door was watching filthy movies all night.'

'Fortunately, I can't hear it from my side,' I said, trying to hide a smile.

'You're lucky. Our bedroom wall is adjoining his.'

'Surely, it isn't that late though. I know that he is usually in bed for ten.'

'Yes, well, Ingrid and I like to be in bed at a reasonable hour. And *then*, when he *has* gone to bed, we get the sound of…well…you know, from those two young uns at the other side of us.'

'Ah, well, there's little I can do about that, I'm afraid.'

'That in itself isn't really the problem. It was when they cranked their music up to mask their sounds. It was one o'clock before we got to sleep last night.'

'Oh…right…well maybe I could…'

'Ingrid!' Seth shouted, interrupting me. 'Have you got Ian's tea yet?'

'There's no rush, honest,' I assured.

'You said to stay in here for ten minutes!' Ingrid shouted back.

'Don't be daft, woman. Get in here,' Seth called back.

Ingrid came into the living area with a single cup of tea on a saucer.

'That's great that, isn't it. Won't that be cold by now?' Seth asked.

'I don't know,' she replied. 'You tell me.'

And with that, Ingrid simply jerked the cup over, spilling the contents on to Seth, who stood up in shock.

'Ever so sorry Ian,' Ingrid apologised. 'I'll make you another one.'

'No, no. It's fine,' I told her. 'I'm not that thirsty. Seth can keep it.'

Seth dried his face and the yellow polo shirt he was wearing with a tea towel. Once finished, he stood behind Ingrid and wrapped the tea towel around each of his hands and made a strangling motion with it, before throwing it over the back of his wooden chair.

'Have you seen what he sits on?' Ingrid said. 'I wish it had been torn asunder during the move. He couldn't even do without it for the short time that we'll be living here.'

'Nothing will ever happen to that chair. It's been around for a very long time,' Seth said, proudly.

'Yes, you can tell. It's an eyesore, an affront to the senses. First chance I get, it's getting tossed from the stairwell window.'

'You'll be doing no such thing. It's my lucky chair!'

'It won't be lucky when it's in pieces on the pavement,' she said, confidently, before changing the subject. 'Have you told him about those noises yet?'

'Yes. I've told him about the old man's videos and I also very delicately told him about…'

'About those two having intercourse all night!' she interrupted.

Caught completely off guard by this comment, I burst into laughter.

'Yes, thank you, dear,' said Seth, embarrassed.

'Like a pair of rabbits, the two of them,' Ingrid said, fuelling my laughter.

'Yes, well…' I struggled, through laughter, '…as I was telling your husband, the old man does go to bed quite early and there is little I can do about the young couple's…erm…lovemaking. I can ask them to turn their music down, but then you'll hear…the…er…'

'Shagging? Copulating? Fornicating? Doing the nasty?' she said, causing me to laugh even harder with each passing word. 'It doesn't bear thinking about.'

I could contain my laughter no more and there were tears streaming down my face.

'This is no laughing matter young man,' she added, sternly. 'I need my beauty sleep.'

'I am sorry. I wish there was more I could do,' I sympathised.

'Couldn't we just move into one of the downstairs flats?'

'I'm afraid not. They still need renovating, so they're not fit for purpose.'

Seth was now clearly getting frustrated too at my lack of options.

'Fine. Just forget it then,' he shouted, startling me.

He suddenly appeared to have a sly thought. This scared me more than the anger.

'Will you just check the flusher on the toilet? It wasn't working earlier,' he said, quite obviously up to something.

'Are you sure, dear? I'm certain it…' said Ingrid, before getting cut short.

'Yes, I'm sure, Ingrid, darling,' he said through gritted teeth.

'But I was just in there, powdering my nose, and it seemed…'

'Trust me, Ingrid,' Seth boomed. 'It needs checking! Would you mind Ian?' he finished, turning to me.

I knew something fishy was going on, but I thought I had better play the part.

'OK, I'll have a quick look,' I said.

I left for the bathroom to carry out my landlordly obligation.

#

As soon as Ian left the room, Seth flew across the coffee table, with surprising agility. He grabbed Ian's briefcase and began to rummage through it.

'What on earth are you doing, dear?' Ingrid asked.

'I'm looking for a key to the neighbour's flat,' he said, checking through multiple keys in the briefcase. 'I'll deal with them myself. Ah-ha!' he said, holding one of the keys in the air. 'The master key! This should let me into both the flats. First chance I get, I'll sneak round next door and cut the wires to that old man's TV. Then, I'll go to the other side and cut the wires on that pair of love-bird's music.'

'Oh Sethy-poos. I just love it when you get creative.'

'It will be up to you to keep an eye on their routines so that you can tell me when they aren't home. I'm off to the races this afternoon with some old work friends so it'll give you something to do whilst I'm out.'

'Give me something to do? Do you think I just sit alone in the flat all day whilst you're off gallivanting with your friends? Did it ever occur to you that I may be having luncheon with the ladies?'

'Well, are you?'

'No!' she said after a slight pause. 'But it would be nice if you did not assume that I have nothing better to do than spy on our neighbours.'

They both panicked when they heard the sound of a toilet flushing. Seth quickly returned the briefcase to its original position, before its owner entered the room.

'It seems to be working fine,' Ian said.

'Oh, well, that's good then,' Seth replied, out of breath.

'Anyway, I need to be going. Thanks for your hospitality.'

'Of course,' Ingrid joined in. 'So sorry about the tea.'

'It's fine, don't worry about it. Sorry I can't do more about the noise.'

'Oh don't worry about it,' said Seth, cockily. 'The *key* to our problem has just presented itself.'

'Right…erm…OK…' said Ian, picking up on the confusing signals Seth clearly didn't realise he was sending out.

'I'll see you out,' he said, guiding Ian towards the front door, leaving Ingrid alone.

She stood for a moment and looked at Seth's chair in disgust, before kicking it over.

Chapter 20 – The Five Door Chaos

'What's gotten in to you?' Lee asked Layla as he stood at her front door. 'If he's not home, why can't I come round?'

'What about Erica? She's still home!' Layla replied, hopefully.

'Yeah, but not for long. She's taking Dad and Isaac out for the afternoon. We should have a bit of time.'

'I don't know,' Layla said, hesitantly.

'What's happened? This is the first time I've seen you since you got back from America and you're acting different. Did something happen over there?'

'I'm sorry, Lee. I'm just not feeling it lately. I'm so confused. I had a good long hard think about it and I need to leave Ian. I know I don't love him anymore, I just need to find the right time to go.'

'So what's the problem then?'

'Just because I don't love Ian anymore, doesn't mean that I suddenly love you.'

'I don't want you to love me. We're just having fun for now, aren't we?'

'I just don't know if it's there for me. Do you know that special feeling you get when you kiss someone you truly love? I've only ever had that once before. I thought it might be there with you, but it isn't.'

'Layla, don't do this. Give it a chance,' Lee pleaded.

'I don't know. I'm sorry, Lee. I don't want to complicate things further.'

'Just let me come round once Erica has gone out. Give me one more chance to show you how special we are together. Please.'

Layla sat and thought for a moment. Regardless of her feelings she really enjoyed being with him, physically; he was very talented in *that* department. Her urges got the better of her and without a thought for her own emotions, or the emotions of the others involved, she agreed. He told her he would be round as soon as Erica left, and to leave the door open for him. Layla returned to her flat to freshen up.

#

The end of the afternoon grew closer. There was a peaceful calm on the corridor that would very soon be disturbed, in more ways than one.

Alex moseyed through his flat door, dressed, with Natalie, still in her pyjamas, draped around him, yet again.

'Please just go later,' she begged.

'I can't. I'm gasping for a cuppa,' he said, desperately. 'Shop's only two minutes away. I'll get some milk and be back before you know it.'

'No, don't, just come back to bed.'

'But we've been there all day!'

'So! Just ask one of the neighbours for a cup of milk.'

Thinking on it briefly, Alex decided that wasn't such a bad idea, 'Yeah, I suppose I could do that.'

'Yay!' said Natalie, letting go of his neck. 'I'll go put the kettle on.'

She skipped back inside their flat. Alex approached the nearest door, the yellow one, and knocked.

'Ah! Hello young man,' said Ingrid who had answered the door 'I expect you're here to apologise for last night.'

Alex, clearly puzzled at this, looked around, thinking that she was perhaps talking to someone else.

'Well, come on in and have a seat,' she said heading into her flat without a word from Alex.

Alex, too confused to contemplate what this was about, simply reached into her flat and pulled the door shut. He gave a little shudder at what had just happened and moved on. Ah! Old blue, he thought. The lot who lived here seemed friendly enough. He gave a jaunty knock. The door was answered by Roger, for once without his wheelchair, standing before Alex like any other able-bodied man.

'Hello nipper,' he said. 'What can I do for you?'

'Hi, I was hoping I could borrow some…' Alex started.

He cut himself short when Roger suddenly brought a carton of milk to his lips and began gulping thirstily from it. Alex just stared in disbelief, before deciding that this was not the flat he wanted to be borrowing milk from. He quickly formulated a poor lie.

'Errrr…' he faltered. 'Sorry, wrong flat. It was this one over here I meant to…'

Roger just slammed the door shut as Alex approached the green door. He prayed that the third time was indeed the charm and that his trusty landlord would sort him out with some milk. He knocked, thinking it couldn't be any worse than his first two attempts, but he was not expecting what came next.

'Come in. I've been waiting for you,' came Layla's voice from inside the flat.

"Odd" Alex thought, but entered the flat regardless, as his short quest for milk grew ever longer.

'In here,' came Layla's voice from the bedroom.

Alex wandered casually in, only to be met by a pleasant surprise. There, stark naked, displaying herself, seductively, was Layla. Alex's jaw dropped as he stared in disbelief.

'Woah!' he bellowed.

Layla's expression changed from a welcoming smile to one of sheer horror as she laid eyes on her unexpected visitor.

'Oh my God!' she screamed as she rolled off the bed out of sight only to pop up moments later covered by a very slinky dressing gown.

'I can explain,' Layla panicked.

'No need to explain,' said Alex, still smirking.

'I'm so embarrassed.'

'Don't be silly you were nice…er I mean…it's nice…fine! You were fine…I mean…you were, it's fine!' he said, stumbling across his words. 'Oh God! I think I'm more embarrassed than you!'

'I'm so sorry,' she said, getting redder.

'Why did you call me in?'

'I was er…waiting for my…er…husband to come home, and when

you knocked I thought you were him and as you saw, I was waiting for him in the…er…the…'

'The buff!' Alex said, completing her sentence.

'Please, can we not mention this to anyone?'

'Yeah, no problem.'

Alex began to leave when he twigged something. He felt stupid for not picking up on it right away.

'Funny!' he said, turning back towards Layla.

'I'm sorry,' she said, confused.

'Oh, it's just, you were waiting for your husband in the nude, yet when I knocked, you thought I was your husband…why would your husband knock?'

That had done it. Layla just sat on the foot of the bead and thrust her face into her hands in floods of tears. Alex rushed over and sat next to her, putting his arm round her. He felt really awkward. He had no idea what to do with a weeping woman, but this was now the second time he had found himself in this situation with this woman.

'What's wrong,' he asked.

'I'm sorry,' she managed.

'What's going on? I'm sorry I pushed you like that.'

'No it's my fault. I didn't realise how obvious I had been…it *is* obvious isn't it?'

'You're having an affair?' he guessed

She began sobbing even louder.

'I'm sorry,' Alex pleaded again.

'It's not your fault. I think wanted to get caught,' she said.

'What do you mean?'

'I'm so messed up lately. This affair is the only thing that's keeping me going. He's coming round soon and I can't wait. I don't even like him that much, but it's the excitement. There's so much other crazy stuff going on in my life at the minute that this affair is the only thing keeping me sane.'

'Is it the bloke from next door? The one with the baby?'

'Yes. It's Lee. How did you know?'

'Just a guess. Based on ages really. It was either gonna be me or him and I don't remember it being me.'

'No,' she chuckled.

'Why would you want to get caught?'

'I just think it would force me into a confrontation with Ian. Like I said, I don't even like Lee that much, but the same goes for Ian. When I met him I thought it was love, but I was just flattered. Lee was just excitement. Neither are the relationship I want. They don't feel right!'

'If you feel like that then they're definitely not right. Natalie and I will be together forever. When you know, you know.'

'The problem is, I think I do know.'

'What do you mean?' Alex asked.

'I was in love once.'

'Why didn't that work?'

'He was engaged to someone else.'

'Another affair?'

'I know, I sound really bad, but I promise I was single that time, so I didn't feel that *I* was doing anything wrong. He said he would leave her for me...then she got pregnant.'

'And he stayed with her?' Alex assumed.

'Yes.'

'And ended things with you?'

'Not exactly,' Layla said, shamefully.

'You carried on seeing him?'

'Yes. Once the baby was born, I started to see sense. I believed him when he said that he loved me, but he was too nice. He would never leave her. When the baby was a few months old I broke things off with him.'

'It's a sad story, but they're a family. I don't know what I can say to help you with that.'

'You don't have to say anything. I don't know why I brought it up. My emotions are all over the place at the minute. So much is stressing me out.'

'Has that got anything to do with when I found you in Kane's flat the other week?'

'Partly. It's lots of things. Something that happened to me ten years ago that I can't seem to forget lately, this whole secret of Kane's, my affair. When I told you that I found that photograph after following Kane upstairs...that was a lie. I was up there with Lee. That's where

133

we'd started going to meet. I stumbled upon that photo by accident. Speaking of which, remember I said that I recognised one of the other men in it?'

'Yes!'

'Well I saw him. Whilst I was in America.'

'Wow! I'd say small world, but you did go quite a long way to see him again.'

'I'd never actually met him before. He's Ian's friend.'

'Really? How are they mixed up in this business?'

'I have no idea. His name is James. I'd seen him in one of Ian's old photos before I'd seen the picture of him that Kane has. That's where I recognised him from in the first place. Then, when I actually saw him in the flesh, I couldn't believe it.'

'That means that he must know my dad too. What is going on here? This whole thing is getting tangled up. And what's that about ten years ago that you mentioned?'

'That is one thing I really can't talk about. I feel guilty just thinking about what I did.'

'I understand. I have skeletons in my closet too. I made a bad choice once, that's probably about ten years ago now too. I understand the need to keep secrets sometimes.'

'Thank you, Alex. I'm glad I could share all of this with you.'

'Well you've shared the sight of your naked body with me already now, so anything else should be easy.'

Layla went bright red and buried her head in her hands again. Alex pulled her in for a tight hug. He felt comfortable with her now and less and less like just a person who lived nearby.

'Chin up, Layla. And I'm just at the end if you ever need to talk.'

'Thank you,' she said smiling up at him.

The sound of a throat being cleared came from the bedroom door. The pair looked up to see Natalie standing looking at them.

'What's going on here?' asked Natalie.

'Natalie!' Alex exclaimed, removing his arm from around Layla. 'What are you doing here?'

'I came looking for *you*. I was wondering how long it took you to get milk, but clearly you're easily distracted,' she said, nodding at Layla's current state of dress.

Layla pulled her gapping dressing gown together.

'Don't be silly, Natalie,' Alex said, disgusted at her presumption. 'I'll explain later. Go and get dressed, we can go to the shop together for some milk.'

Natalie turned around and stormed off. Alex stood and headed towards the door. He turned around one last time to look at Layla.

'Good luck with everything. Don't drive yourself crazy. And...I'm sorry if I've scared your secret lover off.'

'I doubt it,' she laughed. 'He's persistent, he'll be back if you have.'

Alex left to return to his own flat. He saw Erica coming out of hers with her baby and Roger in his wheelchair. She gave him a friendly "hello" as he passed. She seemed nice, he thought. Best not to think about how nice she is though, now that he knows what her boyfriend is up to. Alex returned to his flat after his little afternoon excitement.

Erica was struggling as usual to push Roger, hold Isaac and lock the door at the same time. To add to her troubles, the corridor watchman that was Ingrid Treant came out of her flat to make matters that bit more hectic for her.

'Ah, excuse me, madam!' Ingrid called to Erica.

'Hello?' Erica asked, catching her eye.

'My name is Ingrid, do you remember me from yesterday?'

'How could I forget!'

'I was just hoping to have a little chat with the pair of you.'

'If you're quick,' Roger joined in, uninvited.

'Yes, of course,' Erica replied. 'My name's Erica and the grumpy one's Roger. What can I do for you, love?'

'Where shall I begin?' Ingrid started. 'I had a great deal of trouble sleeping last night due to the old gentleman's adult movies being so loud,' she said, giving Roger a nod. 'I was hoping he would be able to keep the volume to a minimum.'

'I can't do that,' he said, taking an interest in the conversation now. 'My hearing's not what it used to be.'

'Well couldn't you just pop some headphones in?' Ingrid said, turning directly to Roger now.

'I'm not wearing those things. They're uncomfortable.'

Erica tried to aid Ingrid, 'I'm sorry love, I've told him plenty of times how disgusting it is, but there's just no getting through to him. He usually goes to bed at half nine anyway, so I find it's just easier to grin and bear it until then.'

'But if he could just…' Ingrid tried again.

Roger cut her short, 'If you could just go back to your Emmerdale omnibus, love, we can be on our way.'

'Roger!' Erica snapped at him. 'I have no idea how Lee convinced me to take you out with us. You can be so rude sometimes,'

'Me being rude? She's the one that interrupted my afternoon walk!'

'*Your* afternoon walk? More like my afternoon exercise and *your* joyride!'

'That's it! I'm off!' he said, wheeling himself away down the corridor.

'I thought I could smell something funny,' Ingrid dropped in.

'I'm sorry, I have to go,' Erica said to Ingrid, before chasing after Roger. 'Roger! Wait for me!'

'See! I knew you cared. You wouldn't let me go on my own,' Roger smiled.

'It's not that. My purse is on your wheelchair,' Erica said, removing it and hanging it over her shoulder. 'OK…now you can go,' she said with a smile.

'Oh whatever! Get me down these stairs,' he said as they both went through the fire door.

Ingrid remained undefeated, 'With a bit of luck, your boyfriend will be more forthcoming,' she said to herself in the now lonely corridor.

She knocked on the flat that the other two had just left. Lee strolled out, confidently.

'Couldn't wait for me, huh, baby?' he said before hopping back at the sight of Ingrid.

'Hello!' she said. 'My name's Ingrid. You may recall that I recently took up lodgings next door. I just spoke to your girlfriend about the noise problem which your father is causing at night-time.'

Trying to hurry her along, Lee responded, 'My dad doesn't cause a noise problem.'

'He most certainly does, and I'll have you know that it is against the law to have the volume so high at night.'

'Look, love, I'm a police officer and I can assure you that it has to be much later than that to be against the law.'

'You're a police officer?' she asked in disbelief.

'Well…retired!'

'Retired? At your age?' she asked with equal disbelief.

'Look. I quit, OK, and if you don't mind, I have somewhere to be,' he snapped, slamming the door in her face.

'Well, really!' she said, flabbergasted.

Alex, and a now dressed Natalie, joined the seemingly endless string of chaos in the corridor. Alex's phone rang within moments of them stepping out of their door.

'Hello?' he answered. 'Hey up, Mitch, mate! Yeah? I'm just off to the shop with Natalie.'

'Tell him you're busy tonight!' Natalie whispered to him, possessively.

'I'm, er, busy tonight, mate,' he obliged. 'When? Next week! Bring what, sorry?...You want me to bring *that*? Are you sure?'

Natalie was prodding and poking at Alex as he took the phone call, trying to encourage him to hurry up.

'It barely even works any more,' he continued, trying to brush Natalie off him. '…Cause it's really old and knackered…Uh-huh…It starts making a whining sound if you don't give it enough attention…OK…OK, OK, I'll ask,' he turned to Natalie. 'Mitch wants to know if you want to come to a party with us next week?'

Natalie gave Alex a weak slap, smirking as she did, reassuring Alex that he'd not gone too far with his lengthy joke. One person who was not smiling however, was Ingrid, as she looked on in disgust.

'Do you want to go?' Alex asked Natalie. 'It's a celebrity party.'

'Which celebrity?' she replied.

'He won't say. Says we have to go to find out.'

'How are *we* invited?'

'Mitch has hacked the guest list.'

'He wants to be careful doing that. He'll get arrested one day. Anyway, I think I'll pass and I think you'd better wrap up the call,' she said, pointing at Ingrid who was storming down the corridor towards them.

'Right, you two! I want a word,' Ingrid demanded as she loomed towards them.

Alex quickly finished his phone call, hanging up just as Ingrid entered his personal space.

'Hello, neighbour,' Natalie said, cheerily in an attempt to de-escalate Ingrid's obvious high temper before it erupted.

'Don't you "hello neighbour" me!' Ingrid started. 'I didn't get a wink of sleep last night after all the noises you two were making!'

Alex let out a giggle and smirked at Natalie before responding, 'Oh right, yeah, sorry about that, but this is our first time living together, and you know how it is. I bet you and your fella got up to a bit of cheeky in your time, didn't you?'

'We most certainly did not get up to "a bit of cheeky"! We're respectable citizens.'

'All right, dear. Calm down,' said Natalie, joining in.

'I'm trying, but everyone around here is making it so bloody difficult. And I didn't appreciate you shutting the door on my hospitality earlier, either, young man. I'm at the end of my tether.'

'I think we'd better leave her to it,' said Alex as he led Natalie through the stairwell door that was nearest to their flat.

'I'm not finished with you two yet! Come back here this instant!' Ingrid shouted down the stairwell at the pair as they disappeared from view.

She returned to the corridor only to be enraged further at what she saw. At the opposite end of the corridor, leant against the wall next to his flat, was Kane, smoking.

'Erm, excuse me,' Ingrid said, the polite words, not matching her tone. 'Don't you think it's a tad dangerous doing that up here?'

'Don't care,' said Kane, blowing smoke in her face, causing her to wince.

'Well *I* do. I live three doors down and don't want to be burnt to a crisp in my sleep. My husband detests that sort of thing, and if he were home he would...'

Ingrid suddenly realised something. Something that she had meant to do at the first opportunity that she had. How could she have forgotten? Her husband…wasn't home. This was the perfect opportunity to get rid of that God-forsaken chair. She had already tried to squeeze it out of the flat window, but they didn't open far enough. However, she had noticed that the stairwell window was large enough for a whole person to get through, so this chair wouldn't be a problem. She rushed back towards her flat leaving a confused Kane behind. He became even more confused when before her flat door had had time to slowly come to a close, Ingrid had burst back through it carrying the cherished wooden chair. She had headed down the corridor towards the stairwell only a few steps when she heard her husband's voice booming up the stairs. She quickly retreated to her flat and returned the grubby chair to its home. She heard Seth, singing, out in the corridor. Something had clearly made him very jolly.

'What's with all the ruckus?' Ingrid asked, returning to the corridor.

'Crack open the champagne, dear,' came Seth's voice from down the corridor.

He was strolling past Kane when she spotted him.

'Tonight we celebrate!' he called to her again.

Kane tried to tune them out as he enjoyed his quiet afternoon cigarette. Seth had clearly had a little tipple; not yet drunk, but definitely merry.

'Seth! What an earth is going on?' Ingrid asked when he had finally made his way over to her.

'I just won a thousand big ones at the races! We're eating well tonight,' he replied, proudly.

Kane's ears twitched at this. He suddenly took great interest in their conversation as he watched Seth fan out the bank notes for Ingrid to see.

'Oh splendid!' said Ingrid, taking immediate ownership of the pocket money. 'I needed some good news. I aired our concerns to the neighbours in an attempt to resolve our issues, and they were all terribly rude.'

'I told you to watch for when they left the flats. Not confront them,' Seth said, worried that she had made the situation worse.

'Well, the young ones have just left, and there is only the "man of the house" home at the other side of us. And he said he had some-where to be, so he'll most likely be leaving shortly.'

At that, Lee appeared from his flat with impeccable timing. He was somewhat dismayed at the occupied corridor. He was intending to go straight to Layla's flat as arranged, but couldn't with so many people around. Equally, he couldn't return to his own flat now either as this would look odd. Instead he greeted them all with a polite "afternoon" and proceeded to exit the corridor via the stairwell door.

'Smashing,' Ingrid beamed. 'You're all clear,' she told her hus-band.

'Right, get in here. It's time I dealt with these neighbours myself,' said Seth, ushering Ingrid back inside their flat.

Kane was feeling devious. He hadn't resorted to petty crime for some time, but he felt that if the pigeon was going to flaunt its good fortune in front of him, then it deserved to be taught a lesson. He stubbed his cigarette out on the wall and let it drop to the floor before returning inside his own flat. He grabbed his trusty burglary kit, which consisted of a single crowbar, his tool of choice for flimsy flat doors, and returned to his front door. He was about to leave, but he had only opened the door a sliver, when he noticed Lee, sneaking back into the corridor and into his neighbour's flat, looking very suspicious. "What's he up to?" Kane asked himself. Kane stayed in his tactical vantage point where he could see the majority of the corridor. Having heard that Seth and Ingrid were intending to "do something about their neighbours whilst they were out" he felt that he would have ample opportunity to break into the old couple's flat and steal that money. It would most likely be in sight if he got in there quick. Kane worried that he was out of luck as they didn't seem to be leaving, but then, as suspected, Seth poked his head out into the corridor and looked both ways. Kane watched as Seth scurried to flat 3C, holding a pair of wire cutters, and let himself into the flat using the master key. No good, Kane thought. He'd hoped that he and his wife would be doing this together, but with her still in the flat, his chances of robbing them, vanished.

But then, as if the universe was reading Kane's mind, Ingrid's head appeared out in the corridor too. She also looked both ways and emerged carrying the same wooden chair that he had seen her with earlier. She locked her door, and this time, with nothing to stop her, left via the stairwell door with the chair. Kane knew it was now or never. He seized the opportunity and darted towards the old couple's flat, crowbar in hand, and prised open the flimsy yellow door, easily, and entered with gusto, closing it behind him to conceal his actions.

The corridor was silent for less than a single second. Alex and Natalie were the next to disturb the peace when they burst through the stairwell door in a frenzy of heavy petting. Kissing erotically, they rolled along the wall banging into other flat doors and the wall space in between as they went. They attempted to formulate sentences between their broken kisses.

'One of these days…we'll…make it…out of…the building together,' Alex managed.

'I know, but…you looked…so good,' Natalie followed suit.

'Well, we're gonna have to leave sooner or later,' started Alex, coming up for air. 'We need food and milk and supplies. I haven't had breakfast in days. And I need a cuppa!'

'I know, but we've waited for our own place for so long. And besides; I need to remind you what you've got right in front of you. I don't want your eye wandering onto old ladies.'

'She's only thirty two!'

Natalie gave him a stern look.

'But that's not the point,' Alex recovered. 'I told you, Layla and I were just talking about…'

'Blah, blah, blah, I know you've told me it all already. I just think she's a bit of a cougar. And you're mine. Not hers.'

'You know I only have eyes for you. Anyway, you've killed the mood now. Let's go to the shop, like we should have done in the first place.'

'The mood might have been killed for you, but not for me. We'll go after, I promise. Come here, you.'

Natalie pulled Alex back in for another passionate kiss and they continued to fondle along the corridor towards their flat, 3E, which was all the way at the other end. Their vacuumed lips were parted by Kane who barged between them, knocking them apart and causing Natalie to fall to the floor. He was clearly in a rush as he didn't even look back at them. He simply ran inside his own room and shut the door.

'Are you OK?' asked Alex, helping Natalie to her feet.

'Yeah, I'm fine,' she said dusting herself off. 'Idiot!' she shouted at 3A's closed red door.

'I wonder what that was about.'

'Who cares, come here!' she said, grabbing Alex again.

As they continued their throes of passion, banging along the corridor wall, they stumbled through the doorway of 3D. Unbeknownst to them, it had been left open by Kane during his escape.

'Woah!' yelled Alex as they fell to the floor in each other arms.

They struggled to their feet in confusion.

'What's that old bat's door doing wide open?' Natalie pondered.

'That's odd. The lock's been busted open,' Alex pointed out. 'I hope she's OK. Hello!' he called, wandering into the flat for a brief glance. 'I don't think anyone's home,' he told Natalie when he returned to the corridor.

'You know what,' she said, suggestively.

'What?'

'Well, you know the other day you were saying about trying …you know, in different places?'

'But what if she comes back?'

'That's the exciting part.'

Natalie backed into the flat, seductively. Alex was hesitant about following her, but Natalie made the choice for him when she dragged him in by his shirt. They closed the door behind them as best they could. A good thing they did too, as, moments later, Seth returned from flat 3C, wire cutters still in hand, with a satisfied grin on his face. He made for his next target, 3E. He didn't notice the state of his own door as he past it and let himself into 3E, again, with the master key. With more fantastic timing, Lee stuck his head out into the corridor from Layla's flat, 3B, and checked the corridor. Once he was sure it was clear he quickly nipped next door back to his own place, wearing absolutely nothing and concealing his private area with a strategically placed pillow. He wasn't home long before he re-emerged. He checked the corridor and ran back to Layla's flat, however this time it was not the pillow concealing his manhood, but a policeman's helmet. He had also brought a pair of handcuffs with him.

Missing him by only moments, Ingrid returned from her successful mission; the disposal of the long-despised chair. She walked confidently and smugly back to her own flat and pushed at the door. It was already ajar. "Oh no!" she thought. Had Seth got back before her? She scanned the room cautiously to discover, to her horror the sight of Alex's rosy buttocks going up and down on her lavish sofa. Disgust set in. Alex and Natalie were defiling her beloved suite, one of the few home comforts that she had brought to the flat with her. She screamed. Natalie, who lay on her back, turned to look at her for a moment. Alex rolled off and turned to face her, in all his naked glory.

'Police! Police! Aaaaaarh!' she screamed as she ran back out into the corridor. 'Police! I need the police,' she continued to shout at no-one.

She looked around, uncertainly. Then she spotted the blue door. Flat 3C. Remembering that someone who was once a police officer lived there, she ran inside with knocking, continuing to shout her requests for police aid.

Lee had heard the shouting from the other room. He managed to just about don a pair of light blue underwear this time, before rushing out into the corridor to check for the source of the commotion. He was still wearing the policeman's helmet. He spotted his open flat door. Confused, he entered to find Ingrid running around his living room, hysterically.

'Aaaaargh!' she screamed when she spotted him in his almost naked state.

Lee attempted to calm her down, but she pushed past him back out into the corridor. She turned left, back towards her own flat only to be greeted by Alex, hopping out of it, pulling his underwear and jeans up his body as he hopped along. Natalie joined him also clutching her jumper to her chest, concealing her breasts. Ingrid screamed and spun around to see that Lee had followed her out, still in his underwear. She screamed again at this relentless visual onslaught. "The landlord!" she thought. She registered the green door, 3B, and hurtled through it, but barely had she done so when she was greeted by the sight of Layla, pulling up her knickers. They both froze, transfixed. Ingrid screamed yet again and ran back out into the corridor.

'Naked people everywhere,' she screamed, to no-one in particular.

She looked around at all the people now in the corridor in various states of undress; Layla had followed her out dressed in some negligee that she had quickly thrown on, Alex and Natalie, dressed, in a fashion, were giggling in the doorway of Ingrid's flat, and Lee stood tall with all but his private parts on show. Ingrid felt dizzy. She covered her eyes and ran towards the stairwell door nearest to flat 3E. As she passed it however, Seth emerged and grabbed her by the shoulders in an attempt to calm her down. Alex and Natalie looked in surprise at this man who had just come out of their flat. Seth, equally shocked, looked at the pair standing inside the doorway to *his* flat.

'What are you doing in our flat?' The four of them said in unison. The two pairs pushed past each other to return to their own homes, leaving only Layla and Lee in the corridor. Layla quickly bunched up the clothes that Lee had left inside her flat and ran over to him to hand them over, before ushering him back inside his own flat. She turned to return to her own, but locked eyes with Roger, who had just innocently come through the stairwell door and been lucky enough to catch an eyeful of her, barely covered by her sexy apparel.

'Weh-hey! Now this is my kind of party!' he said, cheerfully.

Layla didn't know what to do, so she just ran into her flat. Erica came through the stairwell door shortly after, carrying Isaac.

'What're you going on about now, Roger?' Erica asked, having heard his excitement from the stairwell.

'Just now...a woman...real life...nearly naked!' Roger stammered, at a loss for words.

'You're lucky you saw just the one,' said Ingrid, returning to the corridor in a huff.

'You mean to say there were more of them?' he asked, with a mix of excitement at the prospect, but disappointment at having missed it.

'Not thirty seconds ago, this corridor was full of naked people,' replied Ingrid, unamused.

'What!' yelled Roger, genuinely angry. 'And I missed it? That's your fault, Erica, for being so slow getting me up those stairs.'

144

Erica fired right back at him, 'Well, you should have just walked up then, shouldn't you…hang on,' she paused, realising the ridiculousness of what was being said. 'What do you mean "this corridor was full of naked people"?'

'Like I said. Naked people! Everywhere! Not moments ago!' Ingrid replied.

'Are you sure?' asked Erica in a disbelieving tone.

'Of course I'm sure. In fact, I'm pretty sure one of them was your steady!'

'My what?' asked Erica, confused.

'Your Beau!'

'Like a ribbon?'

'Like your boo!'

'As in ghost?'

'No!' shouted Ingrid, frustrated.

'I have no idea what you're trying to tell me.'

'Your main squeeze.'

'I think she's trying to tell us something,' Erica said to baby Isaac in her arms.

She passed Isaac to Roger to hold whilst she patronised Ingrid. She squatted in front of her and began patting her thighs, speaking to her as though she were a dog, 'What is it girl? What are you trying to say?'

Ingrid responded despondently, 'Well, if you're just going to play silly buggers, I won't tell you what your man was up to.'

'My boyfriend!' said Erica in relief. 'Finally! That wasn't so hard, was it?'

'Well, if that's what you kids are calling it these days.'

'Wait a minute,' said Erica, once the penny had finally dropped, 'you mean to say that *Lee* was out here naked, too?'

'Most certainly!'

'Everything OK out here?' asked Lee, innocently, as he emerged from his flat, fully clothed.

'Ingrid here says that you were out here naked…with others,' Erica quizzed.

'Don't be silly, of course I wasn't!'

'He most certainly was,' Ingrid corrected.

'I was not naked, Erica,' said Lee, ignoring Ingrid.

'Oh, you know what, he's right, he wasn't *completely* naked. I seem to remember him wearing light blue boxer shorts and a policeman's helmet,' fought Ingrid, over Lee's dismissive behaviour.

'Oh that's ridiculous, she must be going senile,' he said, glancing Ingrid up and down now.

'I'm not that old, thank you very much,' she inserted.

'Out of curiosity…' Erica asked, 'what colour underwear *are* you wearing today?'

Lee stood silent. Erica grabbed the waistband of his jeans and pulled it back.

'Hmm,' Erica said, suspiciously. 'Light blue! Coincidence I suppose.'

Lee avoided the issue with the same cheeky grin he had used on Erica a thousand times before. She was too laid back to care or even think he was up to anything untoward.

'Well,' Erica continued, 'whatever you were up to whilst I was out with your father all afternoon, I'm guessing you weren't looking for a job, were you?'

'No, not today, I was er…doing some plastering,' Lee lied. 'We had some cracks I had to fill in.'

'More like the neighbour did!' said Ingrid, aside.

Seth came bursting out into the corridor.

'Right!' he said angrily 'Where are those two little shits!'

'I hope you're not talking about us,' said Natalie, who came rushing out of her flat with Alex upon hearing this.

The residents of flats 3D and E began arguing loudly. The others could barely make out what either party were saying. Ingrid walked over to fight by her husband's side.

'What's going on up here?' said Ian as he burst through the corridor door. 'I could hear you lot from two floors down!'

'I'll tell you what's going on,' started Seth, still seething. 'These two whippersnappers are a pair of thieves. They've stole my race winnings! One thousand pounds worth of hard-won cash, gone!'

'We haven't stolen anything,' said Alex, firmly.

'No we haven't,' Natalie joined in, 'but he's cut the cable on my exotic fish tank! They're all dead!'

146

'Your fish tank? Ooops,' said Seth, awkwardly. 'I was trying to get your music player!'

'So it *was* you? How could you?' she said, angrily.

'Well that's what you get for stealing my money,' justified Seth.

'We haven't touched your money,' reiterated Alex.

'Well, who else could have taken it? And if you weren't stealing, what were you doing in there?' Seth questioned.

'We were just having a bit of fun,' said Alex, cheerfully. 'The only thing we did in there was make a mess of your sofa cushions.'

Ingrid let out a horrified wail upon hearing this.

'Come on, Roger,' said Erica, 'let's get you inside. You don't want to miss your programme, do you?'

'No chance,' he replied, firmly. 'There's more drama out here than in any of my programmes. Besides, I reckon they're all about to get their kit off again.'

'How did you get into our room anyway? We locked it!' Natalie asked Seth.

'I used the master key that I borrowed from Ian when he was at my flat this morning,' he replied.

'Borrowed? Now who's the thief?' Ian interjected.

'It's better than what they did to my flat,' Seth said, pointing at 3D's door. 'Look at the state of our lock. They forced their way in.'

'No, no, no,' Alex panicked. 'That was like that when we got there. That's why we went in.'

'It was probably that shady character you have living at the end!' Ingrid chimed in.

'OK, OK,' commanded Ian, in an attempt to bring order to the noisy corridor. 'It seems that you're all at fault here in one way or another so let's stop pointing fingers. I think it best we all return to our rooms and sort this out later, when everyone has calmed down.'

'How can I calm down?' said Natalie, upset and angry now. 'All my fish are dead.'

She overdramatically called Seth a "murderer" before heading back to her own flat and slamming the door shut on the people in the corridor, including Alex who was about to follow her in.

'I don't know how you convinced us to live here,' Seth said to Ian as he led his wife back into their flat.

'OK, take me back inside, Erica!' ordered Roger. 'I think I missed the best bits.'

'Yes sir!' Erica replied, with a sarcastic salute.

'Please, don't order her around, Dad,' said Lee as the three walked back into their flat carrying a sleeping Isaac.

Alex had been fumbling with his own key to get back into his flat after an angry Natalie had locked the door.

'Sorry about the fish,' Ian apologised to him, as if it were somehow his fault.

'They're not really dead. She's just being dramatic,' he replied. 'It'll take longer than that for them to die...trust me, I know! I'll nip out and buy her a new cable in a minute.'

Alex finally got back into his own flat, leaving Ian alone in the peace and quiet of the corridor which had been such a frantic playground just moments ago. He breathed a sigh of relief thinking that the shenanigans were over...he was wrong. He was about to enter his own flat when Layla appeared at the doorway to block him.

'Hi, baby. What's up?' Layla said, coyly.

'Not much, just a damaged door that needs repairing,' Ian replied. 'I'm nipping to town to buy a new lock. I just need to grab my coat.'

'I'll get that for you,' she said blocking his path into the flat.

'I can get my own coat, Layla,' he said, trying to get past her.

'I know, but it's a mess in here,' she said, continuing to block him, 'and I want it looking nice for when you get back.'

Layla vanished into the flat leaving a bemused Ian out in the corridor. She came back and handed him his coat. Confused, he said his thanks and set off on his way. As he passed the yellow door, Seth ambushed him.

'Oy, Ian!' he called. 'What are you going to do about this door? I've lost enough money for one day!'

'I'm just on my way out to pick up a new lock. And my insurance will cover the cost of your burglary too,' he replied, understandingly.

'Good. It would have cost you an arm and leg by the time you were done with all the repairs and repaid my two thousand pound winnings.'

'*One* thousand pounds was the amount you were moaning about, not long ago, if I remember correctly.'

'Oh yes, of course. Either way you should be more careful of who you have living here,' said Seth as he closed his door.

'Yes, I'm starting to think that!' Ian said to himself when he was alone.

He saw Alex leaving his flat as he continued down the corridor.

'You off out?' Ian asked.

'Yeah, to get that fish tank cable!' Alex replied.

'Oh yeah!' he remembered 'I'm off into town myself. I'll walk down with you if you want!'

'Cool!' Alex replied.

'Ian!' came a voice from behind the pair of them.

Ian spun around to see Erica. Would he ever get out of here, he wondered?

'Yeah?' he responded.

'Could you just have a look at the TV in Roger's room, it's not turning on!' she requested.

'Isn't that a good thing?' Ian joked.

'Definitely not. While ever he's looking at women on there, he leaves me be.'

'Well, I'm just nipping to town with Alex for some bits. I'll have a look at it when I come back.'

'Erica! It's time for my sponge bath,' came Roger's voice from inside her flat.

'Please hurry!' she pleaded before returning into her flat.

Ian and Alex laughed amongst themselves as they left via the stairwell door.

A moment passed where the corridor enjoyed another brief silence. The peace was disturbed, yet again, by Roger this time, rolling into the corridor in his wheelchair. He had a cheeky look on his face and was holding a large, old-fashioned, video camera. He was glad to see that the coast was clear as he had decided to attempt to get a repeat viewing of the mild nudity that he'd caught a glimpse of earlier. He wheeled his way over to Layla's flat and let himself in leaving the door wide open.

Too late to spot Roger, Natalie came into the corridor with a bag of rubbish, again having forgot to get Alex to empty it on his way out. She felt obliged to empty it herself since he was out, buying *her* fish a life-saving present. She walked all the way down to the stairwell door at the far end, as the main bin was closest to that set of stairs. She took note of 3B's open door as she passed, but paid it no mind. She held the corridor door open for Tony who was coming in the opposite direction, but barely acknowledged his presence. However, he definitely noticed her as he glanced at her backside on his way past.

About to knock on his friend's door, he too noticed that flat 3B's door was open and could hear a mild kerfuffle from inside. He rapped on Kane's door, still taking a keen interest in what was going on inside the next flat.

'What do you want?' asked Kane when he answered the door.

'I came for a top-up,' Tony replied.

'Oh good! You know, I could probably run my business off you alone!'

'Look, your neighbour's door's wide open!' Tony informed him, suggestively.

'Just leave it!' Kane tried, as he stepped out of his doorway to have a gander. 'Her husband's the landlord, remember. It's not worth the trouble.'

'We should at least go in and...err...check on her,' said Tony, suggestively.

Kane hesitated for a moment before easily caving, 'Fine, but we're just gonna mess with her, OK? No trouble, got it?'

'Of course!' Tony lied.

The pair of them headed inside Layla's flat without even a courtesy knock. This time however, Natalie arrived back from the bins in time to see them going inside, leaving the door wide open. She thought this odd, but wasn't one to get stuck in the middle of something that didn't involve her. She returned back to her flat, forgetting what she had seen almost instantaneously.

Chapter 21 – The Night of the Fire

'That path's a bit pointless,' commented Alex as we found ourselves intermittently cutting across the grass that ate into the long winding pathway that led from the flats down to the main road.

'You should see the old photos that I have of this place,' I started. 'It looked amazing. Where we're walking now was covered with flowers and plants of all different colours. You'd have stuck to the path then, in fact I'd say it would have been a pleasure to.'

We continued to walk down the hill away from the flats with the terrain swapping from tarmac to grass and back again under our feet as we strolled idly in a straight line towards town.

'Looks like it could rain,' said Alex, looking up towards the murky sky.

'And it's getting dark already,' I added. 'These late afternoons in autumn are becoming less appealing to go out in. We'd better be quick in town.'

We reached the end of the long pathway and transitioned onto the pavement of the main road at the edge of town. We passed from the peace and quiet of the path to a noisy bustling town packed with people finishing work for the day, shoppers carrying an abundance of bags or pushing prams and buggies, all clearly rushing to avoid being caught out by the rain. A large roar of thunder echoed through the town and brought about a sudden urgency amongst the public as they picked up their pace.

'It's good that you came,' Alex said to me. 'It's just dawned on me that I don't know my way around here.'

'Good point,' I chuckled. 'If I'm not mistaken, the place that I pick up most of my D.I.Y. is very close to a pet shop. They should have the cable that you need.'

Our journey took us past Bretton University.

'Bretton Uni!' Alex said. 'I should have gone there. One of my biggest regrets.'

'Why didn't you?' I asked.

'I decided to rush into a job instead. Get some cash together for me and Natalie. Especially with her going to uni too. We'd have been stuck with our parents forever if one of us didn't get a job.'

'Nice of you to martyr yourself like that,' I chuckled.

'Well, she's the brainy one. She was more likely to succeed, and besides, once she's a doctor she can be rich enough for the both of us,' Alex laughed, giving me a nudge.

'Still, you should have gone. Who knows, we could have met sooner.'

'You went there?' quizzed Alex.

'Yeah. Business Studies. I planned to make big money with my own business. Instead I just about manage to scrape it together with those dingy old flats.'

'Give yourself some credit. You haven't done bad for a twenty-two year old. More than most have at your age.'

'Not my friend James. He owns multiple restaurants in America. We shared a dorm together at uni.'

It was either at the mention of his name or maybe being beside the university again that struck up the memory of that bizarre night that James came back to the dorm in a peculiar manner. The whole reason why he owed me one in the first place, and the reason that I could trust him to keep my secret over in America. I won't lie and say that I was never curious about why I was covering for him, though. I'd pondered it on many occasion. Maybe now was the perfect chance to speak about it. I did promise James I wouldn't tell anyone, but it wouldn't matter if I told Alex, I mean, it's not like he will ever meet James anyway. In fact, he would be the perfect candidate to help me shed new light on it. Find out what he thinks about it all.

'Why did your friend start his business in America?' asked Alex. 'Why not here? Does he have family over there or something?'

I mused on this for a moment before responding, 'That's a very good point and something I had always just accepted before, but now that you mention it, I wonder if it's related.'

'Related?'

'Yes. I'm going to recount a memory to you, see what you make of it. You can't tell anyone, because I promised him I wouldn't and he's currently keeping a...secret, we'll say, of mine, so if he finds out I spilled the beans on his, he may be less reserved with mine.'

'I doubt I'll ever meet him, but either way, I won't say anything.'

'That's very true. OK. It was three years ago...'

#

The sound of sirens woke me in the early hours of the morning. Revision books were strewn across my bed as well as several surveillance style photographs, all with handwritten notes clipped to them. I panicked as I looked over towards James,' empty bed. "Phew" I thought realising he wasn't home yet. I need to be more careful. I was foolish for falling asleep with all this stuff left out for anyone to see. I hurriedly shoved anything that wasn't revision work into the shoe box on my bed and returned it to its hiding place at the back of my underwear drawer.

I saw the flash of blue lights across my curtains. I nosily hurried over and parted them. Fire engines, ambulances and police cars were all racing up towards the magnificent Royal Rainford Hotel that sat at the top of the hill on the outskirts of town. I could just about see an orange hue flickering in the windows on the second floor. It was unmistakably on fire and fire engines were hosing the building down heavily.

I was startled when the dorm room door burst open.

'Ian!' exclaimed James, clearly as startled as me. 'You're awake!'

'Well if I wasn't, I would have been when you burst through the door like that,' I commented.

'Sorry about that.'

James turned away from me and stood over the sink, washing his hands. His body language became closed as if he were hiding something.

'What are you doing?' I asked, puzzled.

'Nothing, just go to bed!' he ordered.

'Alright, dad!' I said, sarcastically.

I turned away, but did a double take as I noticed the back of his neck was black, which was hard to see in this dimly lit room at three in the morning.

'What's that?' I asked.

'What's what?' James snapped back at me.

'Is that soot on the back of your neck?'

James quickly covered it with his wet hand causing the soot to fuse with the water making a runny black paste which ran down his neck.

'Have you got something to do with what's going on up at the hotel?' I enquired.

'Look!' James pleaded. 'Ian, as a friend, I need a huge favour; I need you to say that I've have been here the whole night.'

'So you have! What happened up there?'

'Please, Ian. Promise me!'

'I can't! Not until I know what's happened.'

'Something bad. You're going to hear all about it tomorrow, but I swear to you, hand on my heart,' he said, demonstrating the gesture, 'I have no idea what happened. It had nothing to do with me. Please, as a friend, accept that as the truth. Don't ask any more questions and if anyone asks, I have been here with you the whole time. I know it's a lost to ask, but I beg of you. Be my friend. Trust me.'

There was a long silence between the two of us as my mind raced between all the possibilities of what could have happened. I then thought about what this friendship and loyalty could mean. James and I had become fairly good friends in the short time we had known each other, but this could cement it and Lord knows I needed some good friends around me.

'OK!' I agreed.

#

'And we never mentioned it again,' I concluded my story.

'OK,' Alex jumped in at the end of my story. 'No big mystery there. Your friend was obviously involved in the fire and didn't want to be held responsible for the damages.'

'That's the same conclusion that I jumped to. I just feel like there's more to it,' I said, pulling the same inquisitive face I had many a time before when thinking about the subject.

'What makes you say that?'

'Well, this is a long shot, but around the same time a young girl went missing. Janice Todd, I think her name was. Everyone in town was talking about it, but when our teacher told us all at the beginning of class one day, James looked scared. It wasn't that noticeable, but *I* definitely picked up on it. I'd already promised not to say anything so I assumed I was better off not knowing.'

'Why are you telling me if you haven't told anyone else?' he asked. 'I barely know you.'

'It doesn't matter, you won't say anything. I just wanted to know what you thought of it.'

'Well, it's definitely suspicious. Anyway, I notice that you failed to mention that I'm living in a building that has fire damage when you offered it to me,' joked Alex.

I laughed at this indiscretion of mine, wondering how much this *actually* bothered him. Oh well, I wasn't here to make friends. I had a job to do. I kicked a loose flagstone on the pavement and banged quite hard into Alex.

'Steady on, Ian. You nearly knocked me into the road. Good luck getting Natalie to pay the rent if you kill me off,' Alex laughed.

'Sorry about that,' I replied. 'Look at that!' I said, pointing at the slightly raised flagstone. 'Council need to sort stuff like that out.'

'Or you could just watch where you walk,' he jested.

The rest of our journey to the shops was uneventful. I pointed Alex towards the one he needed and we agreed to meet back outside in five. I entered "Jim's D.I.Y." to the charming tinkle of a little bell.

'Ian,' called Jim, popping up from behind the counter.

'Hey Jim!' I replied, earnestly.

'You can't need more stuff surely, you've practically cleared out my electronics department.'

155

'Not today, Jim. Just after a new lock,' I said, heading over to them and grabbing one identical to the casualty. 'One of my tenants has had a little bit of a break-in.'

'I'm not surprised with those flimsy little locks you keep buying. I've told you,' he said coming out from behind the counter and grabbing a different lock next to me, 'you need the SecuriMax. Far better than that load of old tosh you keep picking up.'

'*You* sell it!'

'Yeah, I *sell* it. I don't *recommend* it though.'

'I'll stick with the usual, thanks,' I said, defiantly.

'You are so cheap,' Jim said, disapprovingly, slamming the superior lock back onto its hook. 'I've seen some of the expensive equipment you've bought for that place and then you skimp on the important stuff.'

'"Important stuff" is a matter of opinion, Jim.'

'If you say so. Four ninety five please.'

I handed over the cash with a cheeky grin.

'Smile all you want. You'll end up regretting it one day,' Jim said, slightly annoyed at my smugness. 'How did you get on with all the wiring? Did you call a decent electrician in?'

'Nope,' I sounded off, confidently. 'Did it myself!'

'Remind me never to rent a flat from you.'

'Probably wise,' I laughed as I headed for the door. 'See ya next time.'

I stepped outside. No sign of Alex. I hadn't been that long, though. I headed into the pet shop to see if he had found what he was looking for. It was apparent he wasn't in this tiny shop; I was able to see the entire shop floor as soon as I entered.

'Can I help you?' asked the sales assistant.

'Sorry, I'm just looking for my friend. Came in here to buy a fish tank cable?' I enquired.

'Yeah, young lad. He looked very nervous actually. He grabbed what he wanted and rushed off. Seemed like he was in a hurry.'

'OK. Thanks.'

I left the shop and gave the area another look round. Where could he have got to? A huge flash filled the sky followed by a roar of thunder. Droplets of rain slowly began to gather in the air. It got heavier and faster very quickly. Wherever he is, I'm not getting caught out in this. I hope he's back in time tonight. I wonder what he has to be nervous about. I gave one final look around and began a speedy walk back towards my block of flats.

Chapter 22 – Murder on the Third Floor

Erica left her flat and went towards Ian and Layla's next door, glancing at the heavy rain out of the corridor window as she went. She'd barely reached the door when she was disturbed by Natalie who had snuck onto the corridor without her realising.

'Excuse me! Erica is it?' she asked, politely.

'Yes?' replied Erica, deviating towards Natalie's flat.

'I was just wondering if you'd seen my boyfriend, Alex. He went to town for a power cable for my fish tank. It's only down the road and he's been gone ages. He's not answering his phone either. I'm really starting to worry.'

'Oh, I'm sure he'll be fine.'

'Oh, I'm not worried about *him*. If my fish don't get that cable soon, they could get really poorly.'

'Oh…right,' Erica chuckled, nervously, unable to tell if she was being serious or not. 'Well I saw him leaving with Ian, so maybe they stopped at the pub.'

'Which one's Ian?' Natalie asked, trying to place the face to the name.

'Our landlord!' Erica stated in disbelief.

'Oh yeah, of course,' Natalie said, feeling silly that she could forget. 'Well, he better *not* have stopped at the pub. Not with my fish hanging on for dear life.'

'Have you heard that rain? They may have had to take shelter. I hope they didn't get caught out in it.'

'That's true. The rain could damage the cable.'

'I was thinking more so they wouldn't get wet,' said Erica, unable to tell if Natalie genuinely only cared about the fish and not Alex's health, or if this was her sense of humour.

She was saved from these odd thoughts when an out-of-breath Alex, drenched from head to toe, came through the fire door and onto the corridor. He was holding a plastic carrier bag, presumably holding the much sought-after cable.

'Finally! What took you so long?' Natalie questioned.

'Sorry. I was out with Ian,' he replied.

'Where's Ian?' Erica butted in.

'I dunno. We went into different shops and we were supposed to meet back outside in five minutes. I was in and out of mine within seconds and there was…er…something else I wanted to pick up whilst in town, so I thought whilst Ian was in his shop, I would quickly go get it.'

'What "something else"?' asked Natalie, hopefully. 'A present for me?'

'No they'd sold out anyway so I didn't even get it. Anyway, by the time I'd come out of the second shop, it was hammering it down with rain. I rushed back to where we said we would meet, but he wasn't there. I assumed he didn't want to wait for me in the rain, I know I didn't, so I just came back.'

'Oh good!' Erica said, focussing back on her original destination. 'Ian's probably already back then, which is good. I need to ask him or Layla if they'll watch Isaac for five minutes whilst me and Lee go looking for his dad, Roger. God knows where that lazy old man has got to.'

Erica headed back towards Ian and Layla's flat. Alex couldn't stop thinking about the story Ian had told him. This James character definitely sounded suspicious. It must be the same James that Layla saw in the photograph at Kane's flat. She said he was Ian's friend, and *that* picture puts him at the hotel. It seemed likely that he was involved in the fire. And this girl, Janice Todd, who had been so prominent in the news a few years ago, did it have something to do with her? Should he tell the police? It could be important information.

Erica knocked on flat 3B, not realising that the door had only been pushed to, and so the force of her knock shoved it open further.

'Hm!' mumbled Erica.

'What's up?' Alex asked.

'Nothing. Just the door's been left open.'

Natalie's expression suddenly changed. She'd forgotten all about the two men that she'd seen going into the flat earlier this afternoon. Suddenly overcome by an immense sense of responsibility, she rushed over to the flat door to join Erica.

'I hope she's OK!' Natalie said, starting to sound worried.

'It's only an open door, Natalie,' said Erica, shocked at her seemingly over-the-top reaction. 'You've gone drip white. I'm sure Ian just came and left it open. He's always doing that, and besides, he was probably drenched and wanted to get out of his wet clothes.'

'Yeah, I suppose,' said Natalie, not satisfied with that suggestion. She debated with herself over whether to tell Erica and Alex about what she saw at this point, but didn't want to cause a problem over nothing.

'What's wrong Natalie?' asked Alex, joining the pair.

She didn't answer.

'Look!' Erica said, calmingly. 'Let's just go inside and say hello, then you'll see how much you're overreacting.'

'OK,' Natalie nodded.

'But I tell you this, if we catch Ian naked in here you owe me a drink,' Erica joked, making Natalie grin. 'Ian! Layla? You home? Roger's gone AWOL, I need you to have Isaac for five minutes. I swear…' Erica started, turning back towards the young couple, '…if he's gone out in the rain to get wet on purpose so that I have to bath him, he can get ready.'

'Has he done that before?' chuckled Alex.

'He's done much worse to get a cheap cop, believe me.'

'Never mind that,' butted in Natalie. 'I don't see them. Where are they?'

All three looked towards the closed bedroom door.

'Ian! Layla!' Erica called out again, this time towards the bedroom door. 'We're coming in, so if you two are getting lucky in there, then call out now.'

Nothing. Erica looked surprised. She reached out and opened the bedroom door. She let the door swing itself open, revealing a sight that put shocked faces on all three of them. Erica was the first to scream, followed by Natalie who stumbled backwards. Alex remained still, staring, struggling to process what he was seeing. There. On the bed. Face down with a large knife in her back, was Layla. Dead.

Chapter 23 – The Unknown Consequence

'That recess has thrown me right off. I can't remember where I got up to,' I said, having a good long think.

My thoughts were interrupted when I was asked why I had told Alex such a precious secret about my friend James.

Disappointed in myself for betraying my friend's trust, I replied, 'Well had I known then what was going to transpire, I wouldn't have told him, obviously. At the time I didn't think it would matter. I would never have guessed that the two tales would have intertwined so closely. Maybe if I hadn't had my mind on other things I would have seen what else was going on. The bigger picture. I was too busy with my own life story. Speaking of which, shall I continue?'

A gracious nod was all that I received, and all I needed to continue with my story.

'It was early on Sunday evening. What I didn't know then, was that my life was about to be turned upside down. I returned to a horrific scene inside my third floor flat…

Chapter 24 – Trapped

'Alex!' I exclaimed.

My presence had clearly startled the trio of intruders standing inside my flat. Erica, Alex and Natalie just simply stared at me without a word.

'Thanks for ditching me in town,' I continued, rainwater dripping from the hem of my coat. 'Where the hell did you go? You could have told me if you were just gonna rush back here without me. I was looking everywhere for you,' I told him, as they all stood looking mortified. 'Why are you all in my flat, anyway?' I asked the silent group. 'What's wrong? Why isn't anyone saying anything?'

They moved a little and I saw what they had been obscuring; my wife, lying on the bed with a knife in her back. I dropped the carrier bag containing the replacement lock, resulting in a loud thud, and burst through my tenants. I leapt onto the bed beside her.

'Layla? Layla!' I shouted as I shook her, trying for a response. 'No!' I screamed.

I began to shiver and tears streamed down my face as my lips struggled to formulate anything coherent, 'What happened here?' I yelled at the others, asking for an explanation.

'We don't know,' Erica weakly replied. 'We just found her like this.'

Confused, I eyed the large knife in her back, reaching for it, but deciding against touching it.

'She's been stabbed!' I said, weakly, but my anger soon returned. 'Someone did this! Has anyone rung an ambulance? The police?' I added, furiously.

'No, sorry! I'll go do it now,' Erica said, rushing out of the room.

I continued to cry as I lay down alongside her, looking at her closed eyelids. I snuggled up to her, cuddling her as I cried, being careful not to knock the knife.

'Who would do this to you, Layla?' I managed between sobs. 'Why has this had to happen to us?'

Alex and Natalie were very uncomfortable in the room. I could tell they felt obligated to stay, but had no idea what to say. But who does in that situation? No one expects to see anything like this in their day-to-day life.

'My phone's not working!' exclaimed Erica as she re-entered the room.

'I'll ring them,' said Natalie, clearly eager to leave as she hurried out of the room.

Alex, began to pace the room. Erica joined me on the bed and placed a comforting arm on my shoulder. I had no idea what to do or say. I could taste the salty tears continue to attack my taste buds as I wept for my murdered wife. My mind began to wander. Who discovered her first? Were they together or did one find her and call the others for help. What was going through their heads right now? I stared longingly at Layla's still beautiful face; now empty of the vital essence that had made her who she was.

'Our phone isn't working either!' Natalie informed us as she re-entered the room.

'What?' queried Erica.

'The line is just completely dead.'

'Same as mine.'

'Hello?' came a voice from the living area of the flat, startling us.

'That's Seth!' I said.

The group walked out to meet him. I only came partway to join them, standing in the doorway between the two rooms.

'What's all the screaming about?' he asked.

'Can we use your phone please? It's an emergency,' Erica asked.

'You can't! That's the reason I'm here. Ingrid was on the phone to her sister Martha and the line just went dead. It's not working.'

'When was this?' asked Natalie.

'About ten minutes ago.'

'Look,' I shouted, commanding silence. I collected myself in response to their shocked stares and tried to calm myself. 'Will someone just use their mobile phone? Please!'

I clearly sounded annoyed at the fact that no one had tried or even suggested it. Of course, neither had I, but my wife *had* just been murdered. What did they expect from me?

'I will! Hold on!' Alex quickly responded, apologetically.

He reached into his pocket. A fleeting confused moment turned to panic when he quickly patted the rest of his pockets.

'It's gone!' he realised.

'What?' said Natalie.

'I had it on me when I went into town.'

I looked around my flat for mine and Layla's mobile phone. I pulled up the sofa cushions searching for them there too.

'It looks like ours are missing as well,' I informed the others.

I lifted my landline telephone receiver to my ear to the expected absence of a dialling tone. I tossed the phone across the room in anger, smashing it against the wall and stunning my onlookers.

'What's going on here?' Natalie asked.

'I thought I'd seen enough dead bodies for one lifetime,' Alex moaned.

This seemed to have struck a chord with the young couple. They shared a look that told of a secret between the pair.

'Dead Bodies?' queried Seth.

It was at this that I realised that Seth didn't even know what was going on. Natalie pointed him in the direction of my bedroom. The look on his face was one of profound shock.

'Oh my God! What happened?' he asked.

'No one knows,' explained Erica. 'And all of our phones are either broken or missing.'

'I need to get to the police station, now!' I said, heading out of my front door and into the corridor.

The group followed close behind me, clearly not wanting to be in the flat with the body. I moved at speed only to be stopped dead in my tracks by the locked, and secured, heavy fire door.

'It's locked!' I told the others, puzzled.

I spun around and headed for the opposite side of the corridor.

Natalie snatched the carrier bag that Alex had been holding the whole time, 'Give me that cable!' she demanded. 'There's been enough death for one day without losing all my fish too.'

I had to ignore such a ridiculous comment, otherwise I don't know how I would have reacted. Thankfully she disappeared back inside her own flat. Alex looked embarrassed by her insensitivity.

I met the same fate at the duplicate fire door at the other side, 'This door's locked too,' I informed them.

'You mean we're trapped?' shouted Alex at the realisation of the rapidly worsening situation.

'No, we're not!' I told them. 'Seth, give me the master key back. It unlocks these fire doors too.'

'Hold on!' Seth replied, heading for his flat. 'I left it on the table inside. I'll go and get it.'

Seth went inside his flat. Distraught, again, I rested up against the wall beside my flat.

'I can't believe this is happening,' I heartbreakingly let out. 'Who would want to hurt my Layla?'

Neither Alex, nor Erica, the last two tenants still out here with me, said anything. Alex looked pale and disturbed at being marooned on this floor.

The blue door on my left whipped open and Lee, another unsuspecting victim about to learn of their current predicament, emerged, with Isaac strapped to his chest.

'Erica, have you found my dad yet?' he asked his girlfriend.

'Something's happened,' she informed him. 'Go back inside. I'll fill you in later.'

'What's happened? Is it my dad?'

'No nothing to do with your dad?'

'Well, what then?'

'I'll tell you later.'

'I want to know now. What's going on?'

'Just tell him,' I said. 'Everyone needs to know. We're all in this now. It's not just about me anymore.'

Erica spoke quietly, 'We've just found Ian's wife dead in his bed-room.'

'What?' Lee stammered, clearly very disturbed by this.

'She's been murdered,' Erica finished.

'What? By who? What?' Lee muddled through his words, begin-ning to well up.

I could see that he wasn't taking this well at all. He already looked in a much worse state than the others.

Seth returned with more alarming news, 'It's not there!'

'What?' I shouted at him, pushing myself away from the wall and angrily marching towards him.

'The key! It's not there!'

'You mean you've lost it?' I shouted again, getting angrier still.

'No!' he pleaded. 'It's just gone. I'm certain that I put it on the table in my flat and now it's not there!'

I seethed with anger, shouting even louder than I had up until now, 'If you hadn't stolen it from me in the first place, we wouldn't be having this problem!'

'So we *are* trapped!' Alex concluded.

'What do you mean "trapped"?' Lee said, re-joining the conversa-tion.

Erica explained the situation to him, but he still went through the now familiar motion of searching his flat for either his or Erica's mobile. Of course they'd been taken too.

'Do you think someone is doing this to us?' Erica asked everyone.

Still upset, Lee answered, 'Who would want to kill Layla though? And why lock us in here after they left?'

'Take him back inside, will you!' Erica requested, referring to Isaac.

'OK,' agreed Lee. 'Did you find my dad?'

'No! I have no idea where he would have gone on his own.'

'Do you think he went out?'

'Like he would be bothered to go anywhere by himself. Anyway, just take Isaac inside, away from all this,' she asked again to which obeyed.

I left the others without a word and went back into my flat, but they followed me anyway.

I entered to my bedroom where my dead wife lay and knelt on the floor, resting my cheek on the bed as I spoke to her, 'I don't know what to do, Layla. What shall I do? I need you now more than ever to deal with the one situation you could never help me with. Tell me what happened to you. Who did this to you? Give me a sign! A clue! Anything.' I broke down in front of the others. More tears streamed down my face. 'Please!' I shouted at her. 'Please!' I repeated before crying into her shoulder.

There was a long silence before Seth finally spoke up, 'Maybe you should cover her up, son. Nothing you can do right now. You should preserve her dignity.'

'I'll do it,' Erica volunteered and searched the nearby wardrobe for a spare bed sheet.

'Does no one else have a mobile phone?' I pleaded

'Ha!' snorted Seth. 'We don't own one. Can't work em!'

'Natalie's is broken and off for repairs,' Alex told us.

'So we literally have no way of contacting the outside world then?' Erica concluded as she threw the sheet she'd found over Layla's body.

'What is going on?' started Alex. 'How could someone take all our mobile phones without us seeing them?'

'Because,' I began to explain, 'Seth lost the master key that he stole from me. Whoever did this would have had the run of the place.'

'Now that's not fair, Ian,' Seth defended. 'If they didn't steal it from me, they would have just stolen it from you.'

'You don't know that!' I shouted, storming back out of my flat and into the corridor. 'If it wasn't for you, we wouldn't be trapped up here.'

'Please don't put this on me,' said Seth, pursuing me out into the corridor where I stood with my head in my hands in a fit of rage.

Another unexpected burst of anger caught me by surprise as I felt a violent push in my side causing me to stumble for a few steps.

'You did this, didn't you!' shouted Lee, who had reappeared.

His eyes were red and tears were streaming down his cheeks, but he was very angry.

'What are you talking about?' I asked, panicking.

'You murdered Layla, didn't you!' he accused.

'What?' I shouted back, angered. 'Why the hell would I murder my own wife?' I denied.

'Because you found out about our affair!' Lee revealed.

'What?' I said, genuinely gobsmacked.

I was clearly not the only one that this was news to, 'What?' Erica spat, venomously, also genuinely shocked.

Lee turned his attention on Erica now with an apologetic tone to his voice, 'I'm sorry Erica. I didn't mean for you to find out like this.'

'You're lying!' she said, getting upset and ready to blow. 'Please tell me you're lying!'

'I'm sorry!' was all Lee could muster.

Erica exploded in a fit of rage, 'How could you do this to me? To Isaac?'

Erica slapped Lee, hard across the face causing him to stumble a few paces, before storming inside her flat, slamming the door hard, causing everyone to cringe. Silence reigned. Lee's gaze swivelled slowly to my contorted face.

'You were sleeping with my wife?' I hissed quietly, with controlled fury.

Lee dismissed my question, 'Drop the act! You found out didn't you? That's why you murdered her!'

I burst into a fiery rage again, 'How dare you tell lies about her when she isn't here to defend herself. Layla would never sleep with you.' I paused for a moment to calm my voice. 'And I would never hurt my wife.'

Angry as well now, Lee would not let up, 'Liar! It had to be you. No one else had a reason to!'

This accusation rendered whatever calm I had managed to find, void, as I burst back into a fit of rage, '*I* didn't have a reason to! I didn't even know about you two! And even if I did, why would I stab my wife, leave her in our bedroom and then just lock myself in here with all of you! Maybe *you* killed her!' I countered, switching the focus. 'If you *were* having an affair with my wife, who knows what could have happened between the pair of you. Maybe she told you it was over. *Maybe* she regretted it. *Maybe* you tricked her into it. *Maybe* she'd had enough and *maybe*...you just lost control.'

'I would have never hurt her!' he said, returning fire.

'You don't get to talk about her!' I shouted, taking ownership of the argument.

Lee took a step towards me. I took that as a sign of aggression and pre-emptively lunged at him. Seth stepped between us both and used his bulky arms to easily hold the pair of us apart.

'OK, you two,' he boomed. 'Stop throwing accusations at each other. Whatever has happened I doubt either of you are capable of murder! Let's just figure a way out of the building first. You two can sort your personal problems out later.'

'Well you'd better stay in your room until I sort this mess out,' I demanded, taking charge.

'You think *you* can help us?' Lee laughed. 'You're only a kid!' he undermined.

'I'm more man than you'll ever be.'

'If that was true, your wife wouldn't have come knocking on *my* door!'

Too much! At this I threw a punch at Lee's face, which he narrowly avoided by jumping backwards. Seth positioned himself between us again.

'I think you should go back to your room, son!' Seth suggested to Lee.

'I'm going, I'm going!' Lee agreed returning to his flat.

'I'm gonna kill him!' I said out loud, seething with anger.

'Right, well, I think you should…' Seth started before being interrupted.

'And don't even think about coming back in here,' Erica bellowed, as she shoved Lee back out into the corridor, slamming the door behind him.

I stared at him, ready to say more, but Seth intervened, 'Go on inside my flat, son. You can wait in there for now.'

'Thanks!' Lee replied, going inside 3D.

'What are we gonna do?' asked Alex, reminding me that he was still in the corridor.

Natalie made a reappearance, 'I just tried shouting out of my window to try and get someone's attention, but no one can hear me from all the way up here! The main road is too far away and with the rain bouncing down so hard, there's barely anyone about.'

'Couldn't we all try stamping on the floor, and hope that someone from one of the downstairs flats comes up?' Alex suggested.

'That won't work!' Seth disappointed. 'Ian said that this floor is the only one that has people living on it so far!'

'That's right!' I confirmed

'Well, what about that guy's dad?' said Alex, pointing at Seth's flat where Lee had just taken asylum. 'Didn't they say he wasn't home? Well, when he comes back and he can't get in, surely he'll go and tell someone that we're trapped up here.'

'I have never seen that man go anywhere on his own!' I stated.

'Well they said he wasn't here, so he must be somewhere other than on this floor, right?' he said, sounding desperate now.

'I have no idea, I can't really think at the minute.'

I broke down again. I put my back against the wall and slid down it, looking depressed.

'I just can't believe this is happening,' I moped. 'It doesn't feel real. And if my wife was having an affair, I don't even get the chance to be mad at her. I don't *want* to be mad at her, I just. Urgh!' I slammed my fist into the floor. 'I don't know what to feel. I just want to know what happened. Didn't anyone see *anything*?'

'Nothing,' Seth confirmed.

'No, I was with you most of the time!' Alex added.

'Most of the time!' I said, suspiciously as I got to my feet and moved towards him. 'Where did you disappear to when we were in town together?'

Alex looked flustered, 'I needed to buy something else. I bought the fish tank cable really quickly, so I thought I would have time to grab the other thing I needed before you came out. I'm sorry. I should have waited, or come and told you where I was going before I went for it.'

'It? What's *it*?' I questioned.

'I can't say. It's personal.'

'Well that's very convenient, isn't it?' I said, suspiciously. 'When I went into the pet shop to look for you, the staff member there said you were acting nervously. What was that about?'

'Come on now, Ian,' Seth begged. 'Don't start on him too. We need to keep a level head here.'

'Well, how about you, Natalie? Did you see anything?' I asked, turning my attention on her.

There was a pause. She looked stunned. I asked again, 'Natalie?'

'Well, maybe one thing,' she revealed, nervously.

'What?' I demanded.

'Well, this afternoon I saw two men...er...' she hesitated, as though worried she should have mentioned something sooner, '...going into your flat.'

'What? Who?' I asked, again severely concerned at this revelation.

Two men went into my flat? What has been going on right under my nose in my own building?

'I'm not sure,' Natalie stammered, 'but I think one of them was the guy that lives at the end,' she said, pointing at Kane's red door.

'What?' I replied, again more confusion filled me.

I needed to find out what's been going on. I stormed over to flat 3A and banged on the door.

Kane emerged, 'What have I done now?' he asked, innocently.

'Did you go into my flat this afternoon?' I asked.

'No, of course I didn't!'

'You were seen going in there with another man!'

'Oh yeah, by who?'

Natalie, too scared to say anything, turned away. Tony, Kane's "client", appeared at the door right on cue.

'And he would be the "other man" I presume!' I pointed out.

'That's just a coincidence!' Kane said, dismissively.

I slammed my fist threateningly into the wall by his head, 'My wife has been stabbed. She's dead. So I suggest that if you, or your crony, know anything about it, you tell me now!'

'Dead?' Kane said, a mix of shock and panic on his face. 'OK, look, mate, I'll be straight with you. We did go in there. The door was already open, so we went in to see if everything was all right!'

'Suddenly developed a caring side, have we?' I said, sarcastically.

'OK, fine!' Kane admitted, giving up. 'We were just gonna wind her up a bit, but when we got there, she already had enough to deal with!'

'What do you mean?' I asked, confused.

'Well, that old guy was wheeling around her room trying to film her with a video camera!'

'Who? Roger?'

'I don't know. The one in the wheelchair. Although he did stand up a few times and chase her around on foot. He was asking her to do all sorts. Made *me* look like a gentlemen!'

'That has to have been Roger!' I said to the others.

Seth chimed in with a theory, 'If he had a hand in her death, he may have panicked. Locked us in and removed all contact with the outside world before fleeing the scene. He probably did that to get a head start on us. If he is in a wheelchair, then he may have thought he would need to slow us down to make a decent getaway.'

'I can't believe this!' I said, lost in my thoughts.

'What do you mean "locked us in"?' Kane said. 'I was just about to go out and get some more cigs.'

'We're trapped on this floor!' Alex explained. 'Both stairwell doors are locked, the phone lines are dead and everyone's mobile phones have vanished!'

'Ah-ha!' Tony exclaimed, pointing at Kane. 'I *told* you it wasn't me.' He turned to the rest of us now, 'He's been accusing me of nicking his phone all afternoon.'

'Well this is ridiculous. I'm not staying here,' Kane said.

'I don't think we have a choice for now!' said Seth.

'I can get us out of here, easily,' said Tony, confidently, unsubtly inflating his chest. 'I'll just kick the door down.'

Tony marched towards the locked corridor door with stereotypical cockiness. He kicked it, hard, several times, but it was a fire door; it did not give way. Well, at least my supplier was right when he said nothing could get through them.

The banging soon ceased and he returned to the group, trying to keep his cool, 'It's too heavy. It looks new compared to rest of the place. Is it the same door at the other side?'

'Yeah, they're fire doors,' I confirmed.

'Can't we just all start looking for this master key?' Alex suggested.

'I think it's safe to assume that it was stolen along with the mobile phones,' Seth deduced, gloomily.

'I'm going back to my room!' Natalie said. 'We're not getting anywhere out here and I need to check on the fish. They must be so scared. Are you coming Alex?'

Alex, clearly unable to contain his embarrassment at Natalie's second ridiculous comment in the past ten minutes, burst out, 'They're fish, Natalie! I'm sure they'll be fine!'

Peeved by his disobedience, she simply snapped, 'Alex!' and stormed towards their flat.

'OK, I'm coming,' said Alex following her through 3E's pink door.

'I think we should *all* go back to our rooms!' Seth suggested. 'Ian, why don't you ask Erica if you can stay in her flat until we figure a way out of here? You can't be in your flat on your own after what's happened!'

'Yeah, OK,' I agreed to this sensible suggestion.

'Come on pal,' Kane said to Tony. 'Let's go get high whilst everyone else solves this problem.'

'Yes to that,' chirped Tony, giving Kane a high five on their way back to his flat.

I cringed to think I was allowing that monster to live so close to me. I followed Seth's advice and knocked on Erica's door. It would be nice to have her company tonight and with Lee staying next door I'm sure she could use a hand with Isaac. She answered the door and her smile showed that she needed me.

Chapter 25 – Familiar Faces

Natalie poked her head out of her flat door to check that the corridor was clear. What a difference a few hours makes. The evening had crept up on them and it was now very dark outside.

'It's clear,' she called back into the flat to Alex, before creeping along the corridor.

'You sure?' Alex asked, presenting himself to the corridor.

'Yes, we're fine,' she assured.

Alex locked the door behind him, although after Seth's jolly jaunt in their flat this afternoon, and the fact that the master key was on the loose somewhere, he wasn't very confident of the lock's security.

Alex fell in with Natalie and crept along behind her. They continued down the corridor passing 3D's yellow door, and then 3C's blue door, and then finally stopping in front of their landlord's green door.

'Are you sure you want to do this?' Alex asked.

'I'm telling you, I know her,' Natalie asserted.

'How? Where from?'

'I don't know, but I thought I recognised that Kane guy that lives there,' she said, pointing at Kane's red door, just one flat over, 'and now I'm getting the same feeling about the landlords wife! I just think it's a strange coincidence.'

'So what are you wanting to do?'

'I just need to get a proper look at her, just to be sure,' Natalie said as she pushed open the door to the flat.

She reached for the light switch and flicked it. Nothing happened. She flicked it a couple more times, but the lights were clearly not working.

'That's odd!' said Alex.

'Wait here!' Natalie ordered before running back to her own flat, leaving a baffled Alex behind.

She returned shortly after with a torch, flicking it on to confirm its functionality.

'You still want to go in there?' Alex said, gobsmacked.

'Of course,' she replied.

'You're scared of your own shadow, but you want to go into the conveniently darkened murder flat?'

'It'll drive me crazy if I don't figure out where I know her from.'

Natalie moved into the flat and Alex reluctantly followed. The rain was coming down even heavier now, the noise of it hitting the window sounded throughout the room. Natalie aimed the beam of light around the flat for a moment before settling it on the closed bedroom door. They both slowly moved towards the door, heart rates increasing.

'This is the part in the movies where the body has vanished,' Alex joked.

'Stop it!' Natalie snapped. 'I'm scared enough as it is.'

She got closer to the door and reached out.

'Please be there, please be there, please be there,' she prayed as she slowly pushed the door open.

She shone the torch onto the bed, revealing the sheet that lay flat against a body-like shape underneath it.

'Damn!' she remarked. 'I'd forgotten about the sheet.'

'This is the part in the movies where there's someone different under the sheet,' Alex jested again.

'Alex, stop it, please!' she pleaded, as she walked deeper into the room.

'Don't forget to check everywhere first,' Alex continued. 'There's always someone hiding out of sight.'

Natalie hit him on the shoulder with the torch causing him to wince.

'Ouch!' he cried. 'I'm just saying. Behind the door,' he said, indicating the door that they were currently passing, 'under the bed,' he said pointing there, 'lurking in the toilet,' he said, waving at the open bathroom door.

Having had enough, Natalie ignored him and walked confidently over to the side of the bed and pulled back just enough of the top part of the sheet to reveal, to her relief, Layla's head. She let out a grateful sigh. They stared at her for a while. Natalie turned back to Alex for some assistance in remembering who she was, but his face clearly showed that he already had.

'You remember her too!' cried Natalie.

'You know who that is, don't you?' Alex insisted.

'No,' snapped Natalie, frustrated. 'I can't quite place her.'

'She was at Bretton Quarry when we were kids! When that man fell and died' Alex revealed.

'Oh my God, you're right! She was the paramedic!' Natalie's memory dredged up another worrying issue. 'Oh no!'

'What is it?'

'That's where I know that other guy from too. Kane! He was the one that caused it! The one who said he'd find us if we said anything.'

'Oh shit, you're right. This is insane!' said Alex, baffled. 'Do you think he knows that it's us? Has he come to find us?'

'He can't know it's us,' concluded Natalie. 'He'd have said something otherwise. And we haven't told anyone about what happened that night. Besides, he lived here first. We just happened to walk right onto his turf.'

The straying torch beam lit up a figure as it rose from the other side of the bed. Natalie and Alex screamed in fright.

'What are you talking about?' Lee said, instantly upon his appearance.

'Jesus!' Natalie gasped. 'You scared us! How long have you been hiding there?'

'I got here just a few seconds before you did. I barely even got the chance to look at her before I heard you two coming in here. I thought it might be her husband so I hid under the bed.'

'Told you we should have looked under the bed,' smirked Alex.

'What are you doing here?' Natalie asked.

'I just wanted to see her again,' said Lee, sadly.

'Don't let her husband catch you,' warned Alex.

'Why are you two here?' Lee asked.

'I thought I recognised her from a long time ago,' explained Natalie. 'I wanted to see her again to make sure.'

'Yeah I heard you say. Something about a man falling at Bretton quarry. When was this?'

'It was long time ago. About ten years now. Why?'

'Because I was there too,' Lee revealed.

'What?' said Alex and Natalie in unison.

'Yes. I was a police officer at the time.'

'That was you?' said Natalie.

'Yeah. What were you saying about Layla being there? And that drug dealer guy that lives at the end. I don't remember them.'

'She was the paramedic!' explained Natalie. 'Didn't you recognise her whilst you were both "at it"?'

'I never thought for a second. Are you sure it's her?'

'Yes!' said Natalie getting frustrated.

'I'm just as guilty of that, though,' added Alex. 'I've had a few lengthy conversations with her here and I didn't recognise her at all. But I'd have thought that *you*,' he said, indicating Lee, 'might have conjured up a memory or two whilst you were on top of her.'

'I did only chat with her briefly at the quarry, though. So, if you two were there, you must have been those school kids?'

'Yes!'

'So where does Kane come in to this? I don't remember anyone else being there.'

'You wouldn't. He was…' started Alex, before Natalie shushed him.

'There's no point hiding anything from me now. I heard you talking about him being there. And besides. I'm not a police officer anymore.'

'Why not?' asked Natalie.

'They'd been trying to get rid of me for years. For my lax approach to the job; said I was incompetent, that I wasn't confident enough and that I would just let anyone off to avoid confrontation. They tried to re-train me for years, but they must have given up. About seven years in, the investigations started. It was driving me crazy; I needed the job, but they were trying so hard to weasel me out, it was really depressing. Then, about three years later, it just stopped. All the statements put in against me disappeared, the staff that were giving me grief suddenly got shipped off to other departments and my sergeant was defending everything I did. It was completely out of the blue. I couldn't believe it when I got my ten year service badge. But then, about a year and a half, maybe two, after that, some drugs were found in my locker after a tip was given to my new boss. I had no idea how they got there, but the sergeant who was looking after me had retired by this point, so there was no one to get me off the hook this time, and so, that was the end of me. Someone that I'd pissed off must have finally got what they wanted.'

'Remind me in future,' Natalie began, 'that if I ask a question that's gonna result in a life story, that we do it in a well-lit area without a dead body. I do feel sorry for you though,' said Natalie, beginning to soften towards this man.

'Anyway, that's my sad story, so the least you can do now is tell me how Kane fits into all this.'

'We can't!' refused Natalie.

'Why not?'

'We'll be in danger if we tell anyone.'

'Fine!' Lee said, easily giving up on this line of questioning.

He looked back to Layla. Sadness overwhelmed him, 'I still can't believe this has happened! I think I loved her, you know! My life is pointless without her.'

'What about your own girlfriend?' Alex asked.

'That was just different. I had to stay with Erica for the baby's sake. And my dad, he just loves living with us and his grandson. I couldn't take that away from him.'

'What if your dad really is responsible?' Natalie suggested.

'What?'

Alex carefully explained, 'Some of the others think your dad may be involved in Layla's death.'

'Why would they think that?'

'Kane said that he'd seen him come in here and that he was being a bit perverted with her. And with him being nowhere to be seen, they're assuming he has locked us in and fled.'

'But why would they believe Kane? He could be lying?'

'*Is* there a chance it was your dad?' said Natalie, gently.

'No! Why would he?'

'Well, like you said. He loves living with you and his grandson. If he loved the way things are that much, maybe he didn't want to lose it. If he found out about the affair, would he do anything to protect his way of life?'

'Of course he wouldn't. He's just an old man. And he's out there somewhere, all alone. I need to find him. It's his birthday tomorrow, too. I just...'

Lee froze for a moment before a look of pure joy appeared on his face.

'What is it?' asked Alex.

'Birthday...' Lee began. 'Birthday phone!'

'What?' said Alex, confused.

'Check that drawer,' Lee urged, pointing at the bedside table next to Natalie.

She shone the light on it and opened the single drawer in the unit.

'Ian's underwear,' she remarked. 'Why the excitement?'

'Shine the light over on this side,' he requested.

She did and Lee opened the drawer on the other side. He grabbed a handful of Layla's knickers and threw them on the floor. He then pulled out a wrapped present.

'What's that?' Alex asked, curiously.

'It's the mobile phone that I bought to give to my dad for his birthday,' Lee answered, proudly.

'I can't believe this,' said Natalie, overjoyed. 'Get us out of here!'

Lee unwrapped the present quickly, tossed the paper onto the floor, quickly unboxed the phone and SIM card and dropped the box as well. He shoved the SIM card into the phone excitedly and turned it on. The additional light that the phone's screen provided was very welcome to the scared bunch. He played around with it for a few moments before becoming frustrated.

'I can't dial any numbers,' he said. 'It says that the SIM card isn't connected to the network yet.'

'There should still be a way to make emergency calls!' Natalie advised.

Lee messed with the phone further, and to his relief, found a solution, 'Yes! Here it is!'

Lee began pacing the room on his side of the bed, anxiously. Alex and Natalie embraced each other, happy at the prospect of being freed at last. They waited nervously for Lee to make a connection; Natalie spotlighting him all the while with the beam of her torch.

Suddenly though, Alex noticed something odd.

'Hang on a minute!' he said.

'What's wrong?' asked Natalie.

Alex grabbed her torch hand and pointed the beam at the bed.

'Shouldn't the sheet be raised in the middle?' he said, pointing towards the middle of the sheet that still concealed the majority of Layla.

'What do you mean?'

Alex grabbed the sheet and pulled it back the whole way, revealing a knife wound...but no knife.

'Where's the knife?' he exclaimed.

Lee paused, his face wreathed in smiles, 'It's ringing!' he told them, excitedly.

Then, to their horror, the torch beam illuminated a fourth figure, just behind Lee inside the bathroom. Natalie screamed to get his attention, but the figure swiftly moved up behind him, placed one hand over his mouth and plunged the missing knife straight into his neck with the other, instantly silencing him. Alex and Natalie screamed, hysterically as blood squirted into the room, spraying the walls, the bed sheets and the horrified young couple.

The killer was wearing a black hoodie with a dark material covering their face.

Lee's arms went limp as his life ebbed from him. He dropped the phone to the ground as his grip on it relaxed.

'Run!' Alex shouted at Natalie.

'Get the phone!' she shouted back at him.

Alex started to move around the bed towards the phone on the other side. The killer threw Lee's lifeless body into the bathroom behind them. Alex dived for the phone, but the killer stamped on it, before he could get there, destroying it.

Alex looked straight up at the butcher who wasted no time in kicking him directly in the head knocking him onto his stomach. The killer raised the knife and drove it downwards. Alex rolled onto his back just in time, out of the way of the knife, which stuck, quivering, in the floor. Up it came again. This time all he could do was cover his face with his arms as the killer brought the knife back down. Fortunately however by this point Natalie had jumped up onto the bed. She kicked the assailant hard in the shoulder, causing them stumble sideways away from Alex. The killer quickly recovered and swung the knife at Natalie, making her jump back in fear and fall off the bed. Alex quickly stood, grabbed her arm and pulled her up. They were now at the opposite side of the bed to the killer, with the door opposite the centre of the bed. Alex ran for it, dragging Natalie with him. Their enemy also sprinted for the door, but, luckily for the young couple, stepped into the discarded mobile phone box and slid briefly across the floor and onto the ground, allowing them to run into the living room and flee the flat safely.

They ran back towards their flat, but were stopped by the locked door.

'Hurry, hurry, hurry!' Natalie squealed as Alex fiddled about with his pocket to get the key out of his tight jeans.

The killer burst out into the corridor, looking right first and then left to see the pair struggling at their flat door.

'Alex!' Natalie screamed.

He looked up to see the hooded figure sprinting towards them at great speed with the knife raised high in the air. Leaving the key in his pocket, Alex pushed Natalie behind him. He crouched down and threw his body, sideways, into the speeding person, precipitating them over his back and onto the floor.

Now their opponent was between them, separating them to either side of this menace. The figure stood, aiming its gaze at Natalie first, who stepped back a few paces towards the locked fire door, then at Alex, whose face squinted with determination, and then finally back at Natalie before sprinting towards her. Alex, determined to save the woman he loved, grabbed the thug by the scruff of the neck, taking them off their feet and onto the floor again. He pinned the killer's bicep to the floor with his foot. A mistake! The killer bent its arm at the elbow, shoving the knife into Alex's leg. He cried out in pain. This

182

was followed up by a violent punch to the shin on his other leg, causing him to stumble back a few paces in agony.

The killer spun up into a crouching position and then slowly stood. Deciding that Alex was now the weaker target, the hooded figure sprinted towards the wounded youngster. However, the wound was not deep enough to pierce Alex's resolve, and he managed to grapple the killer's knife-wielding arm and U-turn the villain back around, throwing them head first at the large fire hose box which resounded with a loud metallic clang. Natalie heard this mystery person groan shortly after impact and she thought she recognised the voice, but dismissed it in the desperation of the moment.

Alex reached out over the dazed body to Natalie who took his hand and allowed herself to be helped over it with a little jump. Not taking their chances with the key again they rushed straight into Seth and Ingrid's flat. No fear of that being locked since it had been broken into only hours ago.

Chapter 26 – Unwanted Attention

'As the evening set in more problems began to arise for me,' I told my suddenly engrossed audience. 'With the death of my wife, Layla, and Lee, the man with whom she was having an affair, suspicion, understandably, began to fall upon me. I had to do something to prove myself. To show my tenants that I could be relied upon. And that I was trustworthy…'

Chapter 27 – Revelations

'I just can't believe you've done that!' sobbed Seth.

'It was past its best, Seth, darling,' reasoned Ingrid. 'It had to go, sooner or later.'

'But my lucky chair! You know how much I adored that thing! What did you do with her? Was it dignified?'

'Oh, absolutely!'

'Oh good! A nice lovely burial of some kind?'

'No, I carried it to the stairwell window and graciously cast it from the building!'

'Arrrrgh! How could you do that to Gertrude? Where is she now? What window? I need to know, woman!' said Seth, becoming increasingly irate with every question.

'Oh grow up, Seth. It was just a chair!'

'Just a chair? Just a chair? You have no idea what…'

'Barricade the door, quick!' interrupted Alex, loudly, as he and Natalie burst into the room, moving as far away as they possibly could from the front door, and scaring the life out of the old couple.

'Oh my God! Oh my God!' panicked Natalie.

'What on earth is the matter with you two?' Ingrid asked. 'You can't just barge in here like a herd of elephants.'

'We've just been attacked!' Alex told them. 'And someone else is dead!'

'What? Who?' asked Seth.

'The guy from next door, the one that was having it away with the landlord's wife!' Natalie revealed.

'How? What happened?' asked Seth again.

Still shaking, Natalie answered, 'He was stabbed whilst the three of us were talking! Someone else just showed up. We couldn't see who it was, their face was covered.'

'Oh good heavens!' Ingrid said, getting scared herself now and cuddling up to Seth. 'I thought you said that someone had killed the girl, fled, and locked us in!'

'That's what we assumed had happened,' he said.

'So you mean to say that there is someone still out there? *Killing* people?' Ingrid formulated.

'Unless they're finished!' Alex said, confusing the issue.

'What do you mean?' asked Seth.

'Well, think about it! The landlord finds out that his wife is having an affair, so he kills her, and then he kills the guy that she was sleeping with!'

'Now hang on a minute. You don't know that it was him. You said their face was covered!'

'It was, but he's the only one with a motive *and* he was hiding in *his* room.'

'Yes, but he's staying next door,' Seth argued.

'And he isn't the only one with motive!' Ingrid added.

'What do you mean?' Alex asked.

'The policeman's lover! She would have the exact same motive as the landlord! She discovers that the landlord's wife has obtained a paramour in the form of her boyfriend, so she does away with them both!'

'Of course, yeah!' realised Alex. 'They both have reasons for wanting those two dead! We need to keep away from the pair of them!'

Seth produced a counter argument, 'But if what you're saying is true, then they would have no need to bother us, right? They've killed the ones that they're mad at.'

'Unless they want to get rid of the witnesses,' concluded Alex.

'I think that's being a little dramatic, don't you?' said Seth, incredulously.

'Two people are dead and we're trapped in this building with a murderer…when would you like to start getting dramatic? I mean look at my leg,' Alex said, showing the old couple his wound. 'I'm way past the point of being dramatic. We're lucky to be alive.'

'Good lord!' Ingrid yelped. We need to get you off that right away, young man. Sit here,' she said, gesturing to the sofa. 'We need to get that bandaged up.'

'I'm surprised you'd let me sit down and run the risk of me staining your fine sofa.'

'Trust me, young man. You have left far worse bodily fluids on it already after your little romp in here this afternoon. I intend to have it well and truly destroyed when I get out of here.'

Ingrid produced a first aid kit and began to bandage up the wound.

'Thank you,' said Alex, gratefully.

'I don't know how much this will help, but it should aid in keeping the pressure on it,' Ingrid told him.

'As long as I can still walk, I'm good. I wouldn't want to be a sitting duck when that scorned landlord or policeman's girlfriend come at me swinging a blade about.'

'I'm not so sure it's either of them,' Natalie spoke up.

'Well, who then? The old man? Just because he's missing doesn't mean that it's him,' Alex reasoned.

'He's not missing if he's hiding under a hoodie trying to kill us.'

'What makes you think it's him?'

'When you threw whoever attacked us into the fire box, I heard him groan. I swear it sounded just like Roger.'

'How much can you actually tell from a groan, though?'

'I'm telling you, Alex, it sounded just like him.'

'But the way he attacked us! Sprinted at us! That was no old man.'

'You don't know that. He could be as fit as you or I.'

'But that would mean that he just killed his own son. And remember the motive that you suggested that he had? That he wanted to protect his way of life with his son and grandson. Why would he then destroy that by killing his son.'

'I didn't think of that!' said Natalie, feeling silly.

'Regardless of who it is, as long as the four of us stay in here, together, we should be fine.'

Finding these two unlikely allies had just about managed to mildly calm the young couple down, but their relief was short-lived when a fifth person announced their presence from the doorway to the flat.

#

'Everything alright in here? I thought I heard shouting!' I asked as I walked through the front door into a room of what held a group of clearly very frightened people.

Alex, Natalie and Ingrid all screamed and scrambled behind the sofa, using it as a barrier. Seth, however, remained calm and stood between the two factions.

'Get away from us!' Alex shouted.

'What's wrong?' I asked, confused.

'You killed him, didn't you?'

'Him? Who's him?'

'The one that was at it with your wife. You even said out in the corridor that you were going to kill him!'

'Lee's dead? How? Where?'

'Don't play dumb! You were hiding in your bathroom whilst we were in your flat. You came out and stabbed him.'

'I haven't been anywhere near my room since Layla died. I wouldn't want to,' I assured him.

'You're lying! No one else would have reason to!'

'I swear to you, this has nothing to do with me. *I'm* trying to figure a way out of here.'

'There *is* no way out!' Natalie interrupted. 'We're sticking together in here. Safety in numbers!'

'OK,' I agreed, 'if that's what everyone wants to do, then we should go get the others and bring them all here. Keep *everyone* safe together.'

'You're not bringing those drug peddlers in here,' Ingrid stated, firmly.

'OK, well can I at least get Erica and the baby?'

'She's just as much a suspect as you,' Alex accused. 'Neither you, nor her, are staying here. I think we'll be safer with just the four of us, thanks.'

'Oh come on now, everyone,' Seth intervened. 'This is getting silly. I think we all need to calm...'

Seth was cut short by the others screaming.

'Look out!' shouted Natalie.

I spun around to face the hooded figure which had entered the room behind me. Seth and I backed off to join the group behind the sofa. Admirably, being outnumbered didn't seem deter the intruder; they moved towards me and my terrified tenants. We grabbed vases, sofa cushions and anything we could get our hands on and flung them. Household objects rained down upon the cloaked person, but it managed to shield its face and body, rendering the attack ineffective. It didn't take long for us to run out of things to throw and our attacker advanced once more.

This was my chance to prove to my scared tenants that I am a man who can be trusted, a man who will protect them if need be. I stepped out of the group and shielded them, putting myself between them and the intruder, who wasted no time in thrusting the knife towards my gut. I sidestepped the deadly blow and precisely grappled the wielder's knife arm and twisted it, resulting in the intruder wincing and dropping the knife, which I hastily grabbed from the floor. I began swinging ineptly, but it was enough to cause our adversary to retreat.

'Who are you? What do you want?' I asked.

The killer retreated a few steps before turning and running away from the would-be victims.

'Roger?' I shouted.

On cue, the run faltered for a split second, but it was long enough for everyone to pick up on it; and now, unarmed and outnumbered, our assailant fled the flat.

'Oh my God!' Ingrid panicked. 'What's going on? Who's Roger?'

'He's the old man from next door!' I answered. 'The one that no one can find.'

'Isn't he just an invalid in a wheelchair?'

'He is, but he can walk just fine!'

'But why would he be doing this?' Alex asked.

'I don't know, but we need to move next door fast,' I suggested. 'It's not safe for Erica and the baby on their own.'

Natalie disagreed, 'There's no way we're leaving here with that crazy old man out there!'

'All right stay put! I'll go get them and bring them here!'

I dashed out of the flat into the corridor, but was quickly followed by Alex.

'Wait!' he shouted.

'What's wrong?' I asked.

'Yeah, what is it?' Seth said, joining us as well.

'You shouldn't go back to her,' Alex told me.

'Why not?' I asked, worried.

'You don't still think it could have been her, do you?' Seth asked Alex. 'After what we've just seen.'

'Well, we know it isn't him now don't we,' Alex said pointing at me, clearly not bothered that this might offend me. 'And I can't accept that the old geezer in the wheelchair is doing this, so that just leaves that Erica woman. And you're about to go right to her.'

'But I've been with her in the flat this whole time,' I assured him. 'She didn't hurt me then when she had me all alone. So that rules her out. And, anyway, you said that someone killed Lee between when we all left each other and when I went into the flat with her.'

'That's right!' Alex confirmed.

'Well, I was with her the whole time, so it can't have been her.'

'You never took your eyes off her for a second?'

'Well, she went to the bedroom every now and then to check on Isaac. And she had to go to the toilet a few times for lady business and such.'

'Sethy-poos!' Ingrid said, joining us out in the corridor. 'Come back inside. I'm awfully frightened without you.'

'In a minute, love,' Seth reassured, before turning to me to out Alex's suspicions once and for all. 'Ian. Are you sure she couldn't have got past you and out of the front door at any point?'

'I'm almost positive. She would have to be some kind of ninja to get past me without me knowing. I was sat in the living room; where the front door is, as you all well know.'

'Almost positives are never good in these situations.' Alex pressed, unwavering in his accusation. 'I'm guessing the TV faces the living room door?'

'It does,' I confirmed.

'And I'm guessing the sofa faces the TV.'

'It does.'

'And what were you doing in there?'

I paused for a moment, 'OK, so...I was watching TV, but...she couldn't have got out. Trust me on that. I'd have heard the door go.'

'Fine, but trust her at your own peril,' Alex warned.

Ingrid chimed in with a suggestion, 'Don't forget that drug baron that lives at the end. It could be him. Or his friend.'

Seth offered another alternative, 'Who's to say it's even anyone that lives in these flats?'

'I'll tell you what!' Alex said, knocking on 3A and 3C. 'Let's just get everyone out here. We'll all stay in one flat together and then if the killer shows, we'll know that it's not any of us.'

'Is that wise?' I insisted. 'If it is one of these others, do we really want to be that close to them?'

'They're unlikely to act in front of all of us if it *is* one of them.'

'That's true,' I agreed.

Erica came to the door first, holding Isaac in her arms. She was understandably shocked to see so many people at her door.

'What's going on?' she asked.

'Alex has decided that we're all going to stick together,' Seth told her. 'And it's a good idea. We have to if we want to survive.'

'What makes you think they're still here?' she asked.

'Well because of...oh no! You wouldn't know,' Seth realised.

'What? What's going on?'

'Your boyfriend has been murdered too.'

'What? How? When?'

'Ask the young couple. They saw it.'

'You know what! I don't care. After what he did, he can rot in Hell.'

'That's the baby's father, though,' Ingrid said. 'You must feel something.'

'No! He was dead to me the moment I found out he'd cheated on me.'

'But don't you want to know how...'Alex started.

'No, I don't care. I don't want to know,' she snapped, but a few tears welled up in Erica's eyes.

Tony jumped out of Kane's room holding a sweeping brush like a microphone stand and singing into it like a rock star.

'Oh good Lord!' Ingrid snorted. 'It's a good job none of us have retired for the evening.'

'Loosen up!' said Kane, walking out into the corridor behind Tony. 'Here, love, try some of this, it will calm you down.'

Kane offered Ingrid a drag on his illegal substance. She fixed him with an icy stare and turned her nose up.

'Alright, snob,' Kane said. 'What's up with everyone, anyway?'

'Someone else has been killed,' Alex informed him.

'No shit! Really?'

'Really!' Alex affirmed.

'It wasn't that rocking hot girlfriend of yours was it?'

'No it wasn't, thank God!'

'Who then?'

'Her boyfriend!' Alex said, pointing to Erica.

'*Ex*-boyfriend!' she corrected him.

She really was handling this well, I thought, although her tears were still clearly evident.

'I thought the doors were locked,' Tony pointed out. 'How did someone manage to get in and kill him too?'

'They didn't!' Alex said.

Tony suddenly realised what this meant and let the broom drop to the ground, 'Are we safe?'

'We will be,' Alex assured. 'That's why I knocked on you. We're all gonna go into one flat and stick together. I suggest you knock that off too,' he said, indicating Kane's dodgy cigarette. 'You're gonna need to be focussed for the rest of the night.'

Kane dropped it to the floor and stubbed it out before pointing out, 'If we're all sticking together…where's *your* girlfriend?'

Alex's face dropped, 'Oh shit! Natalie!'

I followed Alex as he ran back in to the old couple's flat and looked around. She was nowhere to be seen.

'Natalie?' he shouted, panicked.

He repeated this several times, before the flush sounded in the bath-room and she came wandering out through the bedroom door.

'What's wrong? What happened?' she asked.

'You're OK!' Alex said, grabbing her.

'Yes I'm fine! I just went to the toilet. Stop overreacting!'

'She's right, Alex,' I agreed. 'We all need to calm down. We're doing as you suggested. We're gonna stick together. We'll be alright now!'

'We're not alright, though,' Alex snapped. 'And if anything we're all underreacting! I'm getting us out of here.'

Alex stormed out of the flat back into the corridor. Natalie and I shared a look. She shrugged as if to say "no idea". We raced out into the corridor to find a very agitated Alex running at one of the fire doors and slamming his whole body into it. It still would not budge. I couldn't help but be impressed at the door's resilience. He began punching and kicking it.

'No offence mate,' Tony started, 'but if I couldn't get through it, you're not gonna stand much of a chance.'

Alex marched up to Tony and squared up to him, staring pointedly. Then, glancing down, he saw the broom that Tony had been playing with earlier. He grabbed it and started banging it into the ceiling, knocking the tiles loose.

'What are you doing,' I shouted. 'Stop wrecking my building.'

Alex ignored me, 'I'm trying to get us out of here. There might be a way up to the next floor through the ceiling.'

'There won't be. It's just a suspended ceiling. It's completely solid above that.'

'It's worth a shot,' he argued.

Alex's poking of the tiles turned more aggressive and he began smacking them off in a rage. As he got closer to us, stood outside Ingrid's flat, we had to step back as he continued to bash the tiles. He reached the ones with the mucky stain on and one tile was all it took; a group of six came crashing down together and something heavy landed between us.

I inhaled a load of unwanted dust as I gasped in shock. Clouds of it filled the corridor, together with the sounds of everyone coughing. Eventually it settled and my horrified eyes fixed on a most unexpected sight. A corpse, decayed beyond recognition, almost skeletal, lay before us in all its gruesome glory with a blue handled screwdriver sticking out of the skull.

The group screamed yet again.

'What on earth!' Ingrid said, mortified.

'What's going on here, Ian?' Seth asked.

'I honestly have no idea,' I replied, truthfully.

What *is* this doing here? I can't be dealing with this right now. Of all the times for something like this to happen! How did I not know about this? If only I had replaced those tiles sooner, although I suppose then I would have had even more to deal with before all this.

'It must have been there long before I took over the building,' I explained.

'And it's just a coincidence that we find this now?' Seth said, disbelievingly.

'It must be. Unless you're saying Alex knew it was up there.'

We all looked at Alex.

'Hey! I had no idea!' Alex defended himself.

I suddenly noticed something that none of us had been aware of up to this point. Kane stared in silence at the ancient corpse.

'Kane! What's wrong?' I asked. 'Do you know something about this?'

'Yes!' he said, to everyone's surprise.

'So *that's* what you've been up to,' Alex said.

'Yes, well, no. Sort of! Not quite this.'

'What do you know about this, Alex?' I asked, getting more and more confused.

'I know that your wife caught him doing something suspicious upstairs,' Alex answered.

'What was she doing upstairs? She had no reason to go up there,' I said, concerned.

'Well she was having that affair, wasn't she! So she'll have been up there…you know!'

'How do you know that's what she was doing?'

'Well…she er…what, sorry?' Alex said, trying to avoid the question.

'You knew?' I asked, angrily.

'I er…what?' he stammered.

'You knew about the affair and you never told me?' I shouted.

'I didn't *really* know, she just mentioned it. I'm new here. I didn't want to cause a problem.'

I was so angry with Alex. If he'd just told me about the affair, I wouldn't have had to deal with so many surprise revelations.

'You never told me about this,' Natalie said, butting in.

'Look, babe,' Alex began sucking up. 'The girl was upset when she told me. I didn't think it was important.'

'Very suspicious if you ask me,' I accused. 'Not telling your own girlfriend about it. Were *you* giving it to her too?'

'Were you?' came a second accusation from Natalie. 'Did I interrupt you both when I walked in on you earlier?'

Alex protested, 'What? No! Of course not. Don't be silly. Look, Ian. I'm sorry I didn't tell you about your wife, but she was so upset about it all and I barely knew you. It's not like I had an allegiance to either of you. All I can say is, sorry!'

'I suppose that's fair,' I decided, calming down. 'I shouldn't blame you for my failings as a husband.'

'Thank you. I'm still sorry.'

'So you said that she caught Kane…' I started.

'Listen, mate!' Kane tried butting in.

'Shut up, you. Every time someone talks it's just more and more lies. Alex. What did my wife catch Kane doing?' I asked, desperate to get to the bottom of this.

'I don't know,' Alex said. 'I don't think she ever found out before she…well!'

I turned my furious gaze onto Kane now.

'Is that why she's dead?' I asked.

'What? No, I…' Kane tried again.

'Is that why you *murdered* my wife? She caught you doing something?'

'Yes she did, but I never…'

'Aaargh!' I screamed him into silence. 'We were safe here. Secure!' I continued to shout. 'Even though we weren't the happiest, I was working at getting my marriage back on track.' I began to cry, choking the words out. 'Then I let you lot live here. With your lies, and deceit, affairs, drugs and whatever else you people have been up to. And now my wife is dead. Dead! I should have screened you all better.' Realisation suddenly drew on my face. 'It's all my fault. I should've never have started this stupid business,' I shouted, crumpling into and ball on the floor, sobbing bitterly.

Erica knelt down next to me and put a consoling arm around me.

'I know you're upset,' she said. 'But this is not the time. We need you to be strong. We need you to be a leader. You know this building better than anyone. We need you to get us out of here.'

'You're not keeping any secrets from me, are you, Erica?'

'Of course not. All I want is to get my baby out of here safely. Can you help us?'

'I'm going to try. But first. No more secrets. I want complete transparency. Anyone that knows anything at all needs to bare it. It's the only way we'll get to the bottom of this.'

'I'll go first,' Kane volunteered. 'I swear to you, I did not kill your wife, Ian.'

'I can vouch for that,' Tony said, butting in. 'He was with me the whole time.'

'How reassuring,' I mocked. 'Well what about this one then?' I asked Kane, pointing at decayed corpse on the corridor floor. 'Did you murder this person?'

'I...' Kane paused at the question. 'I don't know.'

'What do you mean you don't know? Who is it?'

'It's...it was a girl named Janice Todd' he revealed.

Alex and I shared a glance. He must have been thinking what I was thinking. We'd only just been talking about her this afternoon. But how is Kane mixed up in it? I was always sure that her disappearance had something to do with my friend James. What other mysteries are lurking in this building's past?

'Wasn't that the girl from the news a few years ago?' Ingrid queried.

'Yes!' Kane confirmed. 'They never found her. So this must be where she's been.'

'How do you know it's her?' I asked.

'The screwdriver!' he swallowed.

Ingrid moved in closer to the group with a suggestion, 'I can tell there is quite a story to this. Let's move this back to the comfort of my flat. We can all have a much needed cup of tea, and we can hear all about it!'

#

We were now all squeezed into Seth and Ingrid's flat. Rain relentlessly pounded against the window with no signs of letting up. After two deaths, a missing old man and a three year old corpse, we sat down to the much-deserved cup of tea that Ingrid had made for us. Kane and Seth were sitting on the sofa. The rest of us had either found a patch of floor to sit on, or a section of wall to lean against. Kane was clearly very distraught. Whatever he was about to tell us had shaken him to the core.

'It was three years ago. In May. As some of you have already pointed out. Janice Todd's disappearance was all over the news. She was reported missing the day after the fire that happened in this very building. No one could have known that two incidents were connected, but me and my friends were responsible for both. There were five of us. We met up regularly at the hotel every couple of months.'

'Were they the same friends that came to the party last week?' Natalie asked.

'Yes! Well, three of them were,' Kane confirmed.

'What party?' I asked.

'You were on holiday,' Natalie informed me. 'We'll tell you later.'

I gave Erica a stare, airing my disappointment. She apologetically shrugged. I'm sure what ever had gone on here, she had very little say in it. I'd asked her to watch over the place and it's still standing so I decided I wouldn't hold it against her.

'And the fifth person was *his* dad,' Kane said, pointing to Alex.

'I had a feeling you were gonna say that,' Alex said.

'Because of the photo?'

'Yeah! Well, that and the fact that me and Natalie were hiding in the bathroom when you were in Ian's bedroom.'

'So Derek was right, he did see you going in there.'

'You were in my room?' I asked, getting agitated.

'Yeah; we had a party, used a few rooms, tidied up after. Happy?' Kane said, dismissively.

'Not really,' I replied, still concerned.

'Well you'd have never known if she hadn't said anything,' he said, indicating Natalie. 'Anyway, back to my story,' he said, changing the subject. 'We would usually book out an entire floor and just party there. The hotel was usually full of students that went to the university nearby, so they were always up for a party. One night we met a young girl there by the name of Janice Todd. She was very vulnerable. A couple of months before, her mother had passed away after a long illness. From what I gathered from her, she'd spiralled out of control since then. She was staying at the hotel, but was definitely just there for something else. Drugs. *She* approached *us*, begging for some stuff. She had plenty of money, but she also was very fit. We refused to sell her anything, suggesting that she pay…by other means.'

'Other means?' asked Ingrid, confused.

'I'm not proud of it,' Kane continued, 'but we passed that girl around like she was nothing. An object.'

'You vile man,' Ingrid said with disgust.

'Ingrid!' Seth said, to quieten her of her judgemental outbursts.

'Well, that poor girl.'

'Now's not the time to question Kane's morals,' I said. 'We can all make judgements about the type of man he is, but let's just get to the bottom of this for now.'

'Why was she staying at the hotel? Erica asked, moving the story along. 'Where was her father? Didn't he care about her?'

'I don't know about her dad, but her step-father had been up to see her earlier that evening. He was quite high up in the police force. When he saw us talking to her, he warned us to stay away from her. Of course, then we wanted her just to piss him off. She was well up for it too. She didn't seem to like him very much. Said he was getting too over-protective since her mum died. She said that he was making a massive effort to look after her and kept going on about how he'd promised her mother that he would keep an eye on her when she was gone. She felt he was taking it too far. So she'd decided get a room at the hotel and go solo for a while. Anyway, when she came up to our party looking for drugs, she had a friend with her. A young lad that she went to the university with.'

I asked a niggling question, already suspecting the answer, 'His name wouldn't happen to be James by any chance, would it?'

'Yeah, how did you know?' Kane asked.

'He was my roommate at that university. I'd suspected that he was involved for some time.'

Alex and I nodded at each other, confirming the suspicions that I'd shared with him this afternoon.

Kane continued, 'Well, basically, this lad, James, really liked her. You could tell right off. She was going wild, but he was trying to be respectful and trying to get her to stop, but the prospect of finally getting with her so easily after years of trying, blew his morals out of the window. We decided to take him under our wing, you could say. Which we don't do often, but we could see he needed to learn a few life lessons. We hooked him up with some "courage" and gave him a *turn* with Janice.'

Ingrid made a noise to signal her disgust at this, but Kane continued.

'He'd confessed to being a virgin who didn't drink or take drugs. It's brilliant how the lust for a woman can blur a person's morals. He left there a better man thanks to us.'

'Did you know him afterwards?' I asked.

'Well…no!' Kane said.

'Then how can you say he left there a "better" man. He might have been different to you, but you changed him for the worse. He was on the verge of becoming a successful business man. The women would have come anyway as soon as that happened. After that hotel fire he wasn't the same. He was distant for a few days, but then he became over-confident. Cocky! He'd lost all respect for women and for himself. It wasn't long after, that he ran off to America. I'd always suspected he'd ran off out of guilt.'

'He went to America!' Kane said. 'No wonder we could never find him. What's he doing there?'

'He's running a successful restaurant over there.'

'So he *did* become successful, anyway. How do you know that what happened that night wasn't the reason he was able to do all that? We could have been the ones that turned his fortunes around.'

'He was a smart kid. He'd have done it anyway, *without* your help.

Urgh. You make me sick. You just go around ruining lives. I bet you've always been the same.'

'You don't know anything about me!' he shouted.

'I bet I can guess,' I shouted back.

'Calm down you two,' Seth boomed. 'We're here for the truth. To try and get to the bottom of this. Not to cause more problems. Let him tell his story, Ian.'

'Fine,' I agreed.

'Right,' Kane started. 'As I was saying, we met this girl at a party we were having…'

I cut him off, 'Yeah, yeah! We know. Her step-dad warned you off her, you passed her around, did some drugs, corrupted my friend and God knows what else. I'm sure all that's a story for another day. Just tell us how all of that led to her being stuffed in the roof of my building?'

'I don't know that, but what I do know, I'll tell you. I was the first to wake up a little later that night…'

#

Kane awoke on the sofa of room 5D. Janice was still asleep on top of him. His body had gone numb with the dead weight of her. He looked at her silent face. She was stunning. The fact that someone so pretty had turned out this way was sad, but Kane wasn't going to complain. He'd never get to sleep with a girl of her stature in a million years under normal circumstances.

Kane craned his neck to look around the room. Alan, fast asleep in the chair opposite him, was snoring loudly. He was a mostly bald man of average height and build with a big beer belly rising up and down, dramatically, with every breath.

Jack lay passed out on the floor with a rubber band wrapped around his arm and a stray syringe next to him. He was definitely the worst drug user of the group. He didn't help himself though. With the state he was in, if the cops raided this place, he'd be caught red handed, but there was no getting through to him. Kane and his mates had warned him on plenty of occasions.

No sign of Derek or Paul, which was odd. They usually all crashed in the same room together at the end of the night. Their new young friend was here though. Well, in a fashion. Kane chuckled to himself as he saw James, sprawled over the entrance to the hotel room, on his stomach, with his head out into the corridor, resting in a pool of his own vomit. Kane didn't panic as he could see, from the bubbles forming in the liquid, that he was still breathing.

'Lightweight,' Kane said to himself.

Kane suddenly felt Janice drool onto the side of his face.

'Ew,' he shouted. 'Get off me, you minger!'

Janice did not wake up. Not wanting to touch the saliva with his hand, he wiped his cheek on the shoulder of her white top. The red smear showed him that this was in fact...blood. He panicked, quickly slid from underneath her and got to his feet. He looked at Janice, who now lay face down on the sofa. All he could see of the screwdriver lodged into the back of her skull was the blue handle.

'Oh shit,' he said to himself, quietly.

Then he noticed that she was tightly grasping a fistful of long ginger hair.

'Guys! Wake up,' he shouted, moving around the room trying to shake the others awake. He was unsuccessful with James and although Jack *did* wake up, he was too out of it to realise what was happening. Alan, however, *did* wake and joined Kane in shock as the pair looked at Janice's mutilated body.

'What happened?' Alan asked.

'I have no idea. I just woke up and found her like this,' Kane replied.

'What's going on? Is it...my turn,' Jack asked, dazed.

'Get with it, Jack,' Alan said slapping him hard across the face,'

'Ouch! You do that for?' slurred Jack.

'Janice is dead. Do you know anything about this?'

'What? She's dead?'

Jack begun to panic and cry. He was a coward when it came to gritty stuff and this was one of the grittiest the group had ever come across.

'Pull yourself together, Jack,' Alan boomed at him. 'We need to figure out what we're going to do. Kane, wake the kid up.'

Kane had another attempt at rousing James. This time he came around. He squinted in disgust at the stench of the sick that he was lying in.

'Hey, kid! We've got a problem!' Kane told him.

'What?' he replied, but didn't need an answer when he spotted Janice. 'No!' he screamed.

He scurried over to Janice's body and put his face close to hers.

'Janice! No, no, no, no. What have you done to her?' he screamed at the others.

'We haven't done anything. We just found her like this,' Kane told him.

'Janice!' he cried, grabbing her head and turning it to face him. 'Why did you have to come here? What have I done? I wanted you. I thought it was the only way I could have you, but I never knew it would lead to this. I'm so sorry!' he cried, breaking down and sobbing besides her.

'Does anyone have a clue as to what happened here?' Alan asked.

'I can't remember anything since I last shot up,' Jack confessed.

'OK,' Alan said, looking at a clock on the wall. 'It's ten past three now. We only have a couple of hours until it gets light. What are we going to do?'

'What do you mean what are we going to do?' James asked. 'We need to ring the police.'

'No police! Are you stupid?' Alan shouted. 'I'm not going to prison for murder, or manslaughter, or anything I could get for being near this.'

'Did you murder her?' James shouted.

'No I did not!' Alan stated. 'But what about you? Can you say for sure that *you* didn't murder her?'

'Of course I can. I would never hurt Janice,' James defended.

'How can you be so sure? How much did you have throughout the night? What's the last thing you can even remember?'

James was silent. He couldn't actually remember anything for at least the last four hours.

'In fact. I remember you having a pretty big argument with her.'

'I did?'

'Yes. How are you when you're angry, James? None of us knew you before tonight.'

'Oh God!' James panicked. 'What have I done? I should have never come here. What if I *have* killed her?'

'Calm down,' Alan said. 'No one's saying that. We're saying, none of us can remember. We were all pretty wasted last night.'

'This can't be happening,' Kane said, shoving his head into his hands. 'This is just the excuse Laura needs to get what she wants.'

'Kane! Relax! We'll sort it!' Alan assured.

'Where are the others?' Jack asked.

'I don't know, but that's Derek's screwdriver sticking out the back of her head so I'd really like to know.'

'I'll go get them. They're probably in their rooms,' Kane said.

'I'll come with you,' Alan volunteered. 'You two stay here. Don't let anyone else in.

The two cowards quivered as they looked at each other.

'Derek!' Kane shouted, now out on the fifth floor corridor, banging on 5B.

'Paul!' Alan shouted, banging on 5A.

Paul answered fairly quickly. He was missing a large section of his long ginger hair and there were scratch marks down his face that had started to crust over.

'What happened to you, man?' Alan asked.

'I just woke with a killer headache and this,' Paul said pointing at the scratches. 'I think someone must have scratched me. I hurts like hell. And look at the state of my hair. I'm gonna have to shave it now. Years of growing it, down the tubes.'

'Shut up, Paul!' Alan snapped. 'Listen here, something's happened.'

'I think I might know where your hair is,' Kane said.

'What?' said the other two in unison.

Kane walked back to the crime scene and the other two followed.

'Holy shit!' exclaimed Paul when he set eyes on Janice's corpse. 'What happened?'

'Maybe *you* can tell us!' said Kane, pointing to the lock of Paul's hair, firmly clamped in her hand.

'I have no idea how this happened. I don't remember her even scratching me.'

'Well something clearly went down, here!'

'Something's not right,' Alan pondered.

'Alan?' said Jack.

'It looks too staged.'

'What do you mean?' Paul asked.

'Just a feeling.'

'Well that's Derek's screwdriver!' Paul said, pointing at the murder weapon.

'Where is he?' Alan said.

Kane walked back out into the corridor and banged on 5B yet again.

'Derek! You in there?' he called.

Alan joined him out in the corridor.

'Where is he?' Alan asked.

'He's not answering,' Kane replied, trying the door handle to no avail.

'Right! Give me a hand.'

Alan started to shoulder barge into the door. Kane joined him.

'OK. On three,' Alan said.

They counted and barged the door together. It came clean off its hinges and fell to the floor. A startled Derek stood in the room on the other side. Clearly he'd been able to hear their calls, but was ignoring them. The three of them just stared at each other. Alan and Kane looked around the room. It was, unusually for Derek, spotless. Clutter free and smelling fresh. On the sofa was a nearly packed suitcase.

'Going somewhere?' Alan asked.

'Oh shit!' replied Derek.

'What are you doing?' Kane asked.

'I'm getting out of Dodge,' he said, now ignoring them and continuing to pack. 'I take it you've seen the dead girl in your room?'

'Yes! We also saw that *your* screwdriver is what killed her,' Alan stated.

'Yeah! That looks bad! I know.'

'You're erasing any evidence that you were ever here. Aren't you?'

'Damn straight! I walked in there earlier. Saw what I saw and now I'm gone. You guys should do the same.'

'No, Derek! We need to sort this out, together.'

'Like shit! See you later.'

Derek grabbed his case and scurried out of the room and through the stairwell door.

'Derek!' Alan called after him as he disappeared from view. 'That son of a bitch!'

'What are we going to do,' Kane said, panicking again. 'This is a right mess! Maybe James is right. We should call the police. Let them figure it out.'

'You do that, you lose Lisa forever. Look, Kane. You're one of my best friends. You helped me out big time when my kid was born. And now I want to help you out with yours. Get out of here.'

'What?'

'Get out of here. You can't be anywhere near this. If Laura finds out, that's it! You're finished!'

'Are you serious?'

'I'll explain to the others. You just get out of here.'

'I don't know what to say.'

'Just go. Don't ever mention this again. We'll deal with it. Don't ask how.'

Kane hesitated, but thought of Lisa. He turned tail and left the fifth floor. Leaving behind everything but the clothes on his back, he ran down the stairwell and left the hotel.

#

'So you don't even know what actually happened here?' Natalie asked.

'Not really!' Kane confirmed.

'Well that was a colossal waste of our time then, wasn't it!' Erica stated.

'And we still don't know who killed that girl,' Seth said.

'Clearly it was me or one of my friends,' Kane said. 'But I couldn't even begin to guess who. We were all so out of it!'

'What did you do for my dad when I was born?' Alex asked.

'I...' Kane started.

Alex changed his mind, 'You know what! I don't want to know. I made a conscious decision not to learn about my dad. And I'm starting to see that was a good choice.'

'Why would it have been bad for you to stay and help them?' I asked Kane.

'Because of my daughter,' Kane revealed.

'Your daughter?' said Natalie, Erica and Ingrid, simultaneously, gobsmacked.

'My ex-girlfriend Laura was trying to keep me from seeing her. I had to keep out of trouble. One wrong move and they would have had me. Not that it mattered in the end anyway. The judge made a ruling to grant sole custody to Laura. Completely out of the blue. I wasn't allowed to see her at all.' He turned and spoke directly to me now. 'That's what I was doing in the flats upstairs when your wife caught me. I was looking for something in an old hidey hole we'd used on the several times we'd stayed there. I was looking for something that I'd left behind, but I found a note instead and it pointed me to your flat.'

'So it was you who broke into to my flat all those times?' I surmised.

'All those times?' Kane asked, confused.

'Yes! Three times by my reckoning. You gave me a pretty hard smack on the shoulder. And then one of the times you clubbed me on the head and knocked me out. I could get pretty pissed off at you right now if we weren't dealing with bigger issues.'

'You assaulted him?' Ingrid asked.

'What? No!' Kane assured. 'I only broke in the once. I swear. I never even saw you.'

'Why should I believe you?' I accused.

'Why would I admit to one and not the others?'

'That's true,' I said, thinking.

'So let me get this straight,' Natalie confirmed. 'You were burgled three times. Once by Kane, who you never saw. And twice by someone else who attacked you,'

'That's sounds about right!' I agreed.

'It would have been nice to know that when we moved in.'

I looked around at my group of increasingly confused tenants. They were actually coming in handy. Brainstorming all of the things I did not have control of, or even understand, was helping. At least they served some useful purpose.

'Anyway,' Kane said, continuing his story. 'I didn't even find what I was looking for. I'd followed the letter exactly and all I found under the floorboards was a pile of junk I didn't understand. Some documents and something in a box.'

'Did you…look through them?' I asked, worried.

'I did, but I didn't understand them. Were they yours?'

'I think I'm beginning to understand what's happened now.'

'At least somebody does,' Erica said, flabbergasted. 'Are you going to fill the rest of us in?'

'I was hiding something very important in my flat.'

'What was it?' Alex asked.

'*That* is not important,' I stressed. 'Anyway, the first break in I interrupted. I caught the burglar attempting to break into my locked cupboard. They smacked me on the arm and ran off. I was worried about the safety of my secret, so I decided to move the contents of the cupboard. I found a loose floorboard in my bedroom and hid it under that. The second break-in happened only days later. I was bashed on the head inside my flat. When I came to, my cupboard *had* been broken into this time. Luckily for me I'd moved the items to a safe place, outsmarting my attacker.

Erica realised something, 'You told me that you'd only had some jewellery stolen when you had come round to get your cut cleaned up.'

'Yeah. I'm sorry about that. I didn't want to get into it there and then.'

'You lied to me, Ian. Why?'

'Look! Can we discuss that later?'

Erica huffed into a sulk. I was clearly in her bad books now. It would take some work to build back those bridges.

I continued with the story, 'Anyway. As you just heard. I went to Erica's flat to get my cut cleaned and then, when I got back, I had been burgled again! I came home to find the floorboard up and my secret out for all to see. So, I'm guessing that was you then?' I said, looking at Kane.

'Yes. Sorry!' he replied.

'So are you going to tell us this secret of yours?' Alex asked.

'No,' I replied.

'Well, how about I just go under the floorboard and see it for myself?'

'You can't. I've moved it now.'

'Well this all seems very fair!' Alex ranted. 'You've brought us all in here for complete "transparency", and yet, you're refusing to share your own secrets.'

'He's got a point!' Erica agreed, obviously still angry that I'd lied to her.

'Look!' Kane said. 'I really am sorry I went through your stuff. It's just, the note I got led me to believe it would be really important. I couldn't risk not knowing.'

'Well!' I relented. 'Lucky for you I did find something under the floorboard before I claimed the space as my own.'

'You did?' Kane said excitedly. 'What was it? Where is it?'

'I'll let you see for yourself.' I stood before remembering something. 'Oh!'

'What's wrong?'

'It's in my cabinet in my bedroom. Where Layla is. I can't go in there.'

'I'll go!' said Tony, and he jumped up and left the flat before anyone could say anything.

'I'd forgotten that young man was even here.' Ingrid said.

'Me too,' said Natalie. 'He's very quiet.'

'He's gonna die!' said Alex, shocking the room.

We all stared at him.

'What?' he shrugged. 'Everyone knows that the non-descript, unimportant characters, always die in these sorts of movies.'

'Shut up about movies, Alex.' Natalie snapped. 'This is real life.'

'Fine, but when he turns up dead, you'll be...'

'Got it!' interrupted Tony as he re-entered the room. 'One teddy bear and one photo,' he said, tossing the bear to Kane.

'George!' he shouted

'George?' asked Natalie.

'It's my daughter's favourite teddy. She loved this bear. I wonder why it's here.'

'Weren't you scared about the killer?' Natalie asked Tony.

Tony was silent for a moment before responding, 'Oh shit. I'd forgotten about that.'

Everyone stared at him in disbelief.

'Yeah! He *is* that stupid,' Kane confirmed.

'Check the note!' I told Kane.

'Note?' he replied.

'Around the bear's neck.'

Kane found the envelope and quickly removed the note to find the heart-warming crayoned message I'd already read.

'I love you daddy. I miss you,' Kane read out aloud.

Something I never thought I would see, happened. Kane began to cry.

'That's so cute,' Natalie said, shedding a tear of her own.

'It's nice to see you have a soft side,' Ingrid said, beaming.

'I can't believe Lisa sent me this,' Kane said, wiping away tears. 'Alan must have got this without Laura ever knowing. She would never have allowed it.'

'I wonder what this photo is about?' Tony wondered.

'Gimme that!' Kane demanded, snatching the photo.

He read out the message on the back, first, 'This should be all the evidence you need, mate. Good luck! Alan.'

'Dad?' Alex called out.

Kane turned and looked at the photo. A huge grin spread across his face. Natalie caught a glimpse of the photo of the young woman and the old man kissing.

'Ew!' she snorted. 'That's disgusting. He looks old enough to be her granddad. Who is she?'

'That...' Kane said, unable to contain his excitement, 'is Laura. My ex-girlfriend. The mother of my beautiful daughter, the one important thing in my life. And that old man she's with...well...that is none other than the judge who ruled in Laura's favour. Now I see how she got her way!'

'Well, that horrible old man!' Ingrid said.

'Just goes to show that you can't trust our justice system,' Seth added.

'This changes everything,' Kane said, standing. 'My whole life was Lisa,' he continued, overjoyed. 'With this, I can get her back. This proves that the judge was corrupt. Laura obviously seduced him and got him to give her what she wanted...Lisa, all to herself. I need to turn my life around. I need to start now. Come on Tony,' he said, heading for the door.

'Where are we going?' Tony asked.

'Back to my flat!'

'But I was just about to tell everyone my big secret. Once, I was in this car park and...'

'No one cares about that. Come on!'

'You can't go back to your flat on your own. It's not safe,' Alex shouted.

'Tony'll be with me,' Kane assured him. 'We'll look out for each other, don't worry. I need to do this. I'm gonna clean up my act. I'm gonna flush all my drugs. You're gonna see a new me,' he finished as he skipped out of the flat.

'Wait!' panicked Tony, getting up to follow him. 'All of them?' he said, anxiously as he chased after him.

'They shouldn't be on their own,' Alex insisted. 'Never split up like they do in the movies.'

'They'll be fine!' I said.

'Famous last words!'

'I'm having that seat then,' Erica said, standing with a fast asleep baby Isaac in her arms. 'My back's killing me from being sat down there.

Alex, who was sitting on the floor next to the sofa made some pathetic excuse to move. He clearly still suspected Erica.

'Well,' I said, 'I suppose that's enough revelations for one day.'

'I have one more,' Natalie revealed.

'What?' I said!

'Natalie! Don't!' Alex said.

'We have to tell them Alex!' Natalie pleaded, getting very upset.

'What is it?' Erica asked.

'It's nothing,' Alex said, quickly jumping in. 'I don't think we need to worry anyone further.'

Ingrid spoke up, 'It's clearly not nothing, not with how upset your young lady is! Let her speak.'

'Natalie!' Alex said. 'Are you sure about this?'

'Yes!' she insisted. 'I just can't stop thinking that this has something to do with us all sharing a past!'

'What do you mean?' Seth asked.

'When we were younger we did something bad!'

'Are you sure you want to re-live the past?' Alex warned.

'Yes! We might as well now! You've been dying to come clean for the last ten years. I know you only kept quiet because you knew how scared I was.'

'Yes, but now with everything that we've learned. I don't think that this is the right time.'

'It's the perfect time! I honestly think that this is why we're under attack.'

'It's not why!' Alex insisted. 'It's probably got something to do with what we just heard from Kane. It might be Janice Todd's stepfather, come to get revenge on what Kane and them lot did to her.'

'If that was the case, why would he kill his wife,' she said, pointing at me, 'and her boyfriend,' pointing at Erica, 'and nearly you?' she finished, pointing at Alex's bandaged leg.

'OK fine, not that, but maybe it's to do with this big secret that Ian's keeping!'

'It's not that!' I said.

'How do we know that?' Alex re-iterated.

'It's this, Alex!' Natalie asserted. 'Our secret. I know it is! We need to tell them.'

'Natalie!'

'It's time, Alex.'

'Tell us your story, dear,' Ingrid encouraged.

Natalie took a deep breath and began to speak, 'It was ten years ago. Alex and I were only fifteen. After school, we would sometimes head up to the quarry to get drunk. It was the best place to go without getting caught. But what we saw, we never expected...'

Chapter 28 – Ten Years Ago

'Try this one, Alex,' offered Natalie.

She handed him a can of beer. She got excited whenever she tried a new one. She'd been drinking for well over a year now and was becoming quite experienced with alcohol. She was already turning into a young woman and could handle it, no problem. Alex, on the other hand, wasn't doing so well.

'Oh, er, thanks,' he replied, his voice still unbroken.

He took the drink and begrudgingly had a sip. He had only just started drinking himself. With his new girlfriend Natalie being such an experienced drinker, he wanted to try to look cool in front of her. However, he groaned and held his stomach after a few more gulps.

'What's wrong?' she asked.

'I think I've had enough,' he said, defeated.

'Again? You're such a lightweight. You'll get used to it if you keep drinking.'

Pressured, he continued to sup the liquid that he didn't even like. He tried to absorb himself in the view to take his mind off it. The town of Bretton opened out in front of them. The evening was just settling in and the sun was disappearing into the horizon. The barren quarry's brown foliage looked dusty in the dusk July light. The pair were leaning back against the quarry face. It was so steep that they were almost upright, their bottoms firmly planted on a natural shelf. Greenish weeds poked up through the quarry ground where they sat.

Natalie checked her phone to see a few missed calls from her parents. They clearly worried about her, but had got used to her absenting herself after school. Alex checked his phone also, but there was nothing. His mum probably didn't even know he wasn't home. Her most recent boyfriend has just ended things with her and she had no doubt spiralled back into her routine of getting drunk and falling asleep on the sofa.

The public footpath, which they had strayed from to get here, went steeply down the banking from the top, where there was a small village, to the bottom, where the main town was. The path was a fair distance from them now, but they could just about make out some people returning to the village with their shopping, and some others heading out into town for the night.

'Should we do some revision whilst we're here?' Alex suggested.

'Don't be such a geek, Alex. Just enjoy the drink,' she replied, before swigging another huge mouthful.

Alex looked over at their bags, dumped on top of each other a short way away and thought about the vast amount of homework he'd allowed to pile up.

'Oh crap!' Natalie exclaimed, looking at the mucky marks that the quarry dirt had left on her clothes. 'My mother's gonna kill me,' she said, trying to brush dirt from her shirt.

Natalie stood up and dusted herself down. Alex watched her longingly in her white school shirt and grey skirt, dusting down her beautiful body; her long slender legs emerging from her skirt. He'd always fancied her, and couldn't believe that she was actually his girlfriend now. It still seemed surreal to him, but she must have liked him too. Being the rebel that she was, she never wore the school tie that Alex still had around his buttoned up shirt collar. *Her* top couple of buttons on the other hand, were undone.

Her gaze settled on his as she caught him staring at her. He quickly looked away and pretended to brush down his matching white shirt and grey trousers.

'Were you staring at me, Alex?' she asked, coyly.

'No, no! I was just, er, making sure you'd got all the dirt off,' he stammered.

'You're cute!' she said, laughing and sitting down next to him.

'Drink your beer.'

'Why do you want me to drink it so badly?'

'Because it'll give you courage.'

'Courage for what?'

'This!'

Natalie straddled him and began passionately kissing him. Even though they had been going out a couple of months, this was their first "real" kiss. It caught him off guard. He'd never had a passionate kiss with anyone before and had no idea what to do with himself or where to put his hands. He felt completely awkward, but he didn't want to mess it up.

'Do you mind?' came a man's voice causing Natalie to remove herself, hastily from Alex, who was gutted, but somewhat relieved at the same time. It gave him the chance to prepare himself for when she, hopefully, tried again.

'What's wrong?' Natalie asked, spotting a man and his young son, who clutched a kite close to his chest to hide himself.

'Well,' the man started, 'it's just not something I want my son seeing when we are out for a leisurely stroll.'

Natalie stared at the man and his son for a moment. The man, who was in his forties, had a bald head and large ears, but a very jolly smile in contrast to the rest of his mean-looking features. He was quite short, but evenly proportioned and was wearing a brown leather jacket and light denim jeans. His son was short too and very skinny. He was wearing a football shirt and shorts, with white trainers. A small tuft of his blond hair sticking up in a clump at the front. He was young, probably not quite into his teens yet.

'What's the matter?' Natalie asked. 'He'll be up to this sort of thing in a few years himself.'

'Perhaps,' the man chuckled. 'But I'd say you two are too young for that sort of thing yourselves. Anyway, we are just passing through, but, something to think about. We'll get out of your way.'

The son was shy and stayed very close to his dad, and, as they walked away, wouldn't let go of his hand. They walked deeper into the quarry. The terrain began to flatten out further in onto a large open area at the far end. They would be coming back this way any moment, no doubt, Natalie laughed to herself. The only thing over there is a very steep drop to the bottom, so they would be back along this route again when they realised it was a dead end. You'd think they would have spotted the large "Danger!" sign at the end of the dusty trail warning people of the drop. But she soon realised that they were not lost when they began to fly the kite in the large open area.

'Bollocks!' Natalie said.

'What's wrong?' Alex asked.

'They could be there ages.'

'So!' Alex said, not sure what she was getting at.

'Well, I was hoping we could, you know!'

Alex worried about her sexual experience and his own deficiency in that area.

'Oh sod it!' she said, climbing back on top of him.

'We can't here!' said Alex, panicking, but still yearning for her.

'It's fine! They won't hear us!' said Natalie, starting to unbutton his shirt.

'Not too near the edge, son! Come back this way!' they heard the man shout from over the rise.

'You were saying?' Alex chuckled.

Determined not to give up, she scanned the area.

'Come with me,' she said getting to her feet and taking Alex's hand.

They picked up their bags and Natalie led them a short way down the steep embankment to a circle of shrubbery. There was a secluded clearing in the centre. They dumped their bags on the floor and she pulled Alex down on top of her. This time Alex felt a lot more comfortable as their tongues darted between each other's lips and explored each other's mouths. The privacy gave Alex a lot more confidence.

They'd barely got started when Alex heard the dreaded sound of another presence. Of course this was never going to happen for him. Something would always ruin it. The pair knelt up and peered over the shrubbery to see a man in a black hoodie move along the trail that they had just abandoned. He had its hands in the pouch pocket at the front of his hoodie as he walked with purpose towards the same open area as the father and son. They let him pass before returning to more important things.

This was another short experience as the pair were interrupted again by shouting coming from the direction of the dad, his son and this third man.

'What do you think they're arguing about?' Natalie asked.

'I dunno! Let's go see if everything's OK,' Alex suggested, getting to his feet.

'What? Sod that. Leave em to it.'

'They might be in trouble. I'll go. You wait here.'

Alex stepped out of the clearing and cautiously crept in the direction of the disturbance. He dipped behind the large sign; not too close as to be seen, but close enough to just about hear them. He only caught a snippet of what they were saying before he was disturbed.

'Well?' said Natalie, making him jump as she snuck behind the sign with him.

'Jesus, Natalie!' Alex exclaimed.

'And you seemed so brave a few seconds ago. What are they saying?'

'If you keep quiet, I might be able to hear them!'

The pair sat motionless. Each movement or shuffle was enough to block out the faint voices that they could only just make out. They had to remain very still if they wanted to eavesdrop effectively. The son was still clutching his kite close to his chest. He stood behind his dad, very close, only daring to poke his head out from behind him slightly to watch the third person, who had his back to the young couple. There was a lot of aggressive pointing going on from both the dad and the other man. Alex resorted to holding his breath so that he was able to hear what they were arguing about.

'I've already told him! The conversation is over!' insisted the dad.

The other man replied, '*He* doesn't seem to think that it's over! He wants what is rightfully his!'

On this, the other man lowered the hood on his hoodie, perhaps to appear more intimidating.

#

'It was Kane!' Alex blurted out, interrupting Natalie's account of the story.

'Alex!' she snapped. '*I'm* telling the story.'

'You mean it was the drug dealer that lives with us?' Ingrid responded to Alex's outburst.

'Yes!' said Natalie, reclaiming the story.

'What was he doing there?' she asked...

#

The dad continued his defence in this verbal war, 'I've told him numerous times. It's my creation. I will do with it as I see fit.'

'*He* says that you worked on it together,' Kane informed him.

'Well we didn't, I made it alone. I toiled over it night and day, whilst he messed around with his computer and flirted with the cleaner, who, I might add, was far too young for him.'

'*He* says that he *was* involved. He also said that it will make you both very rich men.'

'As I told him, it isn't all about money. I don't want to sell yet. Anyway, I don't know why I'm discussing this with a stranger. I am trying to have a quiet evening with my son. Please leave us alone and tell him that I will discuss it with him at work, tomorrow.'

'I know you've got it on you.'

'What makes you think that?' replied the dad, worried.

'It's in your inside jacket pocket. I know that it goes everywhere with you.'

'Have you been watching me?' said the dad, suspiciously.

'I'll ask you one last time,' Kane said, calmly producing a gun. 'Hand over the invention and I won't kill you.'

'What!' the dad shouted, beginning to panic. 'OK, this is getting way out of hand. I can't believe my partner, my friend, would send you to kill me.'

'He told me to get it by *any* means necessary. Look, mister, I don't care about any of this. As long as I deliver it, I get paid. So hand it over!'

'Dad, I'm scared!' said the son who was beginning to quiver behind his father now.

'It's OK, son, go stand over there,' said the dad, pointing towards a safer location. 'Please, you're scaring my son.'

'Then just hand it over,' Kane demanded.

'Listen,' the dad said, trying to calm the situation. 'He and I have worked together a long time. I never said I won't share the pay-out with him. We're a team. Regardless of his non-existent involvement on the project, I will still split the profit with him, I'm just not ready to sell yet. Tell him to be patient.'

'I don't have time for this,' Kane paused, waiting for any indication that the dad would give in to his demands. It did not come. Kane needed the money and wasn't ready to listen anymore. 'Fine! Have it your way.'

Kane lunged at the dad and they both fell onto the dusty ground. Kane rolled the man onto his back and was reaching inside his jacket pockets in an attempt to take the bounty by force. They continued to wrestle as the dad tried to fight off Kane's attacks. The son was screaming at Kane, begging him to stop, but this simply fell on deaf ears. Alex and Natalie watched intently as the fight unfolded before them. Natalie gasped in horror as they rolled close to the cliff's edge. Alex was about to intervene, but cringed as he worried he was too late. Luckily the pair managed to find their footing and both scrambled to their feet, the dad with his back dangerously close to the cliffs edge, and Kane standing opposite him with the gun firmly trained on him.

'I have to do something,' Alex whispered, urgently to Natalie.

'No, stay here. We need to hide,' said Natalie, cravenly.

'But he's going to *shoot* him,' Alex pleaded with her as she grabbed him by the arm to stop him from leaving her side.

'Enough games!' said Kane, loudly. 'Hand it over. Now! Or I *will* kill you!' he said, with such menace that the onlookers felt themselves holding their breath.

The dad pondered on his relationship with his friend and quietly resisted again, 'I know that he wouldn't ask you to go that far.'

Kane matched his quiet tone, 'I just want my money. I don't care how I get it.' There was a long pause between the two of them after this calmer exchange. But Kane's anger soon got the better of him,

'Fine. You had your chance,' he snapped, aiming the gun squarely at his chest.

Alex plucked up the courage, and with one swift movement, broke free of Natalie's restraining grasp. He darted towards Kane and leapt up onto his back, wrapping one arm around Kane's gun arm to immobilise it and raining a barrage of punches down on him with his free hand. Kane swung him from left to right, violently, in an attempt to shake him off, all the while swearing and threatening him. Alex yelled at the dad to run away, but instead of fleeing, was telling Kane to let the young hero go. Kane ignored him managed to land a punch to the side of Alex's head. Kane himself had lost his bearing with all the spinning. He flung a dazed Alex over his shoulder accidently into the dad, who in turn stumbled over the cliffs edge with a terrifyingly long scream.

'No!' yelled the son, who ran to the edge of the cliff to peer over at his father.

'What have you done?' Kane screamed at Alex.

'Oh my God!' panicked Alex. 'I didn't mean for that to happen.'

The son began to cry and then dashed back towards the part of the cliff which was less steep to make his way down to the bottom. Kane panicked and made a grab for him, missing him by inches. He chased after him, but stopped in his tracks when he heard the sound of a female voice.

'I need an ambulance quick. Someone has fallen off the cliff at Bretton Quarry,' Natalie stammered into her phone.

Kane snatched the phone from her and ended the call. He grabbed her by the scruff of the neck and pulled her out from behind the sign.

'Who are you? What are you doing here?' Kane demanded of her.

'That's my girlfriend,' answered Alex from afar, still a little dazed. 'Please leave her out of this!'

'Right!' Kane snapped, collecting himself. 'You two! To the bottom of the cliff. Now!'

Kane aimed his gun at the pair who held their hands in the air as their captor directed them down the slope to the bottom of the cliff.

'You'd better hope he's still alive!' Kane warned Alex.

Kane spotted their bags on the way down the slope.

'They yours?' he asked.

'Yes,' said Natalie, quietly.

'Bring them with you,' he ordered and they obeyed.

They turned a bend at the bottom of the slope, and found themselves by the vertical cliff face that now loomed high above them. Their worst fears realised; at the bottom of the cliff, with his son, crouched, crying over him, was the loving father, face down in the dirt.

Alex froze in shock at the sight, causing Kane to walk into his back.

'No point getting soft now,' Kane advised. 'You should have thought of the consequences of what you were doing.'

They all heard the sound of a distant siren getting closer to the quarry. Kane began to panic.'

'You were saying?' quipped Natalie.

'Shut up, you!' snapped Kane, striking her across the face.

He pushed the young couple to the ground and told them not to move. Alex held Natalie close, holding her cheek where she'd been hit. Kane ran over to the father and cast the boy aside without a moment's thought. He rolled the motionless dad onto his back and began to rummage through his pockets. By this point the son had got back to his feet and was raining feeble punches and kicks at Kane, which he simply ignored. He eventually removed a small, unmarked, brown box from one of the man's inside jacket pockets, slid it open and peered into it. Satisfied that this was what his client wanted, he closed it and put it inside his own pocket.

Kane heard the sound of a car pulling up. The sirens stopped, but the whole area was filled with flashing blue lights. He grabbed the boy, who was still kicking him, and threw him at the young couple's feet.

'Keep him there,' Kane ordered, giving them a flourish of his gun to remind them who was in charge.

He quickly concealed it when as a young female paramedic came rushing onto the scene.

#

'It was your wife,' Natalie explained to me, breaking the narrative of her story. 'That's where I recognised her from.'

'My wife?' I replied, solemnly wiping my eyes.

'Yes,' Alex joined in. 'We never thought in a million years we would see her again.'

'Why didn't you say anything sooner?' I asked, still shaken from the story so far.

'It was ten years ago. You must understand *I* would have never recognised her if Natalie hadn't. And it's not like we knew her well or anything.'

'I always did wonder what she was like before I met her.'

'A decade has been kind to her,' said Natalie. 'She was as pretty then as she is now. She seemed really confident in her job, well, at first.'

'At first?' I asked. 'What happened next?'

#

Oblivious of the others, Layla made straight for the casualty before her. She dumped her equipment down next to him. Her I.D. badge swung wildly around her neck with her fast movements. She was wearing a plain black top and green paramedic trousers which were held up by braces. Kane and Alex began to panic as Layla checked the man's breathing and felt for a pulse.

'What happened here?' she asked, still not looking at anyone else and attempting to resuscitate the patient.

'Is he dead?' asked Kane, moving uncomfortably close to Layla.

Clearly not appreciating what she had walked into, Layla responded, again without lifting her eyes, 'Step back please and tell me what's happened.'

'He's dead, isn't he?' Kane declared.

There was a pause as Kane quickly tried to think of a way out of this. He made a rash decision, revealed his weapon and pointed it at Layla.

'Right, stop that!' he ordered her.

'Oh my God!' Layla panicked as she stared at the gun. 'What are you doing?' she asked.

'Get away from him!'

'I need to keep trying to resuscitate him until the Ambulance and the police arrive.'

'Police?' Kane panicked again. 'Right. You,' he said to Layla. 'Sit down over there with the other two. Now!'

Too scared to move, Layla stayed frozen by her charge, now certainly dead. An impatient Kane grabbed her and dragged her across the ground, dumping her with a panicked Natalie, a solemn Alex and a heartbroken young boy.

'Right, he's dead!' Kane announced as he stood in front of this small audience. 'Nothing we can do about it now, so we have to get our stories straight. This was an accident, got it?'

'No, it wasn't,' said Alex, springing to life. 'This is *your* fault.'

'I was only trying to scare him. He fell because you knocked into him.'

'I was trying to *save* him.'

A scared Layla butted in, 'OK, I don't know what's happened, but you all just need to calm down and explain everything to the police when they arrive.'

'That's not going to happen,' said Kane, confidently.

He grabbed Layla's I.D. badge and studied it.

'What are you doing?' she said, worryingly.

'Paramedic Layla Kitson,' Kane read aloud. 'Now I know your name and where you work.'

He removed the I.D. from the holder and put it in his pocket. He walked over to the young couple and grabbed their bags. He emptied them both onto the floor and began rifling through various school books and bits of paper there until he found what he needed. He ripped the important information from the books.

'That's names for you two, and the school you go to,' he said, smugly shoving their personal information into his pocket as well.

'What are you doing?' Layla asked again, hoping for some clue to his intentions.

'I'm getting out of here. When the police get here, you're gonna tell them that this man fell. I was never here.'

'We can't do that,' she said, shocked at the prospect.

'Put it this way, if you don't, me and a few of my friends will find you and, well, you'll end up like him,' Kane threatened, pointing at the dead man.

The boy began to sob even louder now, causing Natalie, who'd been attempting to console him, to cry as well.

'She's right!' Alex said, indicating Layla. 'We can't go along with this.

'I think your girlfriend would disagree,' Kane said, indicating Natalie. 'You wouldn't want anything to happen to her, would you?'

At this Kane walked around behind the group and shoved the nozzle of the gun against her temple making her shiver in terror.

'Please don't hurt us,' she screamed. 'We won't say anything, will we Alex?'

'But Natalie, we…' Alex started.

He then realised how upset she was. He placed a comforting arm around her.

'OK,' he agreed. 'We won't say anything.'

'How about you?' Kane asked Layla.

She didn't respond so he headed over to her and dragged her to her knees.

'Did you hear me?' he said, reasserting himself, backed up by the action of shoving his gun under her chin.

'Yes, yes. I promise,' she said, panicking now. 'It was an accident. You were never here,' she reiterated, before dissolving into tears.

'Good!' Kane said, satisfied that he would get away this.

More sirens forced him to pick up his pace, 'I need to get out of here. Just relax and everything will be fine.'

'What about him?' Layla said, indicating the crying child, the one person who would certainly *not* go along with this.

'Just deny everything he says,' Kane said, viciously. 'He's just a kid. No one will believe him over you.'

The sirens grew louder and more blue lights filled the area. Kane had left it too late for comfort. He sprinted deeper into the quarry away from the direction of the vehicles. It didn't take him long to vanish from view into the shrubbery. Layla and Natalie continued to sob whilst Alex stared silently into space. The boy ran back over to his dead father and lay across him, weeping bitterly.

\#

'I'm gonna kill him,' I said, outraged.

I stood and marched for the door.

'Ian, don't!' pleaded Erica, the baby preventing her from stopping me physically.

I allowed her words to stay me.

'Don't do anything rash, Ian,' said Ingrid. 'I know that he isn't the nicest of fellows, but everyone has a bad past. You can tell that he has changed somewhat. And I honestly do believe that he will turn his life around for his daughter.'

'But what he did to Layla! She never deserved that! I wanna hurt him so bad.'

'The killer will probably do that for you,' murmured Alex.

'Alex!' snapped Natalie.

'Well, what are those two thinking going off on their own? We need to all be here, together.'

'If he *had* been in here, *I'd* have killed him,' I said, angrily.

'Seth, are you alright?' Ingrid asked, noticing her husband's quiet demeanour.

'Hm?' he said, clearly in a world of his own.

'What's the matter?' she repeated.

'Oh, er, nothing. I was just concentrating on the story. What happened next?' he asked Natalie.

'Well,' she started, 'the first policeman arrived on his own and it was, yes, you guessed it, your boyfriend,' she said to Erica.

'*Ex*-boyfriend!' she insisted. 'So Lee was there too, was he? All these secrets and lies are really starting to piss me off!'

'Let's just get to the end of this story,' I said. 'Go on, Natalie.'

'OK! So Lee showed up next…'

\#

'Am I the first here?' Officer Lee Wilkinson asked, hesitantly, anxiously surveying the scene.

'Yes,' managed Layla as she dabbed at her tears.

'Are you with the ambulance?'

'No, I'm the first response. The ambulance should be on its way. He was already dead when I arrived.'

Lee walked over to the body and stared at it in shock.

'What happened?' he asked.

Before anyone could attempt to lie, the dead man's son revealed the truth, 'There was a man here. With a gun. It was his fault.'

'What?' said Lee, clearly scared and instilling no confidence whatsoever into the rest of them. 'Where is he?'

'He ran off. He was shouting at those three,' said the child, pointing at the witnesses.

'Are you all OK? Did he hurt you?'

Layla was the first to remember Kane's threat, 'No, no, there was no man. This young couple were out here when they saw him fall off the cliff above.'

'You witnessed him fall?' Lee asked.

'Yes,' said Natalie, joining in, 'he was flying a kite with his kid and he just fell.'

'They're lying!' screamed the young boy. 'There *was* a man here. With a gun!'

'No! There was no one else here,' Layla reiterated.

'Stop it! Stop lying,' pleaded the son, angrily.

'We're not lying,' insisted Natalie again.

'OK,' Lee patronised the boy. 'Something really horrible has happened and you're probably a bit confused. Where do you live? Is your mum home?'

'I don't have a mum,' revealed the boy, piling additional guilt onto Alex and the others.

'Right, well…' Lee said, struggling to think what to do. 'I'll take you with me, but you need to start telling the truth.'

'I *am* telling the truth,' asserted the boy, loudly.

Lee looked at the group at a loss of what to do. He spotted Alex, hitherto silent.

'What about you? You're very quiet?' Lee quizzed.

Alex looked at the group. Seeing his girlfriend upset made him behave out of character. There was a long pause before he gave his lie.

'It's as they say,' he stomached. 'There was no one else here.'

'Liar!' screamed the son.

He began to cry even louder now, pushing past the useless police officer and running away. Lee chased after him and they both disappeared from sight.

'We can't do this! We need to tell the police the truth,' Alex said to the others.

'But that man will find us if we say anything,' said Natalie, still shaking.

'We have to put our trust in the police. They'll help us.'

'The police?' laughed Layla. 'They're not going to help us. Did you see the state of that drippy officer just now? If that's who we have to rely on, then we don't stand a chance.'

'So we're just going deny it ever happened? What about that kid? He just saw his dad die.'

'We can't change that,' said Layla, with a sense of self-preservation. 'But we *can* stop ourselves from being killed.'

'Alex, please. I'm scared!' pleaded Natalie again.

Alex didn't have time to talk the others round as an additional two police cars pulled up at the scene. Several officers climbed out and ran towards them. A few ran towards the body and the rest crowded round the scared liars. Layla gave Alex a look as if to say "follow my lead". Alex decided to remain quiet for fear of letting his conscience defy the others. A few of the police officers were talking to Layla and she lied her way through with ease. A number of other officers began to question Alex and Natalie, but he allowed her to answer most of their inquiries. Alex was concerned at the ease with which she piled on the extra lies to embellish her story.

A door slammed, loudly as a final officer climbed out of one of the police cars. An old plump man, with a large, grey moustache that stretched the width of his face. The epaulettes on his shoulders bore the sign of a higher ranking officer.

'Sergeant!' called one of the officers. 'Looks like an accident. This young couple were up there,' he said, pointing high above his head to the top of the cliff, 'and so was this man who was playing with his son. According to these two, the son lost control of the kite and it nearly blew him over the edge. The old man rushed to help him, but went over the cliff himself.'

'The boy went over too?' questioned the sergeant.

'No, sir. They said he ran off.'

'I see. And you, miss?' the sergeant asked Layla. 'Where is the rest of your team?'

'The ambulance haven't arrived yet,' she said with a shaky voice.

One of the officers brought her something to drink which she swallowed gratefully.

'Correct me if I'm wrong,' began the sergeant, 'but as the first responder, are you not supposed to continue to attempt resuscitation until the main ambulance crew arrive.'

Layla panicked, but quickly found words, 'I am, yes. I'm sorry. I found it too traumatic.'

'Sounds like you're in the wrong job then, sweetheart. Was he like this when you found him?'

'No, he was still conscious when I got here,' she lied. 'I asked him what had happened and he told me how he'd slipped and asked me to make sure we looked after his son.'

'So you heard his dying breath, is that what you're telling me?'

'Yes. I think that's why I couldn't continue working on him. It was awful to see him die. And then the young boy started spouting a load of nonsense about a man with a gun. Said that he shot at him. It's like he just went crazy, as if what he'd seen had traumatised him. The dad lay there and he was trying to get the boy to tell me the truth. He told him that now was not the time for one of his fantasies. That's when he told me what had happened himself.'

The sergeant hummed forcefully. He looked around and continued to survey the scene. His eyes rested on the young couple. Natalie seemed ready to continue her lie some more, but Alex's demeanour caught the sergeant's eye.

'Young man!' he addressed him.

'Yes,' Alex managed.

'Are you OK?'

'Not really,' he replied, soullessly.

'You saw him fall, yes?'

'Yes,' he said with brimming eyes.

'And after this…' the sergeant looked the cliff up and down, 'I'd say…eighty foot fall to his death, he had enough energy to tell you how he fell and to tell his son to stop fantasizing is that correct?'

'Yes, sergeant!' called Natalie.

'Young lady. I wasn't addressing you. Well, young man?'

Alex held his thoughts. He was so shocked at the massive lie that the paramedic had just told. And even more so that his girlfriend could play along so easily. But he saw how scared she was and he wanted to protect her. He decided to back up her story.

'That's what happened, sergeant,' he answered.

'I see,' said the sergeant musing again. 'And where is the man's son now?'

'He ran off. One of the police officers went after him.'

The sergeant turned around and addressed his other officers, 'Who accepted the call first? Whose car is that?' he asked, pointing to the police car which had already been there when this squad arrived.

'Officer Wilkinson, sir,' answered one of the policemen.

'Fantastic!' said the sergeant, sarcastically.

'There he is, sir!' said the officer again as Lee came back to the scene gasping for breath.

'Lee! Where's the boy?' asked the sergeant.

'He gave me the slip, Gordon,' said Lee, between breaths.

'That's Sergeant *Humphrey* to you, boy!' bellowed Gordon, his tone indicating that this was a regular problem with Lee. 'How old was he; did you see where he went?'

'He was about ten or eleven, Sergeant Humphrey. And no, sorry. He was just too fast.'

Gordon spoke very slowly and angrily, 'You mean to tell me, that a small child managed to outrun you? First thing in the morning, you can retake the fitness test.'

'Sorry, sir,' said Lee. 'Anyway. Now that you lot are here, my shift finished half an hour ago. Mind if I clock off?'

Gordon was livid, 'You can go and sit in my car. You're coming back to the station with us.

'What?' said Lee.

'You are the most disgraceful product of the police force I have seen in years. And you need a good kick up the arse about your attitude. Now go and sit in my car.'

The other officers started to laugh.

'You think this is funny, do you?' bellowed Gordon. 'We've got a dead body here. I know it's not something you're used to in Bretton, but it's time for you lot to step it up. Something fishy is going on here,' he said, turning to address the witnesses again. 'We're going to stay here and continue to question you until the ambulance gets here. When that happens, you're all coming back to the station for further questioning.' He turned back to the officers, 'Get another car down here so we can take them back separately. Split these three up and start questioning them now. When the ambulance gets here I need one of you to stay behind with the body. Whoever that is can take Lee's car back to the station later, so make sure you get his keys off him. So, to be clear, we'll take two of the witnesses back to the station with us and when the fourth car gets here they can take the third one. Everyone clear?' he shouted.

'Yes, sir!' The officers called back in unison.

#

We all sat there in silence as we listened intently to Natalie's account. It was extremely hard to hear. We'd all hung on her every word.

Natalie brought her story to a close, 'As the three of us lied to the ambulance crew and police officers, I knew we would have to live with this for the rest of our lives. We lied at the cliff and we lied back at the station. They eventually let us go. I thought Alex would have caved, but when I saw him afterwards I could tell he'd been through Hell having to keep up the lie for so long. Of course, it wasn't only that he felt bad about lying, but he also felt responsible for that man's death. The guilt eventually started to eat away at him. At the time, I was only thinking of myself. I remember thinking I was being punished for sneaking off after school to get drunk. It was stupid to lie. I see that now,' she said, reminiscently as tears collected in her eyes. She managed a final sentence, 'I know what I did was wrong, but I don't want to die here because of something stupid I did as a kid,' she finished, before finally breaking down, burying her face into Alex's chest.

'Oh what an awful tale!' said Ingrid at the conclusion of Natalie's story. 'How peculiar that so many involved ended up living in these flats together?'

'I can't believe how well you remember it!' Alex said to Natalie.

'Do you think Kane knows that you know?' I asked the young couple.

'I don't think so,' Natalie replied, wiping a few of her tears away. 'I thought I recognised him when I first met him, but couldn't place his face. I asked him if we knew each other and he didn't recognise me, so...'

'He knows it was your wife, though,' Alex butted in, only just realising himself. 'I heard them talking about it. I didn't piece it together at the time because they were being secretive, but I see now that they must have been talking about the cliff. The fact that they kept it from me proves that neither Kane, nor your wife, knew that I was actually there myself.'

'Something else I didn't know. Great!' I said sarcastically, but then a thought hit me. 'Wait a minute!'

'What?' asked Alex.

'So you're telling me that Kane realised that my wife was the paramedic from all those years ago?'

'Yes, I presume so. I can't think what else they could have been talking about.'

'What if he did kill her then,' a look of realisation dawned on my face before being masked by the tears I'd produced. 'Did she tell someone maybe? Is that why he did it?'

'I don't think so,' said Alex, in an effort to prevent me jumping to the wrong conclusion. 'Not at the point I heard them talking about it anyway. It seemed her lips had been well and truly sealed.'

'And why would he have killed *her* boyfriend,' Ingrid said, indicating Erica. 'He never even met Kane. In your story you said that he had fled before the policeman had arrived. Is that correct?'

'That's right,' said Alex.

230

'It must have been difficult to keep that a secret all these years,' I said to the sobbing Natalie.

'It was horrible,' she responded. 'I should have let Alex tell some-one, but I was too scared.'

'It's never too late dear,' Ingrid said, magnanimously. 'You can be honest now!'

'She's right,' Natalie said, turning to Alex and composing herself. 'When we get out of here, we should confess everything!'

'Really?' said Alex, pulling her into a hug. 'Oh Natalie, I'm so glad!'

Ingrid happily added another comment, 'I think what's most impressive is how long you kids have been courting. I was wrong about you two.'

Natalie looked adoringly at Alex, 'I think what happened brought us closer together.

Alex returned her loving gaze and stroked her hair, 'I was in such a mess. I wouldn't have got through it without her.'

'No, it's my fault. You wouldn't have been in that state if I had just let you confess like you wanted to.'

'I wonder whatever happened to that poor boy.' Ingrid thought aloud.

'You know what, I've had enough of this!' Erica exploded, unchar-acteristically.

'Erica?' I asked, concerned.

'Me, and my baby have been put at risk, and because of what? All the secrets you lot have kept over the years.'

She stood up and marched with Isaac toward the door.

'Where are you going?' I asked.

'I'm going back to my flat. I'm going to lock myself in and wait until this all blows over.'

'We can't!' I insisted. 'We have to stick together. We need to get to the bottom of this.'

'Get to the bottom of it?' she laughed. 'It's obvious that one of these secrets has come back to haunt you and regardless of why someone is doing this to you lot, it has nothing to do with me. I'm not involved in any of your stories. I'm a target just by being around you and I have a baby to consider.'

231

'How do you know that they're targeting us for any of those reasons? It could be random. Or maybe *you* have a secret that you haven't told us yet?'

'I don't have anything to worry about from my past. I'm going back to my room. You can come and get me if you find a way out of here, other than that, leave me alone.

At this, she stormed out of the door. I attempted to follow her, but she slammed it in my face. I turned to the others.

'I need to make sure she's alright,' I told them.

'Don't, Ian,' Natalie pleaded. 'This is what the killer wants. For us to split up.'

'I know. But Erica isn't thinking straight. I have to go to her. Look, she's on her own now. If I go to her, at least we're a team of two. Kane has *his* friend, so just make sure that you four stick together and we should be OK.'

I gave one final look at them before peering out of the corridor and checking. Then, I rushed over and knocked on Erica's door. I heard Natalie shout to me again as I left, but I had to leave them. Erica couldn't be alone.

Chapter 29 – A Mistake

'As the night set in, my story comes to a close,' I said to the audience, who had remained still and silent throughout the closing chapters of my tale.

This shallow crowd had been waiting to get to the nitty-gritty. Some of them were literally on the edges of their seats. They knew enough about the story to know what came next. But they wanted to hear it directly from me.

'Everyone had more or less paired off by this point,' I continued. 'Kane and his friend were in his flat, Erica and I were in her flat, no one had any idea where Roger had got to, and the old couple and the young ones had stuck together. This wouldn't last however and the foursome would become another two pairs very shortly. And it was when they divided, that they all became very vulnerable. Erica was getting tired and she didn't want to disturb Isaac. She just wanted the night to be over.'

I glanced at my audience yet again. They were so focussed. So intent. I'd just told them that I was reaching the end of my story; that it was nearly over, however, knowing how my story ends, they knew that before I reached the conclusion...another four of us would be dead.

Chapter 30 – Separation

Ingrid stood at the doorway and watched as Ian left their flat.

'It's just the four of us then,' Ingrid said, despairingly. 'I hope you can keep us safe young man,' she said to Alex.

'We will keep each other safe,' he replied.

'And what do you expect *me* to do? What will I do if that perverted, crazy old man comes in here? One look at a glamorous slip of a thing like me and there'll be no stopping him.' A crack of thunder made Ingrid jump, 'Just look at that rain. I can't remember the last time I saw such a downpour.'

'Alex,' addressed Natalie.

'What?' he replied.

'I remembered something else. Something I didn't want to say whilst Ian was here.'

'What is it?'

I don't know how relevant it is, but after they split us up, I saw Layla talking to someone else…'

#

'And there isn't anything else you can tell me?' one of the officers asked Natalie.

'No, I already told you,' she replied.

The officer looked at her, trying to suss her out. He gave up, satisfied that this was all he was going to get from her.

234

'I'll be back in a minute,' he said and walked off.

Natalie had been sitting down in an enclosure of shrubs. Alex was on the other side of the police cars and all the officers, but she could see a few of them giving him a hard grilling. She felt very vulnerable having been separated from the other two. She peered through the bushes next to her. Layla was on the other side of the greenery out of earshot. Natalie watched as the officer who had been interrogating *her* approached the one with Layla and pulled him away. Layla buried her head in her hands. Natalie watched her, hoping she hadn't given them away.

Moments later another man approached her from behind. He was one of the paramedics who had arrived with the ambulance crew. She jumped when he tapped her on the shoulder. They embraced each other long and hard. Natalie tried to stay silent to hear what they were saying, but it wasn't necessary. The man looked around shiftily, before dragging Layla over to the enclosure of shrubs on the other side of Natalie. Natalie dropped low just in case they saw her trying to eavesdrop. They were very close to her now and she could hear everything.

'What's going on?' asked the paramedic.

'What are you doing, Dave?' Layla panicked. 'What if someone sees us?'

'I needed to make sure you were alright,' he said.

He pulled her in for a passionate kiss, but she stopped him and looked around, 'What are you doing? It's too risky,' she said. 'If someone sees us and it gets round at work…'

Unbothered, he cut in, 'My number one concern is you at the minute. What's going on here? I heard the police talking. They think there's more to this story than you're telling them, is that true?'

'Of course not,' she lied. 'Just let them know at the hospital that I probably won't be coming back tonight.'

'Are you OK?' he asked.

'Yes, I…' she started before being interrupted by his phone ringing.

'Hey, babe!' he said, answering the phone. 'Sorry darling, I've got to work a bit later tonight. Say goodnight to my son for me.'

Layla marched off and Dave tried to stop her with an apologetic gesture, but she walked away.

'Is he sleeping OK?' Dave continued, speaking with his unsuspecting girlfriend over the phone.

#

'I doubt it's relevant,' Natalie continued, 'but I listened to them for a while.'

'She was having an affair back then, too?' Ingrid asked, gobsmacked. 'Well, she's certainly a warm one, isn't she?'

'When he got off the phone he and Layla had a whispered argument. She told him to stay away from her and that it wasn't a good time for him to be around her. The policeman came back to me after that so I had to stop listening in. Do you think it could have anything to do with what's happening here now?'

'I doubt it,' concluded Alex. 'This Dave guy must be the one she told me about. The one she fell in love with.'

'When was this?'

'When I was having a little chat with her earlier this afternoon,'

'How many of these "little chats" did you have with her?'

'Only a couple.'

'You learned quite a lot about this stranger from only a *couple* of chats,' Natalie said, sarcastically.

'Don't start that again,' he said.

'Seth, what *is* the matter with you?' Ingrid said, bringing the young couple back to the problem at hand. 'You're being very quiet dear!'

He stood, slowly and spoke, 'I think Natalie is right!'

'About what?' Ingrid asked, confused.

'When she said about why we're in this mess. It can't just be coincidence that we are all linked to this in some way!'

'Well, not us,' said Ingrid, confidently, only to be met by a long pause. 'Seth?' she asked, warily.

'I'm sorry dear. There's something I never told you.'

Ingrid's heart sank at these words, 'Oh no, please don't say that we are involved in these shenanigans in some way!'

'I'm sorry, Ingrid!' said Seth, contrite.

Natalie's earlier panic returned as her theory gained some more substance, 'No, no, no! I knew it! I was right!'

'How could *you* possibly be involved?' doubted Alex.

Seth explained, 'If you recall in your story the man who fell off the cliff had a business partner.'

Ingrid begun to realise, 'Seth...no, it can't be. What are you saying?'

'I was his partner,' Seth revealed. 'The man's name was Damien Frith.'

'But that means...'

'Yes. I'm the reason he's dead today. I hired that thug, Kane, to threaten him. It's my fault that poor boy is without a father. Remember my rainy day fund? The one that I refused to spend?'

'Of course!'

'It's a large portion of the money that I earned when I sold the invention. I intended to give it to the boy if I ever tracked him down. Pass it off as an inheritance fund or some such. That way I could reduce some of my guilt without getting found out.'

'What was it, Seth? What was so important that you went to these lengths?'

He walked away from the group, ashamed, but told them his story, 'Damien and I designed lots of things together, but nothing compared to the thing that he created one day. Damien enjoyed the creative side of things and just did it for the love of the job. He would tinker with his products for ages before taking them to market. Saying they should be perfect before anyone saw them. I, on the other hand, just saw the vast fortune that could be made and I wanted to sell right away. I had so many debts, thanks to Ingrid's frivolous spending. I just needed this one great invention as soon as possible, just to stay afloat.'

'What was the invention?' Ingrid asked, persistently.

'It took off even better than I had ever imagined. It's in something you all use today. It's...'

'Who cares what it was,' Alex interrupted, loudly. 'This is all *your* fault?' he accused Seth.

'I'm so sorry,' he replied, beginning to get upset himself. 'I never meant for him to die. He was my friend. The man that I'd hired turn up on my doorstep later that night. He looked really shaken up, but he handed me the invention, I gave him his money and we didn't say a word to each other. I never heard from him again. When I saw what had happened on the news, I was sure that I would be found out, but when they said that there were witnesses who reported it as an accident, I was so confused.'

'Confused? We lied for you!' Alex snapped.

'I'm so sorry,' Seth began, tears forming and voice shaking. 'No one was supposed to get hurt.'

'Well they did!' Alex shouted. 'Everything that happened that night was because you got greedy. Come on Natalie, we're going!' he said, grabbing her arm and heading for the door.

'Where are you going?' Ingrid asked, panicking.

'We're going back to our own flat!'

'Don't be silly, Alex. Take your own advice. We simply must stick together! Remember?' she pleaded.

'No way,' he said, determined. 'I don't trust any of you.' He turned to Seth, 'You could have set this up yourself, to tie up your loose ends.'

Ingrid answered for her husband, 'Don't be absurd. My husband isn't capable of murder!'

Without another word, Alex stormed off, dragging Natalie with him.

'Come back,' cried Ingrid as their final visitors left the flat. 'Oh Seth, they're gone! We're all alone now. What are we going to do?'

'We'll be OK, darling,' he assured. 'You lock the door and I'll grab us some things to defend ourselves with!'

Ingrid marched towards her flat door.

'Wait!' Seth said, stopping her in her tracks. 'The lock's still broken from earlier. This is not good.'

'Well, I'll at least pop the chain across,' she replied, continuing towards the door.

She stopped in fear as the light from the hallway was blacked out. The hooded figure stood menacingly in the flat doorway. Ingrid screamed as it moved towards her. Seth managed to pull Ingrid further back into the flat and behind him to protect her as they backed away.

The killer moved slowly towards the elderly couple, running a knife along the nearby radiator to produce a horrifying rattle.

Seth ushered Ingrid away from the villain and they eventually found themselves backed into a corner in the kitchen.

'Please don't harm us,' Ingrid squealed.

The killer stood mere feet away from the terrified couple. Seth stood proudly in front of Ingrid, determinedly shielding her as she cowered behind him. There were a few moments silence, but this ended when the killer advanced once again. Seth knew it was futile to resist. He felt the knife slide in and out of his neck at speed.

He clutched at his throat as he crumpled to the floor, barely able to manage words as blood spurted through his fingers, 'Ge...ger...spee...inwar...stop...sha...save...'

The light died from his eyes and he could say no more. Ingrid collapsed on top of him and let out a great wail of despair. The killer stood over her and looked down. Ingrid stared up at the faceless menace. The killer brought the knife up and wiped the blood away with a gloved hand.

'Why?' Ingrid sobbed, anticipating her own immediate demise.

The killer stared down at her for a few moments before turning and walking out of the kitchen area, leaving a confused and devastated Ingrid behind.

The killer left the flat, closed the door and stood outside flat 3D's yellow door in the empty corridor, breathing for a few moments. It looked at Alex and Natalie's pink door, 3E. Then at Erica's family's blue door, 3C, and finally at Kane's red door, 3A. Decision made, the bloody gloved hand reached for the handle of the pink door and tried it. Locked. Not a problem! The killer reached into its pocket and produced the master key. The key slid in smoothly and the killer quietly opened the flat door.

The hooded figure stood in the doorway for a few moments and surveyed the area. The young couple were nowhere to be seen in the immediate area. The lounge and kitchen area were absent of life. Hearing murmurs coming from the bedroom, the killer ambled to the open doorway of the young couple's bedroom, and there, on the edge of the bed, were Alex and Natalie, chatting.

It took them a few seconds to notice the extra presence in the room, but when they did, Natalie's screams could have brought the roof down. The killer flew towards her thrusting the knife at her to silence her. Alex pushed her sideways off the bed out of harm's way and dived off the other side himself as the killer landed flat on the bed. He quickly flipped the duvet over the killer to steal a few moments. As the killer fumbled with the bedding, Alex grabbed Natalie's arm and dragged her towards the doorway and out of the bedroom. However, unbeknownst to Alex, the killer had caught up to them, and as Alex ran out of the front door with Natalie in tow, the killer grabbed her trailing arm, wrenching her from Alex who fell out into the hallway. He quickly got back to his feet, but the killer slammed the door in his face, separating the young lovers. He grabbed the door handle, but only managed to create the tiniest gap, before the killer had grabbed a large cabinet and tipped it sideways to block the door from opening further. Seeing Alex's fingers creeping round the door, the killer gave the cabinet an extra vicious shove. Alex withdrew, escaping with his hand intact.

The predator turned and stared at a motionless Natalie on the floor. Alex was banging loudly on the door from the corridor side and shouting for Natalie, but she had other priorities. Now was not the time to play the scared victim. She made a conscious decision to survive this.

She sprung to her feet and ran towards the bedroom, the killer hot on her heels. She hurled herself inside and managed to shut the door just as the killer barged into it. The door was rammed repeatedly as Natalie attempted to hold it closed with her back, but she could feel her strength failing. Suddenly, the blade of the knife came through the door missing her head by inches. She couldn't stay there. She abandoned the door and sprinted for the bathroom. She kicked it open, but turned and retreated underneath the bed. The killer had managed to push through at this moment and ran towards the swinging bathroom door. Natalie crawled under the bed and out the other side. She stood to see the back of her assailant looking into the empty room. She jumped onto the bed and, with a flying leap, kicked the confused intruder in the back, causing them to stumble into the bathtub and become tangled inside the shower curtain along the way.

She hopped off the bed and ran back towards the front door. Alex was still banging on it.

'Alex!' she screamed.

'Natalie!' he replied. 'Are you OK? Move whatever's blocking the door.'

She crouched down and tried as hard as she could to back the heavy piece of furniture out of the way. It began to move, but unfortunately the killer came sprinting out of the bedroom towards her with its knife high in the air. When they reached her, the knife was brought down towards her. She rolled aside and it plunged into the cabinet. As the killer attempted to remove it, she punched them in the face. Angry, the aggressor wrenched the knife from the cabinet, slicing it through the air and into Natalie's arm causing her to cry out in pain as blood sprayed across the room.

#

Out in the hallway, Alex had used every ounce of his strength to push the door, to no avail. To his left, Ingrid walked out into the corridor in a daze.

'Se...Seth...he's gone. He got my Seth,' she said, dizzily.

She was clearly in shock.

'Come on!' Alex said, determined. 'We need to get help.'

He looked up and down the corridor trying to decide what best to do. The corpse of Janice Todd added an eerie feel to the corridor and it was distracting him, but he had to be quick. He could hear the tussle that Natalie was having in her room. He decided on the red door.

'Quick!' he shouted, dragging Ingrid down the corridor. 'The druggies!'

He banged repeatedly on Kane's door until eventually, he answered.

#

Natalie, squeezing together the deep cut in her arm, quickly retreated to the bedroom once more and leapt up onto the bed. The killer ran through the open doorway and sliced towards her in a big semi-circle.

Natalie jumped off to the side dodging the deadly strike by millimetres causing the killer to overbalance and fall onto the bed. Natalie grabbed the bedside lamp and as the killer attempted to sit up she smashed it over their head, knocking them down again. For good measure she pulled out the drawer from the bedside cabinet and smashed it into pieces over her opponent's head as well. She grabbed a shard from the debris and tried to stab the killer with it before it was kicked from her hand.

She ran back towards the main room leaving a trail of blood from her wounded arm in her wake. She ran around the sofa towards the window and started banging on it hoping to draw some attention. She knew she was spending too much time on this and spun around to see the killer sprinting towards her. They vaulted the sofa, catching her off guard. She felt the vicious thrust of the knife in her stomach causing her to scream out in agony. The killer drew the knife out and went in for the final blow. She raised her wounded arm to defend herself and the knife pierced her palm. The killer was getting increasingly frustrated at not being able to finish the job. Natalie's left arm was almost completely out of action, but she had to buy time for Alex to get through the door.

#

'What have I done now?' said Kane, answering the door to Alex's urgent knocking.

'We're in danger! We need your help!' Alex shouted back at him.

'Danger?' said Tony, joining them in the doorway.

'Yes! The killer's here. They just killed her husband,' Alex said, indicating Ingrid, 'and my Natalie is trapped in our flat with them.'

'What?' said Tony, panicking.

'Who?' asked Kane.

Ingrid chimed in, still hysterical at seeing her husband butchered, 'It's the old man that feigns needing a wheelchair. He's gone stark raving mad.'

'You still think it's him?'

'It doesn't matter who it is,' Alex said, rushing them. 'We need to hurry. I need your help getting back into my flat. Please. Natalie's locked in there with the killer.'

'OK! Hold on,' Kane said before whispering some instructions to Tony who then retreated into the flat.

'What are you doing?' stressed Alex. 'We need to go. Now!'

'Trust me! We're gonna need this!'

#

Feeling determined once more Natalie ignored the throbbing pain on her savaged arm and wound herself around the murderer's arm. She was dragged and pulled around the room before she managed to find her footing up on the sofa. She pushed hard, hurling herself and the killer in a tangled mess towards the window. Their two arms smashed through the glass and Natalie managed to slam the killers,' arm into the side of the window frame, causing the knife to drop down onto the grass in front of the building below.

Furiously, the killer summoned all their strength to finish this scourge of a girl. They grabbed her arm and thrust it down into the jagged glass remaining in the bottom of the window frame. This third wound proved too much for Natalie and she now lost every bit of strength in her mangled arm. She was ragged off of the window frame, bringing the glass with her in her arm, and thrown towards the television cabinet. She banged her head on the unit and fell to the ground. Her wounded arm fell to the floor and her good arm lay over the edge of the cabinet. The killer stamped hard on her good arm forcing it the wrong way over the corner of the furniture and breaking it to the sound of the loudest scream Natalie had given yet. She hunched up in pain on the floor with both arms completely incapacitated. The killer stood over her. She looked fearfully into the faceless hood as it grabbed the large television and tipped it off its stand on a collision course for Natalie's head. She mustered her remaining strength and rolled out of harm's way, but that was her lot. She was too weak to do more.

The killer strode over the broken television and grabbed her by the back of her clothes, lifting her and tossing her over the back of the sofa. They stepped up onto the seating area of the sofa and over the back of it to where Natalie lay. The killer ignored Natalie's cries of pain and surveyed the room looking for a weapon before spotting the fish tank.

Natalie was grabbed by the hair and pulled along towards the fish tank. She screamed, but was powerless to fight back. She was dragged to her feet by her hair and dunked into the fish tank. Her arms flailed feebly as she kicked out wildly at the killer, but she was held firmly in place by the hand on the back of her head. The disturbed fish darted about, crazily, as huge bubbles burst forth from Natalie's mouth.

#

Alex felt that Kane wasn't sensing the urgency of the matter, but that feeling was soon quelled when Tony handed him a gun.

'Right!' said Kane, confidently posing with the weapon. 'Let's see how they likes this!'

'Yes!' said Alex, delighted. 'Now we have a fighting chance. Quick, save Natalie!'

'Come on, mate!' Kane said to Tony. 'Let's save the day.'

Kane led Tony, followed by Alex across the corridor back towards the pink door, leaving Ingrid standing alone at the safe end of the corridor.

#

Natalie's life slipped away as the killer watched the last of the air bubbles touch the surface. Once satisfied that she was dead, she was dropped to the floor. These death throes had taken so long that by the time the killer was able to squint through the sliver of a gap in the front doorway that the overturned cabinet would allow, they saw a band of heroes heading for them with a gun.

The killer quickly took their phone out and touched a few icons on the screen. The corridor blacked out followed by the sound of the tenants panicking.

'Aaaaargh. What's going on?' came the sound of Tony's voice.

'I can't see a thing,' wailed Ingrid. 'What has happened to the lights?'

The killer grabbed the overturned cabinet and, using their remaining strength, dragged it out of the way, and escaped into the darkened corridor, blundering into Kane on the way.

'What was that?' Kane panicked.

'What?' Tony asked, before spotting the hooded figure himself. 'Aaargh. There's someone behind you.'

'Where?' Kane asked before spotting it also, pushing past Tony. 'Wait! I see him!'

'Where is he?' asked Alex.

'He was just there. He's gone!'

They heard a door open and slam shut.

The lights returned. Ingrid was cowering at the far end of the corridor by Kane's door. Alex, Kane and Tony were huddled together in the centre of the corridor.

'What happened?' Ingrid asked, shakily.

'Someone brushed past me!' Kane replied.

'Me too!' Tony added.

'I didn't see or feel anything,' said Alex, before spotting his open flat door, 'Natalie? Natalie!' he shouted and ran into his flat.

The others stood in silence in the corridor as Alex's screams confirmed the worst. Ingrid put her hand over her mouth. She felt for Alex, but she was grieving for her own loss as well. She felt so light and airy. How could she cope with all of this, she thought, wearily. She stood in silence, absent of purpose, empty.

'Tony,' Kane said. 'Go and get him.'

'But, I don't want to go in there,' he replied. 'What could I say to him?'

'You're going to have to. I'll keep watch on the corridor. We need to act fast and we need to stick together. Drag him out here if you have to, but we *are* getting out of this. I'm not finally getting Lisa back for her to lose me now. Go and get him.'

Tony cautiously walked into the young couple's flat. Only inches in, he knew it would be bad. Blood was splattered all over the floors and walls. Then he saw Alex, standing in silence, looking at Natalie's body.

'Alex?' he said, to no response.

He stood beside him not wanting to look at her himself. He tried to guide him away, but Alex wouldn't budge.

'We need to get back together,' Tony told him. 'We need to deal with this whilst we still have control.'

'You're right!' said Alex, to his surprise. 'I can mourn later.' Alex had a determined look about him, 'Right now...I'm angry. I'll get revenge first.'

Tony began to guide him out but he turned back to Natalie.

'I will avenge you Natalie. I promise,' he said, wavering in his determination as tears threatened to fall.

'Come on,' Tony said, forcing him away from the scene.

They both returned to the corridor.

'Right!' said Alex, taking charge. 'We're getting out of here. Natalie's gone and I'm gonna make this bastard pay. Did anyone see anything when the lights went out?'

'I think I saw him!' Kane said. 'He rushed past me in a hoodie,'

'Yeah, that's him!' Alex confirmed. 'Where did he go?'

'I think he went towards your flat,' Tony said to Kane, pointing at 3A.

'No!' said Ingrid. 'I was standing right here the whole time, no one came past me, I assure you.'

'Then it must be this one then,' Tony said, pointing at Ian and Layla's green door, 3B. He definitely went past us.

'He could have doubled back,' said Kane. 'Because I'm pretty sure he went into this one,' he said pointing at the blue door, 3C.

'Oh my, there's a baby in that flat,' said Ingrid.

'It has to be this one, I'm telling you,' said Tony, pointing at 3B again.

'But if it was *that* one,' said Ingrid, pointing at 3C, 'then that baby is in danger.'

'I'll go in and check,' said Kane, cautiously reaching for the door handle.

Just as he was about to open the door however, it swung open.

'What's going on out...' said Erica.

246

In a panic, Kane fired several shots into the young mother's chest. She flew back against the door before falling out into the corridor in a limp bundle.

They all surveyed the scene, shocked. Kane walked backwards from the body, distraught.

'What have I done?' he said, full of remorse. 'I've killed her!'

Chapter 31 – The Truth

As I stood in Erica's bathroom getting changed, I was horrified to hear sounds of gunshots and panic. 'What's happened?' I asked myself, fearfully. I went out into the main room. Isaac was alone in his cot, but as I looked towards the front door I was horrified to see Erica's body lying across the threshold, surrounded by scared tenants, and a smoking gun in Kane's hand.

'What did you do?' I shouted, enraged. I ran towards Erica and slid onto the floor beside her, 'What did you do?' I shouted again, angrier and more desperate than ever.

'It was an accident,' Kane pleaded. 'We were ambushed by the killer. We thought they went into this flat! I thought she was the killer! She came from nowhere! I panicked!'

'We've been in here the whole time, no one came in. How could you be so stupid?' I spat.

'I could have sworn they went in here.'

'I was right then,' Tony said. He must have gone into this one, he said, pointing at my flat door. 'Unless it's some sort of ghost that's attacking us.'

'Don't be ridiculous,' said Kane.

I was very shaken at what was happening. I thought I'd got a handle on this, but clearly I was wrong. I had to get on top of it once and for all.

'What's been going on?' I asked, struggling to curb my reactions.

'My husband is dead, that's what!' yelled Ingrid. 'You brought us here for only a few days and now my Sethy-poos is gone forever. I should have never convinced him to move house. Then we wouldn't have ended up here in the first place.'

Realisation hit Ingrid; she began to sob loudly in the corridor.

'Seth's dead?' I asked.

'Yes, and so is Natalie,' Alex added, angrily. 'We need to find this killer. I'm not letting them get away with this. I want this guy either dead or in prison. That's the only thing I can do for Natalie now.'

'The killer attacked all of you together?' I asked.

'No…well…they snuck up on me and Natalie in our bedroom…'

'You separated?' I asked, incredulously. 'The plan was to stick together.

'We got into an argument. Seth told me that *he* was the one that hired Kane at the cliff that day. *He* was the dead man's partner. I didn't think I could trust him.'

'What?' I said.

'Cliff?' said Kane worriedly. 'How do you know about that?'

'Natalie remembered everything,' Alex said. 'We were the school kids that you threatened at the cliff that day.'

'What? You can't be,' he said, disbelievingly.

'We are! And Seth hired you to confront that man didn't he?'

'I…I never knew. I didn't realise. I recognised your wife,' he said indicating me, 'but I didn't realise you lot were there too.'

'We were just in the wrong place at the wrong time,' said Alex.

'We haven't got time to go over that story again,' I said.

'Is the baby OK?' Ingrid asked.

'Yes. He's fast asleep in his cot, thank God.'

He won't be OK in a few years when he finds out how his mother died. I looked at Kane who was holding the murder weapon and seethed with anger. I could feel myself boiling up again.

'I can't believe what I've done,' said Kane, desperately.

'It was an accident, mate,' said Tony, to my disgust. 'You can't be blamed for that.'

'Of course I can. The police will take one look at me and assume I murdered her.'

'You *did* murder her!' I shouted at him. 'If you are going to carry a

249

loaded weapon around you need to be responsible. You've never taken responsibility for anything in your life!'

'It was an accident,' he repeated.

'I've got your back, mate,' said Tony 'I'll tell 'em how it was.'

'And how was it?' I snapped. 'He shot her. He acted without thinking and now Isaac is without a mother. You're a monster.'

'I'm so sorry,' he said, breaking down in tears. 'I never meant to kill her. I was scared. I was thinking of Lisa. I have a chance to be with her again and the thought of dying now, when I had something to live for, had me on edge. Then when Erica just suddenly appeared, she startled me.'

Kane was weeping openly now at the thought of taking a child's parent away. He must have changed, I thought. This is the second time he has done that now and he didn't get this upset the first time. As far as we know, anyway.

'We've all lost people,' Alex said. 'But we need to focus. We can grieve afterwards. We need to get out of this building and tell the police. We need to stop this killer. That's the only thing we can do for our dead, now.'

'There is no way out,' I said bluntly. 'Short of jumping out the window, we're trapped good and proper.'

'Window…window…' pondered Alex.

He looked around the room for a solution. Then he spotted it. He looked at the red fire box.

'Wait!' he yelled, a spark of hope in his eye. 'Why don't we dangle the fire hose out of the stairwell window, and use it to climb down! Why didn't I think of this before?'

'Of course. You're a genius,' I said. 'Hurry, let's try it,' I encouraged him.

Alex hurried to the fire box housing, unhooked the latch and opened the container. Alex's shocked face told us all that he had found something unexpected.

'What's wrong?' I asked.

Alex reached in and wheeled something out for us all to see. It was Roger! Bound and gagged in his own wheelchair with his large old-fashioned video camera resting on his lap.

'Oh my goodness!' said Ingrid, confused. 'What on earth is going on here? I thought he was the man that's behind all this?'

'Yeah, that's Roger!' I confirmed. 'Is the fire hose still in there?' I asked, already knowing the answer.

Alex peered back inside, 'No! Nothing!' he said, before kicking the box door shut in anger.

Ingrid took Tony, walked over to Roger and began to untie him. Their attempts to rouse him were to no avail.

'So what does this mean?' asked Kane.

'I'll tell you what it means,' Alex suddenly realised. 'It means that whoever is doing this is out here, right now. It's one of you!' he said, with an accusatory point at us all.'

'Or you!' I said, offering an opposing theory. 'When we were in town together and you left me to "buy something". You still haven't told us what you were really doing. Maybe you snuck back here before me and killed Layla. How else can you explain how you got home before me?'

Alex's face crumpled at my accusation. He slowly reached into his pocket and produced a ring box.

'I was buying this,' he said, his words catching in his throat. 'I was going to propose to Natalie.'

He sat down defeated. Ingrid shed a tear herself at this and no one knew what to say. I knew I ought to have said something having being the one who brought this about, but what could I say?

'I'm sorry, Alex,' I said. 'I didn't mean…I just meant that…'

'Trust me,' Alex said, showing me the wound on his leg. 'I didn't stab myself.'

'It *can't* be any of the five of us,' Ingrid assured. 'We have all been present when the killer has struck.'

'Have we?' I asked.

'Yes,' she assured. 'You, Alex and I, were all attacked in my flat.'

'That's right,' I said.

'And those two,' Alex said, indicating Kane and Tony, 'were out here with me and Ingrid when the lights went out and the killer came rushing through.'

'The lights went out?' I asked.

'Yes!'

'That's when I saw the killer,' said Kane.

'Yeah, me too,' said Tony.

'And you saw them too, Alex?' I asked.

'What? Oh, well…no…but I heard…' he replied.

'I didn't see them either,' said Ingrid.

'What are you getting at?' asked Kane.

'Well,' I started, 'we still don't know for certain that either of you two and the killer have ever been in the same place at the same time, do we?'

'Listen here, pal,' said Tony, aggressively. 'We haven't killed any-one.'

'It can't be them, Ian,' Alex said. 'The killer was in my flat when I went to get their help. There's no way he could have gone from my flat to his without me knowing.'

'Fair enough,' I said.

'Like I said before,' Ingrid began, 'who's to say it is anyone that lives in these flat.'

'It could still be him,' Kane said, pointing at Roger, unconscious in the chair.

'I still think it could have been her,' Alex said, pointing at Erica. 'We haven't been attacked since she was accidentally shot. Ian, is there any chance?'

'No,' I said assertively. 'She was with me the whole evening. The whole time that you say these things have happened.

Discussion broke out between everyone. Wild theories were being thrown around the room until something I said stopped them.

'What was that?' I said, turning my attention to my own flat door which had been empty for hours; empty, that is, apart from the body of my wife.

'What was what?' said Kane, who was the closest to me.

'I heard a noise in my flat!' I told them.

'But, everyone that's still alive is out here. Aren't they?'

'As far as I know!' I said.

'I told you!' said Ingrid. 'It's an outside threat.'

'Yes!' said Tony 'And I said it was *that* flat that the killer went into earlier.'

'I should have listened to you,' Kane said, full of regret over Erica's death. 'But you did also suggest it could be a ghost.'

'Perhaps he is right,' Ingrid added. 'What if this *is* some sort of entity.'

'Don't be daft,' said Kane.

'Quiet everyone,' I said. 'This is no time for that. We need to act.'

'I'll go in,' said Kane, poising his gun.

'Do you think that's wise after what you did last time?' I suggested. 'Why don't you give me the gun?'

'Yeah, you're right!' Kane said, giving Erica's body another glance. 'Do you know how to use it?' he asked me?'

'Yes!' I replied as he handed me the gun. 'Oh yes!' I said as I turned it back on its owner.

'What?' yelled Kane.

With the gun in my hands I had regained control. It shouldn't have come to this, but I had already let this go on for far too long. With Kane at one side of me and the rest at the other end of the corridor with Roger. I had to act fast. Kane stared at me as he began to realise the situation that he was in.

'You?' Kane said. 'It was you? Please don't. Lisa! My life. I was going to turn my life around. I was going to be happy.'

I pulled the trigger and fired a single bullet into his chest. The blood seeped slowly onto his white shirt as he slid down the edge of the corridor wall into a crumpled heap on the ground. Dead. I turned menacingly towards the others and stared straight at Alex.

'Ian!' he cried. 'What are you doing?'

'You're the last one!' I said.

'Last what?' said Alex, before realising what I'd done. 'Did you kill Natalie?' he shouted.

'I killed them all,' I revealed. 'I didn't intend to reveal myself to you, but sometimes you have to improvise. I let my emotions get the better of me, I got careless, but that's *twice* Kane has ruined my life. He had to die!'

'But why? What did we ever do to you?'

'Nothing!' I snapped. 'You did nothing! And that's exactly why I did this. You called me a liar. When my dad was laid there at the bottom of that cliff, you all just stood there and lied!'

'That boy!' he realised. 'That was you?'

'Yes, and I've carried that day around with me for the last ten years.'

I stared at the gun in my hand, 'I wonder if this is the same gun that scumbag used to threaten my dad,' I said, indicating Kane.

'That can't be you,' Alex said. 'You look nothing like him. Your hair colour isn't even the same.'

'Hair can change colour during puberty. I'd tell you to look it up, but you won't be alive much longer.'

'But why did you do this?' Alex asked.

'Revenge!' I said, menacingly. 'I wanted revenge on the ones responsible for dad's death and those that prevented justice; the three cowards too scared to confess the truth, the evil man hired to confront my father, that pathetic excuse for a police officer who didn't believe me, and finally, my dad's greedy partner who started all this.'

'Wait! You planned all of this? How?'

'Years of planning. I spent hours awake at night in my university dorm room planning for this day. I had photos of you all, notes, schedules, likes, dislikes, what jobs you had and so on. The point is I made sure I knew everything about you so that I could one day get you all in the same place at the same time. I couldn't risk killing you separately and getting caught before I'd finished. I had to get you all at once. So I used the money that my dad left me, bought this place and spent the last year getting it ready!'

'This is a joke. It would be impossible for you to get us all here together.'

I adopted a soothing voice as I began to reveal all, 'Evidently, it's not impossible,' I snorted at the irony of his question. 'Lee was the hardest as he had a family and a successful job, but that's nothing a few drugs in his locker didn't fix. You and your girlfriend were easy enough. You were already looking for a cheap place together, I just simply made you an offer you couldn't refuse! Same with this guy,' I said, giving Kane a swift kick. 'Unfortunately, I had to marry Layla myself. She lived alone and there was no other way I could see of getting her here. I purposefully made friends with a group of hers, knowing that we would eventually cross paths. She was so blinded by the fact that a younger man found her attractive that she didn't even realise that I never loved her. *She* stopped loving *me* eventually, but this was after we were married and I was already so close to my goal. I just needed to keep her sweet for a few more weeks. Little did I know that she was keeping herself sweet with Lee. I had no idea about that affair, but if it kept them both here, I can't complain. Then for the final piece of the puzzle, I showed Seth and Ingrid a beautiful house that I knew they would want; invented a situation in which they had to be out of their house, but couldn't be in that one just yet, requiring them to live here for the weekend. Of course the house I showed them was never going to be theirs as it was mine. The one my father left me.'

'I can't believe that you manipulated us like that!' said Ingrid.

I turned my attention on Ingrid and Tony now, 'I am sorry that I got you others involved like this, but it was the only way I could get my targets here.'

'So that's why you didn't harm me when you killed my husband?'

'That's correct,' I confirmed. 'The same reason I didn't kill Roger. I have no issue with anyone not involved in my father's death. I mean, I'm not a monster.'

'You *are* a monster. I don't care what my Seth did in the past. He was my husband. I wish you had just killed me rather than leaving me without him.'

'Well I *do* care what he did in the past, I'm afraid,' I snapped, before returning to my calm stance. 'But I am sorry about the effect that it has had on you,' I said, genuinely.

'So let me get this straight,' Tony said, realising the situation, 'I'll be safe as well. You won't hurt me!'

'That's right,' I confirmed.

'Oh, thank you, thank you, thank you,' he said, excitedly, with no concern for anyone else's feelings. 'I promise I won't say anything when I get out of here.'

'Ha,' I laughed, ironically. 'That's the attitude that got some of these into trouble. I would be a bit of a hypocrite if I told you not to say anything.'

'What do you mean?' he asked, confused.

'It doesn't matter,' I dismissed this unimportant bit-player.

'How could you have possibly pulled all of this off?' Alex asked.

I suspected he was trying to stall me and after all the movies I had seen I'd said to myself that I wouldn't get delayed in the end. However, I was itching to show off. I can see why they do it now. I mean, I had put a lot of work into this, and artist's work should be admired.

'Well, that was easy enough,' I said, eager to spill. 'I gave myself full control over the building. Every flat was powered through my own. I have the power to each flat, run up into the one above, along the fourth floor corridor and into 4B where it comes back down into my flat. Specifically my bathroom where I have a power box that controls the lot.'

'I saw that the night of the party,' Alex said, clearly bitter with himself for not suspecting anything.

Shall I finish?' I asked, without waiting for an answer. 'Everything was connected wirelessly to my phone so that I could control everything from anywhere. Oh, and also…locks on the fire doors? You should have thought that was suspicious, surely. I'm surprised nobody mentioned it. By the way, all of this kit is available at Jim's local hardware store if you ever need anything like this.'

I looked around the corridor at my silent tenants.

'Sorry, bad timing for a joke, but I did tell him I'd promote his shop whenever I could, but I suppose the rest of you won't be staying here,' I said, eccentrically. They were scared and unamused so I just carried on, 'Anyway, er, what else…what else,' I pondered, trying to remember my other great feats. 'Oh! When we were walking down to town earlier,' I said to Alex, 'I did the old "stumble into you and pick your pocket" trick. That's how I got *your* phone. I'd already managed to swipe the others from the flats by this point.

Next I needed to find a way to ditch you in town so that I could return to the flats to begin. I couldn't believe my luck when *you* left *me* to buy that engagement ring.

When I did get back to my flats I found *that* perverted old man,' I indicated Roger, still unconscious in his wheel chair, 'harassing my wife. I simply clubbed him on the back of his head. She looked so relieved that I'd saved her. That was short-lived when I stabbed her moments later.

Next I doubled back down the stairs, went outside, round the back of the building and watched for you to return. I followed you upstairs and watched you from the stairwell. Once you all headed into my flat, about to discover my dead wife, I slipped onto the corridor and locked the fire door behind, then went across to the other one and locked that too. Then I conveniently showed up *after* you, making it look like I had been in town all along. Luckily for me, Kane had gone into her flat too, as well as Roger, proving that she was alive *before* I left the building. To everyone else it looked like you had arrived back before me, suspiciously I might add, due to the time inconsistency.

Later that evening, when I was staying in Erica's flat, I moved back to my own to configure the wireless panel in case I needed it later. It wasn't long before I heard someone approaching my flat door. I killed the lights to my flat hoping that this would deter them. It didn't! I hid myself in the bathroom just in time as Lee entered my bedroom. Perfect, I thought. I didn't think it would be so easy to kill my next victim, and he walked right into my lair. I could kill him and leave him in my flat. The chances of anyone else coming into the flat with a dead body was so unlikely, no one need know he'd died.'

'We told him!' Ingrid sobbed. 'Seth and I warned him not to go and see her. We told him you would kill him if he caught you there. I didn't realise how literal that statement was.'

'Ha,' I chuckled. 'I do love irony. Anyway, I was just about to strike when lo and behold, I heard *more* people entering my flat. So much for no-one wanting to come in there, but there you were,' I indicated Alex, 'you and your girlfriend. I decided it best to stay hidden whilst you were looking at my dead wife, hoping that you'd leave soon, but I panicked when Lee produced a mobile phone. Hidden in *my* flat of all places. Irony, again. The one I had missed when I had stolen all the others was right under my nose. Nothing for it, I would have to kill him there and then, but I was outnumbered. I needed one fatal strike to kill him instantly. I took my chances and went for the two of you as well. Unfortunately you managed to escape me. I could have had you too if during our tussle you hadn't thrown me at the fire box, waking Roger.'

'So that's why Natalie was sure she'd heard him!' Alex stated.

'It's because she *did*,' I confirmed. 'I had to let you get away. Once you bolted into Seth and Ingrid's flat, I had to subdue him again,' I said, looking over at the comatose old man. 'Clearly I did a better job this time,' I joked, before telling Alex the rest of plot. 'Later on, once the rest of us had left the four of you in Seth's flat together, you know, after all the story telling, I heard you arguing loudly from inside Erica's flat. Once your trust of Seth began to wane and you returned to your own flat, I took the opportunity to strike whilst you were separated. Unfortunately, *you* managed to slip away again. I had to act fast to escape your flat once you had enlisted Kane's help, so I killed the lights and fled into Erica's flat. And then, well, I think you know the rest.'

'But,' Alex stammered. 'What about when we were in Seth and Ingrid's flat together? You were there when we were attacked by the killer.'

'I think you've stalled me long enough,' I decided. 'It looks like that's one thing you'll never know.'

I walked over and grabbed Alex. I dragged him away from the others and threw him to his knees at the far side of the corridor.

'Goodbye Alex!' I said, as I raised the gun to his head. 'My harrowing nightmare can finally come to an end.'

Alex closed his eyes and Ingrid looked away, too scared to watch. I was about to pull the trigger when I was clubbed hard on the back of the head. I fell to the floor in a daze, dropping my gun. My vision was blurry, but I was still conscious. I scrambled around looking for my gun, but by the time I could focus properly, Alex was standing above me, our positions reversed, gun poised. I saw Roger behind him with his video camera in his hand.

'How do you like it?' he said.

'Stupid old man,' I said. 'I should have hit you harder.'

'What's going on here?' Roger asked, genuinely confused. 'I haven't missed any more naked ladies have I?

His humour turned sour when he spotted the body of Kane, the near skeletal corpse of Janice Todd, and then the body of the mother of his grandchild, Erica.

'Erica?' Roger managed. 'Oh my God, what's happened?'

'I'm afraid we have some more bad news,' Ingrid began. 'It's about your son.'

'No…no! He's not…he's not dead too, is he?'

'Him and many more, including my husband.'

'How? What happened?' he asked, unable to comprehend.

'This bastard killed them!' Alex shouted, the gun still firmly aimed at my head.

'You killed my son?' asked Roger.

'He deserved it,' I spat. 'You don't know anything about what's going on here old man.'

'I know you killed my son! That's all I need to know.'

I ignored him and turned my attention back to the one who held my life in their hands, 'So, what're you going to do now, Alex? Kill me?'

'I should!' Alex said. 'Having you behind bars will never be enough. I want to see you dead. Like Natalie. You murdered her. Murdered her for being a scared kid.'

'I was a kid too!' I shouted back at the irony of his defence. 'I was scared too. No one cared about me when you murdered my dad.'

'It was an accident and I'm sorry. I can't say sorry enough for what happened, but that doesn't mean that everybody else deserved to die.'

I shouted even louder causing Alex to wince a little, 'My dad didn't deserve to die for anything.'

'No, he didn't,' agreed Alex. 'And neither did Natalie,' he said, putting the gun's nozzle, square into the centre of my forehead. 'But you do!'

'Wait, Alex. Please!' Ingrid squealed. 'Don't do this. Don't be like him. Let the authorities deal with him.'

'No!' disagreed Roger. 'Kill him!' he egged on. 'You said he murdered Natalie. Do her justice. End him!'

'No!' shouted Ingrid. 'I lost my Seth too, but this isn't the right way. We're better than him.'

'Do it, Alex,' ordered Roger.

'Don't,' screamed Ingrid.

I could see the conflict going on in Alex's head.

'I can't think!' Alex shouted, angrily. 'There is too much going on. I don't know if I can kill someone.'

I had reached the end. My life was over. I had been found out. I had been caught. I had lost everything. My parents, my love, my freedom. A part of me just wanted everything to be over. I looked up at Alex with hatred in my eyes.

'You're pathetic!' I snapped. 'Just do what you have to do. You've ruined my life already. There's nothing more you can do to me.'

Alex retreated from me slightly, moved by my speech.

'How could you do all this?' he asked. 'I am so sorry about what happened to your dad, but this?' Alex asked. 'What do you want from us?'

'Not *us,*' I told him. 'You! I want *you* dead. I will never forgive you for what you did. My life is over now. I have lost everything. I want you dead. If you don't kill me here, today, I will make sure that you die the very next chance I get. That's the honest truth.'

'What more do you need than that, lad?' Roger said. 'Kill him. Make him pay!'

'Don't let him influence your decision, Alex,' Ingrid reasoned. 'He can't kill you if he's in jail for the rest of his life. Make him suffer *that* way, without staining your own hands.'

I grabbed the gun and put it to my own forehead, 'Do it!' I shouted, preparing for the end.

'I will,' said Alex, to Ingrid's horror and Roger's excitement. 'For Natalie! And for all those you have killed today.'

I looked at the ground. Saddened at the thought of one last loss, 'Just make sure that…that Erica's baby is taken care of. Make sure that Isaac is taken somewhere safe.'

Alex looked into Erica's flat. He could just about see the baby's cot from where he was. He took a step back from me and eased the trigger of the gun.'

Ingrid shouted, 'Don't do it, Alex. This isn't who you are! It won't make things easier,'

Roger followed, 'Don't listen to her, lad. She's right. It won't make things easier, but it will make you feel better. I saved your life just now, remember? Do you think he would have spared you if I hadn't woken up in time?'

'I know I could make a rash decision here,' Alex began. 'I know he deserves to die. But I am partly responsible for his father's death. If the one thing I can do for his father now is to spare his son's life...then I'll do it.'

'You pathetic little worm,' I sneered. 'Call yourself a man? Do you think that Natalie would...'

I was stopped by the butt of the gun. All went black.

#

I awoke shortly after. I saw two blurry figures talking.

'Did you tie him up properly?' Alex's voice said.

'Yes, he's not getting out of that,' replied Tony.

My vision cleared and I saw the pair of them sitting opposite me. My hands were tied behind my back. The three dead bodies were still there, but Ingrid and Roger were nowhere to be seen. I was particularly close to the decaying corpse of Janice Todd, which was pretty gruesome.

'He's awake!' Tony said.

'Still haven't killed me then?' I asked Alex.

'No,' he replied. 'We did find the master key on you though. And a phone. Ingrid had to take Roger outside otherwise he *would* have killed you. She rang the police, too. I think I just heard them pulling up actually. That could have been what woke you.'

I laughed at him, but he didn't respond. I just stared at Erica's body. An innocent victim in all of this. I had gone out of my way to spare Ingrid and Roger, when it would have been easier just to kill them, but they weren't to blame. And Erica certainly wasn't. Such an unfair casualty in my twisted world. She didn't deserve to die.

Armed police arrived at the third floor. They shouted at Alex and Tony to hit the deck. Standard procedure when there is a firearm involved evidently. Once they had secured Kane's gun from Alex, they allowed him and Tony to stand. They explained everything to them. They tried talking to me a few times, but I simply ignored them. There were two officers chatting with Alex and Tony, one with me and an officer at either end of the corridor. Could I escape this situation? Could I in some way get out of this without killing anyone? Unless it was Alex of course. Could I perhaps just kill Alex? Even if I was stopped afterwards it wouldn't matter. Even if I died trying. As long as

I finished my mission. But I could see no way that would be possible. He was too heavily guarded, *but* there was only one guard with *me*. And only one at the closest exit. That was it. If I was going to escape; that was my chance.

I rolled my arms under my legs in one swift move, bringing my tied hands to the front. I clasped my palms around the screwdriver in Janice's head. I drew it from her skull and swiftly plunged it into the nearby officer's thigh, causing him to scream in pain. I dashed towards the officer guarding the door and knocked her over just as she attempted to draw her gun. I looked back to see all the remaining officers chasing me, as well as Tony and Alex.

I ran down the stairs. I heard one of the officers request backup on his radio. I came to the second floor and continued down the narrower staircase towards the first floor. I was stopped in my tracks by a platoon of officers running up towards me single file in this narrower staircase. The leader drew his weapon and asked me to stop. I ignored him and ran back up to the second floor. I ran across the corridor and leapt over the stray fire hose that was strewn across the floor.

'Stop!' I heard the officer yell.

Ignoring it a second time resulted in a bullet being fired into the wall just above my head. I stopped running and raised my hands to surrender. The officers approached me from the far end of the corridor. The exit was so close, but I didn't stand a chance against their weapons. I looked at the fire hose housing that had been ripped from the wall to my side. Chancing it again, I rolled behind it. Moving fast, I retreated to where the fire hose box should have been and saw that the hose itself was still plumbed in. I pulled the lever causing the house to whip wildly around the corridor, throwing the officers into chaos as water sprayed everywhere. I used the commotion to flee to the stairwell at the opposite side and made my escape down the identical narrower staircase.

On the first floor now, I continued down the next set of stairs to the ground floor. Halfway down I saw Alex and Tony, who had clearly come down this side of the building, but gone too far. Alex spun when he heard me behind him, but I punched him in the face, knocking him aside. I ran past him towards Tony, who, scared, stepped aside allowing me to pass.

I burst through the front door where more officers greeted me. I sprinted to my left and turned to run down the side of the building. I glanced back to see officers right behind me. However, these weren't armed and I was faster. I could make this, I thought, but a lapse in concentration caused me to trip over something I had not expected. Seth's old wooden chair, on the ground, down the side of my building. I fumbled and fell to the ground. The officers were on me in seconds, securing me with actual handcuffs this time. I knew that this was truly the end. There was no escape now. I've failed you, dad. I am so sorry.

Chapter 32 – His Audience

'As the officers escorted me past Ingrid, into a police car, she said, "I guess that chair was lucky after all".' I told my audience.

I looked at them all; sitting there, listening to the tale of how I tried to avenge my dad by killing five people. How I had trapped them in my building with the express purpose of doing so. I looked at them again. The same faces I had spent all this time with. I think I will miss them. I have enjoyed their "company". Oh well. I can't stay here forever. I'd better wrap it up.

'And there you have it,' I continued. 'That's the full story. Things worked out very differently from how I had planned! Due to unforeseen circumstances I made the biggest mistake of my life. I lost the woman that I love and I can never get her back! It makes everything I did pointless. I see that now! I was stupid.'

I was asked a question.

'I'm sorry. I refuse to answer that,' I told him.

'Objection!' said the prosecutor who had asked me. 'The defendant cannot omit parts of the story.'

'Objection!' said my defence lawyer. 'It is my client's right to not speak should he not wish to do so. He states that that is a very personal part of his story!'

'Sustained!' said the judge. 'The defendant may refrain from explaining this, however, if he wishes to find leniency in today's sentence, I highly recommend that he tells the whole story.'

I was suddenly very aware of how real all of this had become. I had got so lost in telling my story that I forgot that there were proceedings to follow. This was said to be my last day in court and that a sentence would be handed down today. What could I do? What more could I say? It didn't matter, anyway. I'd come to terms with it. I had almost finished what I set out to do. If it meant a few decades in prison before I could finish what I started, then so be it. I would do everything I could to get out as early as possible. It would take years, but one day, I would be free. That's when Alex will pay.

'Ladies and gentlemen of the jury,' said the prosecutor. 'I'm sure that you, as much as I, wish to know the complete story.' He turned back to me now. 'Please tell us how you managed to appear a victim like everybody else, when several of you were attacked by the figure we now know to be *you*.'

"Leniency" I thought. If this was what I had to do, to allow me freedom one day. Then so be it. I would give them what they wanted.

'I never intended to reveal my accomplice,' I began, 'but the worst has happened now so I suppose it doesn't really matter.'

I thought I could keep it together, but I couldn't. I felt myself welling up and my voice was shaky. Recalling *this* was very upsetting.

'Erica was never supposed to die,' I struggled. 'She was supposed to take care of our baby in case I got caught, or until it was safe for me to return to her.'

The audience looked shocked at this revelation.

'Our baby?' asked my defence lawyer. 'You mean…you're Isaac's real father?'

'Yes!' I answered.

'And Erica was your accomplice?' asked the prosecutor.

'Yes!' I answered again. 'Erica is the love of my life. I met her a few years ago when I had already begun to plan my revenge. We fell for each other straight away and she said she would do anything for me. I told her my story and she agreed to help. What were the odds that I would find the love of my life right in the middle of a crazy revenge plot and manage to convince her to help me! She was so understanding. I started to build my fake relationship with Layla, but tried to see Erica as often as I could. When she got pregnant, I had to hurry my plan along. She quickly seduced Lee and within weeks told him that she was pregnant and that it was his.

Once Lee told me that my wife was having an affair with him, I knew people would begin to suspect me. That's when I asked Erica to step in for me. I said from the start that I would never ask her to take a life. I didn't want that on her conscience, but I found some things that she *could* do. I had her help with stealing some of the mobile phones and I needed her to be the one to find my wife, otherwise she could have been lying dead in my flat for hours, so I asked her to make an excuse to go over there. She even managed to wrangle some witnesses to join her.

She was the one that donned my disguise and pretended to attack me whilst I was with the others, to throw them off the scent. I also told her to react when I shouted Roger's name to help plant the idea in people's minds that it was him. We choreographed the whole thing. The little argument that we had in Ingrid's flat wasn't planned, though. But it was a good bit of improvisation; dismissed any ideas people might have had about us being in cahoots. She was amazing. She wasn't supposed to die.'

I wept. The thought of losing the perfect woman was too much. And I never even spent enough of my time with her. Instead I wasted the years we could have had together, with Layla instead. All for revenge. I felt sick.

'There are still a few things that need clearing up,' the judge said. 'A lot of unanswered questions. What your father's invention was; who the other person was who broke into your flat and what they were trying to steal, but most pressing is the murder of Janice Todd. Can you shed any insight into this? We have heard as much as we can from Alex Kendall and Ingrid Treant, but with Kane dead, her murder remains unsolved. It is a matter of urgency that we find out who killed her.'

'Kane told us nothing more,' I cooperated. 'He simply said that either him or one of friends had killed her, but they were all so drunk and high that they did not who.'

'That is a great shame, Ian. A mitigating statement could have brought about some good from all the hurt and pain you have caused.

Her death still remains a mystery so many years later. And now the potential suspects are to be extradited back to America tonight!'

'I am sorry, your honour. I will never agree that what I did was not right, however, I do hope you find that girl's killer. I wish I could have helped more.'

'We have all those involved in custody. Truth will out, that's what I always say. At least her family have a body now. However, more closure would be gratifying.'

'You say everyone involved? Even my friend, James?'

'Everyone!' the judge, said firmly.

'Then he probably knows that I broke my promise.'

'You refer to the fact that you told Alex, James,' secret, yes? Why *did* you do that anyway?'

'Well, your honour. I expected him to be dead in a few hours. I didn't think it mattered.'

'I see. And are you ready to tell us about your own secret? The nature of your father's invention or what it was you were hiding in your flat?'

'No!'

'Any idea who tried to steal it?'

'None!'

'I see. A great shame that you won't tell us more; I was quite intrigued. However, we accomplished what we came here to do today. I thank you for allowing me to question you further on unrelated matters, but you were our last chance of shedding light on it. Anyway, I think we have heard enough. As trying and as difficult as this case was to hear. It was more of a confession of sorts. This morning's trial involving the murder of Janice Todd was far more complex, I assure you. However, I shall now hand down my sentence. Ian Frith, you have shown severe malice in your campaign for revenge. Whilst what your victims did ten years ago, may seem wrong, it was not your right to exact the punishment of death upon them. It is for this reason that I have decided that you must see the inside of a prison cell, for the rest of your days. Jailors, you may take him away.'

Four Jailors appeared and boxed me in. I was cuffed and marched away. I knew that I would not get to come here again. I wish I had savoured every one of my days out of the prison. I will miss this courtroom. Was it worth it? What would my dad think if he could see me? I have only thoughts, now. I have no family. No love. I have left my child parentless, just like me. How could I do that? I grew up thinking of no-one but myself. I forgot to stop for a moment and consider that I was putting a life that I was responsible for in the same position. I don't deserve life. I will end it the first chance I get. I cannot live in this world where I believe what I did was right, but others do not. I agree I have caused much hurt for the families of my victims, but my hurt was so deep that I could not exorcise it. This was my only chance. And still, now, after all this time, I still want Alex dead.

Chapter 33 – Judicial Banter

'Sorry, your honour!' said the defence lawyer. 'I am not familiar with this morning's proceedings, but I am very invested in *this* story and I am interested to know what is happening with the Janice Todd case.'

'This is a most unusual situation,' the judge said. 'Two very deep stories. Intertwined through time, people and place. I was sure that we would get to the bottom of that mystery, however something that Alan Kendell, Jack Cors, Paul French, and Derek Wellburn did in America has caught the attention of the FBI. I have had to bail them into their custody so that they can be investigated for that. It was very difficult to hold them here with so little evidence and the FBI had arranged for them to fly out this evening. I would have loved to have got to the bottom of Janice Todd's murder before then. Most unfortunate, however...perhaps there will be another chance for this mystery to be solved.'

'What do you mean?' asked the prosecutor.

'The officer in charge of the case suggested that James Ellam join them on their flight back to America.'

'For what purpose?'

'He thinks that, put them all together, truth will indeed, out. I put a request in with the agent in charge of the transfer and he agreed, but...something about that whole case is bugging me.'

'Isn't it strange how small, unrelated details niggle at us.'

'Indeed it is. I can't separate the two cases and I want answers.'

'I know what you mean. During an interview I had with Alex, whilst building my case, he told me about another mystery,' revealed the prosecutor.

'Did he now?'

'Yes. Apparently Officer Lee Wilkinson was due to be fired sometime *before* the drugs incident. All the papers were prepared...and then...to his amazement, all the evidence against him vanished.'

'So he was going to be sacked anyway, *before* the drugs turned up in his locker. I wonder what happened there.'

'So did I, so I followed it up, but there was no trace of what had happened. I eventually gave up once I decided it had no bearing on *this* case, but a part of me really wanted to know.'

'Perhaps a story for another day?' the judge mused. 'Anyway. It has been a long trial. Ian Frith will die in prison, and I have a filet mignon waiting for me at home. Sir!' he said to the prosecutor. 'Madam!' to the defence lawyer. He gave them a slight bow and left the pair alone. With the trial over, the two resumed their usual friendship.

'Well, that was a tale and a half,' remarked the prosecutor.

'It's definitely been one of my more interesting days in court,' replied his counterpart.

'I just can't believe the set of circumstances Ian had to put in motion to achieve his purpose.'

'I know. So much planning. It must have been very difficult.'

'Of course, a lot of coincidences took place too.'

'Speaking of coincidences. Take a look at this,' said the defence lawyer, holding up one of her legal documents that she had been doodling on the back of.

'Perhaps if you'd been paying attention,' he said, seeing her scrawl, 'your client might have done better.'

'Don't be silly,' she replied. 'He was done for from the start. No, I did this when I was bored during the beginning of his story.'

'What is it?'

'Another freaky coincidence. You know how I love my wordplay.' She held up the paper. 'Do you see it?'

'See what?'

'Oh Arthur! You're losing your touch!'

'I take it you're going to tell me?'

'Would I ever pass up the opportunity to show off to you?' She pointed at the drawing. 'This is a map of the third floor. I have written all the tenants names in the flats that they were living in. I have put men first, women second, oh, except for the cripple and the baby, I put them *after* Lee and Erica.'

'What are you getting at?' he said, not seeing where she was going with this.

'Take the first letter of all of their names and I think that you will find a very spooky coincidence!'

He read aloud, 'Kane, Ian, Layla, Lee, Erica, Roger, Isaac, Seth, Ingrid, Alex, Natalie! Killer. Is. Ian.'

'You see,' she said, proudly.

'Yes. Very odd! Only you would spot that,' he laughed.'

'Perhaps. Strange though.'

He stared at the paper and then turned it over.

'What is this anyway?' he asked.

'Oh,' she said, looking at it, 'it's just the police report from when they first arrived at the building to arrest Ian.'

He suddenly realised something. He ran his finger across the report.

'What's wrong?' she asked.

'It can't be!' he said, running back to his folder on his desk.

'What?' she stressed.

'Maybe if you weren't playing word games and actually paid attention to what you had in your hands.'

'What are you talking about, Arthur?'

He pulled out a notepad, 'The body count. It's incorrect.'

'What do you mean?'

He began reading through his own notes and then ran back to her and pointed something out on her documents.

'What are you showing me?' she asked.

'According to the police report, excluding the body of Janice Todd, whose gender they didn't identify until later, there were only two dead females at the scene. One from a stab wound and the other from drowning.'

'What's your point?' she replied.

'In the story we just heard, the defendant claimed that there was a third girl who was shot to death.'

'Of course! Erica! Now that is strange.'

Chapter 34 – From the Ashes

As the four jailors escorted me down the empty corridor, I felt as if I was marching towards my death. No one else here. A long corridor. Several closed doors. And the silent sentries that were marching me.

Just when I'd given up all hope, something odd began to happen. Was I imagining it or was the female jailor on my left stroking my arm? I turned to look at her. Her low cap covered most of her face, but I saw a brief smirk appear. What happened next I could have never predicted. She reached for her baton, drew it and spun around. It extended with the force of her spin, clubbing the guard behind her hard on the head. In one swift movement, she pushed me to the ground to get a clear shot at the other two guards on my right, and clubbed the pair with two fast movements. The three other jailors now lay unconscious on the floor.

My saviour looked at me. She removed her cap and shook out her hair to reveal her identity.

'Erica!' I shouted, confused, before embracing her in a heartfelt hug.

I was filled with a range of emotions. The love of my life, here, in front of me, alive.

'But how? I saw you die!' I said.

She laughed, 'You didn't honestly think I would just walk into the corridor unprotected, did you? Especially when you'd just told me that they had a gun.'

'What do you mean?'

'Back at the flats when you rushed in and told me that they had a gun and that I needed to stall them, I decided to play it safe. Whilst you were in the other room changing back into your normal clothes, I grabbed a bulletproof vest, which Lee had kept from his police days, and put it on. Turns out he did have his uses,' she laughed. 'But when they shot me, the impact must have knocked me unconscious. I came round just as I saw you fleeing. Your timing could not have been better. Everyone chased you, so I dashed back into my flat to grab Isaac, but he wasn't there. Turns out that Ingrid had taken him outside with her earlier. Anyway, trapped, I changed into Lee's old police uniform and just strolled out of the building. There were so many police there that no one even noticed me.'

'I'm so happy to see you. I thought I'd lost you forever,' I said again, embracing her, not able to get enough of her. 'Where's Isaac now?'

'He was placed in foster care…but I know who he's living with. And I know where he is right now. I've been watching the family for some time. We have to grab him now! I have booked us onto a plane out of the country, tonight. We can grab Isaac and then get the hell out of England.'

'I can't believe you've done all of this. You're too good for me!'

'I know,' she laughed. 'Now let's go!'

She dragged me through one of the nearby doors and led me out to safety. I was free. All thanks to the love of my life. I knew we had to act fast. Everything had to happen tonight. Getting Isaac, escaping the country. We needed to do everything before the police could stop us. I didn't want to tell Erica, but I also had one last thing to do before I left the country.

I will have my son, and then, Alex, I shall have my revenge.

The End

A word from the author…

Thank you *so* much for giving this book a chance. As an amateur author it has been very difficult getting this off the ground and I can't thank you enough for contributing towards its future. It needs all the help it can get so please recommend it to friends and family. If you purchased it online then please provide feedback, a rating, reviews etc. Share and talk about it on social media and the official facebook and twitter page. Anything at all that you can do will help me immensely. I hope you enjoyed this novel and will look forward to more books from me and of course, more in the 'Best Served Cold' series.

Part of a theatre group?

'Best Served Cold: The Five Doors' started its life as a stage play before being adapted into a novel. Named, simply, 'Best Served Cold' it captures all the shocking thrills and twists of the book across a two act stage script. With a stronger lean on comic elements for the first act, followed by a more serious second act to conclude the tale, it is a great play for a large mixed cast. Scripts and performance rights, as of February 2016, are available from www.stageplays.com

Acknowledgments

First and foremost, I must thank the person that spent hours trawling the text, finding typos, grammar mistakes and disastrously structured sentences and helping me to fix them. That person is Christine Mulrooney, a fellow member of the amateur dramatics group that I am a member of. Without her this book would have been an unreadable mess. I have learned so much from her and I cannot thank her enough for helping bring the story to life.

Next I must thank my friends and work colleagues who gave the book a test read, provided feedback and ultimately let me know that the book was worth pursuing. It was watching how these people responded so favourably to the book, that gave me a renewed motivation to push ahead with publishing. So I give my thanks to; Kirsty Cox, Lee Merrick, Jane Doughton and Stephanie Gibson. Thank you for helping to polish the final product.

Going back to the story's roots, I must give thanks to Paul Taylor, who agreed to direct and produce the original stage production, giving worth to my initial idea. Ashley Ironmonger also deserves a quick mention here for his large contribution towards Ingrid's vocabulary. I could tell he had a lot of fun playing around with her dialogue in the script. Whilst we're on the subject of the play I should also give thanks to the original cast from whom I based the description of the characters on. They brought life to my characters which allowed me to develop them further in the novel. And they are; Michael Cutts, Peter Horner, Alice Love, Barbara Parkinson, John Parker, Sophie Goddard, Esther Dyson, John Ryall, Chris Wilkinson, Callum Clarke, Jeremy Cutts, Jake Dyson, Joanne Morfitt, Nick Percival, Ian Harley, Jim Parkinson and Neil Barham.

Another man who deserves great thanks is Phillip Johnson. He designed the cover for the novel and allowed me to send him many emails that requested the tiniest of changes to the artwork until I felt it was perfect.

Dale Rivers deserves a special mention for his help with the media side of things, including the production of the trailer which featured many of the original stage cast, as well as: Eloise Daye, Bob Willerton and Yourek Lesniak.

And a great thankyou to many more. So many of my friends and colleagues have contributed in some way over the last two years.

Finally…thankyou to…*you*! The reader. By purchasing this book you have contributed towards my dream of being able to tell stories. I hope you get to read more from me!

About the Author

Andrew Crossland was born in Barnsley, South Yorkshire, England in 1987. He began performing on stage at the age of fourteen before stopping once he got a full time job after college at eighteen. It wasn't until very recently that he was lured back to the stage and decided to write a play of his own. After a sell-out audience, great feedback and a huge attachment to the characters, he immediately began work developing the story further and expanding the universe of the characters drastically.